LA CHAIRE

beyond the Garden Gate

Colin Lever

ELSP

Published in 2011 by
ELSP
11 Regents Place
Bradford on Avon
Wiltshire   BA15 1ED

Origination by Seaflower Books
www.ex-librisbooks.co.uk

Typeset in 9/12 Palatino

Printed by CPI Antony Rowe
Chippenham and Eastbourne

ISBN 978-1-906641-38-2

For my wife Elaine

Preface

The book is based on real events, taken from personal diaries, biographies and actual recollections of events that occurred although some of the scenes are the creation of the writer.

Chapter 1

La Chaire 1945

"Papa, Papa!" Albert shouted to his father as he ran towards him.

"Not now Tabby!" his father reprimanded, "go back to the house this is no place for a little child."

"But Papa, I want to water the plants with you. You always let me water the plants." Albert pleaded as he pulled at his father's trouser leg.

"Not today Tabby, there are too many soldiers and too many wagons. You might get hurt." his father explained, distracted.

Albert sensed his father's agitation and for a moment let go of his trousers. His father continued to water the shrubs and small trees that had been placed in individual pots, in a long line outside the main house. German soldiers strode purposefully this way and that all about the terracing. There were a number of wagons and trucks; their engines, ticking over, waiting to be filled. Officers barked orders as the soldiers went about their work, carrying paintings, rolled up carpets, chairs and other items of furniture. It seemed that just about anything that was not nailed down was being placed in the back of one vehicle or another.

Fascinated by the goings on, Albert wandered away from the safety of his father's side and into the morass of activity. He stopped to stare at a large portrait of a man he had never seen before. He thought that the man was staring at him and looked scary so he quickly moved on. He saw a large rug leaning on the back of a truck waiting to be placed. He was attracted by its bright colours. He touched it gently with his fingers. It had a warm, soft texture that he liked so he touched it some more.

"Out of the way!" a soldier shouted as he brushed past Albert carrying a heavy sculpture that he threw onto the back of the wagon.

Alarmed by the soldier's unfriendly outburst, Albert turned tail and ran back to his father.

"Papa, are the German's leaving?" he asked.

"Yes." his father was very careful not to spill any precious fluid as he watered each plant in turn.

"Are they taking everything with them?" Albert enquired innocently.

"Yes."

"Even the plants?"

"Yes."

"But they are your plants," Albert observed.

"Not any more," came the terse reply.

"Le Bloas have you finished watering the plants yet?" the German officer asked impatiently, his voice barely audible above the furore. Albert clung to his father for comfort.

"Nearly," Albert's father snapped back.

"Then get a move on, they have yet to be loaded and fastened safely," the officer instructed before moving into the house.

Albert's father cursed under his breath.

"Can I water some plants now?" Albert pestered once more.

"I've told you, no," his father shouted at him. "Now stay out of the way."

Albert felt like crying as he shuffled his feet in the gravel of the terrace, moving to the far end of the row of plants where his father had pointed to.

He watched as his father rolled the large plant pots towards the back of one of the lorries. His father then called for help so that they could be hoisted, one at a time, onto the back of the lorry. He then took it upon himself to jump up onto the lorry, place each pot carefully and fasten it to the side of the truck with rope. Albert sucked his thumb as he watched his father toil. Once all the plants had been loaded, his father jumped off the lorry. A soldier raised the tailgate and secured it. He made his way to Albert and pulled him close. Albert reciprocated. The bond between father and son was re-established.

The two of them watched as one lorry after the other manoeuvred in the tight space of the terrace before following the one in front down the drive and onto the lane. Their contents rattled and teetered in the back as the vehicles made their way over the uneven ground. Last to leave was the truck containing the plants. Albert looked up at his father.

"Are you sad, Papa?" he asked.

"A little," his father replied softly.

"Is it because they have taken your plants?"

"It is."

"Will you grow some more?"

"Maybe"

Yves reflected on his son's childlike optimism. He wondered whether he had the strength to start all over again. He had been the latest caretaker of the garden that was La Chaire, a legacy that had begun over one hundred years before.

Chapter 2

Alton, 1798

She stood there, motionless, surrounded by delicate, silk petals; their hue a deepest red fading to pink at their base. A heady aroma, as if carried on the air by a hundred burning candles, scented the air around her. The atmosphere was both expectant and intense.

She was a willing receptacle as she stood naked, Venus like, and pale against the colour of the petals. Her vulvic lips exposed, pouting, ripe and swollen belied her dispassionate nature. Penetration overshadowed her. She was surrounded by masculinity but, although clearly potent, to her they were as Eunuchs, unable to fertilise her deepest recesses. No, she was waiting for a different suitor.

Attracted by the changing colours, and drawn in by the rich scented aroma, a winged steed alighted, drinking deeply from the sweet nectar she had to offer. A stranger alighted and was ensnared by her feminine charms. He was not choosy but, unlike the gigolo, he was about to give his all in cementing this union, stimulated as he was by a powerful sexual chemistry. He was not alone.

She had attracted many other strangers to her bosom but only the chosen few would be allowed to enter her chambers. Once impregnated, her tresses would fade and fall. Her male courtesans, initially so erect and fecund, would droop and die. Her deflowering complete, she would swell up, nourishing the seeds of her union and then she too would die, her seeds dispersed as orphans to survive or to perish in an unforgiving world. Made in her image they had every chance of survival.

Chance was the hand that traditionally guided the coupling, but on this occasion another was the force behind the matchmaking. Sam was skilled in the art of propagation. It needed a steady hand and the softest caress to avoid damaging the delicate organs. Armed only with a pencil-thin brush, made from the finest animal hair, and a hand lens so that he might effect a more precise meeting, he would tease the yellow pollen from the anther and transfer them to the voluptuous mouth of the stigma, from whence he would let nature take its course.

There was a constant hum in the glasshouse as insects of various shapes and sizes went about their lives. Exudent flora let their scent spread throughout, mixing and melding with the mustiness of soil and compost. Around the edges, nearest the glass, opaque with whitewash and condensation, young seedlings turned their emerging leaves to the light, each comfortable in its own little, red clay pot. A narrow, rectangular walkway separated these outer benches from the ones in the middle that, in turn, were cut into sections two tables wide. In the centre were arrays of plants and shrubs at various stages of growth and maturity, some flowering, some not. From canes suspended from the roof, plants were hung out to dry in preparation for their use in lotions, potions and elixirs. In the middle of this jungle, surrounded by a forest of flora, sat Sam. He was hidden in a quiet recess where the air was still and where other distractions might pass him by.

He felt something on his neck. He ignored it. There it was again, irritating, pestering him. He flicked whatever it was away with the back of his hand and continued to look through the mounted hand lens at the plant underneath. Seconds later the pest was back but this time it tickled his right ear lobe. Experience had taught him to ignore such distractions, they usually give up eventually but this little beast was not for quitting. He flicked at his ear to give the critter a hefty whack.

"Ouch!" he exclaimed as he caught his lobe with a force that made it throb.

He settled back to his work, irked at the interruption. With surgeon like precision he held his hands either side of the lens; scalpel in one and tweezers in the other. Just as he was about to make the first emasculating incision, a large 'something' landed right inside his ear. He dropped his instruments immediately stood up in a fit of paranoia knocking his stool over and hit his ear with such a force it made his ear drum pop.

"You!" he shouted as he saw the real hand behind the irritations. "I might have guessed!"

He set off at full tilt after Sarah but, anticipating him, she had run in a zigzag manner along the narrow corridors to avoid capture. With youthful exuberance they played cat and mouse around the benches. Sam possessed the greater agility but Sarah more than matched him with her quick-wittedness. Across one of the central benches they paused for breath.

"Sam, your fingers will turn green if you spend any more time in here!" she teased.

Sam rubbed the dust from his hands onto his trouser legs. Sarah smiled warmly as she teased, little creases appearing around the edges of her eyes. Sam returned the smile whilst watching her every move.

"And you will end up wearing thick spectacles like Mr Barwick, the accountant, if you keep sticking your head in all those books," Sam replied.

For a moment their gazes met across the scented table, Sam was transfixed even as Sarah looked away. For such a tender age, Sarah had a fulsome figure. It was partly disguised by her loose fitting, plain white, chemise dress. Her hourglass shape was accentuated by the long-sleeved Spencer jacket, tight around the waist, hugging her upper body and emphasising her large breasts. Her face was rounded and of a pale complexion with a little puppy fat underneath the chin. Her features could hardly be described as petite, but it did not detract in any way from her youthful beauty. Ruby lips and welcoming hazel eyes drew Sam in. Her hair styled in tight rag curls cascaded from underneath a simple black bonnet tied underneath her chin.

"Knowledge is power and books are a great source of knowledge," Sarah commented head bowed.

"But they aren't the only source of knowledge," Sam's cognitive processing broke the spell.

Sarah looked up at Sam who was still staring at her wide-eyed. He was drawn towards her by feelings he did not quite understand. She lowered her gaze shyly.

"You'll not learn much locked away in a potting shed," she mocked.

"I learn much more than you think," he replied.

"You'll not learn a new language talking to your plants! Nor will you see the world with your head stuck in compost! How will you experience romance if you never go out and meet anyone?" Sarah was keen to show him that she was no push over.

"You read too many novels!" he snapped, blushing.

Sarah stepped slowly towards him and placed a re-assuring hand on his.

"I'm sorry, Sam, it was not my intention to insult you. I was merely teasing. You know I have the greatest respect for what you do." she said.

He was trying so hard to bring the fire that burned inside of him under control but that touch, the softest of caresses, sent shock waves right through him. He blushed even more, if that were possible. It felt like his veins were about to burst.

"Why, Sam, what is the matter?" Sarah spoke with genuine concern seeing him so flushed. "Come, let's get you out of this stuffy place and into the fresh air."

Like a lamb he let her lead him outside. The light was brighter than in

11

the glasshouse, even on a dull day like today. The cooler air was like a cold shower bringing him quickly to his senses. At first he was unusually quiet. He was confused and perplexed by the feelings inside of him. He did not comprehend the emotions that had burst forth.

"Come on, let's go to the house, Father is inside and they are going to have a Friend's Meeting." Sarah skipped away leaving Sam standing motionless by the doorway. She turned and saw that he had not moved so she returned to him and stood close, so close he could smell her sweet breath on his face.

"Come on, silly. If you don't hurry they will have started the meeting without us."

When does play turn into passion? When does liking turn into love? Sam and Sarah had known each other since infancy. Both families lived in Alton and they were related. Her father, the famous botanist William Curtis, was in fact Samuel's first cousin, even though he was thirty three years his senior. Sam's father, James Curtis, the local surgeon and apothecary, was Sarah's great-uncle. All relationships change with time, and the one that bound Sam and Sarah was no exception.

They made their way away from the musty glasshouse and emerged straight into a kaleidoscope of colour. The garden was surrounded by meadowland with its profusion of bright yellow buttercups, delicate blue cornflowers and intermittent pale red, corn poppies all competing to be seen amongst the tall meadow grass. In these fields Sam and Sarah had played chase, allowing grass and flower alike to run through their fingers as they ran. To the south stood the remnants of an ancient British woodland where the two of them played hide and seek behind the old oaks, ash and sycamore trees, the pungent smell of white-belled wild garlic trapped under the canopy. Carpets of bluebells lay motionless and trees with roots exposed were decorated with ground hugging primroses. Patches of silver birch, hazel and willow made ideal frames with which to build secret dens. Nowadays, Sam used the same trees as a source of ingredients for his father's medicines.

Behind the glasshouse, a thicket of prickly gorse and broom, their yellow flowers radiant against the deep green of their leaves, played host to razor sharp brambles that tumbled and tussled with wild honeysuckle. Tucked between the thicket and the glasshouse was a rough grassy corridor. Here, away from inquisitive hands, Sam nurtured the foul smelling henbane. Deadly nightshade, with immature green berries soon to ripen into a deep purple, snaked its way up and around anything it could find. Hemlock grew tall and proud, its purple spotted stems leading up to tiny dense white umbels. Just to one side, away from the glasshouse, lay a large compost heap, laden with a variety of dead plant material, around its perimeter and away from the glasshouse a large bed of stinging nettles waited to ambush unwary passers by.

The apothecary garden itself was a mixture of the functional and ornamental with a strong emphasis on the aesthetic, a style that Sam would adhere to throughout his life. A hedge of hawthorn, holly, mulberry and witch hazel had been boxed cut to offer protection from blustery westerly winds. In front of this was Sam's growing interest in flora not required for the Apothecary. Rhododendrons flush with huge trusses of pink flowers caught the eye. Camellias, the object of Sam's latest experimentations had lost their rich red flowers, but their glossy, dark green leaves glistened in the daylight. A bed of rose bushes running along the length of the west side of the garden completed the sequence. Hardy wild roses with delicate pale pink and white flowers grew next to larger highly scented apothecary roses and fuller old roses with their deep red satin petals. Sarah loved to visit if only to sit in this beautiful garden and read her books. The garden offered peace and tranquillity. The fragrances relaxed the soul and the colours, both vibrant and subtle, inspired the creative mind.

On the opposite side, a fence and trellis had been constructed to protect the garden from cold Easterlies. Clockwise-twining honeysuckle oozed a sweet perfume from tubular two-lipped orange, yellow flowers. Hops twined in the same direction a little further along, their large lobed leaves and inconspicuous male green flowers raised their heads near green female cones.

They stepped over lawn camomile with its profusion of small white flowers and headed towards the ornamental bay tree cut in a pom-pom style. A gravel path led them alongside aromatic English lavender, purple fingers wagging in the breeze. The lavender had been intertwined with bright yellow santolina and common rosemary to make an eye catching knotted garden feature.

"Tell me Sam," Sarah enquired as she linked arms with him.

He felt an awkwardness that had not been there before. Their relationship had lost its innocence. "What career do you hope to pursue? Will you follow in your father's steps?"

"And become a surgeon?" Samuel exclaimed, "I don't think so!"

"Then what do you hope to do with your life?" she asked pausing in front of the bay tree before turning towards the hops and honeysuckle. His father made frequent use of the hops to help relieve gastric complaints and as an antiseptic.

"I'm looking for adventure and excitement," his eyes lit up as he spoke. "I would like to expand my horizons beyond Alton and explore where no other person has set foot. I would like to go to the edge of our glorious empire, where there are no maps and step into uncharted territory."

"And what would you do there, apart from get lost?" she teased, squeezing his arm as they walked past rows of elongated foxgloves, alive with fauna that hummed in harmony, their spires of upturned pink and purple cups disguising the deadly digitalis locked inside.

"I would seek out the most exotic and luxuriant flora, species hitherto unknown to man." he replied gesticulating with both arms, relieving himself of Sarah's continuing affections.

"And how might these discoveries serve you?" she asked grabbing his arm again and sitting him down in the arbour. A heady fragrance of Jasmine filled the space, emanating from the white and yellow flowers that bespeckled the climbing trails. Jasmine oil and Lavender oil were favourites in the shop, bought by ladies to freshen themselves. In front of them, a bed of purple-blue bergamot swayed in the slight breeze. Sam stooped to take in their aroma. He picked off a flower and examined it before passing it to Sarah, an impromptu act he immediately regretted.

"Who knows what treasures such flora may yield," he stuttered, trying to offset the enormity of his gesture. "New medicines and cures for the sick, new materials that might serve mankind, and beautiful blooms to lighten the spirit."

" 'Tis good to have dreams, dearest Sam," Sarah said with a note of caution, blissfully unaware of his gathering insecurity, "but if you attended to your studies you might still become apprentice to your father and have a handsome salary on which to live."

They set off walking once more moving slowly past a mixed bed of bright yellow evening primrose and camomile.

"If a man doesn't have dreams and ambition then his life has no direction." Sam replied.

"Besides, I am not studious enough to apply myself to books. I prefer the outdoors; I don't like being shut in, in a stuffy old room surrounded by dusty old books."

"No! You prefer to be shut in a musty old shed surrounded by grimy old plants!" Sarah quipped.

They both laughed as they passed by a bed of comfrey, their mauvebells hanging in drooping clusters. Alongside, grew some yarrow, its dull white clusters of flowers failing to catch the eye. The leaves of the yarrow provided relief for toothache and other gum disorders.

The final part of the garden was given over to culinary produce laid out in regimented rows. Purple leaved basil caught their eye, alongside white flowering coriander and curly leaved parsley. A bed dedicated to alliums, garlic and chives with their thin stems and bulbous purple heads bobbing this way and that lay alongside another that contained the herbs sage, dill, thyme and coriander with its pale pink clusters of small flowers. All these beds were edged with bright orange marigolds. They provided protection from slug attack and were used as an essential ingredient in ointments as well as being an aesthetic addition to the garden.

"What would you want to do with your life?" Sam asked Sarah.

Sarah mused on the question for a moment.

"Father has bestowed on me the most liberal of educations, so it would be a shame to let it go to waste," she began. "I too would like to travel, before I settle down and raise a family, but not into uncharted territory. I would be happy visiting famous places in the Far-East or the Americas helping the unfortunate and the needy."

"Then perhaps we might go together!" Sam suggested innocently.

"Yes!" Sarah agreed enthusiastically, "I could write about our experiences and publish them in a novel while you catalogued and listed your new discoveries and put them on show in a botanical garden. We would make enough money to buy a little cottage in the country and tell tales of our adventures to our grandchildren!"

"Not forgetting our memoirs!" Sam added.

"Indeed, Sam!" she finished.

Their last steps took them past rows of potatoes, beetroot, cabbage and broccoli and a whole host of other crops. On the other side of the path grew broad-leaved rhubarb, catmint, tall fronds of angelica and ungainly fennel brandishing its pastel yellow florets.

The apothecary garden led to the backdoor of the house itself, its outside walls festooned with nasturtiums, bright orange and yellow flowers rampaging every which way. They stepped into the kitchen where the rest of the family were waiting. Out front was where James Curtis, Samuel's father, made his preparations. The shop had two tall bay windows through which shoppers might view what was available within. The shop led onto the main street of Alton

"Ah, at last you two!" Samuel's father gasped, "I thought you'd never get here."

James Curtis was quite a tall man with a rapidly expanding waistline that befits a man in his middle years. He sat relaxed as best as he could on a balloon-backed Windsor chair. The buttons on his shirt strained under the pressure and his white necktie looked as if it was strangling him. His tricorn hat rested on the tabletop, his bald pate available for all to see. Wisps of white, wavy hair lay loosely about his ears. His face wore a frown, a professional seriousness, following years of intensive consultations and surgical operations. His eyes had a cold fierceness about them although his personality was quite the opposite.

"Well, Master Samuel, what is it that keeps you so busy up the glasshouse?" William Curtis, Sarah's father, enquired, genuinely interested.

William Curtis was not unlike his uncle in looks, if somewhat smaller in height and rounder in the body. He sat directly in front of the back door, turning ninety degrees to the table so that he could see the two teenagers more easily as they spoke. His tricorn hat rested close to James'. His legs were stretched out in front of him, crossed at the ankles, showing the well worn underside of his black buckled shoes. His black breeches disappeared under a large stomach that was just about held in by a plain white cotton shirt. White stockings gripped his meaty calves.

"I am exploring the merits of the camellia." Sam replied.

"A finer species of flora I have yet to discover," William observed, his chubby cheeks and red face breaking into a smile.

"Flowers and blooms are all well and good," Sam's father interrupted, "but they do not put bread on the table."

"I beg to differ uncle," William challenged, turning in his chair to face his adversary. "I have made a handsome living from 'flowers and blooms' as you call them."

"Agreed, nephew, agreed, but you are one of only a few. Others like you do not reap a similar reward for all such labours. Most are servant to the medical profession or in the pay of landscape gardeners," James pointed out.

"But times are changing father, " Sam began as he took up a standing position near the door. "The vast geometric landscapes created by the like of Capability Brown are being broken up into smaller, more aesthetic, units using flowers and shrubs."

"That might be the case, Sam, but all you will ever be is a glorified gardener, a lackey to those with established reputations. It is they that have the status," his father warned, wagging his finger in Sam's direction. "It was not so long ago that my skills as a surgeon and apothecary carried little more status than a butcher or a shopkeeper. Now I am welcomed in most areas of polite society, and that brings with it an improved reputation and a welcome swelling of the coffers. This affords me the opportunity to be generous of spirit when it comes to the poor and needy," James pointed out.

"But young Samuel has such a talent. Surely you can see his inner light shining when he is amongst his beloved flowers," William entreated, opening up the palm of his hand in the direction of his cousin. "He has a way with flora the like of which I have rarely seen. He can get plants to grow that other nurserymen can only dream of. I daresay he could get flowers to bloom in the desert!"

"There you are!" James interjected, "Nurseryman! Is that all his much acclaimed talents will aspire to? As a simple nurseryman he will barely be able to support his own offspring."

"The Landed gentry may be few in number but, as Sam quite rightly said, times are changing." William stood up to add effect and a touch of theatre to his final point. "There has been talk of creating gardens in towns and cities. Not private parks for the gentry as exist already but ornamental or botanical gardens to which everyone might have access."

"And who will pay for these gardens?" James asked.

"Perhaps Samuel might be able to turn the heads of Whigs and Tories. Perhaps he might impinge on their philanthropic nature to build gardens for the masses." Sarah speculated.

"I think you dream too much, young Sarah," James poured cold water on her ideas. "These social climbers are too busy creating follies, idols in honour of their false gods. They are not likely to spend their hard won profits on the poor. Besides, you are assuming Samuel would ever reach such a lofty status in order to impart such influence and persuasion. Enough, let's go into the drawing room and begin our meeting of friends."

Chapter 3

Walworth 1801

The early morning sun stabbed through the windows creating shafts of light around the gaps in the curtains. Light rays illuminated the chair nearest the window, highlighting the weals in the red leather as the chest of drawers cast its shadow on the far wall. A large beam spotlighted the old oak bed. Underneath the plain blue quilt, something stirred. The warmth of the two bodies wrapped up in a generous stuffing of eider had created a cosiness that each was reluctant to disturb. But the freshness of newly wedded bliss transcended other needs and provided a freedom of expression for each to explore the other. Sam and Sarah felt like pioneers, prepared to go where their imaginations and inclinations led them. Sarah took hold of his hand, silently enjoying the moment.

"I love you, Mr Curtis," Sarah sighed, breathless, staring up at the ceiling.

"And you are my heart's desire," Sam replied, also looking upwards.

"You will always stay faithful to me, Sam, won't you?"

"What need have I of another woman, when everything I have ever wanted is lying next to me?" Sam rolled onto his side and kissed her cheek gently.

"Even when my beauty has faded and my face lined with age?"

"By then my dear we'll have shared a life and though your outward appearance might not be what it once was, I will love you as I do now for what you possess within."

Moved by his words Sarah rolled onto her side so that they faced each.

"What was that?" Sarah asked twisting her body round to look at the window.

"Probably a bird striking the glass," Sam mused, "Or maybe a twig."

He took hold of her hour glass frame and pulled her towards him. Another noise rattled the window.

"Oh my goodness!" Sarah jumped. "What was that? Sam go and see will you?"

"If I must!" Sam said reluctantly.

"Isn't it about time you two got out of bed?" a voice shouted up from below. Sarah recognised the mocking tone straight away.

"Don't you think it would be polite to leave us be!" Sam shouted back, laughing.

"I don't know!" came the reply. "You've been married more than a year now. Has the novelty not worn off yet?"

"It might if you keep interrupting like this!" Sam countered.

"Good!" the voice returned, "Perhaps we'll get a full day's work out of you at last."

Sam stepped back from the window, leaving it open to let the fresh morning air flow in.

"I think I had better go." he said smiling at Sarah. "The master calls."

"You think more of your beloved plants than you do of me." Sarah teased.

Sam jumped into his clothes, drawing up breeches, slipping into boots, stretching into a shirt and fastening a necktie. He leant over to kiss his wife goodbye as he struggled with a brown brocade jacket. He stepped out of the house and into the garden. Waiting for him was a man somewhat shorter than he in stature but stocky. He was older than Sam by a good few years, the top of his head quite bald; it shone in the morning sun.

"And what is so urgent that you have to drag me out of bed at this ungodly hour!" Sam complained, keeping his face straight.

"If you are going to learn the nursery business you are going to have to put in the time." the man replied equally straight-faced. "You are going to have to do a lot less frolicking and focus more on learning new skills."

"I am." Sam replied as he stretched his arms upwards and yawned.

"Indeed." the man smiled, blinking as the sunlight caught his eyes.

"So, James, my experienced brother-in-law, what delights do you have in store for me today?" Sam enquired as he moved towards the man and slapped him affectionately on the back.

James Maddock was related to Sam Curtis by the fact that he had married Curtis' sister, Mary. They lived nearby, in a generously sized cottage, just on the edge of Walworth, a small town in the borough of Southwark. Maddock was a talented and experienced nurseryman and Curtis wanted to learn as much as he could. So, having bought the property with its generous acreage already used exclusively for cultivating plants, he apprenticed himself to Maddock.

When Curtis had first purchased Walworth, the flowers had been potted and arranged in symmetrical rows. Small pots were to be found on long wooden trellis tables, larger pots on low lying shelves supported by bricks, and the extra large pots were placed on the ground. The flowers had been simply arranged by variety so that a customer could choose the best from what was on show. It was a system that was simple to manage and one that had provided the previous owner with a fair income. The problem that faced Curtis was that other nurseries had sprung up to meet the growing demand for flowers mainly from the middle classes who would travel from the city to buy their wares.

"If we are going to compete favourably with other nurseries, we need to offer the customer something new." Curtis had said to Maddock.

"You mean new varieties of plants?" Maddock had asked.

"Yes, exactly that!" Curtis had been keen to put his skills in creating new hybrids or 'mules' as he called them.

"That will take time." Maddock had pointed out.

Curtis and Maddock rearranged the pots so that the colours of the flowers complemented each other. Customers that might have just bought one plant now bought matching plants. They could see how reds surrounded by blues brought out the intensity of each and frequent comment was made of purples mixed with pinks and reds.

Not content with simply juggling pots around, Curtis came up with the idea of creating mixed pots of flowers. "But different plants prefer different soils." Maddock had complained in an attempt to dismiss the idea out of hand. Curtis, however, seeing the emergence of a challenge, was not so easily put off.

"Perhaps, James, we can develop a soil, one that will allow most plants to grow." he had speculated.

"I don't suppose it would be impossible," Maddock had admitted hesitantly. "But it won't suffice for all plants." He added.

"We won't know until we try," Curtis had encouraged.

Although pessimistic about the success of such a venture and unsure about its implications, Maddock set about creating the 'perfect soil', one in which all varieties of plants might prosper.

'I think we must start with a loam,' he had instructed. 'It has a good structure, drains well yet retains moisture. If we imbibe it with a plentiful supply of humus then I believe we will get quite close.'

Maddock's research combined with Curtis' talents for creating all manner of mules produced a wide variety of flowers. Plants that could not be found in any other nursery, flowers that blossomed for longer and, it seemed, bigger and brighter than those purchased at other nurseries. Walworth Nursery became synonymous with quality and diversity. People began to flock to the garden.

Their early spring arrays of pansies and polyanthus had just finished and were being cleared away. The purple of the perennial pansies contrasted with the pastel yellow of the evergreen polyanthus. Curtis' beloved Camellias had started to brown and fade. He had placed them in large pots around the edge of the nursery in order to break up the monotony of the hedging. People could buy the traditional plain red Camellia Japonica with its bright yellow stamens or a white variety. However, what proved most popular were the mules created by Curtis himself. These included the Kew Blush, Rose-Coloured and Double White, Double Striped, each with their own particular combination of red and white petals. Curtis and Maddock could not cultivate enough of them to meet the demand and so they fetched a high price. Throughout the year different varieties of roses were placed in between the camellias to maintain the spectacle in front of the hedge.

Springtime moved toward summer and the nursery was alive with colour. At the far end of the garden, just before the glasshouses where Curtis and Maddock propagated plants to a production line schedule, a small orchard could be viewed. At present, all the trees were in bloom. The pale pink apple, cherry, pear and plum attracted a lot of interest but were not for sale. They were part of a project Curtis was working on.

Sarah had designed two flowerbeds in the shape of a flower. A mat of mauve aubrietas marked the perimeter and defined the shape and petal sections. Massed ranks of rich red tulips filled the petal space and the picture was completed with a centre circle containing clusters of pink auriculas. Pots of plants were placed in between the scalloped edges of the display, on shelves shaped like leaves.

Another group of flowerbeds contained a complement of purple and blue, bell shaped hyacinths and French marigolds, showing a mixture of red and orange pompom heads. Finishing touches included pockets of herbaceous flowers to add fragrance to the nursery, this included lines of English and French lavender marking a boundary between the flowerbeds and the outer hedge. The bobbing purple heads ran parallel with a gravel path around the perimeter. To the east, near the wooden outhouse that served as a shop, Curtis had recreated his and Sarah's favourite meeting place: an arboretum draped in scented jasmine and honeysuckle, a reminder of their time spent in his father's Apothecary garden.

"It won't be long before the other nurseries catch on and start to copy us," Curtis had stated.

"What else do you propose Sam?" Maddock had asked. "Surely we have done all that we can to embellish the nursery?"

"Not quite everything," Curtis had replied. "I think we should create our own publication."

"What on Earth for?" Maddock had exclaimed. "Surely we sell enough papers and periodicals without trying to hawk another one."

Maddock had a talent much sought after by others, but when it came to business he lacked intuition.

"If we produce our own publication we can promote the type and range of flowers that we grow here at Walworth," Curtis explained.

"But there are so many publications on the market, including your late uncle's Botanical Magazine, although it has seen better days."

Maddock could not see the point of putting what would be a lot of effort and money into such a risky venture.

"Sarah, what is the best selling magazine on the shelves?" Curtis enquired.

"*Thornton's Temple of Flora*," came the reply. "It is really popular."

"And why is it so popular?" Curtis asked.

"Because it has a few colour prints in it," Sarah informed him.

"Then we must match *Thornton's Temple of Flora* or do even better," Curtis pronounced.

"And how are we going to do that?" Maddock was still very sceptical.

"Do most people that buy from us enquire as to the details of how to maintain the plants or show any interest other than the colour and spectacle of the blooms?" Curtis enquired.

"Some people do!" Maddock was put on the defensive, unsure about where his brother-in-law was leading.

"How many people show an interest in how to maintain or grow the plants? Most people? Half? Less than half? Hardly any?" Curtis' tone was blunt.

"Probably less than half," Maddock admitted reluctantly.

"Then there is your answer!" Curtis stated. "What we need is a periodical that is not so verbose, one that shows off the flowers in all their glory, one that people will look at and admire the blossom."

"A publication without explanations and instructions!" Maddock cried. "Are you mad?"

"Of course we will have some explanations, or at least information about the flowers, but we will keep the language to a minimum," Curtis elaborated. "You see, James, it is all a question of emphasis."

Maddock remained unconvinced.

"Many of our customers buy from us because they do not want the hassle of growing the plants themselves that's why they return time and time again, to replace the plants that have died off. Most of them do not have the inclination to keep the seeds and endeavour to cultivate their own flowers year after year."

"That's profligate," Maddock complained.

"Indeed!" Curtis said. "But these monied people do not seem to bother. They use their new found prosperity to fuel their excesses and the regular purchase of flora happens to be one of them."

"If we do produce a periodical along the lines that you have suggested, the quality of the prints is going to have to be something special," Sarah had mused.

"I agree," Curtis was already thinking along similar lines.

"And that will cost money," Maddock moaned, "Money that we can little afford."

"We will require a highly skilled artist who possesses a keen eye for detail," Curtis ignored his James' bleating.

"And how will we locate such a person?" Maddock continued to try and pour cold water on the idea. "Such artist's do not frequent our social circles; they seek out more lucrative contracts among the rich."

"We shall just have to advertise and see what comes our way," Curtis spoke with confidence but with more than a little bravado.

As the morning wore on their daily routine was halted by one artist after another. Some were quite talented but wanted too much money, others would have worked for peanuts and a quick glance at what they had to offer showed why. It was quite late in the afternoon and business had waned considerably when the last of the prospective artists turned up. Maddock was on his knees leaning over his prized tulips when a voice behind him disturbed his daydream.

"Excuse me, can you tell where I might find Mr Curtis, I am here regarding the paintings?" she said in a squeaky, high-pitched voice. Her enquiry irritated Maddock, not that he needed much encouragement.

"You're too late!" he barked, talking into the flowers and ignoring her.

"I will speak to the master not the servant." she retorted.

Fury rose in Maddock and, as his pulse raced, his face flushed with anger. He threw down his trowel and turned to give this woman a piece of his mind but, as he caught sight of her, his jaw dropped and was lost for words.

There are women whose beauty is fleeting, perhaps a radiance borne out of child-bearing or perhaps a youthful bride veiled in white. Clara was all of these and more. Maddock's eyes rested first on her face. Her sandy hair had been caste in ringlets that hung like catkins around her face and forehead. Her hair had been lifted, fixed in place with a neat little bonnet, revealing a neck of sublime smoothness. She possessed a button nose speckled with a few freckles. Her lips were small and tight, but what snared Maddock were her smiling eyes fixing him to the floor like a statue; their blueness contrasted with the milky, marble white of their surrounding, bearing into him and rendering him speechless. His eyes moved down her body. Her simple, white gown, embroidered with small dots, gave her an elegance that emphasised her petite frame. A neat, little bosom supported by a braided empire line and covered by a bright blue spencer jacket buttoned at the front added shape to her slimness. Her feet wrapped in soft black leather shoes were in proportion with the rest of her body as were her hands, her fingers small and delicate with elegantly manicured fingernails.

"Well?" she scolded not at all amused by his vacant expression. "Where will I find Mr Curtis?"

"Standing right next to you!" Curtis answered making her jump a little.

"Why, Mr Curtis." she replied in a high-pitched squeak, holding her hand to her chest. "You gave me such a fright."

For a moment, just a moment, they shared the briefest of eye contact. In that moment they came together, knowingly, to the exclusion of any other. They held their breath, hearts beating louder, palettes desiccating at the thought. He was captivated by her eyes, unblinking, full of expression, confident, engaging and provoking.

"Then let me ease your palpitations by taking you around our beautiful gardens, it will prove most restful to your emotions I am sure," Curtis sprang back into life, opened up his palm and indicated for her to walk with him.

"Why thank you, Mr Curtis; you are such a gentleman. I would love to walk among these beautiful blooms." she said looking up at him with doe eyes.

Maddock's initial shock gave way to envy as he watched his brother-in-law stroll away with this beauty at his side. Curtis looked over his shoulder and gave Maddock a wink. Maddock returned to his weeding muttering loudly.

"I must apologise for my brother-in-law!" Curtis smiled.

"Oh, I was bit short with him," the woman apologised.

"He has a cantankerous nature, but he is a skilled nurseryman nonetheless and I am most grateful for what he has taught me."

"My name is Clara," she declared, "Clara-Maria Wheatley."

"Not the same Wheatley that created the popular Cries of London?" Curtis asked.

"No, that was my late husband, Francis; he died not long ago."

"Oh I am sorry to hear that," Curtis was genuine in his condolence.

"But I was the model in many of his paintings," she revealed.

"Indeed!" Curtis pretended to be impressed. "But what we require is an artist not an artist's model."

Clara laughed at the misconception.

"You are mistaken Mr Curtis, I am now a painter in my own right, I have had my work exhibited at the Royal Academy on a number of occasions."

"Indeed!" Curtis repeated himself, this time he was impressed. "And you would like to come and paint our humble plants, how so?"

"I have recently taken up painting flora and it is proving to be increasingly popular, so I am keen to take on this project. Besides, work is work, Mr Curtis and I have to earn a living for myself now that I have no husband to support me and with three daughters to raise," Clara explained.

Once they had visited the whole of the garden, Curtis escorted Clara back towards the house. At that same moment Sarah and Mary came out of the shop inquisitive of this vision that was holding their respective husband's attention.

"This is Mrs Clara Wheatley," Curtis introduced Clara to them both. "And this, Mrs Wheatley, is my beautiful wife, Sarah, and my sister-in-law, Mary."

"It is a pleasure to meet you both," Clara greeted them with a broad smile and polite handshake. As she took hold of Sarah's hand, Sarah was made aware of Clara's confidence. Although brief, the handshake was firm and full of vigour. This transference of conviction, aligned to her unquestionable attractiveness, made Sarah feel quite inadequate. Turning to Curtis, Clara said:

"I must make my way home now, Mr Curtis, before dusk sets in."

"Samuel, if you please," Curtis gently corrected her.

"I must get back to my daughters," she explained.

She shook hands with Curtis and Maddock, who could not keep the inane grin off his face. As she walked away from them Curtis shouted to her:

"I will be in touch, Mrs Wheatley, about the arrangement."

She looked over her shoulder and smiled.

"Clara, please call me Clara," she returned

"Clara!" Maddock swooned in jest. "She's as pretty as a picture and that's no lie."

"What is this arrangement she spoke of?" Sarah asked, raising her eyebrows at Curtis. He shifted awkwardly under her gaze.

"I have commissioned her to paint the pictures of the flowers."

"Have you seen any of her work?" Sarah asked.

"No, but she tells me that she has exhibited work at the Royal Academy."

"She has told you this, dear husband, but you haven't seen her work? She might be selling you a tale."

"I intend to travel to her studio tomorrow and see her work for myself." Curtis revealed.

Spring had just turned to summer as Maddock and Curtis removed the fading spring flowers and replanted with emerging summer blooms from seeds sown in early spring, having been propagated in the glasshouses then placed outside in cloches to harden before final planting. Curtis, Maddock and Sarah laid out their plans for their summer arrangements with their usual attention to detail. In the height of the summer there would be rectangular beds displaying spires of bright blue lobelia peeping over purple dahlias with their bronzed leaves, which, in turn, would be surrounded by a flush of much smaller pinks radiating a deep pink hue.

Clara had begun painting. The presence of an artist with such a good reputation added to the interest in the gardens at Walworth and word spread. People would stop and stare at her work in progress. Clara often enjoying the banter of passers by, it was an ideal way to promote her talents and she made the most of it. Curtis and Maddock were no exception when it came to chatting to Clara. Maddock in particular would make a beeline for her, offering his 'expert' opinion, whether she asked for it or not. She took his comments with good grace.

Mary watched Clara from a distance muttering scathingly to Sarah.

"Just look at the woman, she speaks to all and sundry, has she no morals?"

"Does she really need to play up to every gentleman that passes by? She should know better, a woman of her age."

"Her age?" Sarah enquired.

"She must be beyond her thirtieth year at least." Mary speculated.

"How do you come by that?" Sarah was not convinced.

"She told us that she married just before the age of twenty, she has had three daughters, the eldest of which is in her teens, that puts her beyond thirty."

"Well if what you say is true then she has more talents than I first thought and good luck to her, with a face as beautiful as that and a figure to match, she won't be long without a man."

Mary's comments registered with Sarah. She had never before felt the nagging pain of jealousy. Her educated upbringing had taught her to be objective and reasoned in her dealings but call it what you like: instinct, woman's intuition, Sarah felt uneasy about this flirty, sylph like female, especially when she was in close proximity to her husband

Soon after, with Mary's warning ringing in her ears, Sarah watched with dismay as Sam approached Clara. They greeted each other warmly, chatting in a relaxed manner. Sam crouched and plucked a flower from the display she was studying. Clara accepted the gift and gently took in the scent. Sarah's eyes narrowed as her husband took hold of Clara's hand and eased it closer to her face so that she might better detect the flower's fragrance. Clara leant backwards, her effervescent smile evident as she spoke. Sarah frowned at the provocative posturing. As Clara resumed painting, Sam crouched beside her. His chin was almost resting on her left shoulder and he appeared to be whispering in her ear. His arm moved around the back of her neck and rested on her right shoulder. Sarah could not quite make out what his intentions were. Was he pointing to something on the canvas? Again the two shared a joke and Clara turned to face Sam so that their lips were only a fraction away from each other. Sarah was horrified. Her heart raced and she went quite pale. Not long after, Sam stood up, said a few words to Clara and then departed, heading towards the glasshouses with a distinct spring in his step. Sarah was curt with him for the rest of the day.

As they got into bed Sam broke the silence.

"Have I done something to offend you my dear?" he asked tentatively.

There was a long pause until eventually Sarah answered.

"You seemed to be paying Mrs Wheatley a lot of attention this morning?" her voice was terse.

"Not at all, I was merely showing an interest." Sam replied.

"So, what were you talking about that required you to get closer than might be deemed decent?" Sarah's voice was tinged with hurt.

"I am sorry my dear, I wasn't aware that I had gotten 'indecently' close."

"I saw you put your arm around her shoulder!"

Realisation began to dawn on Sam. "I was merely pointing to her artwork and discussing the colour of the pinks she had just painted. Dearest Sarah please don't be so jealous," he pleaded. "You would be so impressed with her efforts, she has captured the deep pink of the petals and their texture but what I liked most was the blue-grey of the narrow leaves and the general composition of the work, it was exquisite."

His effusion irritated Sarah even more and clashed with her own guilt at what seemed to be such a plausible explanation. Mixed emotions created turmoil.

"Then why present her with a flower and then take hold of her hand like that?" Sam was confused.

"I plucked a flower for her so that she could smell the clove-like scent. Her sense of smell must not be as attuned as her visual senses and so I eased the blossom closer for her to get a closer draught. Where is the harm in that?"

He took Sarah in his arms and held her tight in an attempt to reassure her. Soon after, he leaned across her and blew the candle out. They settled under the covers, still cuddling and drifted into sleep both thinking about one person, Clara. Another morning found Sarah alone in bed, her husband gone.

"Where has Sam disappeared to?" Mary asked as she and Sarah pottered in the shop, arranging this and tidying up that.

"Up to Covent Garden and then onto Southwark to see Mrs Wheatley."

"On his own?" Mary's voice sounded surprised.

"Of course on his own, why shouldn't he?" Sarah's tone belied her true feelings

"I wouldn't let my James anywhere near that Wheatley woman."

"And why not?" Sarah tried to hide her own convictions.

"Because the temptation would be too great. I wouldn't trust him and I certainly don't trust her. She's a widow, and that sort of woman has needs, you can see that and she doesn't care how she satisfies them. She'll whip Sam away from right under your nose."

"I trust Sam. He wouldn't even consider such a deed, he loves me." Sarah declared but there was doubt in her reply.

"I don't subscribe to the belief that a man and a woman can have a relationship that is purely platonic, 'tis not natural. There is always more to it than meets the eye."

"Sam is in love with *me*, nobody else." Sarah was genuinely hurt by the inference.

"That might be the case but if you think Sam is different than all other men, then you are as naïve as you are young Sarah. Look how he cannot take his eye off her when she is working. What do you think he is doing, admiring her painting?"

"Enough, Mary!" Sarah asserted. "Sam and I are happily married, and I will not let you poison my mind with idle gossip!"

The two women went about their business once more but this time there was an uneasy silence. Sarah was determined to steer clear of Mary and so be spared anymore damaging talk.

As the days passed Curtis decided that it would be prudent to keep his distance from Clara, even though he felt that he had nothing to hide. He busied himself in his greenhouse doing what he did best, hybridising plants. It was intricate work and demanded lots of concentration as well as time.

Eventually he broke his silence with Clara. She was still working on the pinks as he passed by. Her gown was pastel yellow in colour with a revealing bodice, but the bareness of her chest was hidden in part by an opaque, off white fichu.

"It looks like it might be a wet day, you'd best be careful," he said, speaking at a distance.

"Thank you Sam, I will," Clara replied while she worked another colour into the painting.

"Surely this poor light cannot be conducive to such artwork?" Curtis could not help but step a little closer to see what she had achieved.

"On the contrary, the impending blackness seems to have brought out a radiance in the blossom giving it a hue the like of which I have never seen."

Clara mixed colours on her palette with an urgency that Curtis felt inclined not to interrupt. Was she trying to get the colour right before the heavens opened or was she busy catching the moment before the light changed. He moved away quietly and slowly, careful not to disturb her any more. He strode towards the greenhouse; his mind switching back to the work.

About an hour into his work, he heard the telltale sound of raindrops on glass. At first it was intermittent, lacking rhythm and at its most irritating. His concentration spoiled, he took the opportunity to stand up and give his legs a stretch. He had been sitting, bent over, almost stationary for so long his lower back and thighs were quite stiff. He walked around the glasshouse peering at this and poking at that when he became aware of the rain once more. It had picked up a distinct patter, like the sound of tiny feet running over the glass roof. He thought about Clara and wondered whether she had sought shelter. He stepped to the doorway and leaned out trying not to get caught by any stray droplets. When he saw Clara struggling with canvas, palette and parasol, he burst into action. He reached her in a few steps, grabbing the parasol just as the clouds burst. He directed her towards the safety of the glasshouse, endeavouring to keep the parasol over her and her precious painting as they ran.

"Any damage done?" Curtis was genuinely concerned.

"No, I think we were lucky!" Clara put him at ease as she checked over the painting looking for telltale signs of smudging. "The palette seems to have caught the brunt though."

Clara tipped the palette vertically so that all the excess water drained from it onto the floor. At the same time Curtis released the catch on the parasol and placed it upright against one of the benches. He cleared a couple of plant pots and brushed the dust and dirt away so that Clara could rest the precious canvas. Curtis took hold of the palette and placed it nearby.

"Well, my knight in shining armour, you came to my rescue just in the nick of time," Clara's sunny disposition made light of the inclement weather. "Just look at you! You're soaked. Here, let me wipe away some of the drops from your face with my handkerchief."

Before Curtis could react, she had stepped up to him and, on tiptoes, began to mop his brow with a white cotton handkerchief that she had produced from under her sleeve. Curtis stood rigidly, like an awkward teenager embarrassed by the actions of an over zealous aunt.

"There," Clara concluded, "that should do the trick."

And then she raised herself up once more and kissed him on the cheek.

Before Clara could set her heels back on the floor, Curtis threw his right arm around the small of her back, lifted her off her feet and pulled her close, so near that their noses touched. Without hesitating Curtis kissed her. He placed his left hand behind her head, holding it steady so that he could force home his advantage.

Initially surprised at Curtis' response, Clara eventually relaxed into his arms, allowing herself to feel the power and strength of his muscles as they tensed around her. She opened her mouth a little to soften the pressure of his advance. She could taste his warm breath and she smiled inwardly at the feel of his heartbeat as it thudded against her bosom.

As quickly as Curtis had gathered her up he put her down. He pulled her arms from around his neck and staggered backwards as if shot. He gasped for breath, his face bright red and his eyes wild with emotion.

"I'm sorry, Clara, I don't know what came over me!" he wheezed. "It's so unlike me to, to take advantage of a woman like that."

"Please do not feel guilty on my account," Clara said as she stepped towards him, keen to continue where they left off.

Curtis took a step back, trying to keep a distance between them, fearful that if they embraced again he could not hold back his mania.

"No Clara, this is wrong!" Curtis held up the palms of his hands in an effort to stop her advances. "I am a married man."

He made for the exit, closely followed by Clara. Luckily the rain had eased considerably and so nothing appeared to be amiss as he left. As he reached the doorway, Clara called to him.

"Sam, don't leave!"

"I must!" Curtis said without turning round.

As the torrents fell, Sarah felt a wicked pleasure knowing that Clara was out in the open, exposed and most likely getting a good dousing. As the storm abated, Sarah stepped to the entrance of the shop and peered out in the direction of where Clara had been sitting. All that she saw was an empty easel and two vacant stools. As she stood, cursing her luck, Sam emerged from his greenhouse followed by Clara. Sarah's dismay rose as she saw the anxious look on her husband's face. Something was wrong, something has happened during the storm, in the greenhouse. Her imagination ran riot, fuelling feelings of envy and loathing. A knot in her stomach made her feel light-headed and nauseated. How could he betray her so?

The evening meal brought with it another silence. Sam tolerated the discomfort, principally because of the guilt bubbling inside of him. His thoughts kept returning to his moment of indiscretion. If he said nothing, his own silence might incriminate him.

"Are you angry at me again?" he asked.

"What do you think?" Sarah's retort was telling. He felt himself go pale. Had she seen them together? Was his secret no longer a secret? What did Sarah know?

"Yes, I can see that you are annoyed, but why so?"

"As if you don't know!" Sarah looked down at her meal, picking but not eating. "I saw you, with her!"

"And what exactly did you *see*?" Sam feigned effrontery.

"I saw you stepping out of the greenhouse and her following you." Sarah looked up at him accusingly.

"And what do you deduce from that?" Sam returned her accusing stare. He must remain cautious he thought.

"That you were alone together!" Sarah declared.

"Indeed, we were alone together," Sam admitted. "And do you know the circumstances that led up to us being *alone*?"

Sarah looked back down at her food, embarrassed at her lack of fortitude.

"It was raining!" he declared. "It wasn't just raining if you recall, as you must have done if you were spying, the deluge was torrential. I had run out to give assistance, to help her with her work so that it wouldn't be spoiled, and made for the nearest shelter: the glasshouse."

There was another silence, an uneasy pause as Curtis endeavoured to purvey an air of angst. In reality he was wracked with guilt. Sarah, head bowed, looked fittingly ashamed. Curtis softened his tone.

"Sarah, I don't know why you can't find it within yourself to trust me."

Curtis had always been a man of honesty and integrity but as he uttered these words, he too, was ashamed, his conscience pricking him hard. But the alternative, to tell the whole truth, was something he just could not bring himself to do, for fear of the damage it would cause. Equivocation was as far as he would allow himself to go.

Sarah rose up out of her chair, stepped over to her husband and knelt at his feet, placing her head on his lap.

"I am so sorry for doubting you, Sam," she apologised.

"You are forgiven, my dear," he ran his fingers through her hair. But even now at the point of reconciliation, Clara came between them. Sarah shed no tears, envy simmering inside, but this time deeper, to be kept in check for the sake of their marriage.

Curtis stared into space. What was it about this woman that had turned his head so? Clara offered him something his wife could not give, an element of risk, a dangerous liaison. But it was more than that. He hardly knew the woman but already there was empathy between them, something not yet tangible but it was there nonetheless. He could not describe his feelings for Clara to himself, so there was no way he could begin to explain how he felt about her to Sarah. It was a topic that was best left alone.

Clara visited Walworth on many occasions and Curtis reciprocated, taking time out to visit Clara at her studio above the Milliners shop. He rarely spoke of his visits, not wanting to alarm Sarah. Sarah chose not to enquire of his movements when he went to the city, but in her heart of hearts she knew that the two of them had dealings. The guilt was obvious, in the way that he would avoid her gaze when he first arrived home, his over indulgent greeting and the brief peck on the cheek when he was going to see her.

The Beauties of Flora was published and had the desired effect; bringing many new customers to Walworth. Curtis made a lot of money, capital that he invested wisely. Clara was commissioned to paint for another book 'Monographs on the Family Camellia', a collection of Curtis' prized Camellias.

Never one to rest on his laurels, Curtis started to think beyond Walworth. The nursery was very popular and would, no doubt, have provided him and his family with a steady income for many years. But Curtis had ambitions that had outgrown the limitations imposed by these gardens. Financial prosperity was fine but it would not set him aside from the rest. He wanted much more than to just provide plants for a nouveau riche, he wanted to establish himself as a major name in the world of horticulture, on a par with, or even more famous than, his late Uncle William.

His beloved camellias had given him a flavour of what recognition can bring, affording him cult status among the floral fraternity. But he felt that there was more inside of him, waiting to emerge. Here at Walworth he had discovered the elements of plantsmanship and now a formula was manifesting itself inside his head, one that might just bring with it the acknowledgement he sought.

Like a sorcerer's apprentice, he had absorbed all that Maddock had to teach and more besides. Now he had the ability to create soils that acted like magic potions. When a seedling was eased into the rich mixture even the most stubborn of mules would sprout forth. All plants seemed to have a vigour in both colour and definition that put to shame nurserymen with much greater experience. His own skills in establishing new varieties, a talent that had developed since childhood now had a medium in which it could prosper and with it defy the natural order laid down by the creator.

"Tell me Sam," Clara asked as she applied a delicate brush stroke to her painting. "Do you have any ambitions beyond Walworth?"

"Indeed I do, Clara!" Curtis replied as he lay on the four poster bed watching her at work. "Having learnt as much as James can teach me, I am desirous to unite a perfect knowledge of the best hardy fruits in cultivation, together with a more intimate knowledge of every kind of useful and ornamental gardening that has hitherto been practised in England."

Curtis rose up from the bed and stepped over to see the painting Clara was finishing.

"Here's to the first of the paintings that shall be our latest published work. Here's to the 'Iconographie du Genre Camellia'."

"This book is a strange one indeed Sam." Clara commented.

"Not really," Curtis replied. "It is a natural step after the *Beauties of Flora* publication."

"But it will comprise of only five pictures and will be so large. Who is likely to buy such document at a cost that is bound to be prohibitive?"

"It matters not how many copies are sold Clara." Curtis explained. "What is important is that we record these camellias for posterity so that future generations can marvel at their beauty."

He leant over and gave Clara a kiss on her forehead. Whether Sarah liked it or not, the two of them were bound together in a special relationship of which Sarah could never be a part.

Chapter 4

Glazenwood Essex 1826

The road leading to the gardens at Glazenwood was very busy. It was full of slow moving carriages and horses champing impatiently, eager to reach their destination. There was a whole host of speedy curricles, gigs and even the occasional barouche attracting the attention of the rest. The objective of their sojourn was an entrance directly opposite Coggeshall Road, the one that ran between Overing and Braintree. Like many country estates the original Coggeshall Road had been hijacked and annexed, becoming the driveway that led to Glazenwood House. A pair of parallel five-barred gates prevented access to the uninvited.

The well to do folk that sat patiently in their carriages were, mainly, people with money from the third class of society: clergy, doctors, merchants, bankers, lawyers and the like. These were the nouveau riche aspiring to be pillars of society but lacking somewhat in terms of breeding and pedigree. They had come from London to take in the country air, visit the gardens and maybe buy a plant or two for their own burgeoning grounds, an emphasis of their rising status in society.

Carriages and their occupants were directed to an adjoining field where a large marquee had been erected to stable the horses. Once alighted, the visitors made their way on foot to the main entrance running the gauntlet of a plethora of stalls and booths. Refreshments offering all manner of attractive seductions were on sale. Cut flowers were sold by the bunch; often for buttonholes and as decorations for the ladies' hair. Potted plants of varying shapes and sizes were picked up and haggled over along with baskets laden with fresh fruit and vegetables.

It was a short walk from the field to the entrance, back along the road following the picket fence that marked the boundary of the property. At the entrance, two doormen checked tickets. Being a Quaker, Curtis was not one to sell his customers short. The two guineas annual fee gave the subscriber an entitlement to receive full value for his money in the shape of produce from the gardens or in gardening publications, these were produced by Curtis, of course. People that enquired about trees or plants could have them delivered to their homes in London 'on very liberal terms'. If the subscriber did not have a garden or an interest in studying plants, they could get their value in ripe fruit from a certain Mr John Guildford of Covent Garden.

From the line of traffic, a four-wheeled barouche, drawn by a fine pair of horses, turned and stopped in front of the gates. Their jet black hides sweated from the effort of pulling such a large carriage. The coachman was also dressed in black, complete with cape and tricorn hat. The fact that the carriage had not followed the rest drew particular attention. Those queuing to enter had to move aside to give it way.

The canopy that might have afforded some privacy was intentionally down so everybody could see the occupant. In the rear of the carriage a lady sat upright, shoulders back and head held high, not an easy posture to maintain with all the jogging about. Once attentions were alerted, Clara Maria Pope was one of those people that you could not help but gaze at. She had a propriety and refinement to which so many aspired. Despite her advancing years, she still commanded the beauty of a woman much younger, embellished by clothing that offered discretion and elegance.

She wore a light blue day dress, a pelisse robe made from the finest silk. Unlike similar attire worn by younger women, no flesh was visible around the chest, a white lace fichu eloquently disguised her ageing neckline. Her once lily-white hands now speckled with brown lay hidden beneath short white gloves that finished where the sleeves began. Her hair was arranged in an Apollo knot, plaited into loops revealing a bone structure that had stood the test of time. High cheekbones, a straight jaw, small lips and a nose proportionate with her features. The amazing white of her eyes emphasised the steel blue of her pupils.

The doormen recognised her immediately and proceeded to open the gates. Once ajar, the carriage driver ushered the horses forward. Clara looked along the drive up to the main house, some three hundred yards in length and marvelled at its splendour, situated among so much flora. The track was a sight to behold, almost disappearing as the trees that grew either side swallowed it up.

Behind the Villa to Clara's left hand side grew the American garden. It covered an area of about two acres and was dedicated to shrubs and trees from that continent. Here could be found a fine specimen of black walnut, a giant redwood, still in its infancy, a Western Red cedar and willow oak with its grey-brown bark and slightly furrowed green, willow like leaves each with a tiny bristle at its tip. Male and female catkins dangled lazily, attracting whatever insects happened along, the male flowers, yellowish-green in colour.

Red maple and an American elm could also be spotted, but the real attraction in this part of the garden was the prehistoric Maidenhair tree, the Gingko Biloba. This relic, left over from the carboniferous era, was a must for interested gardeners. It had lobed shaped pale-green leaves that turned an eye-catching yellow in autumn. It also yielded fleshy, plum-like fruits.

Most remarkable about the American garden, however, was not just the fact that it contained so many exotics alien to this country, but that all of them grew to gigantic sizes in a soil that was not their usual peat or heath mould. The secret of their success, and ultimately Samuel Curtis' success, was in the loam they grew in developed by Curtis.

Clara could only just make out the American garden as she was taken up the long gravel drive to the house. She cast a glance in its direction, making a mental note that she would try and take in its atmosphere during her short stay. Her view of the American garden and many of the other attractions was obscured by row after row of fruit trees. She had once been told by Curtis that there were no less than seven thousand apple trees, three thousand pear trees, fifteen hundred cherry trees and a smaller amount of plum trees in addition to several other fruit bearing trees. Each row was alternated with a row of filberts and nuts such as walnut and almond, about ten thousand in total. It was an exhaustive plantation, with all the trees arranged in parallel lines so that, in whatever direction they were viewed, they give a perfect linear perspective; standing to attention like an army of soldiers on parade.

The fact that this was the largest orchard in Britain might have proved to be a big attraction in its own right, but Curtis was not content with merely creating an orchard. Although Clara preferred the ostentatious vista as might have been seen in a landscape garden created by Capability Brown or Repton, she could not help but admire the beauty combined with the functionality of Curtis' creation. True to his word, Curtis had managed to establish just about every hardy fruit tree from around the known world, here at Glazenwood.

Clara, like many others, had often wandered off the beaten track to walk among the falling apple blossom in late spring as it fell from the trees and covered the ground like snow, a white blanket with just a hint of pink. All the walks had been carefully sculptured and lined with flowers to add colour and spectacle to the orchard. There were herbaceous borders containing delphiniums and lavender. Borders based on a cottage garden theme where the visitors could enjoy the deep colour of violets, yellow primroses, blue anemones and purple aubrietas. There were also flowerbeds with bunches of dahlias, delicate red geraniums, carnations, tulips and purple crocuses with deep yellow hearts. Under the boughs laden with produce that could be plucked and tasted, scents and aromas were trapped, intoxicating the passer by with a headiness that remained long after they had made the journey home.

The carriage made its way cautiously along the main drive passing people in their day attire, ladies in peignoir dresses of cashmere, merino or silk ranging in colour from pale pink to bright blue. Some wore short waist length Spencer jackets, others, pelisse cloaks. The men were dressed more soberly and uniformly in charcoal grey or black, outfits consisting of black top hats, Wellington hats, morning coats or frock coats and black trousers or strapped pantaloons over the top of ankle length black boots.

About half way up the road on the right hand side, Clara looked out for the rose beds. They stretched in a long line for over a hundred and fifty yards, their perimeter marked by a rectangular path. She could see lots of people strolling along, stopping to admire the twelve hundred or so varieties that Curtis had planted. There were many roses of French origin, mainly delicate tea-roses of the Noisette variety, coloured peach-pink, saffron yellow and buff, all with a soft musk scent. To contrast these, Curtis had planted richer coloured hybrid roses like the cup-shaped Bourbon rose.

The driveway opened up into a dropping off area covered in loose pebbles. To the left hand side, and arcing around the back of the house, were a number of large cedar trees, their parallel branches sweeping out at right angles from the trunks clothed in a redwood bark. Close to the house on the right hand side a wide variety of magnolias stood guard, the largest of which was Magnolia Grandiflora, a conical tree rising to almost thirty feet. It had huge, creamy white flowers contrasting with the deep, dark-green, glossy leaves.

The house itself was a typical, stone built, regency styled country house. Curtis' modestly designed frontage was luxuriantly clothed with the splendid Wisteria Consequana. The twining stems of this vine had spread all over the one hundred foot frontage of the house snaking upwards over thirty feet high. Clusters of fragrant blue flowers hung about soft, hairy deciduous leaves contrasting with the grey stone of the building. If this was not enough trails of Bignonia Caproeolata made an appearance, their red trumpet shaped flowers with orange throats peeping around the east wall, supported by tendrils clinging to the wisteria vines and anything else they could find.

From an upstairs window Curtis' wife Sarah looked down and saw Clara arriving. Sarah felt her heart drop as old misgivings surfaced. Here she stood, a lone figure, pale and wan and not in the best of health, her father's affliction all too evident. How could he not be affected by Clara, she was beautiful still, flirtatious, a magnet for all men.

"There is nothing between Clara and me," he had said moving nearer to grasp her hand.

"Then why must you invite her? She is nothing to you now; she has served her purpose and has been rewarded handsomely for her work," Sarah enquired.

"She is a friend, dearest," Curtis replied looking directly into eyes which were full of envy and hurt. "It would be rude of me not to invite my friends to share in our success."

"If you loved me, you would not have invited her you know how I feel about her," Sarah became quite tearful.

Sarah and Sam Curtis had brought thirteen children into the world, but every time Clara Maria Pope stepped into their lives, the doubts crept in. Like a leaky tap, they gnawed away at her resolve.

"If you loved me, you would trust me," Curtis replied.

"But she is so promiscuous, flaunting herself at every opportunity," Sarah pointed out.

"She is an artisan, they are all flamboyant that's what makes them so interesting and …." Curtis searched for the word.

"Everything that I am not!" Sarah interrupted.

"Different," Curtis concluded. "They are different and yes I do enjoy her company for that very reason. But if you think that I would replace you and put her in your place you are very much mistaken."

Curtis held her firmly at arms length, paused as he chose his words carefully and tried to smile to alleviate her suffering.

"If I am to be pilloried for spending too much time in the arms of another and lavishing them with the attention that I should have given to you then let's be clear about whom it is I have been so indiscreet with. Who is it that I am truly passionate about? Who is my concubine? My lover? My mistress?"

Sarah looked at him aghast.

"My mistress is my work Sarah. My career has been my only indulgence to the exclusion of everything else at times, even you, I am sorry to say," Curtis admitted.

It was not what Sarah wanted to hear and his revelation left her cold. She stopped shaking and pulled away from his grip.

"You had better go and meet your guest," She said sulkily, turning her back on him.

Curtis could do no more. As he opened the door a young girl no older than seven danced in holding a rag doll at arms length.

"What a beautiful party father, the music is divine. Emily and I are dancing," she said as she spun round and round. Curtis said nothing, he just stopped to let her past, smiled as she pirouetted and then closed the door behind her.

The jollity of the polka played by the Coldstream Guards Band hastened the depression that swept over Sarah, furthermore the music had just woken up Georgiana, their thirteenth child, and she cried loudly straining to be heard over the tune. Curtis dashed down the stairs, across the hall, through the front doors and nipped down the steps in between the two balustrades.

"Clara, it's so good to see you," he said with a joy that he could hardly contain.

Clara glanced up briefly at the window from which Sarah looked down, their gaze locked momentarily before Clara looked away.

"And it is so good to look upon you once more, dearest Sam," she replied, holding onto his hand for longer than might seem decent.

"How have you been?" he enquired as they turned to walk back up the steps.

"I am in good health, all things considered?" she answered pertly.

Curtis stopped at the top of the steps and turned to face her, a handsome man in this his middle age. He had his mop of dark brown curly hair but now it was manicured about his greying temples and his cheeks were ruddy after years spent in the open. He wore a black Newmarket Jacket, buttoned at the front over a white shirt and necktie. Cream pantaloons stretched taut across his beefy thighs were strapped under his black ankle boots.

Clara moved closer to him. They looked so relaxed in each other's company Sarah thought as they exchanged polite conversation. They looked every bit a couple. She could stand the anxiety no more and turned to attend to the young child tugging at her dress, the rag doll hanging limply in her grip.

"What is it Clara? What do you want?" Sarah scolded. She took her anger out on the child, yet another reminder of the woman she so distrusted. Her daughter's name was Clara Maria, named in honour of Mrs Pope, on the insistence of her husband. There was no escape as all around Sarah were reminders of this cuckoo in their nest.

"Come, let me take you through the house and to the garden at the rear; the Band are playing beautiful waltz tunes." Curtis set off with Clara, linking his arm as they moved towards the oak-panelled front door.

They followed the hallway to the rear of the house without speaking. It ended at a pair of large French windows that were already open. The windows led the couple onto a large paved veranda. Lots of people in less formal day wear gathered in eclectic groups sipping wine. Some engrossed in polite conversation, others laughing and lightening the atmosphere around them. The jovial atmosphere was further enhanced by the band as they played a selection of popular waltzes. Curtis entered the throng accompanied by Clara. Heads turned and tongues wagged, making him shift uneasily. Clara on the other hand lapped up the attention. He leant towards Clara as they moved.

"There is somebody I think you might like to meet," he said.

"Is he dashing? Is he rich?" Clara enquired enthusiastically.

"He is both!" Curtis declared. "And he is eligible!"

"Then I must meet him!" Clara replied eagerly, "come, Curtis, introduce me to him."

Curtis led her over to a man who was standing alone seemingly taking in the view of the garden from the veranda, a view much like the front of the house, acres of fruit trees dissected by paths lined with flowers.

"You must take a walk beyond the orchard Sir Henry," Curtis said as he approached.

"And why should I want to do that?" Sir Henry queried, his voice reflecting his obvious breeding.

He turned to face the couple, showing no emotion and appearing quite aloof. "I like what you have done with Glazenwood, Curtis. It's quite functional but there are too many trees for my liking."

"There is a quite exquisite tropical garden, the Australia garden full of exotics beyond the fruit trees opposite the Acre Piece," Clara informed Sir Henry anxious to make her presence known.

As Clara looked at him her pupils dilated invitingly. For his part, Sir Henry returned her gaze then looked her up and down admiring her slim figure and small bosom.

"Pray tell me, Curtis, who is this vision that stands beside you?" he asked standing erect and inhaling so that his chest protruded.

"May I introduce you to Mrs Clara Maria Pope, Sir Henry," Curtis carried out the formalities. "And this is…."

"Sir Henry Pelham Fiennes Pelham Clinton, Fourth Duke of Newcastle," Sir Henry interrupted.

Clara offered her hand. Sir Henry placed his hand over hers in an act of ceremonial dominance. Immediately she stepped up to him.

"It is pleasure to make with your acquaintance," Clara smiled as she spoke.

Sir Henry was a tall man, much taller than Clara. He was of slim build with light, sandy hair. His facial features were as sharp as his manners. Two deep-set, beady eyes stared menacingly beneath a pair of bushy eyebrows. He wore a permanent frown that many a would-be adversary found disconcerting.

"I see that you are married," Sir Henry observed.

"Yes," Clara replied, "to, Alexander Pope, he is one of the best actors in London."

"I am sure he is," Sir Henry's tone was disparaging.

"He is a fine raconteur," Curtis added, as he handed Clara and Sir Henry each a glass of wine.

"No doubt!" Sir Henry remained unimpressed. "I have had occasion to work with a few actors myself!"

"Sir Henry is talking about Parliament and the House of Lords," Curtis enlightened Clara.

"Would you take a stroll with me Mrs Pope?" Sir Henry asked. "Perhaps you could show me the delights of the Australia garden."

"I would be honoured Sir Henry," Clara replied.

She turned to Curtis and said:

"Perhaps we will speak later, Sam?"

"I will look forward to that," Curtis replied, smiling wistfully.

As the couple moved beyond earshot, Curtis heard another voice. It was deep and resonant.

"Are you admiring flora or fauna?" it said.

Curtis recognised the voice immediately.

"Both!" he replied smiling and then as he turned, "Dr Hooker, I presume?"

He took hold of Dr Hooker's hand and shook it warmly. There was a tightness of grip between the two that reflected deep mutual respect.

"And how is the Regius Professor of Botany?" Curtis asked, still holding onto the Man's hand.

"I am well, Samuel, and how are you on this fine day, feeling more than a little pleased with yourself no doubt?"

"That I am, William!" Curtis replied.

Handshakes finished with, Curtis and Hooker walked back towards the house. Hooker was a little rounder in the body than Curtis and not nearly as swarthy. He had a large balding head with whiskers hanging on the side, showing distinct signs of grey. His facial features were bulbous and, like Curtis, he had a ruddy complexion. He was dressed in a plain black morning suit with a white shirt and black necktie.

Once inside they took a right turn into Curtis' study. Three walls were all panelled with oak. The wall furthest from the door was the exception. It was covered from floor to ceiling with shelves full of books. Most of the books were about plants. Some were reference books gathered over the years but most were leather bound manuscripts mapping all his well-documented research since his early explorations at Alton.

In front of the Georgian windows that looked out onto the front of the house sat a splendid Sheraton writing table. His favourite chair, a Heppelwhite, sat empty behind the desk. It was well worn, showing signs of surrender. The only other furniture in the room were two fiddleback chairs in front of the desk and a small plain mahogany side table by the wall opposite.

Curtis was not one for too much fuss, although the merriment going on around him might have made anyone who was not acquainted with him think otherwise. The only decorations around the walls were five portraits of camellias. At first glance they all looked the same, white and red flowers on a backing of greenery, but on closer inspection it was clear that they were all from a different genus. They included the anemone flowered, myrtle leaved and pompom varieties of the Camellia Japonica. The attention to detail provided by the artist was comparable to that given by the grower who had created these hybrids, Curtis. The artist was none other than Clara Maria Pope.

"I still find these monographs quite extraordinary," Hooker exclaimed. "Clara is such a talent."

"Yes, she certainly is!" agreed Curtis.

There was a short period of silence as Hooker analysed each painting in turn. While he was thus occupied Curtis sat down at his desk and shuffled the papers in front of him.

"If we are going to relaunch the *Botanical Magazine* and compete with Sydenham Edward's Botanical Register, we are going to have to give the readers something new, something different, something that will excite them!" Curtis stated with urgency.

"Full colour plates?" Hooker speculated in some amazement as he turned to look at Curtis.

"Why not, it worked for my *Beauties of Flora* publication?" Curtis countered looking directly at Hooker. "If we can get the same quality that you so admire in these paintings it will give us the edge over our rivals. Perhaps I might even persuade Clara to work on this project with us." Curtis continued unperturbed.

"I suppose," Hooker was not convinced.

"And we won't stop there!" Curtis stated, slapping his hand on the desktop as he spoke. "Not only will the *Botanical Magazine* be unequalled in its accuracy of colouring and the number of its coloured plates, it will also be the best with respect to the truth and minuteness of its written detail, enhanced by its beauty of typography."

Their conversation was interrupted as the doors to the room opened. Sir Henry walked in as bold as brass, striding up to them both; his long, slim legs eating up the ground in an instant.

"There you are, Curtis!" he admonished. "What kind of host are you, skulking in darkened rooms and locking yourself away from your guests."

"I'm sure my guests would be better entertained in the presence of such a luminary as yourself, Sir Henry, rather than a boring old gardener like me!" Curtis replied, smiling, "and where is the engaging Mrs Pope?" Curtis could not help enquiring.

"Gone to seek other prey!" Sir Henry commented. "She is a most agreeable woman, if lacking somewhat in breeding, and she is very easy on the eye, although I do prefer to chase much younger fillies." The three of them smiled knowingly.

"Sir Henry, may I introduce Dr William Hooker, Professor of Botanical Science at the University of Glasgow," Curtis said, dealing with the formalities.

"Botanical Science?" Sir Henry exclaimed. "Botany isn't a Science it's women's work!"

Hooker was more than a little taken aback by Sir Henry's brashness and considerably affronted by his comment, but the look on his face did not deter Sir Henry from continuing.

"I mean its status is no higher than flower arranging, painting and embroidery. Pursuits of women with nothing better to do with their time than scour the hedgerows and woods in search of pretty little blooms as keepsakes in their diaries."

"On the contrary, Sir Henry!" Curtis came to his friend's defence, "botany is very much a science."

"How so?" Sir Henry was on the attack, "Where is the experimentation?

Where is the Mathematics? Where is the accuracy and precision that something purporting to be called a science demands?"

"I have built my reputation around experimentation, precision and accuracy," Curtis stated, "my apprenticeship at Walworth was all of these things. I learnt much from my brother-in-law, James Maddock, one of the finest nurserymen in the land."

"Nurseryman!" Sir Henry mocked. "That's not science that's gardening!"

"Gardening it might be to you, Sir, but learning how to culture plants is very much a science," Dr Hooker managed to get a word in. Sir Henry fixed his stare on Hooker.

"Please enlighten!" he asked in a superior tone.

"For any plant to grow it needs soil but plants will not grow in any soil they have to grow in soil that meets their individual needs, it's not such much botany as biology," Hooker began.

"Don't patronise me sir, I know what it takes to get a plant to grow," Sir Henry snapped, his stare fixed on Dr Hooker who began to feel more than a little uncomfortable under his gaze, "and anyway that's trial and error not science!"

"Trial and error *is* experimentation!" Curtis seized the moment.

"If you then add nutrition required by the plant." Hooker added.

"Manure! Call it by its true name man! Horse shit! Pig shit! Cow shit!" Sir Henry was enjoying every moment, arguing his case was his forte and winning the argument was the challenge. "It's all the same"

Sir Henry allowed himself a wry smile. Winning was not just about presenting the facts you had to bully and browbeat your opponent to test his resolve.

"Again you are mistaken Sir Henry," Curtis picked up the gauntlet, "each type of manure contains different ingredients and different plants prefer one combination or another."

"Then there is the amount of water required, quality of light and the time of year," Hooker added.

"These variables determine whether a plant will grow and how well it will grow," Curtis concluded.

They worked as a pair to defend their corner, but Sir Henry was having none of it. Two against one were odds with which he was comfortable.

"And your point is?"

"It is only by experimentation that we can come up with the correct combination of variables to grow each individual species," Curtis elucidated.

Sir Henry broke away from glaring at the two of them and began to pace the room, his hands held together behind his back.

"And what does all this research bring to the scientific table? I can see that you have profited greatly by your endeavours, but it hardly matches up to Newton's Laws. How does it help us understand the fundamentals of nature?" Sir Henry's tone was less aggressive but still direct.

"Of course botany seeks to explain the fundamentals of nature!" Dr Hooker replied.

"And what fundamentals might those be?" Sir Henry enquired.

"We have already dispelled the spurious theory of Special Creation!" Hooker boasted.

"Which is?" Sir Henry enquired.

"That all species have been created by God and that their characteristics are fixed at the time of creation to suit the environment in which they were placed."

"What evidence do you have to support your claims? Without such evidence your words are tantamount to blasphemy!" Sir Henry was objective in his observation as opposed to being zealous.

"Samuel and his ilk have already shown that we can create mules, different genii of plants of the same species. This shows that we can interfere and by the same token that raises the question about Natural Theology," Hooker pointed out.

"And the hand of God as a creator!" Sir Henry interrupted.

"There is an economy of nature. Flora and Fauna have not just been placed in an environment that suits their needs by some supposed creator. If this was the case then nature would be in a state of disorder," Curtis added.

"Is this not the case?" Sir Henry enquired. "If I left my lands alone, it would go to seed quickly enough and be covered in thickets, brambles and all manner of weeds. Surely this is nature in disorder."

"Linnaeus observed that each creature had its allotted place in nature having been assigned its particular food or geographic range. His studies imply a pre-ordained constancy and harmony that is an economy of nature. Robert Brown observed that there is correlation between the variety and number of species and latitude," Hooker lectured

"And Humbolt has provided a comparative study showing that the number of species declines with increasing altitude," Curtis augmented.

"It is called Botanical Arithmetic!" Hooker exclaimed with some satisfaction.

"Don't make me laugh!" Sir Henry mocked. "You give a grandiose title to what is little more than counting plants, and expect people to take you seriously. Your argument just doesn't stand up to scrutiny. This constancy and harmony could be pre-ordained and, in fact, be the hand of God."

"Botanical arithmetic is but one manifestation of a more fundamental law, a natural law that explains the origin of all species," Hooker explained further. "I am sure you are acquainted with the exquisite piece of prose Zoonomia, written by Erasmus Darwin."

"I have had occasion to peruse the book. It is a piece of poetry, not a scientific manual," Sir Henry observed.

"Then you haven't read the notes that accompany the prose Sir Henry," Hooker noted.

"God forbid, no!" exclaimed Sir Henry, "they are incidental meanderings. They are far too exigent for my tastes."

"On the contrary Sir Henry, they are groundbreaking observations!" Hooker pointed out.

"If we can understand the mechanism of plant distribution and add that to our knowledge of plant cultivation then…" Curtis attempted to continue but was interrupted by Sir Henry.

"Then what?" he stopped pacing and glared at Curtis. "You can grow ever more exotic plants for those foolhardy enough to part with their money just so that they keep one step ahead of their high society friends? If I thought your work contributed to our nation like Newcommen's steam engine or Brunel's engineering then I might take you seriously."

"Then we can grow crops like rubber, cotton, timber, sugar, tea, oilseed, spices and fruits and nuts like those that surround us now more efficiently and profitably in order to help sustain our empire and strengthen its foundations," Curtis concluded.

"Curtis' work with mules is not only helping us to understand better the origins of species it is also helping to develop crops closer to home so that we are not as dependent on nations half way across the world," Hooker explained.

"Rubber plantations in Kent?" Sir Henry poked fun at the idea, "and sugar plantations in Devon?"

"Why not?" Curtis speculated, "just imagine being able to grow cotton in Lancashire."

"A very interesting thought Curtis but just how close are you to achieving such admirable aims?" the first sign of recognition from Sir Henry brought a hint of a smile to Hooker and Curtis.

"Research takes time Sir Henry," Curtis explained. "It has taken me twenty years to establish Glazenwood."

"And what are your conclusions?" Sir Henry asked, seeking clarification.

"My conclusions are there for you to see, to taste and to smell!" Curtis pointed an outstretched arm towards the window.

"And what of the other crops you mentioned? Have you begun to grow these in this country?" Sir Henry continued.

"Only under glass and outdoors, with limited success," Curtis revealed.

"Then all that you have is conjecture," Sir Henry concluded.

"With respect to some crops, but with others we have had more success. I am, at present, investigating the growth of New Zealand Flax. If we can grow this in larger amounts we will have no need to ship it from its native country." Curtis explained.

"That would be very beneficial to the Royal Navy," Sir Henry mused.

"Indeed!" Curtis agreed, having already made early overtures to the Royal Navy.

There was a pause while the heat of the argument subsided. The two friends sat in silence awaiting Sir Henry's next comment but it never arrived. He moved towards one of the paintings and stood quietly admiring it.

"That's one of Clara's pieces," Curtis informed him.

"She has a deftness of touch and an eye for detail for one so lacking," Sir Henry stated.

"Perhaps Sir Henry might consider supporting my venture," Hooker asked nervously, chancing his arm.

"And what venture is that?" Sir Henry sniped.

"To restore Kew gardens to its original splendour and develop it into a centre of excellence for botanical research," he explained.

"Are you asking for money?" Sir Henry's response was tart.

"Not directly," Hooker replied, "but it would help enormously if you could use your influence to get the government to fund the project."

"Public money for a science that is not yet proven, I don't think so," Sir Henry dismissed the request out of hand. "We are still paying for the Napoleonic wars, why should we want to fritter away our hard pressed resources on a risky project like that?"

"You do not share our vision then, Sir Henry?" Curtis observed sarcastically.

"Vision?" Sir Henry replied, "tunnel vision more like! You and your kind have eyes only for what is before you. You are blinkered when it comes to broader issues."

There was another pause, eventually broken by Curtis.

"Would you like a cigar Sir Henry?" He enquired pulling open his top drawer.

"No thank you!" Sir Henry's reply was curt. "I can't abide the damn things. All that noxious smoke it's not good for the constitution!"

Another uneasy pause preceded Sir Henry's exit.

"If you don't mind Curtis I will take leave of your fine hospitality," he said.

"Must you leave so soon Sir Henry?" Curtis was genuinely sorry to see him go. Despite his cantankerous nature Curtis found Sir Henry's forthrightness stimulating.

"I have business in London and I would like to get there before nightfall," Sir Henry explained.

Once Sir Henry had left, Hooker turned to speak to Curtis. They sat down in their respective chairs.

"So Samuel, have you achieved all that you set out to achieve?" he asked. "Is this it? Is Glazenwood your Garden of Eden?"

"It's close but it is not quite perfect," Curtis replied. "I still have ambitions to explore further the boundaries of plant propagation."

"Then why don't you come and join me in developing Kew?" Hooker enquired.

"I will help in any way I can William, but I don't think that is the right direction for me. I am looking for a different challenge," Curtis revealed.

"And what new challenge do you seek that Kew would not provide?" Hooker was intrigued. "You will not want for labour. You will be afforded the time and space to do whatever you like and, when I have secured the finances, you will not want for money."

"My dream is not about financial gain; my dream is to push back the boundaries of ignorance surrounding horticulture. I have shown that we can create mules in just about every kind of plant and that we can cultivate most hardy varieties outside of their natural environment using such techniques and the knowledge regarding soils gleaned from my friend and mentor Maddock. The next, and most logical, step is to explore the possibilities of growing more exotic varieties in the open, varieties that do not have to be hardy in order to survive. If I can achieve this aim I will truly have created Eden."

"Where will you begin?" Hooker asked. "Spain or France perhaps?"

"No William," Curtis replied, "I want to see if I can find a place in Britain where such plants may be grown."

"A new frontier for botany, heh?" Hooker stated.

"Indeed William, indeed!" Curtis drew deeply on his cigar and smiled at his friend.

They carried on talking business for a couple of hours, drinking claret and smoking more cigars, until the drawing room was thick with smoke.

Chapter 5

Rozel 1841

Curtis looked landward, studying the area just beyond the shore. Behind him the sea was a blue-green aquamarine with a tidy wave rhythmically ebbing to and fro. The wave stretched to a thin film before retreating, dragging with it a smattering of rounded pebbles, clattering and chattering as they were reluctantly displaced from the rest. Curtis changed his position on the sandy part of the beach in response to the creeping waterline lapping around his feet.

He had travelled as far north as the Isle of Skye in Scotland and worked his way south looking for sheltered bays that were free of hard frosts and strong winds. The Scottish highlands threw up many a hidden gem but strong Westerlies rising up out of the cold North Atlantic, coupled with impermeable black granite through which roots could not penetrate, meant that he had to travel further south in search of the ideal location. His journey took him to Cornwall. The climate was much more forgiving and the Gulf Stream was at its most potent. There were many protected valleys but again the rock strata proved to be pivotal with granite again the main obstacle.

So now he stood on the beach at Rozel, a touch further east than Bouley Bay. It had an interesting valley, with sides not as steep as the others along the north coast but still inclined enough to offer adequate protection from weather extremes. The bay itself pointed north and east meaning that one of its sides faced towards the south, offering long hours of sunlight. The opposite side was, in contrast, more sheltered. Collectively they offered the possibility of growing a wide range of plants and that raised Curtis' interest. He decided to stay a little longer and carry out a thorough study of the valley.

Curtis stumbled his way across the slippery pebbles and larger boulders making his way towards the rock exposed by tidal barrages. Green, slimy algae and masses of bladderwrack made the route particularly treacherous underfoot. Once at the rockface he took out a small knife from his inside pocket and began to dig away at the soft loess that held the pebbles together.

"Conglomerate!" he exclaimed, shouting above the soft sound of the waves. "The rock here is not like the rest of the island. See how the stones pop out like eyes from a socket. This would be ideal for roots and this soil, although it is quite sandy it still has texture."

With this discovery, enthusiasm gripped Curtis. He could barely keep the grin off his face yet he did not want to appear too keen, lest his companion Mr Machon see how enamoured with the land he was and increase the price accordingly. Mr Machon owned the land behind the houses at the head of the valley into which Curtis now progressed, clambering up a grassy slope to gain access.

"Does the valley meet with your requirements Mr Curtis?" Mr Machon asked.

"On first appearances it looks ideal," Curtis replied, "but I need to study it further and in some detail before I can give you a definitive answer."

"Feel free Mr Curtis, and take your time. As you can see the land is not in use at the moment but it has been in my family for generations and has great sentimental value. It would make for good pasture or perhaps a cider apple orchard," Mr Machon gave it the hard sell.

They walked past the small crofting cottages, with their thatched roofs and uneven bleached white walls, all knobbly, having been constructed from the same conglomerate Curtis was so excited about. Outside their doors fishing nets and lobster pots were stacked, exuding a pungent smell that filled the air. A small stream tumbled down from the top of the valley, etching out a narrow channel before it fell onto the pebbly beach, finally surrendering itself to the sea.

"The valley is well watered and the flow suggests a healthy supply," Curtis observed.

"Indeed Mr Curtis," Mr Machon concurred, "it runs with some vigour all year round."

"And what of the weather?" Curtis asked as he looked fleetingly up at the clear blue sky.

"It is a most temperate climate Mr Curtis," Mr Machon could not help sounding like a salesman as he over zealously described the weather. "We enjoy hot, balmy summers and gentle winters. Spring and autumn are very pleasant. I can't deny we do suffer the odd tempest but this valley is protected from all but the most damaging of winds."

"Indeed!" Curtis mused, assuming Mr Machon was telling the truth.

The South facing side of the valley rose steeply overlooking the house below. About a quarter of a mile upstream the cliff face was sheer, its bare rocks poking out from the thin topsoil like skeletal fractures, the exposed bone whitened by the sun. From the cliffs to the shore the land fell in steps, offering natural terracing. Curtis' imagination went into overdrive.

"Look at the way the land lies, it has such a sunny aspect. That sunbaked soil and natural terracing is just the job. With a little work it will support many flowers and shrubs and that would not be out of place in the South of France."

Mr Machon remained silent, walking a couple of paces behind Curtis, content to rub his hands in expectation. All he could see was useless furze. Tufts of grass clinging to rocky outcrops and thickets of green gorse; their bright yellow flowers now faded and replaced by dusty brown seed packets. There was an odd hawthorn bush and oak wizened by the prevailing winds, hanging on for dear life.

Curtis turned to look at the other side of the valley. It reached a similar height but the climb was much gentler, offering a smooth curve from the stream with only the last few yards being awkward to walk up. This north facing side had lush vegetation. Its floor was a thick carpet of grass leading up to a wide variety of small trees and shrubs. Needle sharp gorse were prominent, warning off any unwelcome grazers seeking to munch on their bright yellow flower caps. There were tangles of brambles, their thorns hidden amongst the green ferns that blanketed the area, waiting to snare and scratch thieves who might seek to relieve them of their yet unripened blackberries. Honeysuckle fought a running battle with the brambles as they chased and wove about each others stems. Young saplings, sycamore, elm and beech forced their way out of the morass as did knots of heather, their purple spires just about visible.

"What is this place called?" Curtis asked Mr Machon.

"It bears the name 'Le Mont Crevieu ou La Chaire'," Mr Machon replied.

"Very evocative, but it is too long winded. I shall just call it La Chaire!" Curtis declared with some satisfaction. "Now Mr Machon, if you please, let us return to the carriage and ride back to St Helier. Perhaps on the way we might discuss the details and come to an agreement regarding the purchase of the land."

"My pleasure!" it was Mr Machon's turn to try and keep the smile from his face.

As the carriage made its way past cider apple orchards with Jersey cattle grazing between the trunks and boughs and other fields lined with potato crops sprouting from linear raised beds Mr Machon could not work out how such an eminent gentleman could get so excited about a useless field. A fool and his money are easily parted, he thought, but who was he to complain if he profited as a result. However, even if conscience did not prevail, inquisitiveness did get the better of him. Mr Machon could not resist querying Curtis' motives for wanting to purchase the land.

"If you don't mind me asking Mr Curtis, what exactly are you hoping to do with the land, grow apples or potatoes or perhaps graze cattle?"

"None of those things Mr Machon!" Curtis laughed, "I am going to create a garden."

"A garden eh?" Mr Machon was confused.

"A garden the like you have never seen before!" Curtis bragged, barely containing his excitement. "It will be a testament to man's superiority over nature."

It was spring of the following year before Curtis returned. His daughter, Harriet, had made good all the legal details and the valley was now owned by her father. Mr Machon had been further employed to gather together a workforce capable of carrying out the work Curtis wanted. Today was the day when the workers were introduced to their employer. They had arrived by foot or by cart, standing idly down by the harbour, armed with shovel, pick or axe awaiting the emergence of Curtis.

"I wonder what it is they want doing 'ere?" one swarthy looking man asked, his bowler hat cocked to one side.

"It's not for us to question what they want doin' with it, not while they're payin' two shillings a day." his friend observed.

"Aye, that's a handsome wage for sure!" another man piped in, "It's no wonder there are so many 'ere waitin'."

Curtis strode leisurely towards them carrying a small leather bound book in his right hand.

"Good morning gentlemen!" he greeted them

There were mumbles of 'mornin' in reply, most men just bowed their heads or doffed their headgear as a mark of respect.

"My name is Mr Curtis," Curtis replied, "and if you follow me I will explain what it is I want you do."

Curtis turned on his heels and made his way from the harbour, past the houses at the foot of the valley and proceeded to clamber up the slope that slipped down from the north side of the valley to the shore. The men followed, trampling through bracken, bramble and gorse. Even at sixty two years of age Curtis was no slouch. He led the men at a good pace up to the top, where the steep slope began to level out. He stopped at a rocky outcrop and turned to face them. The men would eventually nickname this place, Pulpit Rock, because it was here that Curtis would gather them together, on occasion and preach to them. Preaching to a mass audience was not part of

Quaker tradition but Curtis felt inspired to give an oration, stimulated as he was by the setting and by his ambition.

"Gentlemen, if you will humour me, I would like to explain to you what it I want to do here," Curtis began. "You are standing in the Garden of Eden."

His revelation did little to appease their confusion.

"If this is the Garden of Eden then I'm a Dutchman!" somebody called out.

"It may not look much like the Garden of Eden at the moment," Curtis continued. "It doesn't look much like a garden at all but with your help we will transform this God forsaken valley into an oasis of splendour, reminiscent of the Garden of Eden. In the beginning the earth was without form, devoid of beauty just like this valley."

"You're not wrong there!" someone piped up.

"At present, the valley has a dampness of spirit, a shadow that brings a shiver to your bones. We will create light in this darkness; a bright light, a resplendent glow of colour that will radiate and reflect around the contours of the valley, dazzling all who feast their eyes upon it."

"You keep telling us what it will be like here, but you still haven't told us exactly what it is you are going to do!" the swarthy man asked.

"In the book of Genesis, God charged us with the task of 'making all plants and animals subjugate to our will. He put forth plants yielding seeds and fruit trees for us to tame."

"We do this already?" the swarthy man pointed out.

"But God placed many plants and trees in places around the world, places where only these plants seem to be able to grow."

"Surely that is God's will?" another man stated. "We are all subject to the will of God."

"Perhaps we are!" Curtis replied, careful not to upset them. "But if God asked us to subjugate plants then surely it is up to us to see if we can grow such flora as and where we want them to grow?"

There was an uneasy mumbling at Curtis' reply as well as some understanding nods.

"And how do you propose to achieve such a feat?" the swarthy man asked.

"If you take a walk around the noble houses of England you will see glasshouses with all manner of exotic plants inside them. There are orangeries, peach houses, houses where pineapples grow in abundance." Curtis sought to reinforce his argument. "To do so is alien to the forces of nature because as soon as you try and grow them outside they wither and die. But if we were to take plants from all corners of the empire and beyond, and grow them here, in the open under the firmament, without the aid of glass then what we will have created is a Garden of Eden, here in Jersey. When God created Eden, in the east, remember, out of the ground he made to grow every tree that is pleasant to the sight and good for food. That is what I am going to do here, in this valley. Look down there, we even have a stream and was there not a stream that worked its way through the Garden of Eden?"

"It's all a bit far fetched if you ask me!" one man whispered.

"I think you're right but who are we to question the why's and wherefore's," came another man's reply.

"Look at the wages he's payin'!" a third man butted in, "For those wages I'd build a castle out of sand on the beach and rebuild it every time it got washed away with the tide."

"Anyway, gentlemen time is money!" Curtis interrupted the chatter that had begun to rise out of the gathering. "If we are to finish the project, first we must begin.

The construction of the gardens started in earnest. Having shared his vision with the workers, gossip soon spread and he was the talk of the island. Most dismissed him as a crank or an eccentric with nothing better to do than to whittle away his children's inheritance. Not long after, a visitor came to look at how the work was progressing.

"Tis good to see you again William!" Curtis shouted as he moved forward to meet his good friend Sir William Hooker. Hooker looked every bit the gentleman in his brown cloth Newmarket tailcoat, paisley patterned waistcoat made from the finest blue silk and lavender coloured moleskin trousers. He was topped off with a brown top hat, which he raised as a greeting to his good friend.

"And you to!" Hooker replied as he shook hands warmly, each grasping the other's hand in a double handshake.

"Now Hooker, let me show you what I have been up to!"

Curtis could barely disguise his enthusiasm. He led him from their carriage to the foot of the valley. From here Hooker saw many men hard at work. Much of the original vegetation had been removed and there was a belt of young saplings almost enveloping the valley. The trees were placed as close together as could be expected. Once established they would prove to be a substantial windbreak.

"This is the most salubrious of locations for your garden!" Hooker stated, standing at the edge of what was no better than a building site.

"It looks more like Sebastopol at present!" Curtis replied.

"Yes, but one must look beyond the here and now and visualise what is to come."

"And what do you see?" Curtis was always eager to glean ideas from his great friend and mentor.

"Well, up there on that North facing slope I can see Rhododendrons. From here the soil looks quite thin and the underlying rock is stony is it not?"

"Purple conglomerate!" Curtis picked up one of the many ovoid pebbles strewn about in the soil.

"They are like fruits of the earth!" Hooker enthused. "Igneous gems rounded by ageless irritation." He stooped to pick a large purple stone. "They look like petrified potatoes!"

"And these are not unlike filberts," Curtis cherry picked some smaller stones.

"And those over there are akin to damsons or plums!" The two men laughed as they tossed the stones away.

"This strata is ideal! Rhododendrons flourish in their native Himalayas at high altitude where the climate is cool. If you are careful with your choice of variety they should be hardy enough to survive anything the Jersey weather can throw at them."

"As you see I have planted a layer of Quercus Ilexa round the edge of the valley," Curtis pointed out.

"Further down the slope should become a little more temperate so you might try establishing less hardy shrubs," Hooker suggested.

"I have heard tell of a Japanese shrub, one that bears exquisite, yellow fruit not unlike miniature pears," Curtis enquired

"Eriobotrya Japonica!" Hooker exclaimed, "or Loquat. An interesting choice but don't expect it to yield any fruit."

"Why not?" Curtis frowned.

"I suspect the climate here will be too cool for it to bear fruit, although it should prove a useful ornament to your garden," Hooker revealed. "Why don't you explore the possibility of raising a crop of Thea Viridis?"

"Green tea?" Curtis looked perplexed. "But its flowers are so inconsequential."

"That is true, but if you could grow the plant out of doors here in Jersey, then maybe you could establish a tea plantation just a stone's throw from England."

"And put myself in competition with all the tea in China?" Curtis laughed at the absurdity of the prospect.

"It would be nothing less than they deserve after they tried to create a monopoly. Thank goodness we discovered the self same plant growing wild in the hills above Assam. Besides," Hooker added, "It would be a fitting memorial to Linnaeus seeing as it was he who introduced Thea Viridis to Europe in the first place."

"Did he really?" Curtis was genuinely intrigued by the fact.

"Yes, but only under glass as part of his botanic collection," Hooker explained.

Hooker turned to face the south side of the valley. The foundations for the house had already been laid, the steep rocky cliff behind it hewn to make a recess for Curtis' new residence.

"Your house looks quite modest in size compared with Glazenwood," Hooker observed.

"What need have I for a mansion any more? My family is grown up and gone. I have only myself and my memories to keep me company and they will be that much closer to my heart in such a small space," Curtis reasoned, "besides, less building means more space for my beloved plants."

"And what is it you are attempting to achieve with this side of the valley?" Hooker asked as he looked up what appeared to be paths winding their way around the natural strata of the rocks.

"I am terracing this side to give it a Mediterranean appearance," Curtis explained. "Having so many trees and shrubs on the north side I think it will provide balance to have smaller shrubs and more flowers on this side, these will enhance the Mediterranean vista don't you think?"

"As we talk I am beginning to realise just how special this location is!" Hooker enthused. "You have an area to the north that is tantamount to the more temperate regions of Indo-China, and to the South you have a distinct Mediterranean or possibly even sub-tropical landscape if you can maintain the temperature and humidity. I have to say Curtis that I can think of few places that could offer such a range of climates and geography in such a relatively small space. At Kew I am in the process of achieving a similar result but only under glass. I am envious of what you are trying to do here, Sam."

"I have achieved nothing yet William, but the ambition is there," Curtis was flattered. "How are the botanical gardens progressing?"

"We have just revolutionised our heating system. We have replaced the old coal-fired flues with pipes through which hot water circulates. It is described by its developer as 'central heating' because the water is heated by coal-fired boilers. This allows us to control the temperature in each glasshouse by the use of valves and stopcocks. We place trays of water on the pipes, allowing us to control the humidity. A gentleman that goes by the name of James Hartley has discovered a method of making much larger pieces of glass, he calls it 'sheet glass'. All free of bubbles and bulges, thus allowing more light into the glasshouses. All in all we are now in complete control of the environment in the glasshouses so that we can grow just about anything!"

"The difference between Kew and here is that I am endeavouring to grow the plants outside under the full exposure of nature, whereas you are making use of man's technological advances to effect a similar outcome. If I were a betting man I would place a wager on which project would be most successful!" Curtis threw down the gauntlet. Hooker placed a firm hand on Curtis' shoulder as they stood side by side.

"I would not want to relieve you of your hard earned money Sam, especially now you have retired!"

Hooker remained on Jersey for a while, working with Curtis on the planning and organisation of the garden. They discussed the type of plants most suited to the environment as well as ones Curtis might 'experiment' with. Orders were placed and it was a few months before they started to arrive.

Curtis leaned over the edge of the harbour wall to watch his merchandise as it was offloaded. Wally had arrived some time before with the horse and cart. He had reversed the cart so that it was about a yard from where the stone steps emerged onto the jetty. Wally, his assistant, remained in the cart to oversee the transfer. The deckhands made their way up the steps, which were slippery from a layer of bright green moss. Under their arms they carried cylindrical packages made from bamboo. Some were quite long and thick, others were considerably smaller and thinner. Curtis was not happy with the treatment they were getting.

"Keep them horizontal," he instructed.

The sailors did not take kindly to his tone of voice but recognised that this was a man of some authority, so their reaction was confined to furrowed brows as they passed by him. Having been chastised they placed the tubes gently onto the cart.

The last parcels to emerge were larger wooden crates with glass sides and top. It took two men to manoeuvre each of these up the steps. The grip the men had on the crates looked decidedly flimsy and Curtis could not resist making his feelings known.

"Careful with those glass crates!" he shouted. "These plants are precious and quite fragile. They do not take any comfort from being shaken around like that."

"Don't worry yourself Mr Curtis, Sir!" the captain called as he oversaw the transfer. He was a thickset, ruddy faced man with a greying beard. His clothes were heavily stained. "My men are steady on their feet, just you see."

" 'cept when we've 'ad a skinful of ale!" one of the deckhands joked as he stepped from the boat. His lack of concentration coincided with a sudden swell that raised the boat up causing him to stumble. As the swell receded, he fell backwards pulling the crate and the deckhand at the other end with him. The pair of them crashed onto the deck with the crate sandwiched between them, miraculously upright.

"Look's like 'e's started early!" one of the other sailors laughed.

The captain turned and scowled, cutting him to the quick.

"No 'arm done 'eh?" he tried to reassure Curtis.

Once the cargo had been offloaded and stacked on the cart Curtis pulled himself up alongside Wally, who, in turn, encouraged the horse forward. The packages had travelled from all over the world. The bamboo tubes had the ends stoppered with clay or rubber. Wax cloth had been wound around to seal in moisture and to prevent salty air getting to the plants inside. Most of these were of oriental origin judging by the lettering stamped on the sides. Some of the large Wardian cases also came out of Indo-China but most of these carried flora from the Americas, Australia and New Holland.

Wally guided the horse and cart past the cottages and turned into the valley road. The white house that was La Chaire was quite distinct among the sandy brown soil that covered the rest of the valley floor. It was a neat and compact residence, virtually box like in shape. Large Georgian windows had been symmetrically placed either side of a large oak door, painted black and housing a robust brass knocker in the shape of a flower. Above the door a small skylight brought welcome daylight into the marbled entrance hall. A short plinth supported by a pair of mock columns surrounded the door itself. The only other visible features that could be seen from the front were two smaller upstairs windows sat directly above the picture windows below, and the tetrahedral slate roof upon which a chimney stack was placed at its apex. A reasonably sized glasshouse had been erected on the side of the house that faced north-east. It was of cast-iron frame construction and had a woven, spiked ridge along the top.

The house had been sited just off the valley road and access was via a path that led in from the south-west. The space for the house had been quarried out of the rocks that towered above it, dwarfing it as they rose vertically behind.

Once at La Chaire, Wally called in a couple of helpers to offload the cart and under Curtis' instruction placed them carefully in the adjoining glasshouse. Wally had tried to look at the contents of the Wardian cases as he moved them but condensation inside had made the glass opaque.

Curtis instructed Wally and the two other men to begin to open them straight away. As each carton revealed its contents Curtis carefully catalogued what had arrived and positioned each as he saw fit. He tugged gently at the stems and almost all of them resisted the gentle force applied. Curtis smiled with some satisfaction; this meant that they had rooted whilst in transit. Many of the plants had been cuttings taken from the original, their time spent in the cool, shady hold of a ship had allowed the roots to develop.

"You can place all these cases around the side of the house, to the west." Curtis told Wally. "This should protect them from strong sunlight and those cold east winds that come off the sea. Raise their lids a couple of inches to help them harden off."

Wally and his two helpers took the cases out of the glasshouse and placed them along the west wall as instructed. The plants in the bamboo tubes proved to be more problematic. As the wax cloth was unravelled, the bamboo that had been split in two to accommodate the plant invariably fell apart, taking with it some of the rooting material.

"These bamboo cases are a pain," Curtis cursed. "You'd best be especially careful with them, we don't want to damage any of the plants."

"Ok Mr Curtis, we'll be careful!" Wally reassured him.

"It's impossible to work out which way is the correct way up so I think it would be helpful to open them as they are, lying flat!" Curtis continued to fuss.

"Will do!" Wally replied busy about his business. "What will we do with the plants once the parcels are opened?"

"We shall have to pot them, water them and leave them here, in the glasshouse for a short time," Curtis informed him.

"Jack, go and fetch two dozen pots will you!" Wally instructed. Jack got up and left to fetch the pots.

"The plants have arrived just in time," Curtis said to Wally as they worked their way through the packages.

"Why's that Mr Curtis?"

"The weather at this time is mild enough to begin the hardening off process and with spring just around the corner we should be able to plant all these saplings in the ground ready for summer."

Curtis used the ground just in front of the house as his nursery. There had been numerous cart loads of good soil brought in from further inland, suitably treated with a combination of pig, cow and horse manure as well as vraic brought in from the beach at Gorey. Here the young plants became more established before being placed in their final home around and about the valley sides.

"Just think Wally," Curtis mused as they viewed their efforts, "only a few months ago these plants were soaking up the rarefied air of the Himalayas or, perhaps, were a roosting post for some rare and exotic bird, deep in the Amazon jungle."

"And now they are here, in Jersey, ready to begin a new life!" Wally concluded.

"These plants shall want for nothing Wally. They'll be pampered beyond belief. They'll not be subject to the vagaries of the wild. In this oasis all their needs will be attended to. They'll receive just the right amount of water, the correct nutrition to develop healthy leaf, root and stem growth and to encourage flower and fruit production. This shall be their Shangri-La."

The temperate nature of the Jersey climate warmed by surrounding seas afforded Curtis, or more specifically the plants, the luxury of a relatively pampered environment, particularly when the plants were in their infancy and at their most vulnerable.

Ten years on, a generation for the less hardy plants to grow in comfort and cosseted in this alien environment, the garden settled into a calm, relaxed state, confident in its development, reassured in that the passage of time had thrown up nothing untoward. But Curtis had been fooled and the threat to his beautiful creation came from above.

A Scotch mist was a portent of things to come. The dense cloud accompanied by persistent drizzle lay heavily on the branches and the spirit alike. The cold, dank air saturated all it enveloped, burdening those who dared to remain in its presence. The mist hung around for days until a breeze blew up from the south-west and cleared it away. A spell of high pressure then settled around the island. Clear blue skies during the day were followed by cloudless starry nights. Curtis and Harriet would don their winter coats, stand outside and marvel at the spectacle. The moon shone bright and the constellations were clear for all to see. Shooting stars flashed for an instant making them linger a little longer in the hope that more would appear. But then the wind changed, blowing in from the east bringing with it freezing air, severe frosts, hail and snow. As the two of them stood and admired the heavens above they became aware of the falling temperatures.

"It's cold when you stand out here!" Harriet complained, shivering as she spoke. Her warm breath condensed on the cold air around her.

"Yes my dear!" Curtis agreed. "It looks like we are in for a cold snap. Come let's go back inside where it is warmer."

What Curtis did not realise until the next morning was just how much the temperature would plummet. He woke to find ice on the inside of the windows. He scurried downstairs, whilst arguing with his dressing gown, trying to find the sleeve so that he could get his right arm in and wrap the garment around him. He drew back the thick blue velvet curtains and peered through the frosted glass of the drawing room window, having to scratch away the ice to see outside. Outside on the window sill he had placed a thermometer and he had to screw his eyes up to get them to focus on the reading.

"Oh my goodness!" he cried, "it's twenty three degrees out there, a full nine degrees below freezing! My poor plants! What shall become of them?"

"What is the matter father?" Harriet asked as she arrived in the room drawn by her father's cries. She too was wrapped in a dressing gown to keep out the cold, her long hair flowing down around her shoulders.

"I thought winters in Jersey were meant to be harmless and so mild that we might enjoy being out of doors in light clothing even in deepest winter but it appears that I was mistaken."

"You have to expect some cold days," Harriet stated as she moved towards the cast iron fireplace and stoked up the embers of the fire trying to revitalise it. Curtis continued to stare out of the gap he had made in the ice on the window as he spoke to Harriet.

"A cold day is one thing but not something this harsh!" Curtis replied. "I am not sure that even the hardiest of my plants can survive such cold temperatures. Twenty three degrees is far too low for what has been growing out there. It will be a miracle if anything survives."

The high pressure kept the freezing air around for days. Every leaf, every twig, every branch strained under the weight of accumulating ice. Leaves hitherto untouched, showed signs of blackening as the frost bit, killing them slowly, remorselessly. A full one and half inches of transparent glass lay on the trees and shrubs, causing bows to snap and break. As they gave way the sound echoed through the silence of the garden, and with every crack Curtis' depression grew.

"Just listen." Curtis cried. "It sounds like muskets being discharged at a distance. We are under attack by an enemy that we cannot beat. If I had a white flag I would open the window and wave it. Oh that we could just surrender and hopefully some of the plants might be spared but I fear this is not a merciful foe and will not cease until everything is destroyed. There is not even a covering of snow that might insulate the plants from the worst of the frost."

Eventually the snows did come but it was so cold the layers soon turned to ice making the terrain slippery under foot. The ground beneath hardened further, the cold frost freezing the moisture it contained. Any roots that were not buried deep underground were lost.

Curtis dressed up in his winter clothes and braved the chill to try and assess the damage it was doing to his plants. He touched leaves and branches as if trying to reassure them that he was near and that help was at hand but the plants just hung limply, slowly being petrified by icy fingers. The snow, if you could call it that, was crunchy underfoot and was sonorous like a drum, eerily echoing around the fortress as he stepped gingerly on it.

He decided to return back to the house. There was nothing he could do but wait and hope. As he turned, the musket fire continued unabated, each discharge was like a shot through his heart. Icy fingers nipped his ears, his chin became numb and even the moisture on his lips froze, sticking them together so that he could not shout out. He stepped into the relative warmth of the marbled hallway a beaten man.

"You're too old to be braving such cold." Harriet said scolding him lightly. "Getting influenza at your age might be the death of you."

"Ah my dearest Harriet!" he smiled warmly as he sat down in his favourite lounge chair. "You are always there to look after my interests, what would I do without you?"

"God only knows!" she replied sitting down in the easy chair opposite him.

"Don't you recall last winter Harriet when we were still eating strawberries from out of the garden?" Curtis reminisced. He took two chestnuts from a pile that he had stored in an old cigar box, placed them on the ends of a long, brass fork and started to roast them in the flames of the fire.

"Yes, and you were put out that they didn't seem to know when to stop?"

Curtis smiled as he remembered and then grimaced as a cold draught snaked around under his chair and over his feet, eventually meeting its nemesis in the flames.

"If this weather continues I shall take myself back to bed and hide under the covers until spring arrives!" he moaned.

Would his plants recover? He did not to have to wait too long for the answer. A thaw set in, the ice melted and the snow disappeared. Snowdrops pushed their way through the softening soil, the green shoots dusted with what was left of the melting ice and snow, their white petals opened up, revealing rich blue and yellow inside. Wild primroses followed their lead, huddled around tree trunks and other sheltered areas, displaying their pale yellow petals. The silent acoustics of the snow were replaced by a cacophony of birdsong. Clucking blackbirds bolted from shrub to shrub, wrens twittered as they darted in between thickets and branches. Blue-tits and robins started to sing from prominent positions at the tops of trees, marking out territories and jostling for space. Spring always arrived early in Jersey.

Was it good luck or sound judgement or just the fact that the cold spell was neither prolonged nor sustained? Whatever the reason the plants in the garden survived virtually unscathed. The Ilex, not normally a tree that enjoys such cold weather, had borne the brunt of the onslaught but had sustained relatively minor damage. Its innermost foliage had remained remarkably frost free and new shoots started to appear. Curtis' potatoes had not survived but his beloved camellias flowered regardless, their red blossoms standing defiant against the cold. He was amazed to see that his exotics had all survived.

La Chaire's burgeoning reputation, along with Curtis' well respected skills in the world of floriculture began to attract visitors to the garden. Some came to judge for themselves the splendour of the gardens that had been passed by word of mouth. Others came to seek Curtis on specific aspects of flower growing, often subjecting him to detailed interrogations, to which most he succumbed willingly.

"It staggers my faith in Australian plants!" he said as he fingered the leaves of the Silver Wattle "I believe that if I invest in a few glasshouses I might be able to defy the seasons completely in this valley."

"A bold statement indeed!" Sir John replied.

"I was under the impression this island never suffered severe cold!" Curtis remarked.

"Then you were mistaken Mr Curtis, although frosts of such severity are rare," Sir John informed him.

The cold of the winter had passed into spring and beyond. The garden was looking as fresh as the two of them strolled together, along the path that led from La Chaire and made towards the garden on the South side. Curtis and Sir John Le Couteur, a local dignitary and president of the Royal Jersey Horticultural Society, were similarly clothed in day dress. Sir John was a tall man with red wavy hair, greying around the edges. His receding hairline revealed a large forehead that was complemented by wild sideburns that he had let grow down his jaw line, until they almost met at his chin. He had a large, pointed nose and eyes that cast a scrutinising look upon everything that he viewed.

"May I take this opportunity to thank you for inviting myself and my wife, Harriet, to your beautiful garden and for judging the flower show at the last society's event."

"It is a pleasure to have you here and I am grateful to yourself and the committee for inviting me to judge the show, the entries were most impressive." Curtis showed Sir John along a path that sloped slowly towards the stream. Behind them walked the two Harriet's. "It is a shame that only a few get to enjoy the beauty that flowers can bring to a garden. Just imagine what the island might look like if every lane and every cottage was alive with blooms all year round?"

"What a splendid thought Mr Curtis." Sir John agreed. "Is that sugar cane that you are growing?"

Sir John pointed to a thicket of perpendicular green shoots rising vertically out of the ground. It had the appearance of tall grass with broad green leaves growing alternately out of a brightly coloured stem.

"Yes," Curtis replied. "It is Chinese sugar cane, Saccharum Officinarum. It is nearly seven feet high already and so dense a cat would have trouble getting amongst it."

"I think you are correct," Sir John agreed, "I have never seen such a tight weave of stems. Is there a reason for growing it or are you just enjoying the challenge?"

"Pigs and horses are really fond of it. I reckon an acre or so would feed a whole farm for two months or more. If you cut it into coarse, green chaff, pigs pick it out from the potatoes. I'm sure it would have more value than those strange looking Jersey cabbages the farmers like to grow."

Curtis bent one of the stems until it snapped with a crack. He took out a knife and sliced off a piece of the stem.

"Here, taste it, its great to chew on," he said as he offered Sir John a wedge.

"No thank you Mr Curtis!" Sir John held his hand up in refusal.

"Ladies?" Curtis asked turning to face them, knife in one hand, stem in the other. Both women shook their heads.

"No thank you father," his daughter replied, "I have had my fill of chewy stems, even if they are sweet to the taste."

"I doubt that you will be able convince the locals to part company with their beloved Brassica Oleracea Longata, or Long Jacks as they like to call them!" Sir John mused. "They use the long stalks as walking sticks you know."

The path they followed led them up a gentle slope.

"In autumn these paths are lined with chrysanthemums," Curtis revealed. "In fact there are thousands of the flowers, lining almost every path on this side of the valley. They are mainly the pompom variety, with large white and red heads, their small petals neatly arranged, like scales facing upwards."

"Chrysanthemum borders are a delight!" Sir John's wife exclaimed. "How many of them have you planted Mr Curtis?"

"Over three thousand!" Curtis informed her as he turned to face her, "I prefer the pompom varieties they have so much more impact, although I do have some more traditional yellows further on."

The four of them moved on towards the rhododendron woods where Curtis had planted a wide variety of Sikkim Rhododendrons. They had grown considerably in the short time they had been planted, bushing outwards, their low lying branches creating a haven for wildlife. The slope rose quite steeply but Curtis had built a zigzag path to lessen the strain. As they approached the rhododendrons Lady Harriet replaced her husband at the side of Curtis.

"Pray tell me Mr Curtis," she began.

"Sam, please call me Sam," he corrected her.

"Pray tell me Sam, what brought you to our island, the weather?"

"In part Lady Harriet that and the location of this exquisite valley."

"I am surprised you did not look to the south of the island, it gets a lot more sun than the north. It can get quite cold around these parts in winter."

"I have noticed!" It was Curtis' turn to sigh in reflection of past troubles.

"We have a beautiful garden at Bel Vue, over looking St Aubin's."

"I have no doubt that your garden is very special but it is the location of this valley here at Rozel that underpins all that I have achieved."

"Would you take my arm Lady Harriet, the light amongst the rhododendrons is limited and there are plenty of stray roots ready to waylay me?"

Harriet linked Curtis and escorted him into the rhododendron woods. As Curtis had anticipated, the bright sunshine was blocked out by the overhanging branches. The shrubs had grown tall and now met above their heads, creating a scented bower, full of colour and spectacle, even in this low light. The white flowers of Rhododendron Edgeworthii shone like beacons, with just a hint of pink. The carmine red of Rhododendron Arboreum glowed eerily, with their fawn stamens peeping out from within the undulating petals. Bundles of bell shaped white flowers of Rhododendron Falconeri hung down from above, looking as if they would ring if a breeze had blown through the bower. Then there was the delicate rose and lilac coloured flowers of the Rhododendron Campanulatum, each bursting forth in great numbers, collected in trusses about the bushes.

"You are such a gentleman Mr Curtis, if you don't mind me being so candid in my observations." Lady Harriet stated. "You have a manner about you that puts a woman at her ease."

"I don't mind your frankness at all!" Curtis replied, "a compliment like that to a person of my advancing years is very special, a keepsake nonetheless." Despite the poor light, Lady Harriet noticed a twinkle in the old man's eyes.

"I bet you were a lady's man in your heyday!" she teased.

"I had my moments!" he said coyly. Her question stirred in him the memory of that kiss, all those years ago.

"Ah, Mr Curtis, I knew you were not all that you seem. You have hidden depths, of that I am sure!" Lady Harriet surmised.

Curtis sidestepped the comment.

"It is in my nature to be methodical, organised and patient. Working with plants does that to you. You don't get the best results by forcing plants you have to be composed if you are looking for the best results. When they are in full bloom it is the plants that relax you otherwise you would not appreciate their beauty. Many flora have attributes that can be easily overlooked if you do not spend time getting to know them. For example, my eyesight is failing and I can no longer see the resplendent detail in many of the flowers, but if I close my eyes my other senses are heightened. I touch the petals and feel their soft silky texture, yet they have such inner strength that it is difficult to actually tear them. Here Lady Harriet, close your eyes and try touching one."

Curtis stretched out and plucked a floret from one of the rhododendrons. As he placed it in her hand his daughter and Sir John passed them by both looking quizzically. Lady Harriet, always game for a little intrigue did as she was bidden. She placed a petal between her left thumb, index finger and second finger.

"It feels like skin," she began. "Skin as soft as velvet, yet there is elasticity about it and fine ridges along its length."

"Now bring the flower towards your nose and gently inhale," Curtis cupped her hand and carefully helped her find a position just beneath her nose. There was something oddly sensual about what they were doing. "Notice how the scent becomes so much stronger and intense as your mind focuses on the olfaction."

"Yes there is an overriding bouquet, a sweet aroma, but as I inhale I notice a more subtle odour, a richness that I cannot quite describe and then another less obtrusive scent," Lady Harriet opened her eyes in genuine wonder. "Why Sam, what a revelation, I would never have realised that this flower, any flower had more than one smell."

The two of them moved out of the bower and strolled into a path lined with acacias. Just before these Antipodean shrubs they came alongside a deodar, a tree belonging to the cedar family. Sir John and Mrs Fothergill had stopped beside it. Sir John had taken a sprig of needles, rubbing them in his fingers and smelling the fragrant pine that emanated.

"Is this not Cedrus Deodara?" he asked Curtis as the other two came alongside.

"Yes it is," Curtis informed him. "It is also known as the Tree of God in its native land."

"India?"

"Not quite. It is common right across Afghanistan to Western Nepal."

"It is quite a size already?" Sir John said looking up into its branches, which seemed to stretch right up to the sky. As Sir John and Mrs Fothergill set off walking again, Curtis and Lady Harriet remained by the cedar.

"Why is it a man cannot befriend a member of the opposite sex without it setting tongues a wagging and becoming the butt of scurrilous innuendo?" Curtis enquired daring to return to his earlier revelation.

"Because, Mr Curtis," Lady Harriet explained, "history shows us otherwise. More often than not innocent affairs are anything but."

"In China, Lady Harriet, the pine tree represents persistence and tenacity!" Curtis quipped, "Qualities much evident in you!"

"I have also heard they represent longevity and dignity, attributes much evident in you!" Lady Harriet returned.

The two moved on as Lady Harriet once more took his arm. The warm sun was a delight, fanning the ambience of their stroll.

"And what type of trees are these?" Lady Harriet asked letting her fingers run through the fern like leaves of the silver wattle.

"They belong to the acacia family. They flower in spring and this one, Acacia Longifolia, has wonderful violet scented flowers." Curtis said as he pointed briefly at the Golden Wattle. "But one of my greatest triumphs is the tree that your husband is standing next to." Curtis boasted, genuinely excited at what he was about to reveal. He quickened his step so that he could reach the tree before her interest waned.

As they approached Lady Harriet admired its beautiful evergreen foliage, its leaves not unlike those of the rhododendrons but a much brighter green and textured on top. Early shoots now appearing were tinged red.

"So why is this tree so special amongst all these other exemplary specimens?" She asked, or more accurately she felt she had to ask. There was a much more interesting conversation to be had and she was not done with that yet.

"This is the Eriobotrya Japonica," Curtis stated. Lady Harriet was unmoved, "commonly called the Loquat." She was still unmoved. He felt her indifference. "The plant is indigenous to China and it is normally only there that it will bear fruit. But look here, you can see clusters of yellowy orange fruit. They have soft, downy skin. Try touching one, they are quite unique." Curtis plucked one from the tree. "Here, try them for taste, they are juicy. Lady Harriet accepted the gift and bit into one of the fruit, gingerly. The flavour brought a smile to her face.

"You may look at the fruit of the tree of knowledge, of good and evil, but you must not eat it!" Lady Harriet quoted as she played with the aftertaste. The quote was not lost on Curtis.

"I managed to grow this fruit here, on Jersey, thousands of miles away from its origin. That is some feat," Curtis was not bragging, merely stating a fact.

"I have to say I am not surprised at this achievement!" she replied. "Marvellous though it might be for any common or garden grower, you, Mr Curtis, are a giant among growers and you have already demonstrated that you can do magic."

"Harriet has made preserves from the fruit," he added. "Perhaps you and Sir John might like to try some along with a pot of tea when you have finished the tour."

"Home made tea?" she teased.

"What else?" he quipped, "I have my own supply of tea trees right next to the camellias in front of the house."

"Whatever next?" Lady Harriet was impressed. "They say that opposites attract." Harriet returned barrister like to the topic of Clara.

As he looked down at his feet and fidgeted with something in his trouser pocket, so preoccupied was he, he almost missed the huge Eucalyptus tree that towered above them to the west of the house.

"Did you know that the eucalyptus is nicknamed the widow maker?" Curtis asked almost rhetorically.

"Why is that?" such an evocative nickname had to be explained.

"Because as it grows, branches sometimes just fall off, without reason and woe betide you if you are underneath at the time!" Curtis could not help but smile and look up at her.

"Are you suggesting I should stand under the tree and test the theory Mr Curtis?" Lady Harriet taunted. She went over to the tree, its broad grey trunk, flashed with brown where some of the outer bark was being shed. It was not unlike an enormous reptilian hydra, its branches stretching upwards and outwards, generously dusted with evergreen leaves.

"They have also been known to spontaneously combust!" he quipped. "Their medicinal oils can explode."

At this point insecurity got the better of Lady Harriet and she made her way hastily back to Curtis. She looked up in awe at this monster of the plant world. As she did so her eyes caught sight of the blue backdrop behind the eucalyptus and high up onto the cliff face to the north. Curtis had planted a herd of hydrangeas, their flock broken only by intermittent white rocks poking out defiantly. The pompom trusses bobbed in the light breeze like heads in a crowd, each vying for the best view of the drama that was unfolding down below. The flowers of the hydrangeas were watercolour blue reflecting the natural acidity of the soil.

"That's quite a spectacle you have up there!" Sir John shouted as Lady Harriet and Curtis approached. "A bit precarious planting them though, I suspect."

"It was not as difficult as you think Sir John, as long as you have a head for heights," Curtis replied. "Would you like to stop for refreshments now or would you rather see the rest of the garden on this north side."

"I don't mind," Sir John shrugged his shoulders. "The walk is splendid, just what the doctor ordered. Besides Mrs Fothergill is a most informative companion. What say you darling?" Sir John asked of his wife. "Shall we rest or carry on?"

"I would like to carry on, Mr Curtis and I have much to talk about," she cast a glance at Curtis who smiled nervously.

Curtis and Lady Harriet followed Sir John and Curtis' daughter past the house and onto a path that led them up the south face of the valley. This side was much steeper than the other. Paths had been cut into the slope to create terracing. To prevent falling debris, Curtis had shored up the parts where there were no rocks jutting out with stones, filling the gaps behind them with soil. He had also packed soil into the gaps between the stones and rocks. He then utilised each and every crevice, placing plants in them and allowing them free reign to wander. Whereas the other side was predominant with herbaceous borders, this side was mainly Mesembryanthemums.

They strode gently past lines of palm trees, interspersed with olive trees and yucca gloriosi that stretched up like columns before opening out into bright green fingers. This rich, verdant backdrop was fronted by an array of colour coming from lines of azaleas. There were mainly deep reds, oranges and yellows. The north side of the valley faced south and with this came the warm sun. The other side of the valley had been distinctly cooler and more humid. The sun baked the land, giving it a dry, Mediterranean feel. The ambience was further enhanced by the terracing and Curtis' choice of plants. He had planted messembryanthemums all along the lower terraces. They had spread over much of the rough stone walling and exposed rock, carpeting it in an iridescent mass of striking magenta, orange and pink.

"Clara was like so many plants in this garden," Curtis began speaking slowly and deliberately as he picked up a bloom "beautiful on the outside, alluring, even mesmerising, on occasion. Her presence was intoxicating, a heady perfume that disarmed you and put you at your ease. But if you scratched away at the surface, poisonous." Curtis used his thumbnail to rough up the surface of a leaf until a pale green sap oozed out.

"They act upon your nerves giving you palpitations until eventually you succumb." Lady Harriet expanded on Curtis' explanation.

Curtis again fell silent as they turned a corner. Even after all this time, the mere mention of Clara's name evoked latent feelings inside of him. For a second he clung onto Lady Harriet's arm for support. Concerned that he might keel over she gripped him tightly by the arm.

"What's the matter Mr Curtis? Are you not well?"

"Pay no heed to me!" he reassured her.

They walked on past the small reservoir, a header tank from which the garden was gravity fed. Lily's floated on its surface, their white flowers opening up to greet the sun. They ignored the silver and golden wattle growing nearby. Curtis made a casual glance at pulpit rock. They pressed on to the summit where they encountered the Monteray pine, a beacon among the greenery. For now it had not grown to greatness although this fast growing tree was in its latter stages of adolescence. Native to the New World, Curtis had planted it here so that people might see it from afar and use it as a landmark to find La Chaire. Its bark was dark brown but fissured with dark grey weals, as if it had been lashed by a thousand cat-o-nine tails. Its needle like leaves shone bright green, gathered in clusters of three. Large oval cones were suspended asymmetrically along its branches. Curtis stood alongside Lady Harriet, under the protection of the branches, using the leaves as a shield against the bright sunlight. He looked out over his domain as he spoke.

"I may see my wife in the structure of La Chaire but the attraction of the garden is all about Clara. The colours, be they vibrant or suggestive. The textures, be they silken or ribbed. The fragrances, be they heavily perfumed or lightly scented, all these senses tantalise the emotions. They are evocative, sensuous, flirtatious and beautiful. Sarah was few of these, Clara was all of them." Curtis paused to catch his breath, his heart beating dangerously in his aged chest. He exuded a sigh that came from deep within. It frightened Lady Harriet, so much so that once more she took hold of his arm, frightened that he might collapse. He turned his gaze away from the beautiful vista and looked directly at Lady Harriet, as if he was going to reveal more but he remained silent.

The four made their way back from the top of the garden to the patio in front of the house. Tea had been prepared and they sat around a cast iron table enjoying the late spring sunshine. The air was rich with fragrance emanating from the clusters of violet flowers hanging above their heads. The wisteria clung, vine like, onto the front of the house, almost covering it. To the south a magnificent magnolia tree displayed its snowy white flowers, blooms larger than a man's hand. It too released a pleasant fragrance that carried on the light breeze. Alongside it a tamarisk tree fought for attention, its delicate pink blossom dwarfed by the magnolia grandiflora. In front of them stood Curtis' favourite, the camellias. Cultivated from the originals that he had first grown at Walworth, they had lost their flowers, leaving behind a healthy, dark green foliage that glistened in the sun.

"This is such a special garden that you have here." Sir John complimented just before he took a sip of his tea.

"It is a magical place, a fairy land, full of exotic rarities, one of the great wonders of the gardening world!" Lady Harriet said in support of her husband's statement. "Where do you get your plants from exactly?" She asked.

"My daughter Maria keeps me generously supplied with flora from Kew but I receive plants from all over the world," Curtis informed her.

A spell of quietude descended on the foursome. The warm spring sunshine, accompanied by the splendour of their surroundings left them lost for words. Curtis looked at his camellias. Even now, lacking decoration they were wonderful to gaze upon. He did not know, as he recalled Clara, sitting at her easel painting them that this would be the last time he would look upon them. For the last time he had watched in childlike anticipation their emergence, sylph like from white buds opening into deep reds their blossom heralding the end of winter and the dawn of spring.

Sir John rose from the table and took his leave.

"Well Sam, this has been a most splendid day!" he began. "I don't think that I have enjoyed a visit to a garden as much as I have this one."

"Before you leave I have something for you!" Curtis announced. "If you will excuse me a moment I will go and fetch them."

Curtis rose up slowly from his chair and made for the greenhouse. He returned a few minutes later followed by Wally and a couple of other gardeners. They all carried wooden boxes, each filled with plant pots, containing young shoots. The coachman brought the gig to the front of the house so that Wally and the others could load it up with the plants.

"You'll find a good variety of exotics in here," Curtis said. "This is loquat, and these are wattles. The larger one there is eucalyptus and those over there are azaleas. Don't worry if you don't recognise all of them, Wally has marked them up for you, with notes on where they are best planted."

Sir John took Curtis' hand and shook it warmly. Curtis rested his other hand on top of Sir John's hand as a mark of friendship and at the same time Lady Harriet bade Mrs Fothergill goodbye.

"Thank you for such an insightful discourse!" Lady Harriet whispered to Curtis as he drew her towards him and placed a kiss on her cheek. The two of them shared a knowing look as the gig turned in the drive.

Chapter 6

January 1889 Ainahua, Hawaii

Princess Ka'iulani sat on the garden chair and looked around in amazement. The uncomfortable nature of the wrought-iron frame did little to temper her wonder at the sight that surrounded her. There was such an abundance of flowers, all packed into such a seemingly small space. La Chaire impressed her as much now as it had when she had first set eyes on the place. It was a comfort to her, a reminder of her own garden at Ainahua, on Hawaii, albeit smaller and quainter. It was set out in very much an English style yet its contents were decidedly exotic. Some of the plants she recognised as being in her own garden. She pictured them now as she sat on the veranda.

In her hand she clutched her diary. Inside the red, leather cover her most intimate thoughts and opinions were revealed. Like most debutantes, she remarked on her perceptions of the people that she met, places that she visited and hopes for the future. She opened the front page as she often did when looking for reassurance. The words that spoke to her were not her own, nor were they written in her smooth, flowing script, honed to perfection by a privileged education. This writer's insignia was much more frenetic. The scrawl displayed an urgency to put pen to paper as if the writer's life had depended upon it, before the ink, or maybe his imagination, had dried up.

She consoled herself with just looking at his signature written in between the preface and the verse below. She voiced the letters in her head.

'R, L, S.'

She knew all the words by heart yet still she held his name in great reverence. She smiled inwardly as she recalled the first time that they had met.

~

The Banyan tree stood alone, its trunk taking on a grey, sickly pallor not unlike sun bleached driftwood, lying dead on the beach. It looked like an enormous, petrified jellyfish, towering thirty feet or so above the freshly cut lawn. It was a tree of many contradictions. Rather than grow upwards, towards the light, it snaked downwards, seeking the dark. Its geotropic roots had felt their way until they had reached the soil below. From the seed, deposited inadvertently by some passing bird in an unsuspecting date palm, roots had criss-crossed around the palm tree, fusing together to create a lattice, eventually squeezing the life out of the unfortunate host.

...us conglomeration of roots, constituting what would be construed by many as its trunk, held up a green canopy of branches and leaves, which, in turn, provided a shaded area underneath of about fifty feet in diameter. Not satisfied with taking over such a large space, the Banyan had sent out new runners from the overhanging branches. Sinuous roots that hung, tentacle like until, they too, found solid ground.

Such a monstrous spectacle might have conferred a sinister mythology upon the Banyan, especially when it was discovered that its flowers grew inside its fruit, where they could only be pollinated by a special type of wasp. However, man has done the opposite, conferring on it a status of tranquillity and hope, a place to meet shaded from the excesses of the midday sun. Up in the branches birds and mammals would feast on the profusion of fig like fruit, ultimately spreading its genes to be deposited anew.

The man who came to rest under the tree was a tall, slim man, complete with a thick moustache and trilby. As a writer it was important not to be disturbed when putting pen to paper. Such intrusions were the cause of many arguments, selfish to the point of obsession. When writing, the writer transmutes into another world, a world where imagination runs at a pace. Ideas chase one another like animals at play, rolling around and fighting for attention. Spontaneously generated, they divide and multiply at a speed that often leaves the writer irritated as they get lost along the way. The mind jumps from one idea to another, sometimes randomly and at other times by logical progression. The whole process is manic, firing adrenalin rushes, creating urgencies, evident only to the outside world by the pained expression on the writer's face. In this nebulous world the writer explores angles and opportunities. It is a private world, an addictive world, aggressively protected, lest ideas should escape and be lost or their embryonic form wither and die for want of nutrition.

"Aloha!" the girl's voice was soft and welcoming but not as appreciated as she might have anticipated.

"Aloha!" he replied brusquely, choosing not to look at her in the hope that she would recognise her intrusion and leave him alone.

"This tree is mine!" she continued irked by his ignorance. "It was given to me by Mama Nui!" she paused. He ignored her so she carried on. "My Godmother was as tall as a tree and as wide!" She giggled.

"That's one big lady!" a response at last, she smiled to herself.

"You wouldn't want to upset my aunt."

"I can imagine why!" he replied, eyes shut, head resting on the trunk behind him, trying to appear relaxed.

"Mama Nui looks after me!" the threat did the trick. He opened his eyes and turned to see who it was that had spoiled his solitude.

"Is she watching now?" he looked around in trepidation.

"Probably, possibly, I don't know for sure!" the young girl was hesitant, nervously walking around him, giving him a wide berth. "She has passed to the other side now and I can never be sure whether she is watching over me all the time or not."

What was it about this man that he should be conferred with the title of 'celebrity'? What was this phenomenon that brought so many people to pay homage to him? She was well acquainted with the fact that status commanded deference, her Uncle, King Kalakaua and his wife, Kapilolani and of course herself, demanded adulation, it was expected. Royalty was in their blood but why would a writer, a person who concocted stories, a dreamer, a storyteller sit aside such giants? She had been with the rest of the crowd that had come to welcome him but only out of intrigue not adulation.

"Then I best assume that she is. I would not want to take the chance of upsetting her that would be foolish!" he said, smiling at the young girl reassuringly.

He took the opportunity to get a good look at her. She was quite young, perhaps thirteen or fourteen years of age, he guessed. Her skin was smooth and tanned a dark shade of mocha. Her body was still very much a child's; long limbed and ungainly but she was beginning to show signs of curvature.

"This is your tree you say?" he asked.

"It is."

"Then if it belongs to you, it must have a name!" the girl looked at him quizzically.

"It is a Banyan tree!" she replied thinking that he was testing her general knowledge.

"I know that," Hhe dismissed, "But what is its name?"

"Don't be silly, trees don't have names."

"Yes they do but they don't want you to find it out in case you put a spell on them."

"A spell?" the young girl was puzzled by the man's strange conversation.

"It's in all the stories. If you cast a spell on something you can get it to do anything that you want but first you must to know its name."

"I know your name!" she replied, staring at him smugly. She flicked her long, wiry black hair from left to right so that it settled over her right shoulder. She had an infectious giggle that he found quite endearing.

"Well, there you have me!" he said, his words carrying a beguiling accent as he spoke. "I am on the way to being under your spell. All you need is a lock of my hair or a thread from my clothing and I will be yours…as long as you know the right words to say as you stir the contents of the pot."

"I'm not a child!" the girl stated indignantly, annoyed at his teasing. Her dark eyes glared at him.

"I am a princess, Princess Victoria Ka'iulani to be exact!"

"And as you already know, I am Robert Louis Balfour Stevenson." Stevenson rose up onto his knees and stretched out his hand for her to shake. She took a step back still undecided. "I wonder who has the longest name? Methinks it is I." he smiled trying to reassure her.

"Actually my full name is Princess Victoria Lunalilo Kalaninuiahilapalapa Ka'iulani Cleghorn!" She declared triumphantly, placing her hand on her hips.

"Got me again!" Stevenson said wistfully "although your surname does not quite fit with the others."

"My father is Scottish, like you."

"You seem to know a lot about me, much more than I do about you. Are you sure that you're not some shaman come to steal my soul?"

"I have read all your books," the princess ignored his tormenting.

"I am impressed by your scholarly nature."

"Why? Do you think I am some native that can barely read or write?"

"Not at all!" he hastened to put her at her ease. "I am impressed that you found it in you to plough your way through all my turgid prose."

"They are not turgid, whatever that means. They are exciting, interesting and most enjoyable."

"Well thank you Princess."

"You can call me Vicky if you like," she told him. She thought it would be good to have a western styled abbreviated name.

"I would not like!" Stevenson remarked. "A woman of your breeding should be addressed with respect. Vicky is hardly a name that instils such virtues. If it pleases you, I will call you Princess."

"That is fine but only when we are alone. When others are present you had best refer to me as Princess Ka'iulani."

"It's a deal."

There was a brief hiatus.

"You are not quite what I expected of as a writer," she observed with some disappointment.

"And what was it you expected?" he replied, "a smart suit, a furrowed brow or a smouldering look?"

Stevenson acted out his suggestions with his usual comical exaggeration. Princess Ka'iulani could not help but laugh at his animated antics.

"I'm not quite sure what I expected but…" she pondered, "you are so…. scruffy!" It was the writer's turn to laugh. The Princess continued. "Your hair is too long and lank, it does you no favours. Your clothes are all creased and you are so pale you look ill."

"Ouch!" Stevenson shouted, jerking suddenly.

"What is it Mr Stevenson? Have you been bitten?"

"Stung more like," came the reply, "by a scorpion!" he looked at her askance.

"I'm sorry," she apologised. "I didn't mean to insult you. It's just that…"

"The reality doesn't live up to the dream," he concluded.

"Well, yes I suppose," she admitted.

Stevenson suddenly tired of the conversation.

"If you will excuse me, Princess, I must take my leave of you. I have pressing issues that I must address before supper."

He was on his way to meet Archie Cleghorn, a fellow countryman and father to Princess Ka'iulani when he encountered the princess for a second time. Cleghorn was a self-made man who had prospered in the island community. Much respected, he had the ear of King Kalakula. Cleghorn was a dour Scot, his stern demeanour was emphasised by his long, untrimmed black beard and his insistence on always wearing formal black regalia atop his white shirt and necktie. Like all folk, Cleghorn had a passion that belied his uncompromising exterior; he loved gardening. The Ainahau estate was the most coveted on the island. Set in ten acres of land, it looked out to the deep blue of the Pacific. Archie Cleghorn had cultivated the grounds around the house with the giant banyan tree having pride of place. This was Princess Ka'iulani's playground. This was where she had taken her first steps and had learned to ride. She was comfortable in her surroundings and was comforted by them.

Stevenson watched her from a distance as she skipped and danced, oblivious to the world outside, running between a soap tree and an Indian tree, its red flowers looking like the claws on a tiger. He shook his head disapprovingly as he looked at her dress, so European with its shaped waist and raised posterior. He watched her twirling and whirling, waltzing with an imaginary partner to a make-believe rhythm. She danced around one of the many islands of flowers that her father had created amidst the verdant green lawns that fell away towards the ocean. She disappeared out of sight and then reappeared on the other side. Still swirling she stooped and plucked a flower from a bush, a bright red hibiscus flower. She smelt its fragrance and felt the soft texture of its petals before placing it behind her left ear.

It was a pleasant sight watching her lost in her childhood, inspired by her innermost thoughts, inquisitive of her surroundings and captured by their sensations. Suddenly she stopped. Stevenson became alert, aware that something was afoot. He eased back behind the trunk of the tree, his senses heightened. The Princess scanned around the garden looking to see whether she was alone or not. Secure in her privacy she performed a cartwheel, not once but twice and then again for good measure, her dress rolled up over her legs. And then she disappeared once more.

"Aloha!" she came upon him from behind and made him jump.

"Aloha, Princess," he returned politely.

"Don't you know it is rude to stare?" she scolded.

"I'm sorry!" Stevenson blushed, having been caught in the act. "I meant no harm."

"What are doing here, in my garden? Have you come to write again?"

"No, Princess, I have a meeting with your father."

"What a shame," her tone changed, "I was hoping that we might talk once more, under the banyan tree."

"Maybe another time when I am not pressed."

"Oh please Mr Stevenson!" she pleaded, looking up at him with doe eyes that he could not ignore.

"Well perhaps if we take the long route, around the garden and make our way slowly to the house. Then at least I can be truthful to your father's wishes and say that I was delayed in transit."

"Thank you Mr Stevenson. Come let's walk towards the sea, it's such a beautiful day and the breeze is so refreshing." Her zest for life was intoxicating as like some whirling dervish she spun around and around in front of him as they walked.

They walked past an oasis containing a large African tulip tree some seven metres in height. Its vivid red trumpet shaped flowers grew in abundance. Princess Ka'iulani pointed in its direction.

"My father calls that a fireball tree."

Around the tree Cleghorn had planted poinsettias. They had pink and red bracts that looked much like flowers atop the pale green or cream and marbled lower leaves. Stevenson paused by the flowers and sat on the grass. The Princess began to feel a little more relaxed in his company and decided to sit down cross legged in front of him but still out of harm's way.

"Mr Stevenson?" she began, looking down at her feet playing with a blade of grass.

"Yes?" he stretched the word.

"Where do you get your ideas from when you write a book?"

"Everywhere. I am a magpie."

"A magpie?"

"In Scotland we have a bird, a very striking bird with white and dark blue feathers."

"Is it like a parrot or a bird of paradise?"

"No Princess, magpies are mischievous birds, thieves no less. They settle on a branch, cock their heads this way and that and look at you cheekily out of one eye. If you leave any trinket out in the open, something that glitters, when your back is turned they swoop down, pick it up with their sharp beak and carry it up into their nest, high up in the tallest tree, where nobody can reach it. Those that have managed to look inside a magpie's nest have often netted a small fortune in gold and silver!" Stevenson again acted out the story with hands, arms and a face full of expressions. Princess Ka'iulani was spellbound.

"Are you telling me another tale?" she found the courage to look right at him. He looked back at her with a dead pan face, giving nothing away.

"On my mother's life, cross my heart and hope to die, I am telling you the truth!" his eyes twinkled all the while, confusing the Princess.

Stevenson rose up and continued to walk in the direction of the ocean. The Princess followed suit. They passed by a profusion of palm trees that had been placed to create a border. Interspersed between them were a number of sago palms, their thick chunky trunks leaning at strange angles in contrast to the regimented date palms that towered above them, their fronds swaying in the breeze.

"So why are you a magpie when it comes to your writing?"

"Most writers are," he informed her. "What we do is to take from what is around us, the flotsam and jetsam of other people's mundane lives, and make alchemy with it."

"Alchemy?"

"Magic!"

"But how do you know what to pick?"

"It's trial and error mostly. Usually something sparks an idea and feeds your imagination," he explained. Stevenson enjoyed describing his art to the uninitiated. Children in particular he loved to instruct, they were uninhibited receptacles. "Here, I shall show you. Let's pick something at random." He stopped and looked around for a likely target. "What about the banyan tree, or those peacocks over there? The banyan tree is old, very old." His voice took on a sinister tone. "Perhaps it hides a menacing secret buried deep within its roots? Or like a protective mother it spreads its limbs to defend them from adversity."

"I must admit, I do take comfort from sitting underneath its branches," the princess wrapped her arms around her chest as she spoke.

"Well there you are, we have the beginning of a story!" he set off again.

"Yes, but it is not exactly a new idea is it?" the Princess said dismissively. "Many stories that Mama Nui told me were like that; tales of sea and shore, of plants and animals that might protect or harm us. Such tales are part of our culture."

"We might be castaways on a desert island."

The look of disappointment was obvious.

"Too much like Treasure island."

"I have a gift for you!" he said changing the subject as they approached the house.

Under his arm he carried a book, a hardback book with a brown cover.

"Why thank you Mr Stevenson!" she said excitedly. "Would you read some of it to me?"

"It would be my pleasure," he returned.

They moved back towards the banyan and sat underneath the protection of its bows, shielding themselves from the strong sunlight. This time Princess Ka'iulani dared to sit a little closer, facing the famous writer. She studied his face as he opened the book. Although he was gaunt and his eyes were bloodshot, she could see a fire in them. He was an imposing figure despite his frailty and he had aura about him that drew her towards him. He chose a page from near the back and began to read.

"Whether upon the garden seat
        You lounge with your uplifted feet
Under the May's whole heaven of blue;
Or whether on the sofa you,
        No grown up person being by'
Do some soft corner occupy;

Take you this volume in your hands"

~

He looked up from the pages briefly, catching her eye before returning to the script. His rhythmic intonation, embellished with a mellow Scottish accent slowly began to remove any insecurities that she had about being in his company. She placed her chin in her cupped hands and just listened, enjoying the moment. When he finished there was a long silence. Princess Ka'iulani was mesmerised by the prose, his voice blending in with the ambience of the garden. She felt like a real princess, with Mr Stevenson, her suitor, reading 'love poems' at her feet. It was so romantic, just like she had imagined in the books she had read.

"If you had one wish, what would you wish for?" she asked dreamily.

"To be free," he replied introspectively. "Free as a bird. Free from prejudice, free from the parasites that make a living criticising my work and free from Bluidy Jack."

"Mr Stevenson if you please! There are ladies present!"

"My apologies Princess!" Stevenson bowed his head in mock deference.

"Why would you choose to be free like a bird and not free like some other animal, a dolphin or a wild cat?"

Stevenson opened up into another poem, gesticulating theatrically with his hands and arms.

"Swallows travel to and fro,
And the great winds come and go,
And the steady breezes blow,
Bearing perfume, bearing love.
Breezes hasten, swallows fly,
Towered clouds forever ply,
And at nobody, you and I
See the same sunshine above.

Let us wander where we will,
Something kindred greets us still;
Something seen on vale or hill
Falls familiar on the heart;"

Again the Princess hung on his every word, her imagination captured as she too soared on the wind. Her dream was broken as he asked.

"What would you wish for?"

"I've often wished for lots of things but now you ask me I cannot think of anything that I really want," she said with an air of disappointment.

"Then you are indeed one of the lucky few!" Stevenson smiled.

"Who is Bluidy Jack?" The Princess asked, in a whisper.

"Bluidy Jack is my shadow!" Stevenson revealed, upon which he flicked through the pages until he found what he was looking for. Princess Ka'iulani waited, like a puppy looking up at its master for treats.

> "I have a little shadow that goes in and out with me,
> And what can be the use of him is more than I can see.
> He is very, very like me from the heels up to my head;
> And I see him jump before me, when I jump into my bed.
>
> The funniest thing about him is the way he likes to grow—
> Not at all like proper children, which is always very slow;
> For he sometimes shoots up taller like an India-rubber ball,
> And he sometimes goes so little that there's none of him at all.
>
> He hasn't got a notion of how children ought to play,
> And can only make a fool of me in every sort of way.
> He stays so close behind me, he's a coward you can see;
> I'd think shame to stick to nursie as that shadow sticks to me!
>
> One morning, very early, before the sun was up,
> I rose and found the shining dew on every buttercup;
> But my lazy little shadow, like an arrant sleepy-head,
> Had stayed at home behind me and was fast asleep in bed."

The Princess applauded instinctively.

"Bluidy Jack, is not really your shadow is he?" the Princess enquired breaking the spell.

"If only he was as benign as that," Stevenson replied. "No Princess, the reality is much darker than my shadow. I have a disease, consumption some call it. I have had it since I was a child, younger than you are now. It has very nearly killed me on more than one occasion. That is why I am here, trying to escape the shadow that is on my lungs."

"Does that mean that you will be staying forever?" the Princess asked eagerly.

84

"Forever is a long time Princess," he tempered.

It was her turn to look wistfully at her feet.

"What is the matter Princess?" he asked. "Would you rather I stayed elsewhere?"

"No, Mr Stevenson, it is not that I don't want you to stay. It is just that I too have to leave my beloved country, in a few weeks."

Stevenson was genuinely taken aback.

"Where is it you are going? And why do you have to leave this paradise? Surely there is no where on earth more suited to a person's well being than here?"

"I am being sent to England, to be educated in preparation for my accession to the throne."

"That is a great honour, Princess and not to be taken lightly!" Stevenson reassured whilst keeping his true feelings to himself. Was there no sanity in this world? Why could a child not enjoy her childhood? You are an adult forever but your youth is fleeting. And why lay the burden of a nation on such young shoulders? "Then we must make the most of what time we have together, eh? Princess?" he said, conjuring up a half smile. "Would you like me to read another poem?"

"Yes please!" she replied. Stevenson passed the book to her. She held it with great reverence, turning the pages slowly, looking at the titles and the sketches, trying to find one that would catch her eye.

How he enjoyed being with children. They had a freedom of thought, much akin to his own. They were not hidebound by social convention or adult reservation, they just followed their feelings. He loved the way they constantly asked questions, even inane ones. For in those questions was the spark that is imagination and he loved to exploit their innocence. Just being around them stimulated his creative juices. Treasure Island, his most successful book to date, had been inspired by the map he had drawn for his step-son, Lloyd, when he was about the same age as the Princess.

Princess Ka'iulani paced her bedroom floor impatiently. She stopped and stared out of the window that overlooked the lawns and the banyan tree with a frequency that amounted to obsession. She had not seen Stevenson for nearly a week and she fretted. She had gotten so close to him that it pained her to be away from him. It was a feeling that was new to her and one that she did not like. When he was not around she missed him terribly. Her sleep rest was disturbed. Throughout the day there was a tight feeling in her stomach, a knot that would not go away. It made her feel nauseous and ruined her appetite. He was constantly on her mind. She was short tempered with everyone in the house, so much so that people began to think that she was ill. Finally she caught sight of him strolling across the grass towards the banyan tree, notebook in his hand and pencil behind his ear. She raced out of the room and down the stairs to greet him.

Stevenson had taken himself to his bed for a few days. Once recovered enough to take the air outside, he had picked up his trusted notebook and gone in search of a familiar place, where he might put his thoughts down on paper. That place was the banyan tree in the grounds of Ainahua.

He had barely settled when the Princess descended on him.

"Close your eyes Mr Stevenson!" she shouted from the other side of the Banyan tree.

"Why?" came his immediate response.

"I have a surprise for you!" she declared.

"What kind of a surprise?"

"Surely there is only one kind of surprise?" she asked quizzically.

"There are nice surprises and nasty surprises and there are big surprises and little surprises." he elucidated.

She was not biting.

"Never mind all that! It will not be much of a surprise if I have to describe it to you!"

"Then I will just have to trust you and hope that it is a pleasant surprise."

"I hope that you won't be disappointed!" she replied a little nervously. "Are your eyes shut?"

"Closed to the world!"

"No peeping now!"

"As if I would forego the opportunity of a surprise from a princess for the sake of a sneaky glance?"

As she came around the tree she saw him seated, legs bent at the knees and drawn up to his body. His elbows rested on his knees and his soft, pale hands covered his eyes.

"You can open them now," she whispered.

Slowly he removed his hands from in front of his face and opened his eyes, blinking in the bright sunshine. What he saw made him blink feverishly once more.

"Now that is a sight for sore eyes!" he remarked.

Princess Ka'iulani stood before him clothed from head to toe in traditional Hawaiian dress. Around her head was a lei, a crown of white and pink flowers, around her neck hung a much larger garland of the same flowers. She also had floral shackles on her wrists and ankles. Her torso was covered by a fabric top upon which a batik pattern of bright yellow flowers had been printed over a red background. Her grass skirt was made from leaves of the tapo and glowed, a verdant green. Stevenson looked down at her bare feet. Like the rest of her they were sublimely tanned. Her perfectly formed toes, gripped the sandy soil as she moved.

"Where have you been? Have you been ill? Is there something the matter? Have I done something to annoy you?" she fired the questions at him in quick succession.

"How could I ever be angry at one as beautiful as you?" he smiled. She melted under his flattery. "Besides, ask yourself why I came here in the first place."

"To see me?"

"What do you think?"

"I don't know," she replied a little insecure.

"Of course that's why I came!" he lied. "What other possible reason would I have to come here?"

"To be alone and to write!" she replied looking at the notebook in his hand and the pencil behind his ear.

"Oh these!" he guffawed. "I only brought these in case you were not around and so that I could occupy myself until you did arrive."

"Really?"

"Really."

"Last time we met you gave me a gift, now it is my turn to return the favour."

"Really Princess, there is no need," he began.

"Please, just relax and allow me to dance for you," she insisted. "Would you like that?"

"I would be delighted!" Stevenson settled and rested his back on the banyan. She began to dance, using her arms and body to tell her story, as is the tradition of the hula. She moved her arms in a wave like fashion to her left whilst her hips swayed to and fro. She then repeated the movement to her right. All the while she chanted, an oral, sometimes guttural sound that touched Stevenson's very soul. He could not take his eyes off her and she in turn looked straight into his. As she had once been mesmerised by his laconic prose, so he was hypnotised by her dancing, all her tones hung on the breeze. The rhythm of the sea provided percussion, the birds in the trees a woodwind section, and the rush of leaves on the branches the tympani.

Together they created a symphony.

She sat down beside him, took hold of his arm and looked up at him. Even at such a tender age, she knew what was expected of her and so, in part, she wanted to do it because that is what being an adult was all about, or so she thought. But the child within her was still strong and was reluctant to be harnessed just yet. In the presence of Stevenson her childishness was unleashed and she felt free, just as she did when she rode her horse or took to the surf on her board.

"Tell me about England."

"I'd much rather talk about Scotland, but then again I guess your father speaks of nothing else."

"He used to do but he is so busy these days he rarely talks of anything but matters of state."

"I don't know if I will ever see Auld Reikie again?" Stevenson seemed to cut across her.

"Is that a person or a place?" she enquired.

"It's a bit of both Princess. Like you and I, it has a beating heart and it breathes life- but for all intents and purposes I would have to say that it is a place, a city to be exact. It is not unlike Hawaii in that it has its own volcano."

"Really? How often does it erupt?"

"It has not blown for thousands of years. It is extinct. They have even built a castle on its top!"

"Pele would not be so pleased with that," the Princess frowned and shook her long black locks in disapproval. "What have the people done to appease her?"

"Created their own smoke!" Stevenson replied with disdain. "It does not go by the name of Auld Reikie for nothing. The city is often full of fumes from the coal fires that so many people burn to keep warm in the cold winter nights. And then there is the stench from the sewers!"

"This Auld Reikie does not sound so nice to me," she observed. "In my culture we learn to respect the land. We do not seek dominance over it, we are taught to treat it as an equal. We believe that the first person came from the land, born of a taro plant that grew from the grave of the deformed son of the god Wakea and goddess Papa."

"I am afraid you will find the western culture no respecter of the land, Princess."

"Auld Reikie, wale o' ilka toun

That Scotland kens beneath the moon;
Whare couthy chiels at e'ening meet
Their bizzing craigs and mous to weet;
And blythly gar auld care gae by
Wi blinkit and bleering eye:"

"I didn't understand any of that." the Princess stated.

"What do you think you will miss, my little Princess?"

"I will miss my horse, Fairy, of course, and my father," she paused to think, "and the peacocks," another pause, "and this lovely garden. I am not sure what else I will miss. I am to school at Great Harrowden Hall in Northamptonshire, but my chaperone lives by the coast at a place called Southport, so I will still have the sea to look upon."

"Of that I am not so sure," Stevenson added a note of caution. "The sea at Southport is so far adrift from the land you can barely catch a glimpse of it and to reach it you have to cross treacherous sands."

"Are you trying to dissuade me from going Mr Stevenson?" the Princess asked, looking up at him questioningly.

Stevenson almost concurred but stopped himself short before he compromised himself. It was not for him to say what he really thought about her pending journey.

"Unlike Scotland, England is a land of rolling hills, soft meadows, painted green and gold. Summer brings with it speckles of reds, purples and oranges so do not be afraid Princess, remember that you are leaving the land of your mother but are going to the land of your father."

On their final morning together, in Hawaii, Princess Ka'iulani sought out Stevenson with more than a degree of urgency. Emotions were running high, fuelled by a nervousness related to her impending voyage.

"Would you sign my diary?" Princess Ka'iulani asked as they settled beneath the shelter of the tree for one last time.

The Princess was dressed in a linen day dress that had a bold blue and white lily print on it. She wore a white bonnet trimmed with blue ribbon and a yellow flower. Her hair was tied up in a bun allowing only a few strands to hang loose. Stevenson noticed that even her dainty, little native feet were covered by white, laced up boots.

"Gladly," Stevenson replied taking the book from her. "And who else's signature are you hoping to get?"

"I thought maybe another famous author like Rudyard Kipling or maybe even Queen Victoria's if I happen to meet her."

He smiled wistfully at her.

"As you happen along the streets of London or perhaps when you are invited to dinner you might just meet the eminent Oscar Wilde."

Stevenson's reassuring words renewed hope to her dismayed features. He opened the book at the first page and began to write. He seemed to spend an age, studying closely what it was he was writing. She watched his expression changing from furrowed brow to raised eyebrows and back again. Once complete, he held it at arms length as if he had just painted her portrait and was reflecting on the colour and tones. Satisfied with his creation he read it out loud.

> "Forth from her land to mine she goes,
> The island maid, the island rose,
> Light of heart and bright of face;
> The daughter of a double race.
>
> Her islands here, in Southern sun'
> Shall mourn their Kaiulani gone,
> And I, in her dear banyan shade,
> Look vainly for my little maid.
>
> But our Scots islands far away
> Shall glitter with unwonted day,
> And cast for once their tempests by
> To smile in Kaiulani's eye."

"Oh Mr Stevenson, a poem dedicated to me!" she cried, leaning over and hugging him tightly. Stevenson blushed openly at the spontaneous show of affection but his feelings were tinged with more than a little sadness. "Please Mr Stevenson may I look upon the words you have penned, I am so honoured, I will cherish it forever!"

He passed the book back to the Princess who read the poem once more. But there was more. Above the poem Stevenson had written a preface. Princess Ka'iulani read it out slowly and deliberately.

"To Princess Ka'iulani. [Written in the April of her age; and at Wiakiki, within easy walk of Ka'iulani's banyan! When she comes to my land and her father's, and the rain beats upon the window (as I fear it will), let her look at this page; it will be like a weed gathered and pressed at home; and she will remember her own islands, and the shadow of the mighty tree; and she will hear the peacocks screaming in the

dusk and the wind blowing in the palms; and she will think of her father sitting there alone.- R.L.S]"

She looked up at him, tears welling up in her sad, dark eyes. They came together for one last embrace. She wrapped her slim arms around his waist and squeezed tightly, turning her head sideways and burying it in his chest so that his chin sat uncomfortably on her head. Hesitantly he folded his arms around her shoulders, resting gently on them, providing a comfort for her that she responded to by tightening her grip. She sobbed openly, her tears soaking into his white, cotton shirt. Her breathing became more laboured, sounding as if she was fighting for air. As she cried on the outside, Stevenson wept on the inside.

"I have a gift for you," he whispered, breaking through the sentiment.

She pulled away and looked up at him, her eyes clouded and with tear marks evident down both cheeks. He took a handkerchief from his pocket and dabbed away the excess. She remained static, arms limp by her side. She looked so vulnerable, he thought. He stooped down and pulled out a box from between the roots of the banyan tree.

"Here, this is for you, perhaps it will remind you a little of our time together

The box was quite large and made from teak or something similar. She took the box from him and turned it in her hand, looking around it for any signs or signatures, but there were none. Holding it upright she opened the lid. As she did so the metallic teeth started to ring on the rotating cylinder as the mechanical gearing started to move. Stevenson kissed her briefly on the forehead.

"Now we must say goodbye and adieu," he said. "You have much to do before you leave tomorrow and I have my writing to attend to."

He turned her around in the direction of the house and in an instant he stepped away from her, making haste in the opposite direction. He strode purposefully across the lawn towards the drive that would take him away from Ainahua. He dared not look back until he was a safe distance away. Once he had reached the drive he could not help but take one last look back. He stopped and turned. There under the banyan tree she stood. She lifted her right hand weakly and waved. He paused long enough to see her place a hibiscus flower behind her right ear. Forcing a half-smile, he too waved goodbye weakly then turned and left.

Now, as she sat in front of La Chaire with her diary open, in her lap she recalled the pain of the moment, as if it were yesterday. The pang of sorrow at the realisation that her first little love affair was over served to fuel the depression that was rising within her. It is said that you always remember the first time that you fall in love and the time she had spent close to Robert Louis Stevenson was no exception. The knowledge that they would never meet again, brought a tear to her eye.

Chapter 7

La Chaire 1892

As Robert Louis Stevenson stepped out of her life she strode into a new one. Stevenson had described England in such fanciful terms that what she was confronted with as the carriage rolled up to the gates of Great Harrowden Hall came as something of a shock. She enjoyed the journey from London, rattling along the country lanes at a generous pace. She loved the rolling hills and the fields decked in yellows and greens, even though there was not as much variety of colour as there had been on her beloved Hawaii and the hills were mounds compared to the precipitous mountainous areas of Oahu. She marvelled at the little village of Great Harrowden with its thatched houses and tiny windows and she stared in wonder at the church with its castellated roof and tower. But as Annie, her half sister, closed the dormitory door behind her for the first time in her life she felt totally alone, a young girl abandoned in a foreign country thousands of miles away from her roots. She took out her diary from her pocket and opened the cover. There she read Stevenson's poem and the preface that he had written. One passage leapt out at her from the rest.

'....*When she comes to my land and her father's and the rain beats upon the window (as I fear it will) let her look at this page; it will be like a weed gathered and preserved at home; and she will remember her own islands...*'

As she looked up, Stevenson's words proved prophetic and it started to rain, hitting the windows with a vengeance. All at once her fears and concerns rose to the surface and she began to cry. She threw herself onto the bed face down and sobbed.

Two years passed without any sign of her imminent return to Hawaii. Even the surprise appearance of her father did not precipitate a call to go home. Eventually she outgrew Great Harrowden Hall and was placed under the governance of a certain Mrs Rooke in order to complete her studies.

Mrs Rooke was a woman of some means, living in a fashionable area of Brighton, which itself was the place for the high society of London to visit and partake of the new trend for 'holidaying' by the sea. She lived in a large terraced house on Cambridge Street, close to the church. Mrs Rooke owned another residence, on Jersey. The place was called La Chaire and she had spoken so highly to the Princess about it on numerous occasions that the Princess could not wait to see it with her own eyes.

The English Channel is renowned for its turbulent seas, irritated by strong winds from the south-west which in turn drive tides coming up from the Atlantic. These are met by colder north-easterlies coming from the North Sea. The outcome can be mammoth waves and any ship that braves the tempestuous swells is tossed unceremoniously about like a rag doll. It was more by good fortune than past experience that Princess Ka'iulani survived the journey from Portsmouth harbour to St Helier, Jersey. She was in no better shape than she had been from the trip from Honolulu to California, or from New York to Liverpool some two years previous. Sea sickness is a terrible malaise as much an illness of the mind as it is of the body. All the sufferer can hope for is to find a place where the motions are not so severe. Princess Ka'iulani had learned to place herself in a cabin out of sight of the waves, somewhere towards the centre where the rolling and pitching were at their least pervasive.

The quayside at St Helier could not come quickly enough and she alighted with great relief, looking quite ashen. A coach awaited them on disembarkation and took them through the town and then the short journey overland to the north of the island to Rozel. She liked the quiet quaintness of the place with its smattering of whitewashed houses fronting onto the tiny pebbled beach and the little fishing boats bobbing up and down laconically in the swell. The coachman took a sharp right off the road and passed between a wall of olive green trees and into the grounds of La Chaire. The garden revealed itself to her in all its glory.

"Oh my goodness Mrs Rooke!" she exclaimed. "This is a sight for sore eyes."

"It is rather splendid isn't it?" Mrs Rooke agreed.

"It is a jewel, and that is a fact!" the Princess remarked. "This is the first time since I have come to Europe that I have seen something that comes close to resembling my native Hawaii. I think even Mr Stevenson would have approved."

The coachman halted in front of the house and let down the steps. As she set foot on terra firma, Princess Ka'iulani took the opportunity to turn around a whole three hundred and sixty degrees, trying to take in as much as she could in one panoramic sweep.

"Why there are plants growing outside here that I recognise from my own garden at Ainahua. The only other time I have seen such flora is under glass at Kew. Not even the Royal Gardens at Windsor can match this place for splendour," she took a few cautious steps this way and that, genuinely interested in the plants that were displayed before her. "How has this place come about? Who is responsible for cultivating it? My father would love to meet him, I am sure."

"My grandfather, Samuel Curtis, designed and built the gardens. It has been here some fifty years now and as you can see it is quite mature."

First impressions are the ones that last, and as Princess Ka'iulani stopped and looked around her she could not help but feel that the garden had warmth about it. It had a welcoming feel, like a comforter, wrapping itself around her and putting her at ease.

"The garden and the house are a little on the small side," she observed critically, "But it is beautiful nonetheless. I am amazed how much flora has been packed into such a tight space."

"Let's get ourselves unpacked and then I will introduce you to the garden properly. Once you have made its proper acquaintance you will grow to love it even more. There are splendid views of the sea and the coast of Normandy from the cliffs behind the house. Across the road the rhododendron walk is exquisite."

The Princess followed Mrs Rooke into the house. They spent the evening unpacking, eating and talking by the fireside. The next day, around about ten o'clock in the morning, Princess Ka'iulani accompanied by Mrs Rooke emerged into the bright sunshine. The Princess wore a long, light coloured pink dress laced with blue ribbon around the waist, cuffs and neckline. The sleeves were short and trimmed with the finest Portuguese lace, creating a ruffed look. The pastel colours gave her tanned skin a radiance that few could ignore. As she strolled gently alongside Mrs Rooke the gardeners heads turned impulsively. At sixteen years of age Princess Ka'iulani, like the flowers around her, was just coming into bloom.

"Why Princess, you look positively radiant!" Mrs Rooke exclaimed.

"I do like these dainty dresses, they are so pretty! " the Princess replied. "Some women dress like men, they look so manly in their plain black robes."

The observation was not lost on Mrs Rooke as she was dressed in her usual black but her garments were cut to emphasise her full figure and trimmed with fine silk and satin. She let the faux pas pass without comment. The two of them made their way across the road to the garden opposite.

"When do you think you will return to Hawaii?" Mrs Rooke asked as they walked past rows of camellias, their blossom mostly wasting on the floor under their feet.

"Who knows? I had been told that I would remain in England for only twelve months but now two years have passed and I am still here. When

King Kalakua died I had presumed that I would be recalled. As it transpires, I appear to be surplus to requirements."

"I am sure your aunt, the Queen, has your best interests at heart."

Princess Ka'iulani was so wrapped up in herself she had never really stopped and looked at her governess. Now, as they passed deeper into the rhododendron walk, she took a good, if discrete look. Mrs Rooke was what might be described as handsome. She was a woman in her middle years and had made many useful connections in high society. She spoke a number of European languages and had entertained people from the highest echelons of society. Her personality was warm and endearing. She was not at all pompous or affected, unlike most of the teachers the Princess had come across at Great Harrowden. Mrs Rooke was worldly wise although she did have an element of the matriarch about her. She was approachable and mellow in her interactions. When they had met for the first time the Princess was immediately impressed.

"When we have finished our stroll I think that we should return to your lessons. Today we will revisit your French and German studies and then maybe tomorrow we will take time out to refine your deportment."

"Mrs Rooke," Princess Ka'iulani began, "how will such lessons help me to tackle the political problems in my country?"

"How you carry yourself is crucial. People will seek to judge you by your demeanour. Rounded shoulders and head bent are a sure sign of poor breeding and weakness of character. Such observations will give your adversaries courage and confidence. A straight back and confident gait will set them on their heels. Mark my words, Princess, holding your head high in times of great stress will rally people around you and in turn, this will give you the confidence you need to win the day. Politics is not just about debating with the opposition. You can win an argument before you even take to the floor. How you conduct yourself in the heat of the battle is just as important as the bullets you fire. Take a look at our noble Queen, Victoria, she influences much of what goes on in parliament without ever having recourse to political argument. She has presence and the respect of her subjects. She does not demand, she enquires, she does not force, she persuades."

"And do you think I will be able to do the same?"

"Who knows Princess?" she replied whimsically. "But I can tell you this, even now at such a tender age, your presence will get attention. What you do afterwards will depend on what other skills you nurture over the coming years."

The following Sunday was bright and clear. The coach had been prepared and was waiting outside the house. The chocolate brown horse stood quietly his ears pricked up in readiness. Mrs Rooke followed by Princess Ka'iulani stepped on board. They were both dressed respectfully in black, their high necked dresses with long sleeves and matching gloves covered almost everything. Atop their head black bonnets were perched slightly left of centre and tilted, just a small fashion statement. The coachman urged the horse forward and the gig jerked into motion. They moved slowly at first, rolling off the forecourt and onto the bumpy road that would take them south up a gradual slope. The large cream flowers of the magnolia caught the Princess's eye.

"The garden has so much to offer!" she observed. "It seems to take on a different appearance every time I look at it. It's as if there is a trick of the light creating an illusion."

"It's no illusion," Mrs Rooke replied. "My grandfather spent a long time designing the garden, leaving nothing to chance, from the arrangement of the flowers right down to the soil that they grow in or so I have been told. Everything in the garden is in place and everything has its place."

"He must have loved La Chaire dearly."

"Indeed he must."

"Did he live here with his wife?"

"No, she died before he ever set eyes on Jersey."

"Perhaps the garden was created in her memory."

"Perhaps," Mrs Rooke's reply suggested that she knew more.

The conversation died as they took a sharp left past rhododendron bushes on both sides flush with pink blossom. Behind them grew the olive green ilex trees, offering their customary protection and shelter.

They came upon a junction and took a right turn. On this narrow road a couple of other carriages moved in the same direction as they were about to go. There were also small groups of people walking along the roadside, who stopped to let the carriages past. After a few minutes they came upon another road. This one was wider and busier. The coachman took a sharp left and eased into the traffic. The princess could see the church a few hundred yards ahead.

Like many of the buildings on Jersey, the church was made from red granite. It gave the place a robust yet parochial feel. The large oak doors at the entrance were stained with a light coloration, giving the timber a yellowish appearance.

They joined other parishioners as they made their way into the church, hesitating briefly before they were ushered into a pew near the front, a place reserved for special guests. They knelt on the cushioned kneelers and awaited the beginning of the ceremony. Once the mass began she followed the service, which was conducted in Jersey French, as best as she could. French was not her best subject but she could make out enough of the language to get a fair understanding of what was being said. Even so her concentration did wan at times and her thoughts returned to her future and what it might hold. She looked around at the faces of the people. One day she would be a queen and a leader of people and they would rely on her to make decisions on their behalf and they would look up to her respectfully. She would be their rock in their hour of need. The prospect was both frightening and exhilarating.

And then the choir sang a beautiful hymn in four part harmony. Their dulcet tones brought her back to reality and she felt the cool of the church, even on such a warm spring morning. She prayed, taking strength from the words she muttered. As she spoke, her thoughts wandered once again. She wondered whether the people in the church even knew that there was a princess in their midst. She was aware that a few glances had been cast in her direction but then this often happened wherever she went. She was a foreigner, her skin was a different colour, people were curious. What she was unaware of was that she was being espied more because of her natural beauty. Even dressed as soberly as she was, she was an eye-catching figure. The black sheen of the silk and satin and the cut of the dress hugging the contours of her slender frame enhanced her attractiveness. Kneeling at prayer gave her an added innocence and then when she began to sing along with the choir all eyes were upon her. Mrs Rooke could not help but feel a sense of satisfaction at having such a rare talent under her wings.

Back at La Chaire Mrs Rooke took the princess on a tour of the North side of the garden. They followed the winding path that would lead them to pulpit rock. They sauntered past tall stems of Yucca Gloriosa and the smaller hydrangea bushes that were just budding. There were also azalias intermingled between the other bushes and shrubs. For a moment Princess Ka'iulani, lost her inhibitions and twirled along the path, much as she used to at Ainahua. Such reflections of her childhood were rare now that she was being educated in what was required to be a young woman but for Mrs Rooke they served as a reminder that there was work yet to be done. The Princess noticed the incredulous expression on Mrs Rooke's face and ceased her pirouette. She obediently returned to pacing alongside her mentor. The Princess stopped by the harbour viewpoint.

"I wonder why the Queen has not called for me to return yet?"

The princess was becoming increasingly aware of her destiny, fuelled by her desire to return home. These were exciting times so full of possibility and she was desperate to be a part of it. The two of them looked out across Rozel harbour. Mrs Rooke took in the view while Princess Ka'iulani stared out beyond the horizon.

"With your beauty and popularity amongst the people of Hawaii, I hear that even your adversaries speak well of you, perhaps the queen sees you as a threat, maybe more so than those who are actually seeking to overthrow the monarchy?"

"That cannot be!" the Princess understood what she was saying but could not agree. "We are family, we are Ali'i. There are not so many of us left. It is beyond reason that aunt Lydia would plot against me."

"Come, let us walk on, I am keen for us to reach the apex of the walk, the view from the top is exemplary."

The two of them carried on along the path. The mesembryanthemums that cascaded over the walls had not yet come into flower. Acacias, palms and wattles lined the walk.

"You are still so young and have so much to learn, princess. It does concern me that somebody of such tender years has to carry so heavy a burden on her shoulders. Politics is a dangerous business and you can never be too sure who you can trust."

"But this is not about politics, it is about family."

"When it comes to presiding over a nation, it is both! And what makes the situation so difficult is that when your heart and your head are at odds it is difficult to discern right from wrong."

"You are so wise Mrs Rooke, I think that you would make a fine ruler yourself."

"I think not Princess!" Mrs Rooke guffawed. "The petty politics of high society are more than enough for me thank you."

"But if you were in my shoes what would you do?" the princess persisted.

Mrs Rooke gave the question some thought before she answered. As she spoke she mimed her response with her hands.

"Take one step at a time and always be aware of what those around you are doing. Be true to yourself and take the high moral ground, that way you can always be sure of having God on your side," she advised.

"If I am not careful I will not be able to trust anyone!" the princess pointed out. "And what then, Mrs Rooke, shall I become so paranoid that I will forever be looking over my shoulder, not knowing who to trust?"

"Politics is about power, and power is a frightening gift. It can be all consuming. Is there not a maxim that says 'power corrupts' and did not the devil tempt Jesus himself almost to the point of capitulation, offering him power over all of mankind?"

"Indeed he did!"

"Then Princess," Mrs Rooke's voice took on an almost evangelical tone. "As your star rises you must also be wary of the temptation power brings. Succumb and your enemies may be least of your problems."

"I will put my trust in God and hope that he will guide me," the Princess concluded.

"Enough of this talk of politics," Mrs Rooke endeavoured to lighten the atmosphere. "We are almost at the summit. If we stand by the Monterey pine and look out to sea we should be able to see the coast of France."

The two women stopped beneath the branches of the pine, with its russet bark and its overhanging branches stretching over them like large, protective hands. It was a clear day and as they looked to the horizon they could see a thin layer of green in the distance with another layer of yellow beneath it.

"That must be the sandy beaches," the Princess enthused. "Which part of France are we looking at?" She asked

"The west coast of Normandy," Mrs Rooke informed her.

"I have yet to go to France, or the rest of Europe for that matter," the Princess revealed.

"It will not be long before you 'come out' and take the well trodden route that many young women before you have done, heading for the cities of Europe, Paris, Vienna, Milan and the rest. Only then will you come of age and truly be recognised as an educated woman of high society."

"I cannot wait!" the princess replied.

The walk back along the snaking path was just as pleasant and somewhat easier as it sloped back towards the house. Once at the house Mrs Rooke began the lessons in earnest.

As spring turned into summer so Princess Ka'iulani moved on. She travelled to the North West of England, to Southport, situated on the coast, just to the North of Liverpool, the city that first welcomed her to England. During her summer recess she stayed at the house of her chaperone, Theo Davies. Mr Davies was once the British ambassador in Hawaii and was well placed to take on the role of chaperone. Princess Ka'iulani had struck up a close friendship with Alice, Mr Davies's daughter and her brother

Clive. During the long summer months they played tennis, a sport at which the Princess excelled. As a young woman in waiting, she attracted lots of attention from family friends and acquaintances. Being a princess however she was shielded from any untoward attractions, although she and Alice had lots of giggles at the expense of possible suitors that dared to step forward and make themselves known. At the family residence, Sundown, Princess Ka'iulani and Alice spent a lot of time around the piano. They both had a love of music and would spend time together entertaining anybody who would listen, performing duets and arias.

The Princess rolled her fingers over the piano, warming up her joints and getting the feel of the keys. She tinkered with scales and then paused before she began. The melody flowed gently out from the wooden framed instrument. Strings resonated as felted wooden hammers hit their mark in tuneful sequence. She played the introductory bars once and then once more for effect before she started to sing. The sound that emerged only served to embellish Alice's wonderment of this young lady. She could not have denied that she was more than a touch envious of Princess Ka'iulani. Not only did the Princess have a royal patronage, she was the most beautiful woman that she had ever seen; so polite and well mannered and interesting to talk with. It was no surprise her sweet soprano voice created a summer breeze on a cold winter's day. But the Princess never did finish the song.

Alice's father entered the room looking grim and full of foreboding.

"Father, whatever is the matter?" Alice enquired seeing the grave look his face.

"Princess, I have just received some disturbing news from Hawaii." He informed them.

"Oh my goodness, Mr Davies, please tell me what it is. Is it about my father, or Aunt Lydia?" Princess Ka'iulani's complexion took on an ashen pallor. Alice stepped over and placed her hands on the Princess's shoulders for reassurance. Tears welled up in Princess Ka'iulani's eyes.

"I have taken receipt of three telegrams!" he began.

"And what do they say?" the Princess interrupted anxiously.

He picked up the first of the three telegrams from the salver that he had carried them in on. He read the words one by one, slowly and deliberately.

"Queen deposed."

"What?" Princess Ka'iulani cried. The terseness of the telegram and the words it contained hit her to the core. Mr Davies picked up the second telegram.

"Monarchy abrogated!" he said reluctantly. The Princess took hold of

Alice's arm.

He picked up the last of the telegrams.

"Break the news to Princess."

There was silence for what seemed like an age before the Princess spoke.

"Aunt Lydia has been removed from office, how awful, I must return home immediately."

Still the immensity of the situation had not sunk in.

"The monarchy has been cancelled you say, by whom? On whose orders?" she carried on in disbelief.

She rose up once more from the piano stool, looking decidedly unsteady on her feet. And then the realisation started to set in.

"If the monarchy has been dissolved then I am no longer a Princess. I have no future, all this education has been for nothing. I am redundant."

Princess Ka'iulani suddenly lost her deportment, her shoulders sagged under the weight of the news and her arms fell loose by her side. She let her head droop and her chin rested on her chest. Tears streamed down her cheeks and spotted her light blue dress. Alice pulled her round and held her in a tight embrace. It was all too much for the Princess and she started to sob uncontrollably. Her cries came from deep within and she shook visibly. Alice looked towards her father for support.

"I am so sorry to break such terrible news to you Princess," he said, not really knowing what to say for the best. "I can only presume that Queen Liliuokalani and your father have not given up the fight."

Princess Ka'iulani fought back the tears and eased herself from the comfort of Alice's embrace.

"Who has done this? What right do they have?" she questioned angrily.

"I am guessing it will be the Hawaiian League, led by Lorrin Thurston and that man Stevens, the snake in the grass," Theo Davies cursed. "I knew he couldn't be trusted."

"What are we to do Mr Davies? I feel so worthless here in England, so far away from my people when they need me most."

"What else can we do Princess? We will have to act quickly and decisively if we are to redress this awful situation. Being over here might be a blessing in disguise." Theo Davies's words held a glimmer of hope amidst the despair that engulfed the Princess.

"What do you mean Mr Davies?" she enquired.

"If the Hawaiian League have taken control of the country then they will have to seek support from congress in America and that will take time. Maybe, just maybe, we can get there before them and you can appeal directly to the American congress."

"Me?" the Princess suddenly felt lonely and overawed by what Mr Davies suggested. All her talk with Mrs Rooke seemed like empty rhetoric. Mr Davies moved towards her and took hold of her hand. He gently raised her chin so that he could look her in the eye. He spoke to her solemnly but with resolution.

"Now is the time for you to step out of the shadows and into the limelight. This, Princess, is what you have been groomed for. This is your destiny."

Chapter 8

New York 1893

Fashioned in the Belfast Shipyard of Harland and Wolff, the SS Teutonic was the proud winner of the Blue Riband; the award bestowed on the fastest ship to cross the Atlantic. Her winning speed was a steady twenty and a half knots. She was an armed merchant cruiser, able to operate as an ocean going liner in peacetime or as an armed vessel in times of conflict. The irony was not lost on Princess Ka'iulani who felt like she was about to go to war in order to keep the peace in her homeland. As far as she was concerned the Teutonic could not cut through the swell fast enough.

The speedy Teutonic had slowed to a crawl as the huge frame of the Statue of Liberty greeted them on their arrival, as if in reverence to the copper lady that towered over them, holding her torch aloft. She gave the Princess a brief moment of hope, in that her task might not be as onerous as she kept imagining it would be. But the feeling did not last long as the Princess espied a huge gathering at the harbour where they were due to dock.

Fuelled by the poisonous rhetoric of the PG's (provisional government in Hawaii) an army of reporters had gathered to see for themselves this Hawaiian princess. Intrigued by the prospect of what such a woman might look like, their opinion primed by descriptions given to them by the PGs, they waited in anticipation.

"What do Polynesians look like anyway?" a fat man asked sucking on a Cuban cigar.

"Well I've only ever seen one and that was Queen Lily whatever. She was as big as her name was long!" nother fat man, standing next to him replied. "I don't know what it is about these coloureds but they look odd tryin' to squeeze their fat butts into a western woman's clothing."

"They look like gorillas in fancy dress!" a third man interjected.

"Yessiree!" agreed the second reporter. "She was one ugly mama!"

The three of them chuckled between bouts of coughing and spitting out tobacco.

"And I bet her ass is as big as a horse's!" the third reporter continued.

"I believe they wear grass skirts on Hawaii!" the second reporter added, stoking up the conversation.

"And not much else!" the third reporter piped in.

"That ain't right and proper!" the first reporter squealed. "Ain't they got no shame? And she's comin' here to ask us to leave them alone? Fat chance!"

The three reporters laughed again at the unfortunate choice of words.

"They ain't much better than monkeys swingin' in a tree!" the second reporter spat. "I reckon Steven's and Thurston and the other members of the PGs are doin' a fine job."

"Here here!" the first reporter declared.

"But surely this so called Princess can't be as difficult on the eye as the queen you spoke of?" the first reporter quizzed. "I mean, Robert Louis Stevenson is a personal friend of hers."

"Well Queen, whatever her name is, is the girl's goddam aunt!" the second reporter replied. "Anyways, rumour has it that Stevenson's gone doolally, built a shack on Tahiti and now lives among these damn natives. He might write a good book, but if you ask me he ain't much of a judge of character."

As she approached the gangway, Princess Ka'iulani hesitated, took a deep breath to steady herself and then stepped onto the boards. As she neared the reporters, the agitated mutterings shrunk in volume, tailing off into a whisper that ceased altogether as it reached the back of the crowd. There was a stunned silence as their eyes feasted on her svelte figure. Jaws dropped and eyes widened in wonder. The Princess was dressed in a conservative day dress, dark blue in colour with a matching wide brimmed hat from which yellow flowers emerged.

Her face was without blemish, her nose sleek and perfectly proportioned. Her lips sallow against the mocha tones of her smooth skin. She wore a slight but welcoming smile and her bright brown eyes displayed an alertness of mind as they briefly scanned the throng. The men, for most of the crowd was of a male persuasion, were totally transfixed. Her hair, almost hidden under her hat, had been lifted up and tied in a bun, revealing delicate ears and a long neck that beat any porcelain princess. They were smitten by her beauty. Mrs Rooke had schooled her well as she walked unerringly towards them. This was obviously a woman of style and poise.

As Princess Ka'iulani stepped effortlessly from the gangway the crowd drew backwards to give her room. Once ensconced on terra firma she beckoned her maid who passed a small sheet of note paper to her. She lowered her head and opened up the paper. At this juncture the reporters instinctively took a step forward, pencils and pads at the ready. Head bowed, she paused to look up appealingly from beneath her manicured eyebrows.

"Excuse me gentlemen," she began softly in perfect Queen's English. "I am not well versed in the art of speaking in public so I have prepared a statement for you, if you don't mind." There were affirmative nods all around, accompanied by reassuring smiles. She had hardly spoken a word, yet she had already won their hearts. The Princess lowered her eyes once more and began to read.

"Unbidden I stand upon your shores today where I had not thought so soon to receive a royal welcome. I come with me over the winter seas. I hear the commissioners from my land have been for many days asking this great nation to take away my little vineyard. They speak no word to me and leave me to find out what I can from the rumours of the air that they would leave me without a home, a name or a nation."

She paused to take a breath, looking up demurely from beneath lowered eyelids. Her voice was clear and her diction precise. There was no hint of an accent and she read with confidence and conviction.

"Seventy years ago, Christian America sent over Christian men and women to give religion and civilisation to Hawaii. Today three sons of those missionaries are at your capital asking you to undo their father's work. Who sent them? Who gave them authority to break the constitution which they swore they would uphold?"

Princess Ka'iulani spoke with a touch of anger as she posed the questions. And she enquired rhetorically of the assembled crowd when, for the first time, she looked directly at them. What they saw in her eyes was a fire and a determination to make her point. They were impressed. She returned to her speech.

"Today, I, a poor weak girl," she started quietly, "with not one of my people near me and all these statesmen against me, have strength to stand up for the rights of my people. Even now I can hear their wail in my heart and it gives me strength and courage and I am strong," she paused for effect, "strong in the faith of God, strong in the knowledge that I am right, strong in the strength of seventy million people who, in this free land, will hear my cry and will refuse to let their flag cause dishonour to mine."

As she folded the paper, the crowd burst into spontaneous applause. There were cries of 'here, here' and 'hooray for the princess'. As the crowd cheered, Theo Davies stepped up to her and whispered in her ear.

"Well done Princess!"

She turned around, smiling at him with satisfaction at a job well done. Her nerves allayed as she turned back to face the press.

How could the PGs have got it so wrong?

The reporters had their story.

"How long are you here for Princess?" the first report cigar butt to one side of his mouth as he spoke.

"Where will you be staying?" the second one asked before she had time to answer the first one.

"Will Prince Koa be there?" the third one asked.

Princess Ka'iulani looked at him incredulously. How could she possibly answer all their questions if they did not give her a chance to speak?

"Is it true that you are getting engaged?" the third reporter fired at her.

For the first time creases appeared on her brow. Then she raised her eyebrows and smiled as if he had just made a joke. She turned to Theo Davies for support.

"That will be all gentlemen we have a carriage waiting and the Princess is anxious to get to her hotel and rest after such a tiresome journey."

The Brevoort Hotel, fashioned from three adjoining houses by a Dutch property developer, was situated near the corner of Fifth Avenue between East Eighth and Ninth Street in the suburb of Manhattan. It was a popular haunt for titled Europeans. The Princess and her group occupied a suite of rooms on the first floor. The next day, Theo Davies sat in a large armchair by the fireplace. In his hands he held a copy of the New York Times, choosing a quiet moment to catch up on what had been said about the troubles in Hawaii. All of a sudden he jumped out of his chair and started to pace around the room in an agitated fashion.

"I don't believe it!" he exclaimed, throwing his hands in the air and flushing with temper.

"Believe what Papa?" Alice asked, genuinely concerned.

"That Prince Koa could do such a stupid thing!" he replied vaguely.

"What has he done?" the Princess enquired, aroused by the mention of her cousin's name.

"He has totally undermined all that we are trying to achieve"

"How so?"

"He has taken it upon himself to speak to the American press and suggest that they should not take much heed of what you say!" he explained pointing at the Princess.

"And why would he say that?" she frowned.

"Because he says that you are no more than a child!"

"He has said that?" it was Princess Ka'iulani's turn to flush with anger, piqued more by her cousin's disparaging slight about her capabilities, than the political ramifications of what he said.

The doors to the Blue Room opened and a tall slim gentleman dressed in a black suit with a white shirt entered. The Blue Room was aptly named, decorated in shades of azure with a dash of yellow and gold here and there to provide a contrast.

"Please rise for the President of the United States!"

Princess Ka'iulani, Theo Davies and his wife did as they were bidden, standing to attention as the President entered. The princess was both excited and nervous. She did not know how she had managed to gain an audience but here she was about to meet the President of the United States. There were those amongst his inner circle who thought that the Hawaiian issue was a waste of time and effort. The situation had been all but resolved and there was little left to be done other than rubber stamp what had been started by the provisional government. A week ago this would certainly have been the path of least resistance, and initial objections would soon have diminished. But then along came the woman that stood before him. As he cast his eyes upon her he saw immediately what all the ballyhoo was about. She looked stunning dressed in her gown of ivory silk.

Grover Cleveland was a large man, weighing in at over two hundred and fifty pounds, his double breasted, three quarter jacket strained under the pressure of holding in his expanding waistline. At thirty six years of age his hair was beginning to recede although it was neatly cut and quite short. A large moustache all but covered his top lip. This, together with his large jowls and heavy eyebrows, gave him a stern exterior. Any reservations Princess Ka'iulani had about him were dispelled. Working his way towards her, shaking hands with her cohort, he produced a broad smile, putting her immediately at ease. She bowed her head and blushed, an action he found very appealing. For him too, the anticipation of finally being introduced to this beauty filled him with nervous excitement, the like of which he could not remember.

"President Cleveland, the Princess Victoria Ka'iulani." Theo Davies completed the formalities.

"Tis an honour to meet with you." The President remarked as he took her hand in his.

"The honour is all mine," Princess Ka'iulani replied allowing her hand to remain in his for a moment.

"Welcome to the White House, Princess."

"Thank you for inviting us."

"May I take this opportunity to introduce my wife Frances," Cleveland indicated in the direction of his wife who stood next to him.

"A pleasure to make your acquaintance," Frances Cleveland said.

"And you, Mrs Cleveland," Princess Ka'iulani returned.

Introductions over with Grover Cleveland boldly took hold of the Princess' arm.

"May I take a few minutes of your time?" he asked politely.

"It is I who should be asking you," she replied apologetically. "I am so grateful that you have afforded me an audience when your itinerary is so very full."

He ushered her towards the large windows that overlooked the White House lawns.

"I know that this has been arranged as a personal visit but I cannot let the moment pass without enlightening you as to what I have just put in place."

"And what pray have you done?"

"Well, Princess," he began. "On top of withdrawing the Hawaiian treaty awaiting ratification by the senate…"

"You have done what?" She exclaimed, stopping them both in her tracks. The look of amazement on her filled him with pride. She looked just like a child that has received the present that they had always wanted. She felt the urge to hug him affectionately but she resisted.

"How are you able to do that?"

"You know Princess in essence this job is easy. You only have to do one thing and that is to do it right." He explained as he looked out towards the city at the end of the lawn, and then with a wink in her direction he added, "And as President I do have the power of veto. My greatest accomplishments are blocking other people's bad ideas and in the case of the annexation of Hawaii that was a one of the worst! The United States is a democracy and we must uphold and promote the principles of democracy wherever and whenever we can. I dislike corruption in whatever form it occurs and this man Stevens' appears to have corruptly gained control of Hawaii and slighted the name of America into the bargain. And so I come onto to my next piece of information." Princess Ka'iulani listened intently. "I am going to send an impartial observer to your island to assess the situation and he will be instructed to report directly to me." She paused a second to absorb all that she been told.

"Mr Cleveland, I don't know how to thank you."

"You don't have to thank me Princess, your being here is thanks enough."

Again she felt the urge to hug him, he was like some cuddly relation but she kept her composure. "If you will excuse me Princess, I would speak with your advisor Mr Davies and fill him in on some of the technical details."

"Thank you again, Mr Cleveland.," she said quietly. "The people of Hawaii will be forever in your debt."

Princess Ka'iulani watched as he moved in the direction of Theo. She was agog at the surprise news. She could not believe that she had achieved all that she had set out to do and so effortlessly. Was politics really this easy?

"Why Princess Ka'iulani you have created quite a stir since your arrival!" Mrs Cleveland brought her back to reality. "That is a beautiful dress you are wearing Princess," Frances Cleveland observed. "Where did you get it, Paris?"

"Yes, it was made especially for me."

"Then you must give me their address, it looks absolutely divine!" Frances took another sip of her drink. "Do you visit Paris a lot?"

"From time to time, as the mood takes me."

"Do you have a residence there?"

"We do have an apartment but I have discovered a little jewel of a place, just off the Normandy coast. It is on an island called Jersey."

"And you travel from there to Paris?"

"Yes I do. It's about a day's journey but it is worth it. The place is called La Chaire. The house is a little compact but the gardens, they are exquisite and the nearest thing to home that I have found. I feel so relaxed there."

"But it is still not home though is it?"

"Unfortunately no," the Princess bowed her head.

"Will you not being travelling onto Hawaii from here?"

"No, I will have to return to Europe. I am advised that it is still not safe for me to return to Hawaii."

"So you will head for Jersey and the gardens of La Chaire?"

"Possibly," the Princess was unsure. "Although I am of a mind to explore the continent of Europe with a little more adventure than I have been able to so far."

Frances rested her hand on the Princess for reassurance. "Let's hope that what my husband has set in motion will come to fruition quickly so that you can return to Hawaii before too long."

"I am so grateful to the President for what he is doing. You will convey to him just how thankful we all are for his help?"

"I shall my dear."

"You must be very proud of him."

"Always," Frances Cleveland smiled. "He is an honest man and has great integrity. It was those qualities that attracted me to him in the first place."

Grover Cleveland stepped across from his discourse with Theo Davies and invited Princess Ka'iulani to follow him into another room. Here she was wined, dined and entertained into the early evening. She spent much of her time talking with Frances Cleveland, building up a friendship as they chatted.

At the end of the evening she returned to the hotel in a jubilant mood. Waiting to ambush her at the door was a bevy of reporters each jostling for the most advantageous position from which to get her attention. Theo Davies did his best to keep them away and at the same time make a path through which the princess might escape into the safety of the hotel lobby. Questions rained down on her as she passed.

"How did you find the President?" one shouted.

Before she could answer another question was fired at her.

"What did you speak about?"

"Has he agreed to remove the annexation treaty?"

"Did you speak with Mrs Cleveland?"

As she reached the hotel door, the Princess turned to face the reporters. Slowly but surely their clamour diminished until there was silence. Taking a deep breath she raised her head and began to speak, looking each of them in the eye as she spoke.

"I was simply infatuated with Mrs Cleveland. She is very beautiful, although not all beautiful women are sweet. But Mrs Cleveland is both and I have fallen in love with her. Mr Cleveland too is also very entertaining. He treated us to a personal display of mimicry." There were laughs and nudges at this revelation, all of which were avidly written down. The princess continued. "Before I leave this land, I want to thank all those whose kindness has made my visit such a happy one. Not only the hundreds of hands that I have clasped, not only the kind smiles that I have seen, but the written words of sympathy that have been sent to me from so many homes. They have made me feel that whatever happens to me I shall never be a stranger to you again. It was to all the American people I spoke and they heard me as I knew they would. And now God bless you for it, from the beautiful home where your first lady reigns to the little crippled boy who sent his loving letter and prayer."

Having made her statement she turned to enter the hotel, the voices and shouts of the reporters ringing in her ears. Once inside she visibly relaxed. She had had such a wonderful day and the adrenalin was still coursing through her.

Flushed with a new sense of hope Princess Ka'iulani sailed back across the Atlantic, determined to complete her 'coming out'. She and Alice, suitably chaperoned by their respective parents, danced and partied their way across Europe. Each city threw up a new paramour and the gossip columns were full of possible liaisons. Each suitor was attracted by her elegance, beauty and status. For her part, Princess Ka'iulani corresponded with most of them on a purely platonic level but in truth she was not really attracted to any of them.

Her new found confidence coincided with her growing sense of identity. For so long she had been a princess in name only, a child on the periphery. Now, as she visited one palace after another, she was treated as her status demanded, as royalty. She was greeted by all as 'your highness', a title that she easily grew into. Her reputation was further enhanced as word spread of her diplomatic skills. Meeting with the President of the United States was one thing, influencing foreign policy was something else. Everyone wanted to be seen with this enigmatic princess. It was during her tour that word came of the death of Robert Louis Stevenson. She smiled with fondness as she recalled her childhood infatuation with this man of letters. She had been so naive back then but now she was a woman of substance, courted by the rich and famous.

The euphoria of her American visit, that had initially propelled her across the continent of Europe, started to wane. Such an indulgent lifestyle has its limits. One party begins to look like another and the whole merry go round becomes tiresome. Her yearning to return to Hawaii grew stronger as each day passed and as each day dawned she grew more and more depressed at the lack of movement. London, Paris and Vienna offered much, but none of them could give her what she really wanted; a home. The Davies' residence in England was welcoming but it was not home, only La Chaire with its quaint little house and garden offered her something akin to what she was after. But even here, cocooned in its floral splendour, she felt trapped.

In the winter of ninety five, before she had completely tired of socialising a great winter storm blew up. It gathered ferocity as it passed across the continent, a mass of low pressure with winds gusting up to gale force and beyond. By the time it reached the Normandy coast it was at its most vehement and it spared nothing. Torrential blizzards, snow and hail storms hammered down from dark, malevolent skies, whipping all who failed to find shelter. Buildings that were not constructed robustly enough were rent asunder and left in tatters. As the eye of the storm passed overhead, its unblinking gaze brought with it any icy glare, causing temperatures to plummet to well below zero. So cold was its stare that it snuffed the life out of the vulnerable, the very young, the elderly the sick.

The front of the storm was, by and large, rebuffed by the thick wall of ilex that Curtis had been wise enough to plant. Any damage was superficial and would have been quickly repaired come springtime. But the garden's Achilles heel was the skies above and as the 'all seeing' eye slowly got La Chaire in focus, it petrified everything within. The salty breeze that might have tempered its freezing excesses was itself shut out by the over protective ilex, leaving the most fragile of the flora exposed to the harsh sub zero temperatures that settled from above.

Many of the exotics, the loquat, silver wattle and sugar cane stood little chance, they were just not hardy enough to survive and when the tail of the storm blew up, lashing at everything in its path, it wreaked havoc, leaving a trail of devastation in its wake. The Eucalyptus tree that had grown to an astonishing eighty feet was unceremoniously cut down to size by the bough splitting frost and the severe gales that ripped the weathered branches from the trunk before eventually toppling it. All that remained was a small stump, its grey exterior reflecting the deadness inside.

Fortunately, by the time Princess Ka'iulani returned, much of the damage had been repaired.

The garden offered her a sanctuary of a different sort. Here Princess Ka'iulani could walk with impunity, alone with her thoughts, dreams and emotions, here she felt protected from the rigours of the outside world. She took the opportunity to dig out Stevenson's book of poetry, enjoying the recollection of her time spent with him at Ainahua. For her La Chaire became a garden of remembrance, a place where her mind would be stimulated by familiar fragrances and flora. In the bright sunshine the purples appeared positively radiant, reminding her of the bright reds and yellows she danced among whilst playing with her peacocks. And then there was the smell of the sea. She would close her eyes and take in the rich aroma of the ozone. On occasion she would venture out of the garden and walk by the shore enjoying the clear, blue water as it passed over the sandy sea bed beneath. The waters were so inviting. At times there were waves large enough to surf upon, if only she had had a board!

The waves and their gentle but persistent rush provided another warm recollection of Ainahua. The sound often lulled the Princess into a state of meditation, transporting her back to where the soft sands and palmed beaches met the warm currents of the Pacific. In her dreams she would paddle in the warm sea, immune to everything that was being played out around her. But then reality would set in; a voice, a shout, a call to arms would break the silence and with it that fleeting moment of peace. For La Chaire had become the centre of operations for the final push to oust the provisional government and restore the monarchy even though Queen Liliuokalani knew little of what was afoot.

Theo Davies and Princess Ka'iulani's father, Archie Cleghorn, paced up the winding path that led up from the house towards pulpit rock. Theo largely ignored the luxurious shrubs that lined their passage. Archie could not help but turn his head at every opportunity to enjoy one plant or another, much to the chagrin of Theo.

"The Republican government will never hold!" Theo declared, hands held behind his back as he marched.

"I agree!" Archie replied, struggling to keep pace. "It's so despised in Hawaii."

"I should think so!" Theo pontificated. "I mean, over one hundred and fifty thousand people on the island and yet only eight hundred eligible to vote, it makes a mockery of democracy!"

"They are within their rights under the law!" Archie reminded him.

"A law that they themselves declared! It's scandalous Archie. I cannot understand why President Cleveland does not assert his authority and send in the troops!"

"Because he doesn't have enough political backing in the senate to activate the military!"

"So we are at an impasse?" Theo paused and sighed.

"For now."

"But we have to be careful how we progress Theo, the queen views the Princess as a threat."

"And so she should!" Theo was unforgiving. "Vike holds the key to the future of Hawaii. If we were to act decisively now the people would rally round the Princess, and we could shift the balance of power away from this self-styled Republican Government in favour of the monarchy."

"The American public certainly prefer her to Queen Liliuokulani!" Archie added but he was still not convinced that such a move was wise.

"Even some of the Republicans have spoken well of her."

"There is some mileage in seeking a compromise," Archie suggested.

"It has been mooted before, perhaps having Princess Ka'ulani as a head of state, much like the role played by Queen Victoria would not be a bad thing."

"But there is the extremist element amongst the Republicans, what lengths will they go to stop the Princess acceding to the throne?"

"You are not suggesting that they would harm the Princess in any way are you? It would be folly to do so and would likely turn the American public and the Hawaiians against them."

"They acted decisively enough to thwart President Cleveland when he sent Paramount Blount to investigate their dealings. Even when Blount sent their leader packing they managed to prevent any progress being made."

"Yes, declaring themselves no longer American citizens was a shrewd move, although a risky one." Theo said with begrudging respect.

"I believe that they are opportunists and acted more in hope that the American people would not want troops firing on their own people. Have you taken a good look at her recently?" Theo changed the subject.

"What do you mean?" Archie stopped in his tracks.

"She continues to be her usual witty self, full of life and vitality but have you not noticed the sadness in her eyes?"

"I can't say that I have Theo?"

"I think she is pining to go home. Remember Archie she has been away from her home for the best part of eight years. That is a long time in anybody's life let alone a young woman like Princess Ka'iulani."

"Hmm," Archie was alerted. "I see what you mean."

Back down the hill, surrounded by the cliffs behind and the Chinese garden at the front, La Chaire was in full bloom. Birds flitted from bush to bush. Sparrows chattered among the dense foliage, blue tits hung upside down feeding on a variety of insects that lay hidden under leaves and twigs. Blackbirds and thrushes rustled in the leaf litter. Collared doves cooed high up in the trees bringing a calm atmosphere to complement the warm gentle breeze that found its way in from the sea.

Princess Ka'iulani and Alice had just finished their tea on the veranda overlooking the Chinese garden to the south. The magnolia tree was just beginning to blossom and the scent from the tamarisk wafted intermittently on the breeze. Behind them, covering almost the full frontage of the white house that was La Chaire, the wisteria was in blossom. From a youthful vine full of adventure and mischievousness it had matured into an old and ancient tree. Its boughs, some as thick as a man's thigh stretched out horizontally, placing the bulk of their weight on the walls of the house. Gone was much of the light green shoots of yesteryear, replaced by a grainy grey bark, whitening with the passage of time. But this old man of the trees was not some fading star whose flower bundles were limp and inconsistent, this sage of the garden captured the hearts and minds of all that set eyes upon it with its profusion of pale violet florets. It was so heavily laden that the air around was thick with its sweet olfaction. All manner of insects flocked to pay homage to it. Early butterflies such as the Red Admiral and the Painted Lady, large bumble bees and thousands of worker bees and hoverflies adding to the spectacle as they created a wall of sound that gave the old man a voice. To the stranger it manifested itself as an angry growl, constant and threatening but to the initiated it was a reassuring hum. This was another place where Princess Ka'iulani liked to sit, a soft breeze bringing waves of perfume around her, creating a relaxing ambience to ease her melancholy. A line of camellias in front were almost bereft of their red and white flowers but still, their sumptuous green leaves caught the eye.

"La Chaire is such a beautiful place. I do enjoy its quietude and the little birds that flit to and fro. It reminds me of home and I take comfort from being here."

If Archie had any doubt about what their next move should be it was removed as he noticed the cheerless expression on his daughter's face.

"Well Victoria!" her father announced as the two men sat down beside their respective daughters. "I think the time has come for us to return."

Princess Ka'iulani's expression changed in an instant.

"You mean we are to return to Hawaii?" she asked in quiet disbelief.

"That is exactly what I mean."

"Are we leaving now, this minute? Shall I pack?" the Princess started to rise from her chair, but Archie put out a hand to restrain her.

"Not so hasty my dear, you have waited eight years to get to this point, a little longer won't go amiss."

"How long exactly?" the Princess began to doubt the reality of her father's words.

"A few weeks, no longer," he explained.

"How many times have I heard that before?" the Princess' initial excitement soon changed into another bout of depression.

"I didn't mean to raise your hopes unnecessarily." Archie explained as he held her hand, "but we do need to prepare the way for your return."

"Why? What has changed?" she frowned

"The Queen's stance for one!" Theo announced.

"As you are aware," Archie explained. "She was against you returning as regent."

"I thought that she still was against me."

"We have been given indications that her position is starting to change on this matter." Archie continued.

"She is, at last, beginning to see the light!" Theo added. "There is also the need to get you in situ before Grover Cleveland's tenure as president is finished."

"Don't talk to me about President Cleveland!" Princess Ka'iulani remarked with teenage angst. "He seemed such an honest man and he has let us down so."

"Don't be too harsh in your criticism of the President. His hands were tied. He did what he could and he is still on our side," Theo explained.

"However, Victoria, the same cannot be said of the next incumbent!" Archie continued. "William McInlay. It is rumoured that he is a committed expansionist and if..."

"Or when!" Theo interjected.

"...he gets in, he will no doubt rescind all Cleveland's good work."

"That is what the Republicans are stalling for, in the hope that once Cleveland's tenure is done they can reintroduce the annexation treaty." Theo was once more becoming animated. "If that happens we will lose the island forever." He added.

"So why can't we leave on the next tide?" The Princess asked in all earnest.

"We must first write to queen Liliuokulani and inform her that you are to return. This will give her time to adjust."

"So we will make our way slowly," Archie added softly.

"Via America to bolster opinion," Theo's tone was almost excitable in contrast. "You are sure to make the same impact as your first visit, possibly more if we play it right."

Archie saw the reluctance in his daughter's expression.

"That should only take a couple of weeks and then we will sail home from California."

"And what will the Republicans make of my imminent return?" For the first time Princess Ka'iulani was worried about going home.

"They are likely to do everything in their power to stop you but the one thing they will not do is try and harm you physically." Theo reassured her.

"How can you be so sure?" Alice asked.

"To do so would turn everyone against them, the Hawaiian people the American press and likely even members of their own party."

The thought of difficult times to come scared the Princess a little but it faded into insignificance when weighed against the realisation that, at last, she was actually returning home. The sadness in her eyes was replaced by a sparkle, those hangdog shoulders that she had to consciously adjust were effortlessly thrust back and her head was held high. Even the debilitating headaches that had plagued her over recent months seemed to miraculously disappear.

She looked around the garden in all its splendour and recalled the last time she had skipped and danced in amongst the flora. She smiled as she remembered the look of disapproval on Mrs Rooke's face at her act of juvenile indiscipline. That same urge to jump up and twirl freely, without inhibition came upon her but this time she used her new found experience to temper such excess. She contented herself with a broad smile and deep sip of tea from her cup.

Chapter 9

La Chaire 1897

It was a fine, sunny day. Princess Ka'iulani decided to make one last journey to St. Martin's church on her own.

"Are you sure that you will be okay?" her father asked with genuine concern.

"Quite sure father," she insisted. "I feel much better today, more like my old self. I am so sorry that I caused you such distress yesterday, I don't know what came over me, fainting like that."

"It is not the first time Victoria is it?"

"No," she admitted, "but I have eaten a hearty breakfast and I have no doubt that the exercise will be most beneficial."

"Why not allow Alice to accompany you?"

"Really father, I would prefer it if I went alone, I am in need of the solitude."

"Well, if you must," Archie reluctantly agreed, "but if you feel at all distressed you must return home immediately, promise?"

"I promise father." She touched his hand lightly and then turned to make her way up the lane. She was dressed in a light, white dress, inlaid with white flowers. She carried a matching white parasol to shield her from the sun should it become too hot. It was late summer but the temperature was still quite fierce in the absence of any wind.

She admired the chrysanthemums that burned as orange as the sun, growing either side of the lane as it gently rose away from the house. Eventually the lane turned a sharp left and became steeper. The cultivated garden gave way to a more overgrown area, flanked by ilex, sycamore and oak trees to the rear and fronted by a forest of rhododendrons that overhung the lane on both sides. This copse of greenery made the lane much shadier and cooler than the garden.

She was glad to reach the sunshine at the top of the hill, pausing for a moment to catch her breath. The climb had been more difficult than she had at first anticipated, even though she had done it so many times before. The princess put it down to her present state of ill health. Once recovered, she strolled gently along the lanes that eventually led her to the church.

Inside, she walked down the aisle towards the front and knelt in one of the pews. In silence she began to pray, private words, thoughts and wishes for her forthcoming journey and the future that lay ahead of her. Her eyes were tight shut and her hands clasped together, elbows leaning on the backrest of the pew in front of her. She looked so innocent in her virginal white, how could a caring creator ignore pleas from one as beautiful as her? She pleaded that her ill fortune would turn and that God would grant her wish, a free Hawaii.

After about half an hour she decided to finish. She got up, walked back down the aisle past the large oak font and stepped into the bright sunshine. The contrast in the light blinded her so she opened up the parasol for protection. She made her way around the side of the pink granite walls, heading towards an old yew tree that grew by the far wall. Under the shadow of its broad, leaf laden branches she was able to release the catch on her parasol. She studied the headstones briefly.

Such was the ambience of the day that she felt at ease sitting on the grass that grew around the graves. A profusion of daisies popped their white heads up from the morass of green, their yellow centres vibrant in the light of day. She plucked one and played with it between thumb and forefinger. She looked up and recognised the headstone immediately in front of her as the one that marked the resting place of Samuel Curtis. It was quite weathered, if the truth be told, its original smooth grey stone blotched with dark patches, from a combination of wind, rain and soot from the chimneys close by.

"I hope that you don't think ill of me wanting to return home," she began, talking to the headstone as if its owner was actually listening. As the princess spoke, softly and from the heart she unconsciously started to pick more daisies, weaving their thin stems into a chain.

"You have your island paradise, now a place of repose for your soul. How I wish I could have the same and to find the peace that you now enjoy."

Having finished her daisy chain Princess Ka'iulani sensed that it was time to leave. She picked herself up from the lawn and dusted off the debris that had attached itself to her dress.

"Now it is time for me to leave this place forever and if you will allow me, I would like a little corner of my heart to remain here with you as a token of my appreciation for what you have done. For me La Chaire was an affair of the heart, my very own little love affair but alas, like all affairs, this one has run its course."

Princess Ka'iulani stepped along the edge of the grave till she could touch the headstone, upon which she leant over and kissed it affectionately, the cold of the stone seemed to warm to her touch. She then placed her completed daisy chain on the headstone before stepping back once more and bowing her head in respect.

She left La Chaire with mixed feelings. The happy go lucky outlook of her teenage years had faded and La Chaire was the only place that gave her the solace that she sought. As her carriage pulled away from the house she knew that she was never going to return. The finality of the situation brought with it a surge of emotion. She had not tarried that long, about twelve months all said and done, but in that short time she had become attached to the place. There was no goodbye party, no crowds weeping and wailing at her departure. La Chaire said its farewell with a peace and tranquillity that only it knew how to do.

Travelling from New York to California brought with it reminders of her last visit as the press rode shotgun, seeking interviews at every possible juncture. She had not lost her touch and the American public had not tired of her story. The princess' expedition back to Hawaii was played out in advance but there was one meeting that she could not avoid. She was compelled to take a detour to Washington, not at the invitation of the White House this time but to meet with Queen Liliuokalani, who had set up home in Washington at the Ebbett House. From here the queen had hoped to pressure the American government further in order to stop the annexation treaty once and for all.

As Princess Ka'iulani entered the hotel room she was immediately confronted with her aunt, who sat in a wide armchair facing into the room with the windows behind her and Prince Koa, who stood by her side.

"Why Victoria how you have grown!" she observed. "The newspapers do not do you justice, you are more striking than I could ever have imagined."

Queen Liliuokalani was an imposing woman. She was smaller and more squat than the Princess and was much broader across the shoulders. Weighing in at over two hundred pounds, she was thick around the waist and heavy breasted. The queen looked at her with a fierce stare from under bushy eyebrows.

Princess Ka'iulani walked up to the queen, leant over and gave her a hug. She then moved to Prince Koa. Their embrace was polite but lacking in affection.

"I am so pleased to see you again after all this time Aunt Lydia!" she smiled, tilting her head to one side as she spoke.

It had been a long time since the two of them had met, and now, standing in front of her was a woman as formidable as herself.

"Come closer and sit by me!" she pointed to a chair close by. Theo rushed to fetch the chair and slipped it underneath the princess as she sat down.

"Thank you Theo." The princess said.

"Yes, the American press were not far wrong when they described you as, now what was it they said?" she paused to seek out the precise phrase. "Ah, I remember now, 'her accent says London, her figure says New York and her heart says Hawaii'," Princess Ka'iulani flushed. "I hear the first." The queen continued. "And I can see the second but how can I be sure of the third?" The tone of her voice changed in subtlety. "What does your heart really say Victoria?"

The princess hesitated, knowing that what would follow would be determined by how she responded.

"Everything that I have done, or wanted to do," the Princess concluded looking directly at the queen as she spoke, "has been in the best interest of Hawaii. Hawaii is my home and it is where my heart lies. I have never subscribed to replacing you as leader, it is yours by birthright and I respect that as any citizen of Hawaii should." Koa grumbled, desperate to have his say but to do so would have incurred the wrath of the queen, so he kept quiet.

"I have never doubted your allegiance to the throne Victoria but there are others who might advise you to the contrary," the Queen cast a glance at Archie and Theo, "and it may surprise you that I would advise much the same." There was an audible gasp, coming principally from Koa. "I may be stubborn but I am no fool," she started to explain. "I recognise that my presence, as Queen, is beginning to become an obstacle to progress and if it is in the interest of our island for me to step aside then I will do so gladly," although she spoke candidly there was a definite air of regret in her voice. "There are those who believe that the middle ground is the way forward, a compromise."

The queen leant back in her chair and rolled her hands a few times.

"But I would advise that you seek nothing less than the full and total restoration of the monarchy," she declared tersely.

There was a long pause while all parties absorbed the enormity of what the queen had said. Princess Ka'iulani was the first to break the silence.

"I respect your wisdom on this matter and although I have friends and family who have given me much advice, I must respectfully say that I do not think that you or I, or anybody else in this room for that matter, should make the final decision."

"I quite agree!" Queen Liliuokalani pre-empted what the princess was going to say. "It must be the people of Hawaii that decide."

"By all accounts the treaty is dead in the water!" Theo informed them.

"Then perhaps I can return to writing my autobiography!" The Queen concluded and then added, raising her eyebrows, "There is so much to tell."

Archie and Theo shared a worried look at each other. Surely she could not mess things up again? The queen saw the look they gave to each other and was not pleased.

"If you will excuse me, I have other matters to attend to!" she announced, rising up from her chair.

Princess Ka'iulani and the two gentlemen paid their respects and left.

~

By the time she rounded the coast of Hawaii and saw the dockside at Honolulu harbour fast approaching the hyperbola surrounding, her homecoming had almost reached hysterical proportions. As she disembarked the band played, all dressed up in their finery. She smiled inwardly as they struggled to keep in tune and together. As she made her way towards the awaiting carriage she pressed palms with many of the people that lined the way. More and more garlands found their way around her neck until she was almost swamped by them. Such were the numbers of people her carriage had to move at a snail's pace. Princess Ka'iulani was awestruck at just how many people had made the effort to turn up, it was quite humbling. She had never seen so many smiling faces before as they pushed and shoved just to try and get a glimpse of her. This was a woman that they had heard so much about but had never seen before. Was she really as beautiful as the stories had described? Did she really take on the might of America singlehandedly? Has she really returned to give Hawaii back to its people? In a land that is built on legend, to have a living one walk amongst them gave credibility to all that had gone before.

She saw the look of anticipation written on every one of their faces. There was hope in the eyes of the elderly, and wonder in the expression of the youth. If she had been daunted by the reporters she was faced with on the quayside of New York harbour she was terrified by the expectation that she witnessed before her now. She reached for her father's hand and squeezed it tightly. He cast a reassuring glance in her direction, masking his paternal concern. Prince Koa observed her trepidation and proffered a knowing smirk.

It seemed an age before the carriage worked its way through the crowd.

As the mass finally thinned she noticed a small gathering of well dressed men, loitering suspiciously by one of the wooden buildings. They each bore an expression of cold calculation. They were not at all welcoming.

"Even the PG's have turned out to greet you" Koa observed. "You are privileged!"

Princess Ka'iulani said nothing, she just returned their stare.

In the days that followed Princess Ka'iulani spent a lot of time reacquainting herself with her favourite places on the island. Where ever she went she was mobbed by enthusiastic crowds. On one of these sojourns she travelled into Honolulu itself and passed by the Iolani palace. She had always been in awe of the building, recalling the huge chandeliers, impressive not only by their size but also by the fact they had electric lights. The place still looked magnificent, set in its own grounds. Built by King Kalakaua, it stood as a monument to his memory. It was constructed in a gothic style with a large tower marking the front entrance and four smaller towers, one at each corner of its rectangular structure. Now it was the centre of government for the Republicans. The thought of them taking up residence in this most iconic of buildings felt like a sacrilege to the Princess.

Her fascination for the building drew her out of the carriage and across the large lawn. She stopped in front of the steps that led up to the main entrance and looked up at the architecture. People walking by recognised her and slowly but surely a small crowd started to gather, accumulating others who wandered across out of curiosity. The Princess was too wrapped up in her thoughts to notice them, however the growing mass alerted those within and an official was sent out with two armed guards to see what was amiss. The princess was recognised immediately and the official, a small weedy little man with a thick moustache, challenged her from the top of the steps, armed militia flanking him either side.

"Is this a Royalist gathering?" he barked, arms folded across his chest.

"I beg your pardon?" the Princess retorted, irritated by his lack of manners and protocol. "Do you not know who I am?"

"I do indeed madam!" Hhe replied unbending. "That is why I asked the question."

"Then please have the decency to address me in the proper manner!" she endeavoured to assert her authority but the job's worth was having none of it.

"Royalist gatherings are prohibited on this island so please disperse now or we will have to arrest you!" he stated.

"On whose authority?"

"On the authority of the Republican government of Hawaii!"

"Arrest me?" the princess started to lose her cool. "You would arrest a woman for walking freely in the street. Put me in prison like you did with my aunt? Is this what you must do to keep yourselves in power?"

The crowd jeered at the man's intransigence and cheered in equal measure at the Princess's defiance, which aggravated the man and his guards who began to fidget threateningly.

Alerted by the growing noise outside of the building another man appeared. In contrast to the first official this gentleman had an immediate effect on the crowd. He was taller and a few years older than his colleague, sporting a very long and rather unkempt white beard which appeared to have a parting down its centre. The moustache above his top lip was very large and bushy, trained into a handlebar style. In contrast, the hair on his head was neatly cropped and short with an off centre parting.

"What seems to be the problem William?" he asked.

"We seem to have an illegal gathering Mr Dole!" the man answered taking confidence from the obvious authority of the man standing behind him.

Dole scanned the crowd and set his eyes upon the princess.

"Why Princes Ka'iulani, what a pleasant surprise!" he said politely. "Is this an official visit?"

"Not at all!" the Princess replied respectfully, recognising that Dole was a man to be reckoned with.

"I was merely out for a ride when I happened past the palace and thought that I would renew my relationship with the place."

"Then please Princess, do not tarry at the foot of the stairs, come inside and get acquainted once more with this magnificent building."

The crowd waited on her next move. The princess sensed their mood and despite a childish curiosity to go inside and see the palace in all its glory she stayed her ground.

"I thank you for your kind offer Mr Dole, but I am afraid that I will have to decline!" she was at her most diplomatic.

"Why so Princess?" he enquired.

"No offence intended but it would be remiss of me to be seen fraternising with your selves when as yet we are on opposite sides and therefore it would be hypocritical to enter into the palace until it has been returned to its rightful owners."

"But we are the elected government!" Dole could not resist the opportunity cross swords.

"By a small minority!" the Princess pointed out.

"Nevertheless!" Dole began to reply but was cut short by the Princess.

"Come now Mister Dole!" she asserted, "let's not be under any illusions. You occupy the palace only because you have displaced the monarchy."

"And we were forced to do so because of their mismanagement of the country."

"You did so because your own selfish interests were compromised!" she corrected him.

Within the confines of the palace the PGs felt safe, outside of its protection they were quite fearful. They were seen as an occupying force and although they had superior weaponry they took great care when they were out and about. The arrival of the Princess on the island had marked a turning point in their fortunes. For the first time they really began to feel that control was slipping away from them. She had galvanised the public in a way they had not anticipated. They were now being subtly resisted at every juncture.

"Have you heard that the American fleet is sailing towards the Philippines to encounter the Spanish fleet?" Dole called out to her as she made her way back to her carriage.

"Men at war!" Princess Ka'iulani returned. "If only people would sit and talk then perhaps lives would not be lost so easily."

"There is a time to talk princess and a time for action." Dole's voice hardened a little. "The Spanish stopped talking when they sank the Maine off Havana and now it falls upon us to act in the only way that will stop them doing anything like that again. They need to be taught a lesson!"

"It has been a pleasure making your acquaintance Mr Dole but if you will excuse me I must take leave."

She was applauded all the way to her carriage. Dole was left to ponder the implications of her popularity.

After the rout of the Spanish fleet in Manilla harbour, the American fleet returned to the nearest port of call, Honolulu, to tend to the wounded and make good any repairs. Their ships were continually employed patrolling the Pacific Ocean looking out for rogue Spanish vessels. The Princess tended to some of the wounded sailors in the tents that were dotted around the garden at Ainahau, even though the naval presence on the island felt more like an invading army. If it were not for the imminent resolution of the annexation treaty she and the rest of the Hawaiian people would have been more than a little concerned. So everyone accepted the overwhelming presence of a foreign force on the island with their usual Hawaiian welcome. Once in town and in such numbers, the PGs grew visibly in confidence, moving freely and openly in the street.

"What is the name of the ship that lies moored out to sea?" she asked one of the sailors as she checked him over.

"That's the Cisco your highness!" he answered confidently, honoured to be able to exchange words with an actual princess. He was a young man with short, cropped hair and a fresh face. His leg was heavily bandaged and bloody but it was his right arm that she was looking at, having removed a bandage.

"Let me know if I hurt you," she said cleaning the open wound gently. The lightness of her touch was not lost on the sailor. His compatriots lying around him in the open air on makeshift beds raised their eyebrows knowingly, and he reacted by leaning back and enjoying the attention.

The distinctive double chimney and twin rigged battle cruiser had a panoply of guns. Those fore and aft were larger than the ones to port starboard. Like the sailors the Princess looked after, it bore a few scars of the recent conflict but nothing too serious. On the front mast there was a pair of crow's nests and into the lower of the nests a sailor had clambered in. He stood facing to shore and began to wave a pair of flags.

"Why is that sailor waving those flags?" she asked.

"He is sending a message your highness, it is called semaphore," he informed her, sitting up gingerly so that he too could see.

"Can you read the message?" the Princess was intrigued.

"I shall try," the sailor missed the early part of the message but then he began to translate for her. "The right hand is at seven o'clock and his left hand is at ten o'clock, that's the letter 'I' by my reckoning." He paused to watch. "Next one is right hand at nine o'clock and left hand down at five o'clock and that's the letter 'S'.

"Is the next letter an 'L'?" the Princess asked with mounting anticipation.

"Yes your highness it is!" the sailor was happy to please the princess.

"I bet he is spelling out the word 'island'!" she predicted excitedly. "He is going to tell us something about the island, I wonder what it is?"

"I think that you are right your highness!" the sailor told her. "I have an 'A' and an 'N' and now, yes, a 'D' followed by an 'S'.

"Islands!" the Princess put the letters together, "I wonder what is coming next?"

She waited with baited breath, as did the sailor. Everyone else around them got caught up in the excitement.

"It's another 'A'." the sailor shouted as if this was becoming some sort of game.

"Island's are..." Princess Ka'iulani guessed.

"No your highness the next letter is an 'N'," he corrected her gently, "followed by another 'N'."

The Princess' heart began to sink. From being full of hope her emotions swung to the opposite end of the spectrum. Now she was in complete despair, hardly daring to believe what the word was that was being spelt out. The voice of the enthusiastic sailor, who was trying so hard to please her started to fade into the distance as nausea and light headedness took over.

"Here comes an 'E' and now an 'X' and another one," his colleagues saw the look on her face and read the semaphore for themselves before the unfortunate sailor realised what he was actually spelling out. The end result was unequivocal.

"Annexed," he said almost in a whisper as the penny finally dropped.

He turned to look at Princess Ka'iulani who stood above him, arms limp by her sides, glassy eyed and looking very pale. Tears streamed down her face in silent acknowledgement.

"Hawaii, USA!" someone else shouted joyfully, completing the coded message, unaware of the Princess' feelings. Eyes glared at him and he clammed up immediately.

"If you will excuse me gentlemen I have some pressing business that I just remembered that I need to attend to," she said, trying to keep her composure when inside all she really wanted to do was to scream out loud. She started with a slow walk until she was free of the prostrate sailors and then she started to jog as the upsurge of despair grew and her own self control started to break down. As she neared the sanctuary of the house the flood gates opened and her heart started to crumble into a thousand pieces. By the time she fell into her father's arms she was inconsolable.

"What is the matter my dear?" Archie asked, at a complete loss as to why she should be so distraught. She coughed out the message that had been translated from the Cisco, in between huge gasps and sobs.

"Islands annexed, Hawaii USA," she cried.

"What?" Archie himself shouted in total disbelief.

"Islands annexed, Hawaii USA," she repeated.

"How do you know this Victoria? Who has told you?"

Eventually she calmed down enough to sit by his side on the couch near to the open grate. She informed him as to what had transpired. From the arms of her father she retired to the isolation of her own rooms. Here alone, the full implication of what had been decided hit home. Dogged with headaches and depression over recent years the blackness swept through her with a vengeance.

Lying on her bed looking up at the ornate ceiling she reflected on the consequences. In an instant she had gone from being the new queen of Hawaii to nothing. She had been stripped bare. No title, no identity, no future, nothing. The adulation she had so much enjoyed since her return, meeting influential people the likes of which would now, most likely, drop her like a stone. How could she ever show her face in public again? The people of Hawaii had put their faith in her and she had failed them.

She recalled her mother's prophecy. The final part of the prediction had come to pass. She had been told that she would go far away for a very long time. She had been away from Hawaii for eight years and that was long enough. Her mother then said that she would never marry. All those friends and paramours, from Robert Louis Stevenson, the German Count, Toby De Courcy and, God forbid, even Prince Koa. She had been so wrapped up in trying to do the right thing, standing by her nation that she had not given enough time to her private life. And finally, her mother had said that she would never be queen and now she would not.

Everyone closest to her had gone, Mama Nui, her mother and King Kalakua, Annie her half-sister and, just recently, Theo Davies, for so long her chaperone. Even Alice had returned to England. Only her father remained. All that she valued was but dust in her hand.

"I must have been born under an unlucky star," she said quietly to herself. When her weeping was done all that remained was emptiness, a void that was blacker and deeper than anything that she had known before.

She had been championed as the hope of a nation and the heart of the people. Now they were both hopeless and heartbroken. She sat at her dresser and looked into the mirror. She saw the trails left by her tears and the redness of her eyes.

"And your name is?" she asked of her reflection.

"Victoria Cleghorn," she replied.

"Weren't you once a beautiful princess?" she enquired.

"In another life," she whimpered and then started to cry once more.

~

As President Dole's carriage drew up at the front entrance, Victoria was feeding her peacocks. She saw him arrive and her first thought was to run and hide. In her mind's eye she saw Mrs Rooke in the garden at La Chaire, remonstrating with her for lacking manners so she scattered the last of the seeds on the grass in front of the birds and turned to meet him. She forced a weak smile which he returned, standing before him as he alighted. A second or two later her father appeared in the doorway.

"Good day to you both!" the President greeted them, trying not to sound too cheery. He raised his top hat to Victoria and stepped forward to shake hands with Archie.

"Oh that these were good days, Mr Dole," Archie said showing his support for his daughter.

"Indeed so Mr Cleghorn and Miss Victoria," he replied apologetically.

Victoria could not decide whether he was being genuinely magnanimous or whether he had an ulterior motive so she kept her counsel, as did her father.

"Is this an unofficial visit Mr Dole or do you have business with us?" Archie's question was direct yet polite.

"A bit of both, if the truth be told," Dole replied looking down at the floor and raising Victoria's concerns. "There are some important matters that I need to share with you both before any final decisions are made."

"In that case shall we go inside where it is a little more private?" Archie put out an arm to invite him indoors.

Once seated, Victoria did not hesitate to press President Dole on matters leading up to the annexation.

"Mr Dole, perhaps you might enlighten me as to why the American government reneged on their decision to quash the annexation treaty?"

"Because once war had been declared with the Spanish, the government realised that it had to protect its Pacific coast in case of attack, and also stop the Spanish forces in Cuba being reinforced from the west."

"But how does Hawaii fit in?" Victoria asked.

"The government of the United States realised that the island of Hawaii was strategically placed in the Pacific. It is a place where they can refresh and restock ships, a place where they can actually launch attacks from and it is also the first line of defence in case of attack." Dole sounded almost apologetic in his explanation."

"I see," Archie now understood and nodded his acknowledgement.

"And what of the monarchy?" Victoria queried somewhat tersely.

"It will be dissolved," Dole said coldly. "But of course you will not be left destitute." He added softening his tone. "You will be allocated significant land, including Ainahua and a pension commensurate with your position." He looked up at Victoria to gauge her reaction. "You still have an important role to play on the island, the people look up to you and we value any contribution you might make to the people of Hawaii."

"You mean that you are trying to save face and want me to help you gain acceptance from the people of Hawaii?" Victoria's harsh words were matched by her glare. "Or perhaps you are attempting to buy my allegiance?"

"Victoria, we do not need your approval. All we are doing is giving you the chance to retire from public office gracefully, so you will accept?"

Victoria hung her head for a few moments before replying.

"What choice do I have?" she answered. "I have no capital of my own to speak of so without your handout I am destitute."

"My thoughts exactly," Dole replied not even trying to hide the satisfaction in his voice.

His business over, he made his way back to his carriage and left.

Victoria's humiliation was complete.

"This is black father," she said coldly, her thoughts distant. "Today our country died and I shall wear black from now on. No longer shall I be seen in any gay apparel. The colour I shall wear will reflect the feeling in my heart."

Her father hugged her tightly and then she retired back upstairs to the privacy of her rooms closing curtains so she might shut out the world.

True to her word, not only did she dress in black but the only ink she would use to write was also black, on black headed notepaper. As she mourned, so the people of Hawaii mourned with her. Her health deteriorated visibly as she retreated to the safety of Ainahua.

"You do not look well," her aunt observed as she visited soon after.

"No, Aunt Lydia, recent events have taken their toll."

"No doubt they have my dear, as they have on all of us," Lydia replied unsympathetically.

"Victoria is finding her return to Hawaii somewhat uncomfortable," Archie explained.

"Yes," Victoria continued, "I find the air most distressing, the humidity exhausts me."

"We have kept you away from the island for too long!" Lydia observed. "Perhaps we should have brought you home sooner."

"I think I now prefer the cold winters of La Chaire to the oppression of Ainahau," Victoria admitted.

The only time Victoria was seen in public was when she was riding her pony and wherever she went she was continually harassed by American soldiers, staring at her through unshaven faces, they seemed to have little respect for her position. Some went beyond all measure of common decency and asked if they could be photographed standing beside her. The final straw came when a ramshackle band of renegades rode up to Ainahau and rattled on the door demanding that she appear and stand beside them.

"This is too much!" she complained to her father. "They are so brazen! Do they have no manners at all? And they say it is us that are the uncivilised ones! I think I will have to take some time away from here, until everything settles."

Her father agreed and so she went across to a friend's ranch on another island, a place where her privacy would not be so compromised.

The weather here was mixed as she took her favourite pony, Fairy, out for a gallop, accompanied by Andrew Adams, her latest beau, Eva Parker and a few others.

"Come on Victoria, let's go back!" Andrew shouted his voice barely audible alongside the thundering hooves and the rain that gusted around them.

"No!" Victoria shouted back. "You return with the rest, I am going to ride on a little further."

"I will ride with you then!" he called. She looked at him affectionately. He cut such a handsome figure, even though he was becoming completely sodden by the rain.

"There is no need," she smiled at him. "Go back to the ranch and I will meet with you in a short while. I just want to ride alone."

She paused to watch him turn and go back down the slope, in the direction of the ranch. Then she turned and galloped in the opposite direction, riding into the gathering gloom that poured over the mountains, black fingers releasing torrents of rain as they passed over head. The path narrowed even more as she climbed but she was not for turning. For the first time for a long time she felt free. The rain on her face invigorated her. She enjoyed the thrill of riding headlong into the elements without a care, unburdened by the worries that had surrounded her, free of any responsibility other than to herself. Her riding clothes became saturated as she climbed higher and higher. She grinned, like a woman possessed, at the adventure that she was having. Eventually she slowed Fairy to a trot as the path became a little more precarious. Her adrenalin fuelled body began to relax. High up on the mountainside was a lot cooler than at sea level and her sodden apparel started to draw the heat from her body causing her to shiver. She turned Fairy around and set off back down the track.

By the time she arrived at the farm she looked a sight. Her clothes adhered to the contours of her body and torrents of water ran from every edge. Her bedraggled hair was matted around her face, which had taken on a ghostly pallor, and her fingers were white with the cold. She started to shake uncontrollably, offering a weak but apologetic grimace as Andrew and the rest stood in the archway to greet her.

"What a sight you are!" Eva laughed, masking her concern. "Come on let's get you inside and into something drier before you catch your death."

~

Whereas Curtis's mark was everywhere around La Chaire, there was no sign that Princess Victoria Ka'iulani had ever been to stay, except for one. A little way along the path from the house, that winds its way gently up the slope to the summit, a small evergreen shrub had taken root. It had been brought by her father the last time he had visited her, given as a reminder of home and one of a number of plants he had tried to bring from Hawaii. Its survival as others faltered, was a testament to its hardy nature. Princess Ka'iulani had been delighted, and had received it like some long lost friend.

Even as the Princess passed from this world, La Chaire did not hold its breath. Like Princess Ka'iulani, the plant that her father brought, Ali'i dodonaea viscosa began its new life in a foreign land without too much fuss, establishing itself alongside its more illustrious neighbours. Like the Princess it had resilience in the face of competition and it had a determination to succeed against the odds. Yet flourish it did, blossoming into a healthy plant with vibrant, evergreen leaves and deep red flowers that were delicate to behold. Its flash of colour caught the eye among the plainer shrubbery around it. Like Princess Ka'iulani, it grew best in the light, if put in the shade it would become quite sickly. It enjoyed the exposure to its maritime environment reminding it of its island heritage, refreshed by the sea spray and the ozone filled air. However, like the Princess its life would eventually be cut short by the cold.

As Princess Ka'iulani lay in her confin, shrouded in white, the chapel adorned with ivory lilies and pure white orange blossom so the chill of winter blew in off the continent of Europe and bit deeply into La Chaire, wiping away forever the last vestige of Princess Ka'iulani in this her garden of remembrance. But the same was not true on Hawaii, for on Hawaii she would never be forgotten.

Chapter 10

London 1893

Ethel sat in the chair and pulled on the first of her silk stockings carefully; if she damaged them she would have to replace them and that would be a week's wages. A tug of excitement gripped her as she felt their sheer texture against the smoothness of her pale leg. The persistent chatter of her colleagues echoed like tinnitus inside her head and it took all of her will to sit herself in front of the mirror and put on her make-up. Curtain up was imminent and its deadline served to focus the mind on the need for routine. Foundation, rouge and finally carmine lipstick to emphasise her fulsome lips was applied.

When the final call came her fears suddenly started to subside, and she focussed her mind on the job at hand as she tip-toed, along with the other Gaiety Girls, up the stone steps from the changing rooms to the wings and onto centre stage. This was the famous Gaiety Theatre and its impresario, George Edwardes had set the standards very high. She had to compete with girls much younger, women with far more heart breaking stories to tell as well as ladies from privileged backgrounds who had their eye on the men in the front stalls. All her associates were fiercely competitive and ruthless in their pursuit of personal gain. It was a world of bitchiness and of in-fighting but once the curtain was up, they worked the audience collectively to put on a show the crowd would not forget.

The theatre was situated at the eastern end of the Strand, just around the corner from Covent Garden. If the punters wanted excitement then they would go to the Lyceum, if it was entertainment they were after then the Haymarket was the place. The Gaiety was all about pretty girls and light relief. Its shows had no pretentions, they worked to a formula with threadbare storylines and were an excuse for titillation and humour but with a refinement that was absent in their predecessor, the burlesque show.

Crowds made their way past shops and restaurants to the entrance, a linten light crystal illumination hanging over its frontage to mark the way. The throng was funnelled through its narrow porch and into the theatre itself. Inside the hall the space rose up to the chandeliered ceiling, cathedral like in volume. The stalls were the most expensive outside of the private boxes and these were almost all taken by young men of impeccable breeding dressed in their evening wear. Their hair style, cut short and parted in the middle, was almost identical, although many sported a waxed moustache of varying proportions.

The overture was met with a resounding cheer as the curtains drew back and the Gaiety girls skipped lightly into the limelight, exposed to the full glare of an audience that analysed their every move. They started to dance whilst singing to the opening tune, 'When a masculine stranger goes by, arranged in a uniform smart'. Edwardes' captivating choreography, embellished by the girls, Gibson garb, gave them a mesmerizing charm. There was no bare skin, no scanty clothing, just a virginal innocence that sent the blood racing.

As the song finished the next refrain began and on stepped Kate Vaughan. The crowd rose to their feet and cheered loudly. She wore a long, clinging skirt of red silk, white blouse, long black gloves and carried a white lace handkerchief. The band played the refrain once more as she toyed with her audience. She lifted up the lace handkerchief as if to signal the start of a race, and at the gesture all the young bucks shot their black gloved hands into the air and waggled them vociferously in salute, as Edwardes himself watched imperiously from the wings.

Charles Fletcher sat in one of the boxes behind the dress circle. He was accompanied by Harenc, Algy Howard and Archie Hamilton, all school friends from his days at Eton. Their box offered them privileged views of the stage and of the crowd in the stalls below. He took up the theatre glasses to get a closer look at the line of Gaiety girls that danced behind Kate Vaughan. He scanned from right to left, pausing only briefly to look at each of the girls in turn. Ethel was the one that he was looking for and he focussed his glasses on her as she danced, totally unaware that she was being scrutinised so closely. She was light on her feet, deft in her actions and smooth across the stage floor. Her smile was endearing, unlike the fixed grimaces of some of the others.

Eight costume changes later they reached the finale before dancing off stage and leaving the audience wanting more. It was an exhausting two hours. However there was little time for rest as each girl took off her costume and sat in front of the long, horizontal mirror that they shared, reapplying the make-up in readiness for the last act of the evening, out of the theatre and into the waiting arms of whichever stage door Johnnie took their fancy. This time the powder and paint were employed more discretely.

Like the costumes that she wore in the show, her evening dress was the latest Bond Street fashion. The outfit was one of only two that she possessed. They had cost her nearly six months wages and she was still paying for them now. The slimness of her body was borne out of her capacity to exist on a near starvation diet as she struggled to make ends meet. The girls gave a collective intake of breath before stepping out into the narrow side street. Each footstep was placed deliberately, one in front of the other, creating a swagger that proved highly provocative for the testosterone fuelled young men who lined either side of the alley.

Most of these well heeled gents had the manners to accompany their status but a few were less than gentlemanly in their approach. One such man stepped across to block Ethel. He got so close she could smell the alcohol on his breath.

"Ah there you are darling!" Charles said as he breezed in between them and took her by the arm. "I have a table ready and waiting at Romano's." He continued as if he had known her for ages.

Charles acknowledged the man as he led Ethel away. Bemused, Ethel let herself be taken as arm in arm they strode into the Strand.

"Cigarette?" Charles asked Ethel as they strolled.

"Yes please," she replied, still clinging onto his arm.

He gave her a cigarette and took one for himself, stopping briefly to light them both.

"Would you care to have supper with me?" Charles asked as they continued walking.

"How could I refuse my knight in shining armour?" Ethel mocked with a tinge of rebuke in her voice.

"Romano's?"

"Why not?"

Romano's restaurant was a short stroll down the Strand from the Gaiety theatre so they were almost upon the place before they had had a chance to get acquainted.

"Would it be remiss of me to enquire of your name?" Charles asked, breaking the ice a little more.

"I am Ethel, Ethel Beddowe," Ethel revealed, looking down at her feet coyly.

"And I am Charles Arthur Fletcher, though most people call me Charlie." He informed Ethel confidently.

His self assured nature put Ethel at her ease, even though their introduction had been somewhat fortuitous. It was not like her to just latch onto any Tom, Dick or Harry but it had been a while since she had eaten a proper meal.

The butter coloured entrance to Romano's was covered by a lintel that stretched out over the pavement, its presence on the Strand was unmistakable. As Ethel and Charles entered they were greeted by Signeur Antonelli, Romano's maitre dix.

"Good evening Mr Fletcher!" Antonelli looked like a military man. He was tall, with a stiffened posture, chest pushed out as he stood to attention. His hair was greased flat to his head with the requisite centre parting. He too, sported a grand moustache, waxed at the ends. "Mr Harenc, Mr Bethell and Mr Palmer have a table inside if you would care to join them."

Antonelli led them through the restaurant. It was a long and narrow restaurant with many tables pressed into a small space, adding to its bohemian atmosphere. Once at the table Charles' introduced Ethel to his friends.

"May I take your coat madam?" Antonelli asked Ethel, having first pulled out the chair for her to sit on.

"Of course," Ethel acknowledged, removing the short velvet coat from her shoulders. Once exposed, the full impact of Ethel's outfit was revealed. It was a pale green in colour and made of the finest silk. It had trimmings of Brussels lace around the neckline and cuffs.

"Absolutely stunning!" Bethel could not help but exclaim.

"Where did you pick this peach up from, Charlie, you sly fox, she's positively ravishing!" Palmer added.

"May I have the pleasure of introducing you to Miss Ethel Beddowe," Charles stammered, still coming to terms with Ethel's appearance.

"Our pleasure!" Harenc stood up and leant across the table to kiss her hand, the other men followed suit.

"Would you like to order a drink sir?" Antonelli asked.

"A bottle of St Marceaux, if you have one." Charles enquired.

"I'll get one sent over straight away." Antonelli replied, turning to the wine waiter and clicking his fingers. The waiter swivelled and went off in search of the wine.

"I'm famished!" Charles exclaimed. "How about you Ethel, would you like a bite to eat?"

"I think I might manage a little something," Ethel's reply was an understatement.

"What would you like?" Charles enquired, "perhaps the Huitres Natives?" Ethel looked at him blankly, "or better still why not try the Creme Pink 'un?" Ethel frowned. "It's a bisque soup made from crayfish, one of Romano's specialities.

"Sounds delicious," Ethel was not convinced, but she was hungry and would try anything if it removed her hunger pangs.

"Then perhaps the lamb cutlets or would you prefer something fishy like, Truite au bleu?" Charles saw Ethel's puzzled face. "Trout." He explained.

"I think I would prefer the lamb."

"Good choice."

Throughout the meal Charles did not take his eyes off her, the way she played seductively with her earrings, the way she touched his friends, lightly yet provocatively as they teased and taunted her and the way she would bow her head and look up at them submissively, like a naughty puppy. All the while the wine flowed and it proved to be an evening of repartee and indulgence. Later on Bethel whispered to a waiter as he was passing. The waiter nodded and returned a short while later carrying a crystal decanter in which a luminous green liquid swayed in time with the waiter's motions. As he placed the decanter in the middle of the table Harenc, having just exhaled a large cloud of smoke from his cigar, cried out with excitement.

"Ah La fee verte!"

Ethel was perplexed. She looked at the contents of the decanter with interest.

"What is it?" she asked aloud.

"La fee verte, or the Green Fairy as it is known. In English it is commonly called Absinthe." Charles translated.

"Is it a liqueur?" she asked.

"It is much more than that!" Charles replied. "It is a whole new experience."

The rest of the men around the table nodded in agreement.

"Oscar Wilde described its properties so eloquently," Bethel enthused. "After the first glass, you see things as you wish they were. After the second glass you see things as they are not. Finally, you see things as they really are and that is the most horrible thing in the world."

All the men laughed in a knowing sort of way.

The waiter returned and placed a pontalier glass in front of each person. Ethel noted the bulbous reservoir in the base of the glass. The waiter then reached for the decanter and poured a measure of the green liquid into each glass, being careful not to fill it beyond the upper edge of the reservoir. Having placed the decanter back in the middle of the table he then took the spoons and put one across the rim of each of the glasses. Ethel was drawn to their design, she had never seen a spoon like this before. The handle was much like any other spoon but it was flattened at the end and punctured with cross shaped perforations. Into this recess the waiter placed a single sugar cube. As he did so there was an audible gasp of expectancy as the final part of the ritual unfolded. The waiter took the silver jug and began to pour ice cold water over the sugar cube. This he did very slowly almost one drop at a time. As the icy water hit the sugar cube so the cube began to dissolve and the liquor dripped into the absinthe, turning it cloudy. As it went opaque so its green colouration faded to a milky white.

"What is happening to it?" Ethel enquired.

"The ice cold water is causing the essential oils of the anise and fennel to precipitate." Charles explained in a whisper, cautious not to break the spell, "it is described as louching. It is important to the quality of the drink that it starts to louche slowly."

"This appears to be a fine bottle of absinthe!" Harenc declared as he studied the translucent liquid before him, "Hoorah to Romano!"

The others joined in, in a loud hoorah. Romano acknowledged their cry from behind the bar.

"When you drink the absinthe you must sip it very slowly and show it great respect." Charles instructed Ethel.

Ethel picked up her glass gingerly and put it to her lips. She took the most delicate of sips before placing the glass back on the table. Having savoured its taste she allowed it to trickle slowly down her throat as Charles and the others watched in anticipation.

"It is very sweet but not at all unpleasant," she proclaimed. "I can taste the aniseed."

She paused for a moment before raising the glass to her lips once more. The others smiled and followed suit. As the absinthe was absorbed into her system she began to feel less inebriated and more alert. Everything around her increased in intensity, colours were more vibrant, conversations distinct and shadows transformed into three dimensional shapes. The laughter around the tables seemed quite infectious and she found herself giggling whilst wide eyed with amazement. The whole atmosphere in the room gradually became exciting and invigorating. The group had a second round of absinthe and then a third. Eventually, with the restaurant virtually empty, Charles reluctantly succumbed to Romano's pleas, paid the bill and stumbled back out into the Strand with the rest of the diners. The night was cold and damp so Ethel tightened her velvet coat as best she could around her shoulders.

"Where to next Ethel?" Charles was starting to slur his words. "Perhaps a turn or two at the tables or maybe you would like to dance until dawn?"

"Much as I would like to join you, I'm afraid that I should make my way home," she replied reluctantly, her inhibitions all but evaporating under the influence of the absinthe.

"Why leave so soon?" Charles seemed genuinely sorry to part company.

"I have to be up early and back at the theatre," Ethel explained. "I have to earn a living you know."

"Forget the theatre and come with me," he slurred, as he wobbled.

"That's very kind of you but I think its time that I took my leave, so if you would hail me a cab?" Ethel was becoming a little embarrassed by Charles' affections but drunk as he was he still managed to recognise her discomfort, so he stepped into the busy thoroughfare and waved down a hansom cab.

As Ethel stepped into the cab, Charles proffered a helping hand.

"May I see you again?" he asked hesitantly.

"I would like that," Ethel said as he closed the door. Charles stepped over to the driver, a thick set man clothed in a long black cape and spoke to him. Ethel did not hear what was said.

She wiggled her gloved fingers at him as the cab set off.

'I would like that'

'I would like that.'

Her words rang in is ears as he almost skipped down the Strand.

Ethel awakened bleary eyed early the next morning, her head still woozy. The biting cold in the room that she called home nipped at her extremities. 'If he could see me now' she thought as she stood in front of the little mirror, viewing her smudged make-up and tatty nightwear. Her bedraggled hair was in need of a good brushing. She drew back her threadbare curtains and looked out onto a cobbled street already alive with people going about their business. In the dank daylight few smiled, everything seemed grey and depressing.

Her wage did not go far once the rent for lodgings had been taken out. Then there came the costumes and essential repairs. Ethel only got paid when the show was underway, there was no pay for rehearsals and her wages had been reduced over recent weeks. Management utilised a take it or leave it approach as more and more young women were being drawn to the theatre, and competition for places was getting fiercer by the day. Following a meagre breakfast consisting of a glass of milk and a slice of bread smeared with the last of a raspberry preserve she had treated herself to some weeks ago, she washed in cold water before putting on her tawdry work clothes. As she put on her coat to brave the expected cold outside there was a knock on the door. She opened it to find her landlady, dressed in her customary black, standing before her.

"There's a coachman outside waiting for you!" the landlady stated.

"For me?" Ethel was mystified.

"That's what the man said!" the landlady replied bluntly before turning her back on Ethel and returning back from whence she came.

Ethel locked the door to her flat and followed the old woman down the bare wooden stairs before opening the front door and coming face to face with the same coachman that had brought her home the previous evening.

"Have you been here all night?" Ethel joked.

"Not bloody likely!" he retorted. "Mr Fletcher asked me to return this morning and take you to the Savoy for breakfast."

"The Savoy?"

"The very place madam!"

"But I am not dressed for the Savoy!" Ethel pointed out.

"You look okay to me miss if you don't mind me saying," the driver replied cheekily. "Are you getting in the cab or shall I tell Mr Fletcher that you can't make it?"

Ethel deliberated a moment before succumbing to her sense of adventure. Once back in the driver's seat he set off at a pace, skilfully dodging carriages and pedestrians alike in his rush to get his customer to her destination.

The coachman pulled into the carriage entrance to the Hotel, on Savoy Hill. Charles was standing in the middle of the large courtyard, by the fountain, which was adorned with masses of flowers, drawing heavily on his cigarette. On seeing Ethel's cab he tossed the cigarette away and rushed to greet her.

"What on earth are you up to Charles?" she asked as he helped her from the carriage.

"I know it seems a little impulsive..." he began, as he paid the cabbie.

"A little!" Ethel stated.

"But I couldn't wait to see you again and so I thought you might do me the honour of having breakfast with me," Charles held out his hand in the hope that she would accede.

"I am afraid that I have already eaten," she said, not able to look him in the eye.

"Oh that is a shame!" he replied removing his outstretched hand. "Surely it would not be detrimental to share at least a coffee with me." He pleaded.

"Okay then," Ethel conceded. "But I cannot dally too long or I will be late for work."

She took his arm as they stepped towards the glazed white brick edifice. Inside, she looked all around her. The sense of space was intimidating as Charles led her up the great staircase, past the banqueting hall on the mezzanine floor and onto the first floor proper where the restaurant was situated. The maitre d□hôtel led them to a table in the middle of the room. Ethel was reluctant to let the man take her coat. Charles recognised her unease and took her hand as they sat offering her some reassurance.

"You look like you've been up all night," Ethel whispered, trying not to attract attention.

"I have!" Charles smiled. "I have been wandering the streets thinking about you." She gave him a look of disbelief. He continued, "I thought that if I went to sleep I would forget what you looked like and so I resolved to stay up all night and wait here for you."

Charles called the waiter over.

□We would like a tray of canapés Moscovites and a bottle of Dom Perignon."

"Certainly Sir!" the waiter replied.

He returned soon after with a silver salver loaded with canapés. He put out two champagne glasses and half-filled them both. Ethel was shocked and embarrassed as heads turned to look at them but she could not help feeling a little excited.

"Do you always live to such excess?" she said as he offered her one of the canapés.

"A champagne breakfast is hardly excessive my dear," he dismissed. "Would you prefer a bowl of porridge?"

He lifted up the bottle from its iced bucket and moved to fill her glass up. Ethel, put her hand over her glass.

"I really shouldn't, I have work to do today. I don't want to be full of gas."

"Come now, indulge yourself a little!" he entreated. "If you have too much you can forget work and spend the day with me instead. We could ride out and take a trip into the Sussex Downs or even to the coast, how does Brighton sound?"

"I would love to but I have to be at the Gaiety. I must work or else I will lose my job!" Ethel explained.

"Surely they would not miss you for one day. How about I speak to the manager to see if I can persuade him to release you? I'm sure if I make it worth his while he would come round to our way of thinking."

"You must not!" Ethel raised her voice for the first time. "I need to work to survive. Have you never been in such a position yourself?"

"I am a man of independent means!" Charles revealed.

"What does that entail?"

"It means that I am not beholden on another for employment."

"Then you are indeed a fortunate man!" Ethel affirmed. "Are you rich?" She asked as she turned the glass around between finger and thumb.

"Men never ask a lady her age and a woman should not concern herself with a man's riches!" Charles replied, raising his glass and winking at the same time.

"I'll take that as a yes then," she returned the knowing look.

"I am the eldest son of a wealthy businessman," he disclosed. "Being the heir to such a fortune comes with great responsibility but it is not without it compensations." Charles leaned back in his chair and quaffed the last of his champagne before stretching to refill his glass.

That evening Charles was again at the theatre to watch Ethel. He waited with the stage door Johnnies and collected her safely before whisking her off to the Cafe Royal for supper. Their romance blossomed, as Charles lavished his affections and his money on Ethel. They dined at the finest restaurants in London, breakfasting at the Savoy then luncheon at the Carlton, dinner at the Cafe Royal, and finally, supper at Cecil's. When she did have time off he would take her to Daly's, the Lyric or the Empire to watch other theatrical shows. He had a great affection for gardens and would take her riding in Regent's Park or for a stroll through Kew.

With each passing day they grew closer until eventually she succumbed to the inevitable and moved out of her draughty flat in Brixham and into Charles' apartment in Beaufort Street, Chelsea. It was a far cry from what she had been used to.

"Why don't you leave your work at the Gaiety and then we can shoot off to France, perhaps visit Paris or Monte Carlo?"

"I still have my commitments at the Gaiety," Ethel poured cold water on the idea even though the suggestion filled her with romantic thoughts.

"The Gaiety! All I hear is the damned Gaiety, when will you put me before that god awful theatre?" Charles' harsh words took her aback as he visibly flushed with anger only restraining himself when he saw the look of concern in her eyes.

"I'm so sorry Ethel," he apologised, "I don't know what came over me. It's just that I want to spend all my days with you, you must realise that. I have the means to make you very happy and we could sail around the world forever, just the two of us but you will not leave the place. It's so, so frustrating."

Ethel stretched out a hand across the table and placed it on his.

"I know that you care for me and that you have given me so much but it might all end tomorrow, and if it does I will have nothing to fall back on. I will be jobless and homeless," her soft voice and delicate touch burned a hole in his angst.

"Then what do I have to do to get you to come with me, marry you?" he said the words without really thinking.

They hit Ethel hard.

A tear rolled down her cheek.

"I cannot marry you Charles," she whimpered, still looking down at the table, avoiding his gaze.

"You're not married already are you?"

"No, I am not."

"Then what's the problem?" he was perplexed.

"I have a child, a boy called *Charlie*, he is four years old," she confessed.

☐Is that all?☐ Charles was relieved to find out that he was not part of a ménage a trios. ☐Where is the child?☐

"With my Aunts in Essex. They have looked after him since I came up to London. I visit him when I can but recently, since I have met you, not as often as I would like."

"I see," Charles mused. A silence ensued, each of them nibbled at their food but both had lost their appetite. "If you are happy with the status quo then why should we change anything?" He piped up.

"What are you inferring?" Ethel asked him, unsure of his reasoning.

"Well if the child," Charles could not bring himself to name the boy, "is happily ensconced with your relatives, surely there is no need to uproot the boy and cause him any more worry than he has had already in his short life?"

"But if we get married then my situation will change and it will no longer be proper to leave him in the care of others," Ethel was perturbed at the choice that was starting to unfold.

"Look Ethel, my dearest," Charles took hold of her hand. "I worship you and I am not sure that I would have broken off our relationship even if you had told me of your situation earlier but I can see why you kept this information from me. You are correct to assume that if the existence of your child becomes common knowledge it will be difficult for us to marry. A man in my position cannot be seen getting betrothed to someone who has had a child out of wedlock."

"That's what I was trying to tell you."

"But if the boy stays where he is then nobody need be any the wiser."

"You are saying..."

"I am saying that if you decide to marry me, you will have to give the boy up." Ethel's face went pale once more. "But there's no reason why you can't go and see him, on occasion, much as you do now and he will be well provided for, I will see to that."

Ethel held Charles' hand tightly across the table. What was she to do, lose the man she had fallen in love with or give up the child? But she had to make that choice and she had to decide here and now, there could be no vacillating. Ethel looked up at Charles with her soulful eyes shimmering with tears.

"If you will still have me, I would love to become your wife!" she cried.

"Then so be it!" Charles' smile lit up the room. He could barely contain his joy. He demolished his drink, poured another and then demolished that "Let's celebrate!" He pronounced, "Waiter a bottle of your finest champagne over here, we are to be married!" He shouted so that all the others in the restaurant could hear him. There was a spontaneous round of applause at his announcement and cries of 'congratulations old chap' from one or two.

~

As the phaeton sped south out of London, heading towards Crawley, Ethel reflected on the disposition of her newly acquired fiancée. She sat by his side, holding his arm tightly as the carriage rocked and rolled over the uneven road surface. He had a devil may care attitude that bordered on recklessness but being alongside such a man filled her with excitement. That air of unpredictability and impetuousness was a heady cocktail that she found intoxicating. Charles felt the warmth exuding from Ethel□s embrace. There was something about her that set her apart from the others that he had met. The hunter had himself been entrapped. He was convinced that his parents would also fall under her spell. How could they not do so? Was she not the most exquisite creature ever to have walked the surface of this earth?

The coachman steered the carriage through Crawley, onto Horsham and then Petworth. The Sussex Downs rolled out before them. Forested hillsides mingled with yellow corn fields and green pastures, creating a patchwork picture that Ethel found refreshing after the greyness of the city, and even the air seemed cleaner. Charles also felt his spirits rise, if that were possible.

"Not long now my love," he said breaking the silence.

The carriage slowed a little and trotted respectfully through the village of Midhurst before turning off onto a long, raking drive that took them down into a dale and past a clump of trees, before emerging into an open common where Dale Park could be seen atop the hillside in front of them.

It was a grand edifice, commanding an elevated view at the top of the hill. It stood stark and forbidding against the greenery of the hills beneath and surrounded by forest behind. It was positively palatial in size. Its line of Greco-roman columns supporting the long balcony above added to its grandeur. A line of enormous arched windows on the first floor took the eye towards the roof and a series of tall chimneys, sitting like a crown that seemed almost to touch the clouds above. The sight made Ethel's heart beat faster with trepidation. She clinched Charles' arm and he placed a reassuring hand on hers.

As she stepped from the phaeton and onto the gravel in front of the mansion she looked at the expanse of land undulating before her. Charles stood by her side and pointed out some of the landmarks.

"The town in the distance is Chichester and beyond that you can make out Arundel and finally the English Channel."

"How much does your family own?" Ethel enquired, awestruck at the panorama.

"Almost all you can see down the hill and a little beyond."

Charles escorted Ethel around the carriage, through the baronial doors and into the entrance hall. Servants greeted him as they scuttled to fetch the couple's belongings. He nodded affectionately as they passed. A plump lady appeared in a blue and white linen day dress. Her hair was gathered up and she sported a small, white bonnet.

"Charles!" she greeted her son. "To what do we owe this surprise?"

"Hello mother," Charles left Ethel's side to go and kiss his mother.

"And who is this delightful young lady?" she enquired as the embrace subsided.

"Mother, may I introduce you to Miss Ethel Beddowe!" he stated with pride. The two ladies touched hands.

"It is a pleasure to make with your acquaintance ma'am," Ethel said shyly.

"Come, let's go into the drawing room, father is there, he will be delighted to see you. It has been quite a while since you last came to visit us. What do you get up to in London? Or perhaps I shouldn't ask?" His mother led them into the drawing room.

The floor was heavily carpeted from one edge to the other. Rococo panelled walls stretched up to the high ceilings where they were edged with elaborate coving. A big mirror hung over the fireplace and large windows extended from the floor to the ceiling letting in ambient amounts of light. The room was dotted with antique furniture. Over by the windows an elderly gentleman, distinctly portly in shape, sat by a sofa table writing. On seeing Charles enter he rose up immediately to meet him.

"Why Charlie, my boy, it's so good to see you!" he hobbled over and shook the hand extended by Charles, slapping him on the other shoulder with his free hand.

"I see you are still limping," Charles observed.

"It's the gout!" he complained. "I can't seem to shift it."

"You need to stay off the claret." His wife commented.

"Away with you woman!" he exclaimed. "Can a man have no pleasure in his old age?"

His father caught sight of Ethel. "Well Charles you have surpassed yourself this time." He observed looking Ethel up and down. His bushy eyebrows exacerbated his stare and made Ethel blush. She looked down at the floor in embarrassment.

"Come let's sit over by the fire where it is more comfortable," Charles' mother insisted.

"I will call for some tea and perhaps something to eat you must both be ready for a little sustenance after your journey."

"That would be lovely mother, thank you," Charles replied.

Ethel took off her yellow overcoat to reveal her silk, lavender carriage dress. Charles' father gasped at the sight.

"Is this a casual visit or do you have a motive for gracing us with your presence?" Charles' father probed.

"Mother!" Charles looked at his mother.

"Father!" he turned to acknowledge his father. "I, we," he corrected himself, "have something to tell you."

"Pray, what is it Charles?" Hhis mother sat on the edge of her chair.

"Ethel and I are engaged and we are going to get married!" Charles delivered the information with an air of vacant self assuredness.

"Oh that is marvellous news!" his mother gripped Ethel's hand and leant over to give her a kiss on the cheek. "But why didn't you tell us earlier and we could have had a party to celebrate?"

"It has all been so sudden, mother," Charles explained.

"So who introduced you?" his mother enquired innocently.

"We were not formally introduced, we met."

At that moment the servant arrived with a tray on which she carried a tea service. She placed the tray on the table.

"Oh how romantic!" his mother sighed as she sorted out the crockery ready to pour the beverage. "I bet it was love at first sight."

The comment resonated with the two lovers.

"You've been reading too many novels my dear!" Charles' father mocked.

"Where did you meet?" his mother continued the interrogation.

"At the theatre," Charles informed her.

"The theatre?" his mother repeated, dreaming up her conspiracy theory as she poured the teas. "Milk and sugar dear?" she asked Ethel

"Yes please," Ethel was mouse like in her behaviour, hardly daring to move.

"Ethel is an actress," Charles revealed.

"Really!" his mother barely hid her disappointment.

"Yes, I am."

"So which theatre do you work at?" Charles' father dug deeper.

"She works at the Gaiety Theatre father," Charles divulged with some petulance. "Not that it matters any."

His rancour drew a cloud over the gathering. For a long while all that could be heard was the sipping of tea.

"Will you be staying for dinner?" his mother changed the subject and the awkward atmosphere was dispelled, for the moment at least.

"If we may" Charles replied, "we will stop over night and return to London tomorrow."

"I will get the housemaids to make up your rooms."

A tense atmosphere prevailed through the evening meal. Charles drank copious amounts of wine, compensating for the lack of dialogue and attempting to deflect his anger by getting himself into a stupor, his father was not so far behind. Ethel was left feeling most uneasy and could not wait to reach the sanctuary of her bedroom.

"Would you mind if I retired to my room, I am quite tired?" she asked meekly once they had finished the meal.

Ethel bade them all good evening and made her way out of the dining room and up the stairs. Once in the bedroom the plush floral chintz and upholstered furniture did little to allay her fears. Charles' mother followed soon after, kissing him goodnight and leaving him with a wistful look to emphasise her concern. On his father's recommendation they retired to the smoking room. Neither spoke a word as they went. Once inside his father closed the panelled doors so that what might ensue would be private.

Charles' father went over to the decanter on the portmanteau and poured them each a large brandy. He then opened the cigar box and offered his son first choice. They strode over to the hearth, inside of which a hearty fire crackled and burned. Cigars lit, they sat looking into the flames, like two adversaries preparing for a show down. Charles did not have long to wait before the hostilities began.

"The Gaiety is a burlesque club," his father spoke into the flames.

"Father, it has not been used for that type of show since before Edwardes took over." Charles swatted away the comment but was irked by its implication.

"Then what is it?"

"The Gaiety puts on light entertainment," Charles elucidated

"Then you don't have to have much talent to get yourself hired. All you need are the requisite assets and a pretty face and I can see she has them both!" His father drew heavily on his cigar, still looking into the fire. Charles sat on the edge of his seat looking directly at his father.

"There's no need to be so rude father. I was hoping that I would get your approval but I can see it is not forthcoming."

"She is no better than a serving girl and you have the audacity to bring her through the front door!" His father growled.

"She has a name father and she is my fiancée!" Charles defended Ethel's honour.

"She is your floosie and nothing more!" his father barked, coughing with the growing stress.

"How can you be so indelicate?" Charles retorted. "She is the daughter of a civil engineer not some cheap tart I picked up down a back alley." The irony of what he just said was not lost on Charles. He took a large gulp of his brandy.

"A civil engineer eh, Royalty indeed!"

Charles sneered at his father's sarcasm.

"And that is supposed to impress your mother and I?"

"Father, I am over twenty one years of age and I can do as I pleas!." Charles threw himself back into the luxurious upholstery of the chair.

"Cissy and Alan have both made attachments suited to their standing so why can't you? God forbid Charles, you are my eldest son, heir to all that you see around you, when will you grow up and start to take your responsibilities seriously?"

"I am well aware of my commitments father, you don't have to keep reminding me, but what that has got to do with whom I choose to marry is beyond me." Charles lied.

"You could have been an officer in the army by now, like your brother Alan, but no, you chose to hot foot it to London and indulge yourself with all manner of nocturnal pursuits instead." His father turned and looked Charles straight in the eye. "Look Charles," He softened his tone, "I know that you are a young man and that you feel the need to go and sow your wild oats. God knows we have all been there." His father winked. "But there is a time to settle down, and at twenty two you should be thinking about doing just that."

"That is what I am doing father, with Ethel!" Charles affirmed. "Once married we will settle down, perhaps even here at Dale Park and I will help you run the place and take on more of your business if you wish?"

"That is not going to happen!" his father spoke with menace.

"What do you mean?"

"I know of these so called 'Gaiety Girls'.!" Hhe began drinking heavily from his glass and then sucking on his cigar. He wagged his finger as he continued. "They are nothing short of gold diggers. They are after one thing and one thing only; your money."

Charles guffawed.

"You could not be further from the truth, Ethel loves me."

"How can you be so sure?" his father sought to sow doubt in his mind. "She is so pretty she could turn any man's head. You will get bored with her eventually and toss her aside like the rest."

"Again father you are way off the mark!" Charles scoffed. "I have never felt this way about anybody else before. I love her, she loves me and there is nothing you can say or do that will stop us."

"Is that so?" his father replied, his tone becoming quite threatening.

"Father, I am tired of this conversation and I am going to bed. Do your worst, why don't you?"

"Is that your final answer?"

"It is!" Charles concluded as he placed the empty glass on the table and tossed the cigar stub into the fire.

"Then hear this Charles Arthur, because what I am going to say to you is not an idle threat."

"Stop being so melodramatic father it doesn't suit you. You've had too much to drink, go to bed and we'll talk again in the morning!" Charles rose out of the chair ready to leave.

"Stay where you are!" his father commanded. Taken aback Charles did as he was told. His father spoke slowly and deliberately, picking his words carefully as he fought through the alcoholic fog that was misting up his brain. "If you marry this woman…"

"Ethel father, she is called Ethel!" Charles interrupted.

"If you marry this woman," his father continued, "I shall disinherit you and you shall get nothing."

"Have you quite finished father? I am tired and I want to go to bed!" Charles dismissed the threat. "If you feel the same way in the morning then so be it, Ethel and I will leave and we will not darken your doorstep ever again!" Charles called his bluff but could not help feeling that he had miscalculated his father's mood.

The next morning Charles and Ethel were up and ready for leaving before his father had arisen. His mother saw them off. She was at her most polite with Ethel and then she turned to say goodbye to Charles.

"Your father meant what he said last night," she said quietly as she hugged him.

"And I meant what I said!" Charles replied.

"You are both as stubborn as each other!" she commented.

"That's as maybe mother but I love Ethel and nothing you or father say or do will stand in our way."

"If you are so adamant then I will speak to him to see if I can talk him round."

"Thank you mother," Charles kissed her on the cheek and then left putting his arm around Ethel as they walked to the carriage.

Chapter 11

1897

Charles' mother wrote to him asking him to meet her at their London residence in Grosvenor Place. Her letter carried a rider requesting that he came alone. Charles arrived outside the Georgian residence, he did not bother to be announced but rather swept in and found his mother in the drawing room having tea with his sister Cissy. He greeted her and Cissy with a kiss, although his antipathy was there for all to see. Pleasantries out of the way, his mother broached the issue that she had summoned him about.

"Father is adamant that unless you disassociate yourself from," she paused, "this woman...."

"Ethel!" Charles interrupted. "She is called Ethel, mother!"

"Forgive me Charles," his mother apologised "I did not intend to cause you any distress." Charles fidgeted uncomfortably. "You know what your father has said."

"He made himself quite clear and so did I. If he wants to disinherit me then so be it, I will have to make my own way in life that's all!" Charles was defiant.

"You are so stubborn Charles," Cissy observed just before she put the cup to her lips.

"I have some securities and bonds that I can cash in." He declared unconvincingly.

"That won't sustain you for long with your lifestyle!" Cissy mocked as she placed her cup and saucer back on the occasional table.

"Then I will have to get a job!" he countered.

"Don't be absurd!" Cissy laughed at the suggestion. "You wouldn't know where to start."

"I suppose," Charles agreed feeling a little browbeaten. "Nevertheless, I will have to find a way to survive because I am not giving Ethel up, not for you, not for father, not for anybody!"

"I thought you might say something like that," his mother lowered her eyes in resignation. "So your father and I have spoken on the matter and have come up with a compromise."

"Which is?" Charles looked at her with suspicion.

"We will provide you with an allowance, a one off payment however once it is gone you will not be able to come back for any more."

Charles paused to gather his thoughts. His instinct was to dismiss the offer in an act of pride but Ethel's voice of reason echoed in the background.

"And how much will this sum be?" he felt a little like he was selling his soul.

"Sixty four thousand pounds," his mother disclosed matter of factly.

"That is a generous offer." Cissy pointed out.

"But a mere fraction of what my inheritance would likely amount to!" Charles was not impressed.

"That is our one and only offer Charles you must take it or leave it, the choice is yours," his mother was dispassionate.

"If that is the value you place on my head to appease your own consciences then so be it. I will accept the money for the sake of Ethel, I would not want to see her destitute."

"There is one proviso!" his melodramatics cut no ice with his mother.

"Which is?" Charles shrugged his shoulders and raised his eyebrows insubordinately.

"Ethel," his mother was careful to use her name this time "will not be allowed to set foot in Dale Park or here at Grosvenor Place."

"That is fine!" Charles retorted. "But neither shall I."

He bade them both a terse goodbye.

"Keep in touch Charlie," Cissy called out just before the front door slammed shut.

The couple were married at Chelsea registry office. Neither of their families attended, just a few of Charles' friends. Charles bought a yacht, The Wayward, a cutter, having sold the apartment in Beaufort Street to fund his investment.

"Who needs lodgings in London when we can live a life of luxury and travel aboard a yacht as fine as this?" he declared as he strode onto the yacht as it was moored in Southampton harbour.

"And what happens when we return to London?" Ethel was a tad annoyed at this indulgence and the fact that he had not discussed either transaction with her.

"We will just have to stay in the best hotels my love!" he replied without a care.

They spent the next few months commuting between the coast of France and England, stopping now and again in Ostend. It was a time of excess, staying at the most expensive hotels, eating the finest cuisine and spending long hours in the casinos. In the course of their sojourns they stopped off in the Channel Islands, their favourite was Jersey. It was while they were at dinner at the Grand Hotel, situated on the sea front in St Helier, that Ethel gave Charles the surprise news.

"I'm pregnant!" she disclosed.

Charles did not react at first he continued to focus on his steak, cutting off a small section ready to eat.

"Are you not pleased with the news?" she asked.

"Of course I am my dear," he replied unconvincingly as he consumed a piece of steak.

"Then what is the problem?" she persisted, placing her knife and fork on the plate in a gesture of ire.

"There is no problem," he smiled weakly. "I was just weighing up the repercussions."

"Which are?"

"Well first of all, with a child in tow we will have to find a place to live."

"I agree," her tone softened at the realisation that he did care after all. "And we will need a wet nurse."

"Of course," he nodded. They picked at their food in silence, each ruminating on the news.

"Do you think it will cramp our style?" he enquired insensitively.

"Well, what do you think?" her sarcasm was cutting.

"I don't see why it should?" he continued talking to himself. "We can always take baby and wet nurse with us. I mean, why should we let a small thing like a child get in our way?"

Charles took Ethel on a carriage ride around the island. They stopped to promenade along the breakwater at St. Catherine's and took a stroll to the end of the breakwater, stared into the choppy water that lapped around it and then strolled back to the carriage.

"Isn't the garden that people have spoken of somewhere around here?" he asked as they settled into their seats. Charles had heard many glowing recommendations of the place over dinner at the hotel.

"La Chaire?" Ethel remembered the name.

"Yes, that's it, La Chaire," he repeated. "It is to be found near the little harbour of Rozel if I remember rightly."

Charles took the carriage past Rozel Manor and Ville es Nouaux along La Pallootterie, following the road around the coast until they came down into Rozel itself. They turned left at the barracks and into the track that led past La Chaire.

"Do you think the owners will let us walk around the gardens?" Ethel asked Charles as she looked around her at once becoming enamoured by the place.

"I don't see why not, the place comes highly recommended, therefore one can presume that they do take visitors," he mused. "The house is quite small." Charles observed.

"But fetching nonetheless," Ethel thought the house was magical with its covering of wisteria, wrapped around its frontage like a fossilised hydra.

The owner heard the carriage pull up outside and was quick to emerge and greet the strangers.

"Good afternoon," her smile was most welcoming.

"Good afternoon," Charles replied leaping off the carriage in a display of youthful vigour. Ethel's disembarkation was a good deal more discrete. "We have heard so many pleasing anecdotes about your garden and we were wondering whether we might be so bold as to ask for your permission to take a stroll about the place?"

"I would be delighted," Mrs Rooke replied. "Feel free to wander where you wish. When you have finished perhaps you and the lady might like to join me for a cup of tea on the veranda?"

"That would be wonderful, Mrs....?" Charles enquired.

"Mrs Rooke and my husband is Captain Rooke but he is back in Brighton at present."

"And I am Charles Fletcher and this is my wife Ethel."

"A pleasure to make your acquaintance!" Mrs Rooke took Ethel's hand briefly.

The introductions complete Charles and Ethel took themselves to the south of the garden. It was mid May and the garden would soon be putting on its finest show. Charles was taken by the luxuriant nature of the plants as they fell over each other, competing for light and space.

"The place is a tad overgrown!" he criticised, "but a wonderful sight nonetheless."

"The fragrances are divine!" Ethel could not resist smelling each and every flower that she passed by, from rich rhododendrons to blooming begonias. The colours radiated in the bright sun of the day, creating a spectacle that kept them spell bound. Having finished their stroll they made their way back to the house where Mrs Rooke had a pot of tea ready, along with a variety of cakes and biscuits. The three of them shared polite conversation about the island and the various places of interest.

"Would you ever consider selling La Chaire?" Charles' question came as a bolt out of the blue, taking both Mrs Rooke and Ethel by surprise.

"As I explained earlier, Mr Fletcher, La Chaire is part of my family's heritage, how could I really think of selling it, even if it is a burden at times?"

Ethel glanced across at Charles, expressing her displeasure at his bluntness.

"Not even for a good price?" Charles ignored his wife's glare and persisted.

"Well, I suppose if the right offer came along I might consider it," Mrs Rooke conceded, feeling a little bullied by Charles' questioning. "But it would have to be a very tempting offer in order to compensate me for my loss."

"It must be a burden on your finances, having to maintain two residencies," Charles detected an opportunity.

"Charles must you be so transparent?" Ethel reprimanded him and then turned to Mrs Rooke. "You will have to forgive my husband, Mrs Rooke, once he gets something in his head it rattles around like a pea in a drum."

Mrs Rooke laughed.

"Please don't be concerned Mrs Fletcher, your husband is not the first person to ask my price and I doubt that he will be the last."

On the way back to St Helier Ethel queried Charles about his questioning of Mrs Rooke.

"Why were you pressing the woman about selling the house?"

"You are going to have a baby and so we will need a place to live," he explained.

"But why there?"

"Why not, it's an ideal place to raise a family? It's quiet, private and it has a harbour within walking distance, ideal for mooring the yacht."

~

Hugh was born two days before Christmas Day. Following a short convalescence the new family carried on much as before, frequenting upmarket hotels in England and France and meeting high society wherever they put up residence. One week it was London then onto Paris or Ostend and down to Monte Carlo to spend time in the casinos. All the while Charles was plotting his next acquisition, the procurement of La Chaire. He had fallen in love with the place the first time he had seen it and he was determined to buy the house and its exquisite gardens.

He hired Le Gallais, in town, to pursue the purchase with Mrs Rooke but she was proving to be a canny adversary. She rebutted all his initial offers and the latest letter that came from Le Gallais, whilst they took breakfast at the Hotel Angst in Bordighera, made him spit out his morning coffee.

"Damn the woman, she still refuses to budge!" he exclaimed

"Perhaps she really doesn't want to sell," Ethel observed.

"I will offer her three thousand pounds and that's my limit!" he declared wiping down the mess caused by the spilt drink. "If she does not accept that then we will look elsewhere."

His increase on his last offer was enough to persuade Mrs Rooke to sell and by January La Chaire was theirs.

~

Springate had a reputation.

Fletcher accompanied by his solicitor, E.B Renouf brought Springate the architectural drawings prepared by Graham and Bank. It did not raise any concern in either of them when Springate agreed to do the work with hardly a glance at the sketches.

"Don't worry about a thing Mr Fletcher," Springate reassured him, "your house will be in good hands."

As Springate shook hands with Fletcher he smiled to himself. These toffs are so gullible he thought. A fool and his money are easily parted and he was going to tease as much money out of this one as he could.

The journey through France was not without incident. By the time they reached Bordighera, south west of Monte Carlo, Charles was cursing the expense of the venture.

"Baby is a frightful inconvenience!" he complained, "and a burden on our finances."

Having dressed for dinner Charles and Ethel visited the nurse's room to check on the baby.

"Do you know Charles I think baby's looking a little seedy," Ethel observed, raising him up to get a better view. "His cheeks are flushed and he is quite hot."

"Perhaps he has caught the nurse's flu."

"Possibly," she said giving him a thorough check. "Are those spots on his face and neck?"

"Surely not!" Charles got up to get a better look, although cautious not to get too close.

"I'll phone for the doctor straight away." Charles started to panic. "And we will have to get the hotel to spray Sanitis about the room."

"Don't get carried away dear!" Ethel reassured him. "Let's wait till tomorrow and see how he is then."

"Are you sure?"

"Quite sure," she replied. "You go on down and have some fun and try not to lose too much, we have a budget remember."

Charles kissed her on the cheek and then made his way towards the door.

"Wish me luck!" he called as he left.

Charles returned a short while later, looking quite out of breath.

"The Empress Frederic is in the restaurant and she is asking to see baby," he gasped as he burst through the door.

"The Empress Frederic, she wants to see baby?" Ethel was perplexed. "Why so?"

"I don't know but you had better bring him down straight away!" Charles instructed.

"But he is in his pyjamas!"

"She has asked to see him in his pyjamas!" Charles revealed.

"Why?"

"I don't know!" Charles replied in a higher voice, his tone becoming somewhat strident.

"But I am not dressed to be received by the Empress?" Ethel suddenly realised the enormity of the situation. The thought of meeting actual royalty filled her with terror.

"Well just throw something on but whatever you do, be quick about it, we can't keep her waiting!" Charles said waving his arms about.

Eventually Ethel found something to wear that she thought was appropriate and dressed as quickly as she could. She dashed to the mirror that hung over the fireplace in order to put on her make-up and tidy her hair.

"There's no time for that, she'll be wondering where we are!" the hysteria in Charles's voice unnerved Ethel.

"Do I look presentable?" she asked in earnest.

"You look beautiful as always," he replied.

She kissed him on the cheek, grabbed Hugh and made for the door. Charles followed. They ran down the corridor and hurriedly swept down the stairs, Ethel clutching Hugh tightly all the way. They rushed into the restaurant before coming to an abrupt halt. There sitting amongst her entourage, was the Empress Frederic. She was an imposing woman despite her age. Although she was slight in height and rather dumpy in figure she held herself on the edge of her seat with a posture perfected over the years. She had an air that befits the royal household and she looked quite like her mother, Queen Victoria. The image filled Ethel with trepidation as she approached.

Tired of being carried Hugh wriggled free. He paused to get his balance before staggering forward at an ever increasing rate towards the Empress. Ethel held her breath, hoping beyond hope that his pyjama trousers would not slide down about his ankles as they were wont to do. The look of delight on the Empress' face grew as she realised that young Hugh was making a bee line for her.

"How endearing," she declared as she swept Hugh up in her arms.

She cupped his little face in her chubby hands and kissed him full on the lips. Not content with being held, Hugh again wriggled free of his captor. He wobbled on his feet, tottered around staring at the ogling adults before returning to the empress for another embrace. She clapped her hands in delight as once more she raised him up. This time he sat still for a while, enjoying all the attention.

"I saw this little treasure with your nursemaid in the foyer as I arrived and I was so taken with him, I wondered what he might look like dressed in his night attire and how adorable he looks!" the empress observed as she felt their soft, silk texture. "He is a charming child. Thank you for bringing him down to see me, now you must get him back to bed before he gets a chill."

Ethel and Charles took their leave and rushed back to the hotel room, adrenalin still coursing through their veins. Their elation was short lived because the rest of the night was an uncomfortable one for both of them. Baby cried and moaned as his fever started to take hold and in the absence of the nurse it was left to them to console him, what had started as a night of great fulfilment turned sour very quickly.

The doctor called in the morning and allayed their fears that baby had measles. The nurse also resumed her duties, her sickness having receded enough for her to resume her chores. Charles and Ethel took the opportunity to get out into the fresh air of the surrounding countryside. Once up in the mountains they stopped frequently to take in the views. Charles took out his pocket Kodak, a wooden box with brass fittings, mounted it on the metal foot that came with it and proceeded to take pictures of Ethel, with the mountains as the backdrop.

After a few days they returned to Jersey and booked in at the Grand, Charles wasting no time in going to La Chaire, taking his friend Parish with him to view the progress being made on the gardens. When they arrived there were workmen busy tiling the roof, putting in sash windows and digging out the foundations at the back of the house.

"Mornin' Mr Fletcher!" Springate greeted him in his usual brusque manner.

"Good morning Springate!" Fletcher replied assertively." How are things progressing?"

"Not so good Sir!" Fletcher could not help feeling that Springate's tone was evasive.

"How so?"

"Well Mr Fletcher Sir, the foundations at the back are proving troublesome. The house has been built almost butt onto the cliff behind and the ground underneath is virtually all rock. It's difficult for the men to break through and so it is slowing everything down."

"Banks and Graham have informed me that you are not following the original plans." Fletcher added curtly.

"That's true Sir!" Springate replied bluntly.

"I don't pay you to think Springate, I pay you to build!" Fletcher sought to stamp his authority on the man. "If you come up with any problems then get in touch with me, E.B. Renouf or Banks and Graham before you proceed!" Fletcher instructed.

"Enjoy your stroll," Springate muttered sarcastically as Fletcher and Parish set off up the northern slope to take in the garden.

"I swear that I will swing for that man!" Fletcher seethed to Parish as they began to climb the slope. "I would sack him tomorrow if I were not bound by a contract."

Under Fletcher's stewardship work on the house increased in pace. Out went the old conservatory where Curtis had once cultivated his fledgling plants from around the world, to be replaced by a smoking room. The new foundations at the back supported two new bedrooms and offices. The ragged driveway out front that led up to the house became a veranda that worked its way around the side of the house. The old house was extended upwards with the help of new internal walls and reinforcement of the existing ones. The roof was removed and rebuilt and the sash windows that were put in were made from oak. No expense was spared to get the things Fletcher wanted. In between times Fletcher could not just sit idly and supervise. He and Ethel took frequent trips to France and to London, buying up essentials for the house. Money was not an object as they pursued an avaricious approach to shopping.

With the house well under reconstruction Fletcher set about redesigning the garden. He was looking for something on a much grander scale, Curtis' original layout was sound but it had been nearly forty years since the great man had passed away and the place was in need of more than just a makeover. Fletcher, influenced by his sojourns in Southern France and Italy felt that the terracing needed to be far more sculpted and defined than it was at present. He had discussed the possibilities with Springate on one of their more amicable days. Springate had suggested using pink granite, knowing that this option would likely be the most expensive. Fletcher toyed with the idea but then settled on using the local puddlestone, the same underlying rock that had attracted Curtis to Rozel in the first place. Much to Springate's chagrin Fletcher eventually gave the task to a builder by the name of Green.

"I thought I was going to build the walls and garden?" Springate complained to Fletcher when Green's men turned up.

"You have the house to complete!" Fletcher replied dismissing Springate's moaning.

Soon after the basics were completed plants started to arrive. Bamboos were placed along the lower path in the form of an avenue. Some were also put in the top pockets, around the reservoir to act as a screen. Dotted along the terraces that had been built he put cacti and ajavis. This started to give this part of the garden a more Mediterranean feel, akin to his favourite haunts in and around Monte Carlo. Palms were placed in the ground around the old eucalyptus stump near the house.

The large Dracoena, planted by Curtis was transferred higher up the garden as Fletcher started to fine tune his creation. To increase light in the smoking room a large rhododendron was unceremoniously cut down. Not happy with the old eucalyptus stump he had it blasted out and removed. The palms he replanted so that the path around the house could be widened.

Fletcher commissioned Green to move the greenhouse. Springate was charged with building two cottages, one for the coachman and the other for the butler, down near the old barracks. He then asked Green to build the stables in preparation for the arrival of the horses and coaches he had just purchased. As work progressed Fletcher took himself and the family off to France. On the way back he pondered with the problem of extending the house. It was as he boarded the boat from St Malo that he resolved the issue.

Rozel was the sleepiest of harbours. It nestled quietly in the north east of the island, where the only sounds to be heard were the waves rattling the pebbles on the beach, and the seagulls guarding their territory around the shore. As Green's men set off the first explosion the whole place jumped.

Gulls screamed and took to the air, locals, startled, stood motionless, momentarily trying to work out what the hell the noise was and where it had come from. The blast echoed up the narrow valley before disappearing up and over towards St Martins. Green's men drilled more holes, laid more charges and set off more detonations. With each round the locals, realising what was happening, got on with their chores, albeit irked by the inconvenience of it all.

Walton was one of Fletcher's neighbours whose property adjoined La Chaire directly. The old man used his land for farming, mainly subsistence and had been resident for many a year. Now in the latter stages of his mundane life, he took exception to anything that remotely involved change.

Fletcher was deep in discussion with Green as Walton approached.

"My name's Walton!" he pronounced as he strode, uninvited, onto the open terrace in front of La Chaire.

"I beg your pardon?" Fletcher was taken aback by Walton's interruption. Undeterred Walton continued.

"Are you the owner of this place?" he enquired bluntly.

"I am indeed!" Fletcher replied.

"You know, Mr..?" Walton fished for Fletcher's name.

"Fletcher, Charles Fletcher, of Dale Park Sussex."

"You know Mr Fletcher," Walton carried on unimpressed, "I'm interested to know what it is you are doing here."

"We are landscaping the garden and refurbishing the house," Fletcher felt obliged to answer the old man.

"I can't see the point myself!" The old man did not worry whether his opinion was welcomed or not. "I remember old man Curtis planting this here and cultivating that there. I said at the time the land was only good for grazing and nothing has occurred to change my mind. It was a pretty garden I grant you that." Walton agreed reluctantly.

Fletcher had an overriding urge to take Walton to task. He turned briefly to Green and sent him on his way before returning to Walton.

"Come with me Mr...?" Fletcher had not registered Walton's name.

"Walton!" Walton repeated gruffly.

"I will show you around and then perhaps I might convince you of the efficacy of building such an environment."

The contrast between the two men could not have been more marked. Fletcher was young, slim and dressed in a well cut black suit, white shirt, tie and sported shiny black shoes. Walton, on the other hand, was quite unkempt in his appearance. His stained, baggy trousers were tied with a belt underneath a large pot belly that hid where it was fastened. His brown, checked jacket was ripped and tattered and tied with string about the waist. He sported a pair of old boots, without laces, the tongue poking out of his left boot. He wore a cap that sat at an angle on his head revealing his bald pate, surrounded by a thicket of grey hair. As Fletcher's young limbs propelled him up steps and along avenues at a healthy pace, so Walton waddled along, bow legged, a few feet behind trying to keep up. Even so, Walton kept Fletcher talking right through to dinner in the evening.

"What an old bore!" Fletcher announced as he eagerly tucked into his evening meal.

"Then why did you humour him so?" Ethel asked.

"He is a neighbour and there might come a time when I need to ask a favour of him."

"So you were buttering him up?" Ethel smiled knowingly.

"A little," Charles returned the smile. "One has to be diplomatic now and again, even if the person you are talking to is something of a country bumpkin."

As work continued on the house Springate approached Fletcher.

"There seems to be a problem," Springate began.

"What with?" Fletcher felt another expense coming on.

"The drains aren't working properly," Springate informed him.

"So what do you propose?"

"Piping them into the brook."

"But the brook goes through Walton's land!" Fletcher informed him. He thought a moment and then added. "Leave it to me and I will clear it with the old man."

Springate went back to his chores as Fletcher set off to see Walton. He arrived to find Walton tending to his small holding.

"Good morning Walton!" Fletcher announced his presence. "I have a problem with the drains from the house and my builder tells me that the only way to solve the problem is to direct the waste into the brook."

"It will cost you!" Walton said without lifting is head.

Fletcher stopped in his tracks.

"Cost me?" he queried turning to face the old man once more.

"Well what do you expect?" Walton elaborated. "If you siphon your drains into the brook it's going to inconvenience me no end because I will have to get my water from further upstream. A little compensation isn't much to ask now is it?"

"Compensation be damned!" Fletcher could hardly contain his ire. Walton laughed to himself and resumed his tilling as his neighbour returned to La Chaire cursing.

Fletcher took down all of the trees in front of La Chaire in order to extend the terrace and create more light, as well as exposing the house in all of its emerging splendour. To the same end the quarrying created space between the back of the house and the cliff face. Fletcher, keen to extend the view in front of the building further paid a visit to his neighbours. Renouf, who lived close by was persuaded to cut back the larger trees that bordered their properties but when Fletcher approached Walton he was met with a flat refusal.

"I'm not cutting anything down just so that you can improve your view!" Walton stated.

There was a particularly stubborn outcrop of rock that refused all attempts to budge it. Green made Fletcher aware of the problem.

"Just blast the blighter!" Fletcher told him, still irked at Walton's intransigence.

Green drilled extra holes into the rock, deeper than normal. Just about lunchtime, when everybody in the village was settling down to eat, the charge was detonated. The blast resonated right through the valley. Buildings shook, some of the newly laid terracing collapsed and pieces of the Louis the Fifteenth interior design work came away from the interior walls. Plumes of dust and rubble were sent up into the air, to fall like hailstones all about. Everybody was cursing but one more so than Walton as the force of the blast took out some of the trees that bordered his land with Fletcher's.

Angered by his new neighbour's arrogance, Walton set about thwarting Fletcher's advancing empire at every juncture. As Green busied himself building the stables, Walton decided that he would construct a perimeter wall which was angled so that it cut off much of the entrance to the stables. He constantly harassed and complained to the builders as they went about their business, telling them what they could and could not do.

Despite the blast there were still some trees remaining, mainly ilex, sycamore and beech, standing in the way of Fletcher's view. Not one to give up, he decided to approach Walton once more but this time through an intermediary, E.B. Renouf, his solicitor. Renouf returned directly from his meeting with Walton and reported back to Fletcher.

"Well, what did the old fool have to say?" Fletcher enquired as they strode along some of the newly widened path leading to the upper terraces.

"He is not willing to cut them down," Renouf told him.

"I thought as much, the stubborn so and so!" Fletcher interrupted.

"But he has made you an offer," Renouf revealed.

"Which is?"

"He will sell you the strip of land upon which they sit."

"And the price?" Fletcher asked knowing that there would be a sting in the tail.

"A thousand pounds!" Renouf could not disguise his thoughts on the matter and raised a smile.

"What?" Fletcher cursed stamping his feet on the ground. "And what would you value the land at?"

"About a hundred and fifty pounds at most," Renouf said after a moment's deliberation.

"I think we might be able to negotiate him down from his original price."

"He'll have to come down a lot more if I am to consider anything at all!" Fletcher declared.

He sent the solicitor back to Walton to see if he would lower his price. Renouf returned huffing and puffing. He was a rotund gentleman and the climb up and down the terracing made him flush.

"He has asked me to ask you what your bottom price is," Renouf gasped as he caught up with Fletcher supervising the planting of some of the shrubs.

"Tell him one hundred and fifty pounds is my top price," Fletcher declared. "I don't know, these Jersey folk are all thieves."

Even as all the construction work was taking place Fletcher never lost sight of his real focus, the garden, but standing in his way were two immovable objects, Old Walton out front and the rock face to the rear.

Where the rock had been blasted away the steep cliff face now became sheer in places. On this blank canvas Fletcher directed the builders to extend the terracing that would eventually house the garden. To the east of the house the terracing took the form of three large descents of around fifteen feet, taking the terracing from the upper slopes to the lane below. These drops were reinforced by large boulders cemented into the rock and to each other to create an impenetrable barrier. The puddlestone from which they were made offered an uneven texture that toned in with the rocky outcrops that remained. The lowest terrace was itself divided into three shallower terraces that ran parallel with each other and the lane beneath.

Directly above them Fletcher had the path widened and included a pergola to run along its length from the wide, open terrace at the front of the house to the easterly edge, leading the visitor into the maze like array of paths that would meander their way all around the northern slope of the valley. Victorian gardens had, for a long time, used covered alleys made from hornbeam or wych elm to create an uninterrupted arched trellis upon which ramblers and vines would grow. Wanting to create a more Mediterranean feel Fletcher built his pergola using upright pillars of larch wood with horizontal beams that were fitted into recesses dug out of the walls. Running along the pergola wall was small terraced edging, filled with soil.

Above the path another higher terraced wall some five feet taller than the first rose sheer behind the pergola. Its stark linear descent was broken by smaller pockets of terracing shaped in semi circles emerging from the larger wall. These smaller pockets and all the other shallower walls that lined the intricate paths were made from much less significant puddlestone rocks. At one end Fletcher had placed his waterfall which would cascade down and around an original rocky outcrop. At the source of the waterfall was a small lily pond over which a rustic wooden bridge passed.

As the garden moved around to face Rozel harbour and the open sea, so the terraced paths melded into each other via adjoining steps, some long and steep others shallow, consisting only of a few steps. The paths followed the contours sloping ever upwards towards the peak. Along the eastern fringe, rock had been removed to create an alcove which would house a stoned cross that had been specially commissioned. Higher up, near the top of the garden, Fletcher had placed the summerhouse which overlooked the other side of the valley. At the very top he created a viewing point, behind which the top rose garden would be planted.

The sheer cliff to the rear of the house that had been created by the blasting had been left untouched, a precarious precipice dropping a good forty feet to the floor below. To the west of the house this precipice had been walled, access to it was by way of a sweeping stairway at the far end. A smaller, two foot wall skirted its base allowing plants to be placed that would eventually clamber up to the top.

Fletcher oversaw the construction of the house, the other buildings and the garden much like a pharaoh might have watched over the creation of a monolith built in his honour. Before any serious planting could take place Fletcher had some more features to add to his framework. The wrought iron arches at the entrance were put in place as was the rustic railing along the walls. The reservoir at the top of the garden was filled by a pump, driven by an engine housed in a shed by the old well. The water from this was then fed by pipes throughout the garden so that it could be watered more efficiently. The key water feature was the waterfall that fell a good ten feet over a rocky outcrop. Fletcher played with the flow until he achieved a moderate cascade. To complete the water feature he placed a rustic bridge over the pond.

Chapter 12

La Chaire 1900

Although Charles was self indulgent in respect of the house and garden he was as much besotted with his wife. It was not so much that he thought of her as some prized possession, he adored her too much to think as arrogantly as that, but he did get great satisfaction knowing that he had someone that his peers could only look at through envious eyes. Ethel's sunny outlook and convivial nature was infectious. She had an innocence and a naivety about her that men found most attractive.

"How is La Chaire coming along?" Stevens asked as he ushered the carriage onto the drive in front of La Chaire.

"Very well," Ethel replied. "No doubt Charles will take you round the place."

Fletcher happened to be at the front entrance as they arrived.

"What a sight you three look like!" he proclaimed. "I surmise that the drinking did not stop after I left."

"And why should it?" Ethel laughed loudly, clinging to her two guardians.

"You best not have any more my dear you'll be seedy in the morning!"

"You are a spoil sport Charlie!" she said as she let go of the two men and sidled up to her husband. He took her hand and led her towards the house, the two guests followed behind.

"The inside of the house is nearly finished, would you like to see what it is like?"

"What did I say?" Ethel raised her eyebrows in their direction.

Having built around Curtis' house and extended it to the point at which he could go no further, Fletcher was still not satisfied that the building reflected his status even though it was now more than twice its original size. It could never compete with the family home at Dale Park but he felt driven to prove to his father, and others, that he could command a home that made a statement in its own way, albeit less palatial. If it was not feasible to extend outwards any further then perhaps he might look inside the building to satisfy his desire. To achieve these aims he had moved everybody out whilst the inside was refurbished, taking up residence in a modest house called 'Ingleside' at Green Cliff.

He had the entrance to La Chaire moved and created an archway using pink granite slabs. The group followed Fletcher through the archway, over the black and white chequered floor and into the vestibule. The oak panelled lobby with its recess containing a Chinese vase was heated by a fire that burned warmly in the hearth in font of them. To their left an oak stairway led back and then turned on itself leading to the first floor bedrooms.

"The far door leads to the offices, to the right is the smoking room and billiard room but I would like to show you the drawing room first."

Fletcher led them through the double doors to their left. Once inside they all stepped into the centre of the room before stopping to look around them.

"Why Charles, this is quite magnificent!" Lempriere exclaimed as he tried to take in as much detail as he could.

Curtis' original drawing room had been extended to take in another bay window so that the two of them now looked out onto the wide gravel terrace in front of the house. To support the ceiling two large pillars had been placed in the middle of the room, each with vertical lines chiselled from top to bottom. The walls were designed in a mock rococo style panelling, their raised features painted in a soft pink and blue over a cream background. Cherubs and angel faces looked down from the top of the larger panels, whilst the smaller panels sported a simple floral design. The ceiling was decorated with plaster cornices the same colour. Large floral plastering had been placed around two large chandeliers that hung from the ceiling.

He had spared no expense in bringing La Chaire up to the required standard. A bespoke, carved oak, Louis the Fifteenth fireplace from Arrowsmiths of London, took pride of place on the far wall, just below the large mirror. This was the focal point in the drawing room. To complement the 'three Louis' theme he had placed his cabinet and other antique furniture purchased whilst touring through France, around the space.

"Why Charles, the room is most delightful!" Colonel Stevens exclaimed.

"You have indeed excelled yourself!" Lempriere added.

"Do you really think so?" Fletcher was genuinely flattered by their comments.

"You can rely on our honesty old chap," Lempriere reassured him.

Flushed with their positive comments he took them back across the vestibule and into the smoking room. There was no furniture in here yet and so the sound of their footsteps echoed on the newly laid block flooring. In the dining and drawing rooms Fletcher had had parquet flooring laid but here and in the billiard room that adjoined the smoking room a slightly less expensive choice had been made.

"I have the billiard table on order and it should arrive soon, along with a pianola for the drawing room," Fletcher informed them.

In the billiard and smoking room oak panelling had been fitted. The panelling darkened both rooms considerably but then he revealed to them his secret.

"What does this switch on the wall do?" Lempriere enquired.

"Try it and find out!" Fletcher could hardly conceal his excitement.

Lempriere flicked the switch and immediately lights came on around the walls.

"You have had electricity installed!" Lempriere was impressed.

"As we were going to have the telephone cabling system put in I decided to go the whole hog and get wired up for electricity. Walter, the butler and I are having lessons on how to keep the generator running."

"If you keep on spending like this you'll have no money left!" Lempriere cautioned.

"I'm glad you said that!" Ethel interrupted, taking hold of her husband. "I keep telling him to be thrifty but he just ignores me and carries on like money is running out of fashion."

"Shall I begin with your birthday present?" Fletcher teased as he looked lovingly into her eyes.

"Perhaps just a modest expenditure?" Colonel Steven's added, smiling.

"Yes!" Charles concurred. "Maybe I should forego buying anything at all?" Fletcher kissed her affectionately.

Charles took them up to the first floor and showed them the three bedrooms, each with its own fireplace made from wrought iron, and from each ceiling hung a chandelier.

"I presume the servants quarters are up the next flight of stairs?" Colonel Stevens enquired.

"Yes, there are four bedrooms up there," Fletcher replied. "They are a good size as well."

"If you spare the rod you'll spoil the child!" Stevens warned, "unless you are thinking of putting more than one servant in each room?"

"If I need to I will but don't forget I am building two cottages, one for the butler and the other for the head coachman."

"And is all the building work finished?" Lempriere enquired.

"Just about," Fletcher replied. "I'm still not satisfied with this house yet so I have instructed the builders to alter the roof, put granite sills in the windows, create ornamental brickwork on the chimneys and build a veranda balcony by the billiard room. I've abandoned the idea of having a driveway up to the house, that's why I had the entrance moved further down the lane. I have ordered Green to build a granite archway and a broad flight of granite steps there. This will lead onto the terrace."

Lempriere shook his head in disbelief.

"I thought your father only gave you a fixed allowance?" he said.

"He did." Fletcher replied. "But if I manage my accounts properly and the bank rate is favourable we should be quite comfortable." Fletcher hugged Ethel who was still by his side, concerned at Lempriere's observation.

As they stepped out into the light of late afternoon the two men paused to look at the garden around the house. The walls were nearing completion but Fletcher looked up with some dismay.

"It's so bare!" he declared with Ethel standing by his side. "It looks like a Roman amphitheatre."

"It will not look so stark when you have covered it with plants," Lempriere reminded him.

"I do hope so," Fletcher, being a perfectionist, had his doubts.

With the house almost complete Fletcher's attention returned to the garden. Like an artist he had constructed the outline in the form of terracing and the special features like the stone cross and the waterfall. His next task was to start filling in the background with a wash of colour in the form of trees and large shrubs.

Having dispensed with the incompetent Sharman, the new gardeners, Smith and Baal, were set to, pushing wheelbarrows as they added manure to the new soil. Fletcher was not frightened to get his own hands dirty and did his bit, unnerving the workers as he dug alongside them. He had the mesembryanthemums moved up to the pond area and placed in pockets along the walls. More bamboo and aloes were planted around the stone cross that looked out over Rozel harbour creating a green backdrop.

Fletcher's perception of the garden was one of a place that was too overgrown and out of control. It lacked diversity in both colour and spectacle. Curtis's 'curious' additions, the exotics that he had so carefully nurtured had all but disappeared. Only the deodar, dracoena, the Monterey pine and few smaller shrubs, mainly hydrangea and Rhododendrons and a couple of camellias had survived. There was the magnificent Magnolia Campbelli, reputed to be the best in Europe but that had been planted by Curtis' daughter, Mrs Fothergill. It was this marvellous tree, in full bloom that had first caught Fletcher's eye. It would be the rock upon which he would build a garden to be envied by all. He may not have realised it but

Fletcher was true to the spirit of Curtis. His passion and his creativity had their roots, both literally and metaphorically, in the actual garden where the pursuit of modern gardening had all begun, some fifty years previous.

Fletcher's plan was grandiose in its design and flamboyant in its anticipated display. What he envisaged was a continuum of growth, from the largest trees to the tiniest of flowers. There would be a cornucopia of textures and fragrances and his pied de resistance, a cascade of colour from one season to the next so that the garden would attract attention, even in the dead of winter.

The pathways were finished as were the nooks and crannies, hidden alcoves and expansive vistas for the unwary to discover and marvel at as they promenaded. Fletcher shopped at the finest nurseries and sought out the most eye catching plants. Like Curtis he loved the idea of growing exotica but unlike Curtis his flora was entirely for display. There was no scientific investigation just an indulgence that would, hopefully, gain the recognition of his contemporaries.

As the plants arrived so they were planted. The blue green leaves of the phoenix palms at the front of the house, a native of the Indian sub-continent, complemented the other palms, bamboos and cacti. Their outer skirt of old leaves rustling in the breeze. The Canary date palm which would eventually produce bundles of cream coloured, bowl shaped flowers in the summer and sat alongside the fast growing Cocas Australia palm.

He planted a Japanese ash also known as the Golden ash whose beauty would brighten up a cold winter's day, standing golden against a white blanket of frost or snow. He got excited at the prospect of its stunning yellow foliage that would appear in the autumn. He placed it just above the pergola near to a silver poplar whose pale green catkins would hang in bundles, bridging the gap between summer and autumn. He bought an American oak, another tree that would display a distinctly coloured foliage in autumn, this time red orange, as would the purple beech with its leaves turning a rich copper at the same time. Completing this autumn display was the laburnum, offering up its brown seed pods in winter and the Rhus Cotinus, revealing wine red foliage in late autumn, fading eventually to a shimmering pink as a sunset finale to the year. All these were placed in pockets around the garden.

Choosing the plants to give a spring and summer exhibition was much easier. Fletcher purchased a flowering peach and a flowering cherry, both Japanese in their origin. The peach would blossom in March putting on a show of pink followed in April by the cherry tree with a similar display. In this location Fletcher anticipated that the first buds of the flowering peach might emerge as early as January. The variegated sycamore would unfold its shrimp like pink leaves in spring and eventually they would turn a pale yellow green before finally turning a dark green with yellow marbling in summer.

A weeping willow was placed by the lily pond, its slender branches hanging down to release yellow catkins in April. By late spring the laburnum should have revealed its yellow, pea-like leaves, hanging in long chains like golden raindrops and the Rhus Cotinu should also have started its cycle of colour by growing lollipop shaped leaves.

The large tulip tree, native of North America, named because of the creamy yellow, tulip shaped blossoms that would truly be a sight to behold, caused Fletcher some consternation because he had been told that it might take twenty years before it blossomed. However he took a risk that this would not be the case.

He had the gardeners place more lily of the valley and mesem-bryanthemums in the spaces on the walls. These would all flower in late spring giving a dash of white and a spectrum of colours along the walkways. He had also purchased a number of lilac bushes that would bloom around this time, exuding a heavy fragrance along the cloistered paths as well as giving clusters of lavender blue flowers.

Summer would welcome in the three terraces of delphiniums, planted in the long terrace near the lily pond. A mass of deep purple, multi headed stems providing a short but eye catching spectacle. Wrapped around the arches and the pergola, rambling roses would wind their way, the Paul's Scarlet rose a vigorous climber producing an abundance of bright red flowers. Fletcher had placed clematis plants to cover some of the walls the most prized being the 'Madam Eduard Andre' which displayed beautiful red flowers in late summer. It was named after its cultivator, whom he met whilst in France.

Ethel's birthday passed without any sign of a present, much to her consternation.

"Aren't you going to wish me happy birthday?" she prompted.

"Happy birthday darling!" he replied from behind the newspaper.

"Is that it?" she complained. "Not even a kiss?"

Charles closed the paper and folded it in half before standing and placing it on his seat. He stepped around the table, leaned over and gave her a kiss before returning to read the news. Ethel was dumb struck. She sat opposite him, unable to eat her toast as her stomach churned caused by a mixture of anger and frustration. She had to know.

"Do you have anything for me?" she asked curtly.

"Beside's the kiss?"

"Yes," she bit, and then more controlled, "beside's the kiss."

"I had been meaning to speak to you about our expenses," he began, his body still obscured by the large broadsheet.

"What about them?" Ethel kept her poise, just. If he was about to tell her that she would have to forego her present because he had spent all of his money on this godforsaken place, she would give him a piece of her mind!

"Well, I have spent a great deal on the house recently there have been so many unforeseen extras, as you well know."

Ethel started to bristle. She wished he would put the paper down and look her in the eye so that he would know how she felt but he did not.

"So I'm afraid we will both have to tighten our belts!" she was just about to tear the paper away from his grip in a fit of petulance when he continued. "However, I have booked us two seats on the boat to Southampton in order that we might go up to London."

Ethel relaxed a little.

"I believe mother will be at Grosvenor Place and I have arranged an appointment with the agency to interview staff for the house."

Ethel bristled once more.

"So perhaps," he started to lower the paper slowly, "we might pick you up a little something while we are in London."

He lowered the paper to reveal a broad smile. Realising that she had been duped she stared at him, pretending to be angry. Inside she felt a surge of affection for him, so much so she leapt up and ran round to give him a kiss.

"Happy birthday darling!" he spluttered out between embraces.

The sailing to Southampton aboard the Veronica was not comfortable. Both Charles and Ethel were experienced sailors and the choppy sea crossing was not new to them, having to share the journey with a large crowd however was. There was a lot of jostling as people sought the best places to sit and combined with the ship's movement it made for a bumpy ride.

"I abhor all these folk!" Charles complained. "They are so ill mannered."

"Oh Charles, you are such a snob!" Ethel laughed.

"Why don't you watch where you are going?" Charles called after a man who spilt the ash from his cigarette over Charles' trouser leg. His voice was lost in the noise of so many other people bustling along.

"It's like a cattle market!" Charles continued to moan. "Do these people not know how to conduct themselves? Let's go up to the bridge dear where there is likely to be a better class of company."

Feeling threatened by those close by him he almost dragged Ethel along the deck and up the steps that led to the bridge. The difference in atmosphere was tangible. From this privileged position all that could be heard was the crash of the waves on the hull of the ship and the intermittent dialogue of the sailors going about their work. In the relative sanctuary of the bridge they were attended to by the captain himself.

They arrived in London to the usual hustle and bustle. They booked in at the Carlton and sought out old friends to share their first night in town with. The next day saw Charles up and ready to visit his mother. That evening he returned to the hotel room to find Ethel had not arrived. He was a touch disappointed but it was not long before she did appear, a little tipsy but in good spirits.

"How was your mother?" she asked as she took off her mink stole and threw it on the back of the settee.

"She's fine but father is bad with the gout again," Charles replied as he sat in front of the blazing fire sipping at a large whisky he had just poured. Ethel took off her coat and placed it next to the stole.

"And what about you my dear, did you have a good time?"

Before she could answer, Charles pulled a small black jewellery box from his trouser pocket and passed it to her. Taken aback, Ethel took the box and proceeded to open it with great anticipation.

"Oh Charles!" she exclaimed, throwing her arms around his neck and planting a big kiss on his lips. "It's exquisite!" she enthused. "Would you put it on for me?"

Charles took the star shaped brooch out of its package and pinned it onto her white blouse. She jumped up and ran to the mirror.

"You approve?" he asked softly.

"Approve?" she could hardly contain her joy, "I absolutely adore it." She proclaimed.

She ran to him once more and kissed him.

"I hope these are the only kisses you've been giving?" he taunted.

"Charles!" she slapped him on the shoulder, "you are incorrigible!"

The rest of the visit to London was taken up with shopping. Ethel went in search of more clothes, while Charles interviewed prospective staff for La Chaire in their hotel room. He got himself a cook, some maids and a coachman named Fenton.

Rather than return to Jersey, they took the boat to Ostend to partake of a little pigeon shooting and then made their way south to Monte Carlo, staying at Ciros Hotel. All this was part of Ethel's birthday treat. They wined and dined from lunch until the early hours, always finishing at the casino.

Not long after their return to Jersey, the carriages that Charles had ordered whilst in London arrived. The three of them took pride of place alongside the pony cart. Charles and Ethel strolled up to the stables, which had been built to the west of the main house, adjoining Walton's property. It was along this border that Walton waged a continuous guerrilla war against his neighbour.

"Aren't four carriages an unnecessary extravagance?" Ethel queried as her concerns in relation to her husband's continued indulgences were raised.

"Do not worry," Charles replied, not completely oblivious to her anxiety. "I would not purchase anything that was not essential."

"But why so many," Ethel persisted, "surely one would suffice?"

Charles expelled a large sigh at his wife's lack of understanding when it came to societal matters. Should he chastise her for daring to question his judgment or should he humour her and educate her inability to comprehend the need for the carriages? He decided on the latter.

"Oh my dearest Ethel would you have us visit friends in the luggage cart over yonder?" He cast a flailing arm in the direction of the open backed cart tucked away in the far corner. "Each carriage is fit for its own purpose." He began. "The Brougham is a must." He stated as they walked towards a claret coloured carriage. "And this is the Victoria, such an elegant French carriage don't you think? It is popular with the ladies." he said giving Ethel a sideways glance. "This is one that you will want to be seen in."

"It is quite beautiful!" she agreed.

He stepped across to the last one, almost hidden by the Victoria.

"Ah, the Phaeton," he explained, excitement evident in his voice. "This is the chariot of all carriages. It is so swift it takes one's breath away as one speeds along the narrow country lanes. Its name is taken from the son of Helios, it is said that he set the earth on fire whilst trying to drive the chariot of the sun."

"Reckless like its owner!" Ethel interjected. "And the pony cart?"

"It is there for everyday use," he explained. "Now let's go back to the house and celebrate with a glass or two of bubbly."

They made good use of the carriages. As Charles had hoped, Ethel fell in love with the Victoria and made it her own, always using it when going into town. She would take Hugh to his dance lessons in it and call on her society friends. It made Ethel feel like royalty as she was driven here and there by Fenton, the senior coachman, or his understudy Everett. True to form, Charles insisted that both men wore a uniform when driving the Victoria, adding to Ethel's sense of grandeur. It was a far cry from dodging guttersnipes in the East End of London she thought to herself on more than one occasion.

~

As La Chaire was being constructed Britain was fighting a colonial war in South Africa. Military regiments were sent to all corners of the empire in order to get the soldiers prepared for battle and Jersey was no exception. The number of men in uniform seen in Jersey increased. The barracks at Greve de Lecq were in constant use as regiments were put through their paces before being shipped off to fight. When given leave, the soldiers sought entertainment according to their social status. Being a familiar figure in high society circles, Fletcher was acquainted directly or indirectly through friends, with many of the officers. He would share a brandy and a cigar with them at the Victoria club. One such officer was Major Drumbeck of the South Devons, a handsome man with a mat of blond hair, parted in the middle. In his red uniform, with its gold epaulets and buttons he cut a dashing figure, his thick thighs bulging inside of tight white breeches, tucked into jet black jack boots which emphasised his sturdy frame. Fletcher could not wait to show off La Chaire to the major. He, in turn, could not wait to meet the renowned Mrs Fletcher and so with different motives they arrived at speed at La Chaire, skidding to a halt on the stones outside the house.

"I see you have wined and dined already!" Ethel observed as the two men disembarked from the carriage, laughing and speaking loudly.

"This is my wife, Ethel." Fletcher made the formal introductions.

"It is a pleasure to meet you Mrs Fletcher," Drumbeck leant forward and took her hand, giving it a gentle kiss on the back.

"Will you stay and have afternoon tea?" she asked, eager to get to know the officer.

"I would be delighted!" Drumbeck was equally as eager to get more acquainted with Ethel.

"Would you like me to show around the garden?" Fletcher was oblivious to the attraction, so keen was he to show off the place.

"Only if your lovely wife will join us," Drumbeck declared.

"What do think Ethel, would you like to come with us?"

"I think the fresh air would do us all good," she replied with a sideways glance. Ethel situated herself between the two men.

The threesome entered the garden via the pergola which was already covered with rambling roses. The odour this abundance of flowers produced was noticeable in the cloistered aisle.

"These are all pillar roses," Fletcher felt obliged to provide a commentary as they walked.

"What an array of colour!" Drumbeck endeavoured to show an interest. He stopped and stood close to one of the plants, leaning over to get a smell of its aroma. "Their fragrance is as light as their colour."

"That variety is called Ard's Rover," Fletcher informed him. "And the ones on the far side are called Reine Olga de Wurtemberg and Paul's Carmine Pillar."

"The red ones?" Drumbeck humoured him.

"Yes. They are called pillar roses because they are trained up a pillar or post in such a way that they give a column of blossom from top to bottom."

"Well they have certainly achieved that!" Drumbeck declared.

"Charles dearest," Ethel interrupted." I don't think Major Drumbeck needs to be told every last detail. Just let him enjoy the ambience of the beautiful garden."

"You're quite right my dear," Charles blushed at his over zealousness.

Suitably chastised and more than a touch embarrassed, Charles fell silent. They set off at a stroll once more, enjoying the warmth of the late spring sunshine. Through the gaps in the pergola, Drumbeck could see the tall wall of the terracing behind.

"And what type of roses are those?" he pointed to the growing fingers of rambling roses that were winding their way up the wall. He was not the least bit interested but felt that he had to placate his host.

"They are all different varieties of Wichuraiana ramblers they originate from France and provide a lot of fragrance. The large white ones you can see are called Alberic Barbier and the salmon pink coloured flowers are Paul Transon. I have over fifty different types placed around the walls. "

Ethel caught Charles' eye and gave him a disapproving frown. Drumbeck saw the look and moved to suppress any angst. He picked a blossom from one of the bushes on the pergola and passed it to Ethel.

"A rose for a rose!" he smiled warmly at her. Ethel returned the smile and placed the stem through a space in her beige, lace bertha, her figure accentuated by the light brown, velvet belt that pulled in her woollen day dress. Drumbeck took the opportunity to again look her up and down. "Tell me Charles, have you never thought about signing up and doing your bit for queen and country?"

The change of subject caught Fletcher off his guard.

"I did my service with the Sussex militia but to be perfectly frank, a soldier's life is not for me. However my brother, Alan, has picked up the baton and has carried our good family name into battle."

"Indeed!" he had now got Drumbeck's attention.

"He fought at Ladysmith."

"And where is he now?" Drumbeck enquired.

"He has been quite seedy of late," Fletcher revealed.

"How so?"

"He has had two bouts of enteric and has just gone down with dysentery."

"Damned bad luck!" Drumbeck cursed. "Let's hope the old chap is back on his feet again soon. God knows its bad enough fighting these foreign Johnnies without having to fend off sickness and disease as well."

"I suppose it goes with the territory," Fletcher replied wistfully.

"Indeed it does!" Drumbeck agreed. "Where does this path lead to?" He asked changing the subject again.

They had reached the end of the pergola and passed by the waterfall. A golden bamboo, still in its immature stage had sent up large, dark green canes. Eventually these would mature to a golden yellow. Alongside the bamboo grew a variegated holly bush and further along the path an almond tree was to be found, its pink blossom making it almost indistinguishable from the peach tree that grew further to the west. This path met the lower one just before the stone cross. At this juncture Drumbeck paused to take the view over Rozel.

"This garden is a veritable maze but a splendid one at that." The magnificence of the place was beginning to get to him. "I have to admit that most gardens leave me cold but this place is quite different, there seems to be something to discover around every corner, and the colours and fragrances, well.." he was lost for words, "I am forced to change my opinion."

Drumbeck's epiphany was music to Fletcher's ears. Ethel prompted them to finish their trek at the summerhouse.

"Do you know when you will be getting the call to go to South Africa?" Ethel enquired as she poured the tea.

"I'm not sure but I expect that it will be some time soon," Drumbeck replied as he extended his white gloved hand to accept the bone china tea cup and saucer. "Did I hear correctly that the island is to create its own militia in response to the situation in South Africa?"

Again Charles shifted uncomfortably.

"The island has decided to create a militia following pressure from the British government," Charles revealed. "It has come as some relief that the Jersey government decided not to conscript any person that has not been on the island for less than a year. I have only just employed many of my house staff and I was worried that they might be called up and therefore be unavailable for service before I had had a chance to make use of them."

"That would have been unfortunate," Drumbeck replied, taking a sip from his cup and looking with smiling eyes at Ethel. Was he being sincere or did Charles detect a hint of sarcasm in the officer's voice?

Charles' insecurities in respect of Drumbeck nagged at Fletcher. This was the case as Charles and Ethel set off to attend a meal at the officer's mess. They approached the barracks at a canter. Major Drumbeck was waiting outside to greet them.

"You are looking as alluring as ever." He said to Ethel as he took her hand to help her off the carriage.

"Why thank you Major Drumbeck!" she replied. "You are very pleasing to the eye yourself, if I may be so bold." She held his gaze as she spoke.

"And a good afternoon to you Charles!" Drumbeck called from the other side of the buggy. Charles could only find the face to grunt a begrudging reply.

The three of them stepped slowly across the parade towards the officers' mess, a single storey building housed between the other buildings that made up these small barracks. Ethel took the officer by the arm, with her husband keeping pace on the other side.

"I have news for you," Drumbeck said as they walked.

"Pray tell us what it is?" Ethel asked intrigued.

"The South Devons have been called up to go to South Africa."

"That is sad news," Ethel admitted, disappointed.

"In some ways we will be relieved to go after all it is what we have been trained for." He declared.

"When will you be leaving?" Charles enquired.

"Within the week," the officer revealed. "Come let's go inside."

As the meal ensued the wine flowed with Drumbeck taking a personal interest in keeping Ethel's glass full.

"Did you hear about the disturbance in town?" Charles asked Drumbeck as he took a large gulp of red wine.

"The rioting you mean?"

"Yes, apparently the local Froggie community were insulting the masses as they celebrated the news of the relief of Mafeking so the crowd turned on them and started to smash the windows of their shops and houses."

"Were their many injuries?" Ethel enquired.

"A few but nothing serious," Charles informed her.

"It looks like you will be getting your call up papers after all Fletcher old chap!" Drumbeck teased as they sat down at the table.

Charles visibly blanched.

"I do hope not!" he baulked. "Poor Guthrie and Ross of the Wilshires died of enteric at Maintzburg and I lost another good friend, Matthews of the Gloucesters as well. I don't want to go the same way."

Charles' comments drew a silence over the throng. Ethel cast him a disapproving glance.

"I hear they are going to raise a militia in Jersey after all," Drumbeck continued to provoke Charles. It was not that he disliked the man it was more out of envy as he saw Fletcher, married to a beautiful woman like Ethel, whilst he was serving queen and country.

Charles winced once again, the prospect of having to serve filled him with dread.

"They cannot seem to make up their minds," he replied, playing down the situation. "First they said that they were not going to use casual Englishmen then I get a letter asking for most of my staff to attend the militia."

"In times like these everybody should be prepared to do their duty!" Drumbeck pointed out.

"I now hear that the Governor is asking personally for me to be enrolled even though I have done my time with the Sussex militia." Charles became noticeably louder and animated as he tried to defend his reputation. "It is the very devil." He declared after demolishing the remainder of his wine. "I have already done my bit for Queen and country. I don't see why I have to do more." Although quite inebriated he recognised that there was an atmosphere being created around the table. "I did tell Le Gallais to inform the Governor that if I did have to serve he was to put me down on the reserve list for officers."

"Good on you old chap!" Drumbeck patted him on the back. "We all knew that you had it in you."

Charles smiled wanly, tugging at his starched collar as he sweated uncomfortably.

After the meal was finished and everything had been cleared away, a decanter containing absinthe was place in the centre of the table, to a resounding cheer by the officers. The absinthe ritual was followed to the letter, traditional French style of course. There was much clapping followed by raucous laughter and cheering as reluctant participants were encouraged to keep up with the rest. Eventually Ethel encouraged Charles to make an exit. As they left they paid their respects, albeit hurriedly to Drumbeck, and wished him well for the future. In the coach going home Charles passed barely a word to her, it was only when they entered the drawing room at La Chaire that he broke his silence.

"Will you really be putting your name down?" Ethel conjured up the courage to ask the thorny question that had nagged away at her all the way home. "I don't think I could bear us being apart and what if you were wounded, or worse?" She added before he got a chance to reply to her first question.

Charles made straight for the decanter, pouring himself a large brandy as Ethel spoke.

"I am not going to serve in any militia my dear!" he replied through gritted teeth.

"But I thought that you had put your name on a list?" Ethel was perplexed.

"A name on a list means nothing!" Charles growled. "If I am asked to sign up I will decline to serve in any capacity."

"Will you be able to do that?"

"I cannot be made to do anything that I don't want to do!" he affirmed. "The governor wants me to take a commission but I will see him dead first!"

Charles threw back the brandy and poured another, larger than the first.

"Charles!" Ethel gripped his free hand tightly. "There is no need to be so incensed."

Charles pulled his hand away much to Ethel's dismay.

"I am sick of Jersey and its small island mentality!" he barked. "I think we will have to leave this place and return to England."

Once more he demolished his drink and poured himself a third glass.

"And abandon your beloved garden?"

"If we must!" Charles did not sound convincing and he was beginning to slur his words. "We can start again elsewhere."

"Just think of the expense!" Ethel tried to reason with him. "Could we afford to start all over again?" Her voice hinted a little of desperation.

"Probably not!" Charles declared as he slumped into his armchair, spilling a little of the whisky. "I suppose we would have to live more austerely but as long as we have each other what does it matter?"

Encouraged by this glimmer of affection Ethel moved towards him.

"You know my dear I feel a little seedy," he muttered as she knelt by his side.

"Probably all the alcohol that you have consumed!" she cautioned. "Let's get you to bed and see how you are in the morning."

Ethel took the glass out of his hand and placed it on the small table by the side of the chair. By now Charles was in a stupor so she hoisted him up onto his feet as best she could and threw his limp arm around her shoulder. They had moved no more than two paces when suddenly she felt him buckle. His dead weight forced her to let go and he collapsed on the floor in a heap. To all intent and purposes he looked dead. For a moment she stood over him not knowing what to do, she held her hand to her mouth in horror.

"Walter!" she cried out loud. "Walter!"

The butler, no spring chicken himself strode purposefully into the room and on seeing his employer prostrate on the floor ran the last few steps. Walter checked him over.

"Is he dead?" Ethel asked fearful of the answer.

"He's not dead madam but he does appear to be in need of a doctor."

"Go and fetch Everett and get him to take you to the doctors in town. I will stay and see if I can make him a little more comfortable."

Chapter 13

La Chaire 1900

The church bells rang out across the island. They could be heard from St Peters to St Helier. In the harbour the steam boats blew their horns, creating a cacophony of noise that was painful to the ears. The clamour was to mark the declaration of peace in South Africa. The news came as a welcome relief to Fletcher as he recovered from his malady. His independence was no longer compromised by the threat of a call up to the Jersey militia. It also meant that he did not have to leave his treasured La Chaire, the house and in particular, the garden that he had invested so much of his personal fortune, time and affection into.

So much had happened since his collapse. Queen Victoria had died, to be replaced by her son, Edward, Cecil Rhodes had also passed away. Closer to home, the parlour maid and cook had been dismissed for insubordination and Fenton, the head coachman, had also been sacked, with immediate effect as it had come to Fletcher's attention that the man was an inebriate and was wont to beat his wife. Fletcher promoted the inexperienced Everett to Fenton's position despite his youthfulness but unbeknown to the young lad even his days as a coachman were numbered.

Charles and Ethel, along with their son, Hugh, embarked on a period in their life where everything was a lot more settled. Old Walton had drawn in his horns and an uneasy peace broke out between them, Springate's work was all but complete, all that remained was the settlement of the final bill. Fletcher's health improved considerably and as a result of medical advice he had been placed on a strict diet as well as being prescribed medication. Following his sudden attack he had had further bouts of giddiness and nausea.

"You must reduce your bouts of excess," Doctor Hird instructed as he packed away his instruments. "It is your liver that is ailing you. You must cut down on the amount of alcohol that you drink, especially the strong stuff, the spirits."

He shook Charles' hand before making his exit from the bedroom.

"I'll escort you to your carriage, Doctor Hird!" Ethel declared, rushing to the door to catch him up.

"How serious is his condition?" she asked the doctor as they descended the stairs.

"I cannot tell for sure," The doctor replied. "If he follows my advice then it is not beyond the bounds of possibility that he will recover but in my experience liver damage is usually terminal."

The doctor's brutal honesty, albeit couched in his calm delivery, brought home to Ethel the gravity of the situation.

Ensconced in his office across the corridor from the drawing room, Fletcher sat behind his mahogany desk trying to make sense of all the piles of papers that were strewn around in front of him. There were a myriad of invoices and bills, almost all of them relating to the house and garden. The telegram in front of him filled him with dread. The bank rate had risen to five per cent.

"This is most worrying!" he mumbled to himself. "Such a high rate will put an extra burden on my dwindling finances."

So precarious was Fletcher's financial position that he had to sell off some of his assets to pay off the interest on some of the loans he had taken out to pay for alterations to the house and garden. It stuck in his craw that most of the money that he was paying out was going to Springate.

"I might as well give him the details of my bank account and be done with it!" he complained as he looked at one invoice after another.

He strode purposefully out of the office, across the corridor and into the drawing room, Ethel followed behind. He went straight to the decanter and poured himself a large brandy, taking a large swig and then another to finish off the glass before reaching for the decanter once more and pouring himself a second.

"Charles, take it easy with the drink!" Ethel warned him. "You know what the doctor advised."

"Damn the doctor and damn my liver!" he exclaimed. "That man Springate is a thief and bounder." He cursed.

"What has he done to rile you this time?" Ethel enquired.

"He has sent me his final account and it is twenty times above what it should be, according to Lloyd."

"How can he do such a thing?" Ethel asked.

"I am at a loss to comprehend his actions!" Charles shook his head in disbelief. "The man must think that I am made of money."

Following days of analysis, many secretive visits to the brandy decanter and frequent burning of the midnight oil, Charles emerged from the stacks of papers, tired and drawn.

"I have checked the accounts and they are most alarming!" he told Ethel over their evening meal. "If we are to survive it will mean a strict economy for a long tome to come. I have written to the bank to ask if they will lend me some more money on my Natal three and a half percent and on my East Indian Railway stock that should give us enough capital to pay off Springate and settle all my other debts."

It came as welcome news when the bank sanctioned the advance against his assets. This set the tone for the next few months as the financial tide did start to turn in his favour. The bank rate fell by one per cent, followed quickly by another one per cent drop. On the back of this Charles was able to negotiate extra cash on the sale of some of his actuaries.

When Lloyd contacted Fletcher with the news that Springate's bill was only going to be around seven hundred pounds, Charles was positively euphoric. His change in fortunes had a pronounced effect and his countenance became profoundly more upbeat, his enthusiasm returned and he spent a lot of time tinkering in the garden as a result. Springate did try to up the bill to nine hundred pounds but Fletcher was adamant that he was not going to get a penny more than that calculated by Lloyd.

The turn of the century had brought with it lots of new innovations and experiences as he and Ethel stepped back into London society, re-establishing old acquaintances and making new ones. They attended the latest theatre shows, wining and dining as much as they had done before. The spectre of war had disappeared and everybody seemed flush with a new enthusiasm. There was a vibrancy about the capital that they both found invigorating and this was reflected in the latest must have technology, the motor car and, unsurprisingly, Fletcher was one of the first in the queue to get one.

He carried out meticulous research before he committed himself to purchasing his first motor car, eventually settling for a Wolseley Tonneau. It was a ten horse power vehicle made at the company's Long Acre plant. It was black around its main chassis with yellow trimmings on its bonnet, side panels and wheels. Its windscreen folded in half and at full stretch could be attached to the retractable hood when the weather turned inclement. Both front and rear seats were double seats, upholstered like the finest armchairs.

Eager to show off his new acquisition, Fletcher drove to the coast and had to negotiate his passage on the ferry because he had not bothered to book a berth for the motor car. There was a tense stand off as a bureaucratic 'jobsworth' gave him the run around. Once at St Helier, he was eager to show off his new 'toy'. He honked his horn at anything and everything that got in his way; pedestrians, livestock, horses pulling carriages, nothing was spared as he steered recklessly through the cobbled streets, and the locals had seen nothing like this before. Being the first car on the island brought with it a certain status which Fletcher was all too keen to exploit.

The loud, flatulent exhaust belched out acrid smoke, choking passers by. Horses shied, careering into motionless objects dotted along the roadside. Unflustered, Fletcher tootled along, irritated by the apparent stupidity of those blocking his way. He tooted his horn time and again, steering violently to avoid possible catastrophes. Angry victims shook their fists or tried to chase after him but their angst was to no avail as he drove on, oblivious to their anguish.

He eventually made his way out of town and took the road up Trinity Hill, past the parish church and down into the harbour at Rozel. As he pulled up outside La Chaire he honked his car horn vigorously, attracting the attention of everyone. Faces peered at windows and bodies looked over walls as he sat regal like in his chariot. As Ethel emerged he leapt out of the vehicle, with the engine ticking over, and stepped forward to embrace her.

"Well, what do you think?" he asked, hardly able to curtail his glee "not a bad acquisition eh?"

"Please don't tell me that you have purchased this, this," she searched for the right description, "machine."

"I have indeed!" he replied sensing that Ethel was not as excited about the car as he was. "It cost me a hundred pounds more than I initially wanted to pay for it but I still got a good deal."

"But we have all the transport that we need!" she pointed out.

"I have decided that the carriages are going!" he declared snootily.

"And this is what you are going to replace them with?" she mocked.

"It is!" he affirmed. Seeing the look of incredulity on her face he softened his stance, taking hold of her hand. "Look, let me take you for a ride, once you have experienced what it is like to travel in a motor vehicle you will come around."

Ethel agreed to his proposal. She returned to the house to fetch her coat and hat. Once next to him in the car, Fletcher released the hand brake and set off at a moderate speed. Walton was in his garden tending to his vegetables, Fletcher honked the horn as loudly as he could, making Walton jump with fright. Fletcher laughed as Ethel reprimanded him. Walton shook his fist and shouted retribution but neither of them could hear him over the noise of the engine.

"Quite invigorating don't you think?" Charles shouted.

"It's not very tranquil is it?" she observed, having to raise her voice as well.

"It's not intended to be," he laughed. "It is supposed to be exciting, exhilarating and adventurous, a little like galloping on horseback without all the worry of falling off."

Charles sold the horses and moth balled the carriages in preparation for their eventual sale. He employed Everett as his chauffeur on thirty five shillings a week, providing him with lessons on how to drive the car.

He drove to Parish's house and picked him up with the purpose of going to the Victoria Club in St Helier. As he pulled up the Parishes rushed out to greet him.

"Come on old chap!" he beckoned to Parish. "Hop in and I will take you for a ride."

Fletcher was in his element as his friend nervously clambered in alongside him.

"Don't be so anxious, I won't kill you."

He set off with a jerk and a stammer as he clunked the gears, searching for the right one. The exhaust eventually coughed and left Mrs Parish trying to disperse a large plume of noxious gas that wafted all around her.

The two men shared the latest gossip as Fletcher took them along the coast road around by La Hocq. As they nattered, the engine suddenly ceased turning. It spluttered briefly before silently slowing to a standstill. Parish looked at Fletcher, who returned his perplexed gaze. Fletcher jumped out of the car and went to the bonnet. Once opened, he performed a meticulous check of everything inside. Parish was impressed. Having completed his studies, he stood up in front of the car and scratched his head. He could find nothing amiss.

"What's the matter?" Parish enquired.

"The devil I know!" Fletcher replied. "I've checked everything and all seems to be in order. I can't think what has happened."

Parish felt the need to get involved and offer his colleague some intellectual support. He knew nothing about motor cars but maybe they worked a little like steam engines and he knew something about those, but not a lot.

"Perhaps you've run out of fuel," he shouted, stating the obvious.

"Petrol!" Fletcher exclaimed, slapping his forehead in disgust at his own shortcomings. "I am such an idiot."

Prompted by Parish he checked the petrol tank and found that it was indeed empty.

"Well done Parish, old boy!" he smiled with relief that it was not something major that had befallen his beloved motor car.

"So where will we get some?" Parish asked naively.

Fletcher scratched his head.

"You know Parish, I have no idea," he admitted. "This is the only car on the island to my knowledge so who on earth will have any?"

It was an ignominious end to such a promising day as their search for that elusive store of petrol proved futile. The moribund vehicle had to be towed back to La Chaire. Fletcher wrote to the Wolseley Company at Long Acre for eight gallons of petrol to tide him over.

Fletcher's shrinking finances coincided with an upsurge in popularity of the garden at La Chaire. Fed by this swell of interest he continued to lavish attention on the place, indulging himself as he looked to maintain the finest garden of its kind. Many people were now holidaying in Jersey and of those that ventured across the channel most paid a visit to the now famous 'La Chaire Gardens'.

As they sat in the drawing room it was Ethel who discerned the Victoria pulling up on the terrace, her attention gained as she heard the clatter of hooves and crunch of wheels on the pebbles outside. She looked up from her embroidery as she sat at one of the bay windows overlooking the terrace.

"We have a visitor Charles!" she informed him. "Oh my goodness look who it is!"

"And who exactly is it?"

"It's Jeanne Langtry Malcolm!" Ethel informed him, speaking each of the component names, clearly and precisely.

"And who is she?" Charles was a touch irked at Ethel's interruption. He was trying to read the paper.

"None other than Lily Langtry's illegitimate daughter!" Ethel revealed.

Mrs Langtry Malcolm was helped out from the carriage by her coachman and was looking around the terrace endeavouring to find her bearings.

"There are all sorts of rumours about who her father is!" Ethel gossiped. "Some say it is King Edward himself."

"Poppycock! The king would not have been so indiscrete!" Charles blurted out, exasperated by Ethel's hearsay. He folded his paper roughly to express his discontent and then strode over to the window to see for himself.

"But Prince Louis of Battenburg paid support money for her as a child." Ethel continued, now standing at the window shielded from the lady's view by the large velvet curtains.

"Then he must be the father." Charles now stood beside his wife, looking out of the window.

"Not necessarily," Ethel whispered, "rumours persist."

"Idle gossip," Charles replied, also finding himself whispering, "tittle-tattle, complete bunkum."

"We must not leave her standing outside waiting!" Ethel announced in a panic. It was situations like these when Ethel's insecurities surfaced, much to Charles' annoyance.

Together they emerged from the main door and waited at the entrance of the porch to greet their surprise visitor.

"Good morning," Mrs Langtry-Malcolm greeted them.

"Good morning," they replied in unison.

"If I may introduce myself," the lady began, "I am Mrs Jeanne Langtry-Malcolm but you may call me Jeanne."

"Welcome Mrs Langtry-Malcolm, Jeanne," Charles replied politely, taking her hand briefly." I am Charles Fletcher and this is my wife, Ethel."

"A pleasure," Ethel said as she took Mrs Langtry-Malcolm's hand.

"To what do we owe this visit?" Charles asked.

"I have heard so much about your beautiful garden, I was wondering if I might be so bold as to ask if I may take a look, it is such a fine day and a stroll would prove quite relaxing?"

Charles escorted his guest through the pergola and then up one of the many sets of stone steps. At frequent junctures Jeanne Langtry-Malcolm stopped to admire the plants that had been placed along the walkways.

"Your garden is quite extraordinary!" she complimented.

"It is my aim that in time not a vestige of the walls will be seen in summer or winter!" Charles declared.

"You mean that the garden is like this all year round?" Jeanne exclaimed in amazement, stopping in her tracks as she spoke.

"Well, not quite yet," Charles admitted. "But I am getting closer to my goal as the plants establish themselves. If you were to visit in autumn or winter you would be presented with a different array of colour and spectacle."

"That will be some achievement!" Jeanne confessed.

"I am going to put up two rose arches in the top rose garden!" he informed her.

"Traditional arches?"

"Yes, made using some young trees that I will plant."

"I do so enjoy walking along a covered avenue whether it be cherry blossom in Spring, in London or an arbour in a quiet garden such as yours.

190

There is something magical about such passages. It's like taking a walk in a fairy wonderland." Jeanne said dreamily. "How many gardeners do you employ?" She enquired making conversation.

"Two, Baal and Smith," he informed her. "Baal is the senior gardener, although he is dense and his pigheadedness drives me mad at times."

"It is such a trial getting the right staff."

"That is a fact Mrs Langtry-Malcolm." Charles concurred. "I've had to dismiss so many since I bought La Chaire, I'm beginning to lose count."

The three of them spent the rest of the morning in the summerhouse, eventually deciding to call it a day just before lunch. Charles and Ethel waved her off from the terrace, pleased that they had made a new contact and such a famous one to boot.

The garden almost looked after itself now, although he could not help meddling with it here and there, a habit that he would never grow out of. But the place no longer occupied the bulk of his waking day. Not one to rest on his laurels Fletcher sought new avenues along which to challenge his energies and none were more timely than the motor car. If his garden was the talk of the island for all the right reasons, his cars became the object of much derision for all the wrong reasons.

Dressed as a predecessor to Toad of Toad Hall, Fletcher donned his leather driving cap, tweeds and goggles and proceeded to trouble commuters who frequented the lanes and byways around the island, especially those along the northern coast. It was with some trepidation that Everett, his one time apprentice coachman, stood beside the car awaiting the arrival of his lord and master.

"Come on lad!" Fletcher barked as he strode past Everett and jumped into the driver's seat. "Stop dithering and climb in alongside me, you'll not learn anything standing there."

Reluctantly Everett sidled into the front passenger seat. Being tall and slim the young man could barely fit into the seat. His head touched the roof of the car and his long legs were squashed up, concertina like, so that they almost touched his chin.

"Once you have got the hang of driving, it becomes second nature," Fletcher reassured him.

"I still think I would feel safer on a horse!" Everett admitted.

As they neared Trinity church a horse drawn carriage pulled out into the lane in front of them. Fletcher honked his horn loudly, causing the horse to shy which, in turn, sent the carriage and its occupants careering through a thorny hedge. The people sat in total shock as the carriage came to an abrupt halt and proceeded to shout in the direction of Fletcher and curse bitterly at their misfortune. Their complaints fell on deaf ears as they puttered on with total disregard.

"Pay them no mind," he said casually to Everett, who could not help but look back nervously at the situation they had caused. "We have as much right to use the thoroughfare as anybody else and besides, it was their recklessness that caused the problem, fancy pulling out like that."

A few days later a letter arrived at La Chaire that had Fletcher complaining once more.

"What is it my dear?" Ethel enquired as she sat in her favourite spot by the bay window reading the newspaper.

"I have a letter here from Le Vesconte, the Connetable of Trinity."

"In connection with what?"

"In connection with the motor car, or more precisely the way that I drive."

"Well I can't say that I am surprised!" Ethel stated.

"He has cautioned me against furious driving, I mean, what utter rot!" Charles mocked.

"Well you do drive rather quickly."

"I had wind at the Victoria Club that there was going to be a summons out for me. Whatever does he mean by 'furious driving'? It's nothing more than a trumped up charge made by a land owner with nothing better to do with his time than to harass me."

"Just be careful Charles!" Ethel warned. "The Connetables carry a lot of influence in the parishes. He could make life very difficult for you."

"I shall take no notice of him what so ever!" Charles declared and tossed the letter in the hearth.

The next morning Charles could not get out of bed. He lay weak and immobile as Ethel drew back the curtains to welcome in a bright new morning.

"I feel decidedly seedy my dear," he said in a whisper.

It took Charles a good couple of days to recover to a point where he felt able to get back to his business. He decided to offload the Wolseley and purchased another car, a De Dion Bouton. He put it through its paces on Barnes Common and having passed its trials, Fletcher wasted no time in sending the vehicle by train to the south of France, so that he might explore the area in the comfort of this, his latest automobile.

"Did you hear about all the casualties in the Paris Madrid race?" Hennessy asked as Fletcher raced around the uneven roads of the Estorils.

It was hardly the most reassuring topic of conversation as Ethel and Mrs Hennessy in the back held on for dear life. The motion of the car was enhanced by the hairpin bends and the sheer terrain of the mountains. Mrs Hennessy in particular was extremely nervous.

"Yes, it was a pretty awful to do," Fletcher replied, shouting above the noise of the engine, not daring to take his eyes off the road as it wound this way and then that. "They had to stop the race didn't they? Eight killed and seventeen injured was the last I'd heard."

Fletcher turned sharply, misjudging his speed slightly. The car skidded on the loose stones that lubricated the already treacherous roadway. Mrs Hennessy let out a muffled scream as Ethel took her arm. Above them, the mountainside loomed, grey, craggy and forbidding. Below them a steep crevasse fell away, its ravine like slopes, vertiginous as boulders, both large and small clung to its edges.

"Charles!" Ethel called from the back of the car. "Do you really have to drive so recklessly? You'll be the death of us all."

Having worked their way up a steep rise in the road it now started to descend just as steeply on the other side. Throwing off the mantle of prudence he threw caution to the wind. The faster he went, the greater the thrill. Unlike his passengers, this adrenalin filled experience was something to be experienced. His concentration was total, his demeanour almost demonic, as they skirted past unwary travellers and skidded over the loose terrain. The lumps and bumps added to the joy ride. He whizzed round one bend after another, gaining momentum as they careered down the hill. Eventually the road started to level out and they all breathed a sigh of relief as the car began to slow, all except Fletcher that is.

As they took one more corner, still travelling at speed, another car appeared in front of them. Fletcher took action to avoid the impending collision, swerving instinctively. The front offside wheel hit a divot and pitched the steering out of control. The car slipped on the chippings and took a trajectory some forty five degrees to the direction of the road. It rattled and rolled until it came to a sudden halt, pitching them out as the inertia took over. Only Fletcher escaped as the steering column held him in place. Steam effused from the damaged radiator and hissed as cool water leaked onto the hot, cast iron engine.

Fletcher eased himself out from behind the wheel, making a mental check of his body as he flexed each part. Finding nothing untoward he turned his attention to his passengers. Hennessy seemed relatively unscathed, if a little shocked at the accident. Ethel had a cut on her forehead and her dress looked torn in places but she was otherwise untroubled.

"How could you be so reckless?" she scolded.

"Are there any bones broken?" e asked sheepishly

"I don't think so, no thanks to you!" she replied.

Mrs Hennessy appeared to have come off worst. She lay in a heap, moaning and clutching her right leg.

"Are you hurt?" he asked Mrs Hennessy.

"It's my leg," she cried, "I think it might be broken, I can't move it."

"Just stay where you are and I will summon help," Fletcher reassured her.

As he got up, he caught a glimpse of Ethel glowering at him. Riddled with guilt, he made for the road to flag assistance. A carriage pulled over and offered help. Fletcher thanked them. Hennessy tried to lift his wife onto her feet but as soon as she put any weight on her right leg she winced in pain

"It's my knee!" she cried. "I can't put any weight on it."

Again Fletcher caught sight of Ethel, still frowning disapprovingly at him. Eventually they managed to help her into the carriage and she was whisked off towards Monte Carlo to seek medical help.

Following the accident, Fletcher had a number of bouts of ill health. He was laid up in his hotel room for lengthy periods of time. Ethel put it down to the after shock of the accident but Fletcher knew that the accident had nothing to do with his health. He kept his thoughts to himself.

Back in Jersey his attention turned to issues financial. He had put his finances in some sort of order but his money was running low and he felt it important to make sure that both Ethel and Hugh were accounted for. There was also the matter of Hugh's education.

"I would like to get Hughie into Eton if I could," he said to Ethel as they dined out at the Grand."

"Can we afford the fees?" she asked innocently.

"We will have to find a way, my dear, even if it means cutting back elsewhere."

"Like on the number of cars that we seem to be accumulating!" Ethel said cheekily.

"I have also contacted Wellington school, another fine educational institution to see if there are any vacancies."

As Charles was speaking he suddenly felt very giddy. He dropped his cutlery and placed both hands on the table to steady himself.

"Charles!" Ethel jumped up out of her seat to attend to him. "Are you alright?"

"I feel quite seedy all of a sudden," he replied weakly.

"You do look very pale," Ethel observed. "Come, let's get you home."

Charles managed to get up and make his way without any fuss to the exit. Ethel chaperoned him in case he fell. Once back at La Chaire she saw him straight into bed.

The following weeks saw Fletcher's health ebb this way and that. Bouts of light headedness and nausea increased in frequency. Despite his malaise Fletcher was determined that his life should carry on as normal. He perceived his sickness as something that would eventually pass.

"I think that I will always find something to do in this garden." He said to Ethel and Mrs Lempriere as they prepared for a foray into the vegetation. "The Ceanothus Floribunda is in fine bloom," he informed them, "as is the pink pearl rhododendron. We shall have to make sure that you see them as we walk."

"I shall remind you if you forget!" Mrs Lempreire joked.

"The arches are up at the top rose garden and I am in the middle of replacing the old rustic railing and the ramblers nearby."

"Did I hear that you got rid of the rustic bridge?" she enquired as they took the steps up to the higher slopes.

"It was rotten and so I brought Le Huquet in to repair it and the railings alongside. He has used larch instead of the oak that we had originally."

"And did I also hear that you have purchased another motor car?" she glanced at Ethel knowingly.

"Yes!" he said proudly. "It's a ten horse power Renault. It has the quietest engine that I have ever heard."

"That should be a relief to all around here." She quipped. They all laughed.

"I got it on this new fangled easy payment scheme." He revealed.

"Is that where you spread the payments over a period of time?" Mrs Lempriere asked.

"Yes, it's quite convenient for us at this present time."

As they walked and talked, Ethel noticed that Charles was becoming increasingly distraught. He was fidgeting, wiping his face with his hands constantly, his eyes shifting wildly in their sockets. Mrs Lempiere appeared not to notice so Ethel guided them back towards the house where she sat her friend in the drawing room whilst she escorted her husband upstairs into the bedroom.

"You look awful!" she said as he slumped onto the bed.

"I don't feel at all well," he replied. "I keep thinking I'm going to have a fit."

"I will take care of our guest, you just lie down and get some rest," Ethel instructed.

It took a few days before Fletcher was up and about again, carrying on as if nothing had happened. They ventured across to the mainland to carry out the business of purchasing the car. They returned by ferry and were met by Hugh, their son, and the nanny at the quayside in St Helier.

"Well Hugh what do you think of her?" Fletcher asked as Hugh stood by the car giving it the once over.

"It looks very handsome." He declared, not really knowing what to say.

"Hop in and we'll drive back to the house." Fletcher said. "You are looking well Hugh." He observed as Hugh settled into the seat next to him.

Hugh smiled, excited at the prospect of being driven back to La Chaire in the new car. However his pleasure was tempered by a feeling that not all was as it should be with his father. As he met his papa he noticed that his skin was a strange colour and that his face looked drawn and haggard, almost like an old man's.

"This car is not as easy to drive as one would imagine," his father complained, as they took the road up St Saviour's Hill. "The seat is cramped and it has a bad change of speed lever, I will have to get it altered."

After an uncomfortable evening not feeling well, Fletcher was back at his desk in the morning looking pale and tired. He opened the letters from the bank but they made for difficult reading. Once more rises in interest rates coincided with falls in his stocks and shares, his financial outlook was not good. The whole situation added to his depression and there was only one way to ease the gloom; alcohol. However there was one piece of good news and he shared it with Ethel as he replenished his whiskey glass.

"I have news from Eton," he said as she entered the drawing room, frowning at the drink he held in his hand.

"What does it say?"

"It is from Lyttleton, the headmaster at Eton. He has reserved a place for Hugh to start in the autumn of nineteen hundred and ten."

Fletcher's health continued to deteriorate to the point at which, following much discussion, he agreed to seek specialist medical help. This meant residing in London for a period of time. His parents offered him the use of Grosvenor Place but he was adamant that he would not be beholden to them and so rented a house about a quarter of a mile away, number three Basil Mansions.

Basil Mansions was a touch more modest than Grosvenor Place. It lay on Basil Street which was situated between Brompton Road and Sloane Street, just south of Knightsbridge. The building was four stories high with a basement and an attic for staff accommodation. The three main floors had large bay windows that hung over the street.

"It is so depressing here!" Fletcher moaned as he fell into an armchair, in front of the hearth. "Fetch me a drink will you." He called to the maid who waited on them.

Doctors visited him almost on a daily basis. He was given one type of medication after another as they endeavoured to treat his ailment.

Fletcher did as he was bidden and, coupled with complete rest he started to show signs of recovery. The yellowness of his skin started to fade and he gained in energy. He still picked up coughs and colds with alarming frequency but he put that down to the London smog that dogged the air around them.

"These damned pea soupers!" he cursed. "They do you more harm than good. They sit on your chest so. Give me the fresh air of La Chaire, how I long for those clean sea breezes."

As Fletcher battled with life itself, the garden also fought its own war. He worried about how it would cope in his absence. The feathery blossoms of spring gave way to the rich grandeur of summer which in turn, eased into the coppers and bronzes of autumn before the austerity of winter bit hard, striping bare so many branches and causing even the most vibrant, green foliage to appear pale and sickly, all of this Fletcher missed. However the careful construction and consideration given to the garden managed to stave off the worst the weather threw at it in his absence. Now, in this his hour of need, his garden was not accessible to him and so the strength and comfort he might have drawn from walking its pathways was reduced to memories of what had gone before.

Through rain or shine, sleet or snow there was always something beauteous that he could take from the garden. The weather might, intermittently, throw up rainbows, fanning its tail like some prize peacock high up in the firmament but the garden responded by providing its own spectrum of colour, stoically defying the transience of the weather, whether it be the intense greenery of brand new rhododendron leaves or the iridescent exhibition given by cascading mesembryanthemums. The spectacle changed as the seasons changed, a commitment to the collaboration of nature and nurture. But even the floral decor of the wallpapered rooms and the bright colours of the peripheral woodwork could not cut through the greyness that seemed to dull each and every room at number three Basil Mansions. With each passing day, Fletcher's demeanour sank into depression from which Ethel found it almost impossible to shake him. From being a committed socialite pursuing excitement and adventure at every turn, he now shunned all but those closest to him. His face became distinctly more jaundiced and his stomach distended as his illness took a final hold.

Fletcher had maintained a belief that he would, at some stage recover but it was not to be. The liver has a natural capacity to regenerate of its own volition but when someone has cirrhosis the damaged cells do not replace themselves with new ones. Fletcher's liver had been on the receiving end of his excesses for many years and had deteriorated to the point of no return, until eventually he fell into a coma and died. As Fletcher's life slipped away so the limelight faded on La Chaire and slowly and irrevocably it once more became a hidden treasure, lost in the folds in the north east corner of a small island somewhere off the French coast.

~

The funeral cortege had started from the family home of Dale Park where Fletcher's body had lain in repose. Now the cortege pulled up outside the church of Saint Mary Magdalene. The hearse drawn by two jet black shire horses, with feathered plumes atop their heads, stopped abruptly causing the pursuing entourage to do the same. It was a procession of black. Old and young, beauty and beast marked Fletcher's passing with customary respect, the only white were the lilies that bedecked the coffin. The church itself was a relatively small building built from local flint, its red roof tiles, standing out against the grey of the stone walls. The pall bearers carried the coffin with solemnity through the church doorway followed by immediate family and then by others, including distant relatives and friends. The family took pride of place in the front pews. His father and mother sat to the right, along with Eleanor and her husband, Ronald. Evelyn and her husband, Jersey De Knoop sat on the other side with Cissy and her fiancé, Gerald. At the far end Alan, his brother stood out from the others, his bright red army regalia contrasting with their sombre black outfits. Behind them the pews filled up to capacity. There was Harenc and Duckworth, the Hennessy's and the Lempriere's. It seemed like all of the friends and acquaintances that he had acquired over his fast and furious, but brief thirty six years of his life had come to see him off on this, his final adventure.

Conspicuous by her absence was Ethel. Their son Hugh was also missing. It was not until the church organ quietened, the throng hushed and the vicar began his opening eulogy that the two absentees sneaked in, unseen through the servant's entrance.

After Charles' peaceful slide into oblivion at Basil Mansions, his family acted quickly. Jersey de Knoop had called for the doctor and had signed the death certificate, even though Ethel was standing right beside her deceased husband.

"I will have to arrange for his body to be brought back to Jersey," Ethel stated.

"Why on earth would you want to do that?" Cissy retorted, coldly.

"Because that is where his home is. He would want to be buried near to his beloved garden and home at La Chaire," she explained.

"The idea is preposterous!" Cissy declared arrogantly. "He will be buried in the family plot in Madehurst churchyard, alongside his relatives and that is the end of it!"

"I see," Ethel had not known of the family plot, neither had they ever discussed his final wishes. "On reflection then it would be moot for you to take care of things," Ethel conceded. "Just let me know if I can be of help and of course keep me in touch with arrangements as they progress." She added in a conciliatory tone, not wanting to antagonise what was already a difficult situation.

"I am afraid we won't be doing anything of the sort." Cissy asserted.

"Why ever not?" Ethel was taken aback by Cissy's attitude.

"Because it will be a family affair and as such you are not family." Cissy's words were harsh and unforgiving.

"But I am his wife." Ethel cried.

"You were his wife!" Cissy corrected her. "Now he is gone, that tie no longer exists, so make your peace with him now because this is the last time that you shall ever lay eyes on him."

"How can you be so cruel?" Ethel wept. Cissy did not look her in the eye, choosing to sit on the settee and proffer a cold shoulder.

Ethel knew that this was a battle that ultimately she could not win. She took a deep breath and said farewell to the man she had shared so much with and had adored for so long. She had crossed the tracks and dared to fall in love despite society's disapproval.

"Goodbye my love!" she said stroking Charles limp hand, tears trickling down her cheeks and onto his nightgown.

Standing at the back of the church she wept once more. She was afforded no respect from the immediate family, either in the church or afterwards as the interment took place. It was as if she was not there, a ghost, a shadow whose presence was shunned. She had to stand some distance away whilst prayers were said and then as Charles was lowered into his grave. Eventually people started to leave one by one and she had to wait until they had all gone before she could pay her own and Hugh's last respects. The Lempriere's held out a comforting hand but such a token response did little to soothe her. With Hugh clutching her hand tightly she threw a few grains of soil onto the coffin before turning and leaving the workmen to start filling in the grave.

Chapter 14

Corsica 1941

The shell landed about a hundred yards from where Yves crouched. The shock wave made his ears pop violently and the ground beneath his feet shook forcibly. The derelict building around him shuddered, releasing debris that fell alarmingly all around. Clouds of dust were raised up and he could taste the powder as it desiccated his parched lips. He endeavoured to regain his sight as he peered through gritted lenses, blinking ferociously so that he might see more clearly. Wide eyed with panic, his blood shot stare searched the horizon, looking for tell tale signs of the advancing enemy. His hands trembled uncontrollably at the thought of the impending onslaught. How could he aim to kill when he could not even stop the tremor in his hands? Up until this moment, the proximity of the enemy had forced Yves to concentrate on one thing only, survival, but now, for some unknown reason, his mind started to wander.

It had been with a heavy heart that he had left his family and his home to go and fight a war that had already taken a huge toll on human life. He had recalled the tales of an older generation who had spoken so candidly about the 'Great War' and all its atrocities, so he had realised that his prospects of returning home were limited. But then people had survived to tell the tales in the first place so there was hope.

It was an irony that he had been conscripted into the French army in the first place, particularly since he was not actually French. He was born in Guernsey but was sent, along with his brothers to go and live with their aunt in Brittany. As he grew up he had taken various jobs in farming, eventually following the migration of Bretons across the Manche to Jersey to go and pick potatoes. He was an avid reader of educational books and it was through such learning that he found his true vocation, gardening. It satisfied his thirst for knowledge fuelled by an intelligence that in a later life might have led to something more salubrious. But his was a time of little opportunity and so he grasped whatever came along. Lady luck had dealt him another opening when he got the job of gardener at La Chaire. With the job came a house, a substantial property. He settled down with Bertha, his wife, and started to raise a family. What a contrast between those heady days when the world was at his feet only for his dreams to be shattered by the onset of war.

He recalled the heartbreaking moment when he had had to say goodbye to Bertha and their two children, Agnes and Albert or Tabby as he liked to call his son. The couple had exchanged a long, heartfelt kiss. Such an open show of emotion was not something Yves did lightly, he was a man like many of those of his generation, who frowned open displays of affection. Bertha had gripped him tightly and was reluctant to release him. Their parting had an air of finality about it which made the embrace all the more poignant. Tears ran freely down Bertha's cheeks as he extricated himself. He too had to fight back the tears as he threw his knapsack over his shoulder and waved them a last goodbye. Bertha held the two children close as he turned and left them not knowing when, if ever, he would return.

The fighting intensified, bringing Yves back to the present. Bullets whistled past with alarming frequency, pinning him down to the point at which he dared not move a muscle for fear of catching one with his name on it. Cannon fire and mortar shells increased in ferocity, raining down all around them. It was a cacophony of fear and terror, and for the first time in his life he began to pray.

Chapter 15

Rozel 1942

It had been a tiresome trek from the harbour, up the shallow but persistent climb towards the north of the island. Looking back, the journey across France had seemed far less exhaustive and even the slow sailing from St. Malo had not felt as draining. Perhaps it was because this was the last leg of his travails that he felt so fatigued. The psychology of reaching the summit filled him with relief. Yves paused to take in this most familiar of views, his knapsack tossed over his shoulder, he savoured the wide expanse of water that stretched out before him. The blue-grey hues of the sea, its textured surface rippled with the lightest touch of a breeze, drew his eye right across to the coast of Normandy in the distance. His war had been an all too brief affair. He had done his duty when conscripted into the army to fight the Germans but like so many of his compatriots, his unit was disbanded soon after the Vichy government had been set up. He had been left to make his own way and like a homing pigeon he had no trouble finding it. The familiarity of this, the final stage of his journey, filled Yves with a mixture of joy and relief. Joy in the fact that he would soon be re-united with his family and that at last he would set his eyes upon his beautiful garden, and relief that he had, unbelievably, survived the war and the hazardous journey home.

It was a warm spring day with barely a cloud in the sky. He could see the gulls circling overhead and calling to those by the cliffs. In the bushes that bordered the road, he could hear the robins, warblers and blue tits all singing their signature tunes. He paused to watch them flitting from shrub to shrub, seeking out the tallest branches from which to gain the best vantage point to mark their territory. The hedgerows, mainly hawthorn, were laden with small white blossom, bees, hover flies, butterflies and a myriad of other insects moved from flower to flower, creating a vibrant buzz of activity as he passed by. A large horse chestnut, looking like a decorated Christmas tree, displayed its candelabra of creamy pink flowers proudly in the corner of a far field. Various flying insects flitted among the iridescent yellow gorse, so full of blossom that its sharp green leaves were barely distinguishable. Along the grass verges by the side of the road, red campion, bluebells and blue cornflower competed with the tall grass for space, all of them swaying in unison in the breeze that blew in from the sea.

In sheltered bowers, where trees overhung the roadside, the pungent smell of the wild garlic clearly discernable.

He was home.

The realisation that he was at his journey's end spurred him on. What little energy he had coursed through his veins, loosening tired muscles, soothing aching joints and anaesthetising blistered feet. There was a distinct spring in his step as he made light of the steep road that took him down towards Rozel. Here, in this picturesque little harbour, he knew that he would find comfort.

He turned off the road and stepped back into his old life, his thoughts turning immediately to his beloved garden. He looked around, not sure what to expect. Everything seemed much as he had left it in nineteen thirty nine. For him the war was over and he could not wait to resume his love affair with this garden. As he approached the large house he stopped to take in the magnificence of its design. The whiteness of its walls and pillars matched the white rocks behind it, giving the impression that La Chaire was much larger than it actually was.

Two young children ran out from a house a few yards up the valley, running alongside them was a small black spaniel. The house was also painted white but it was much smaller in size than La Chaire and nowhere near as grand. Its welcoming nature was embellished by the rambling wisteria that bedecked its walls, enveloping the doorway in a mass of hanging bunches of purple florets. The two children, one boy and one girl, saw the stranger and immediately ran up to him, stopping a safe distance away. The black spaniel was much more inquisitive, running up to him and sniffing him around his legs whilst its tail wagged furiously. They stood side by side and stared at Yves, their necks craned as they looked upwards. He was such a tall man. He returned their stare with eyes that held little emotion.

"Who are you?" the girl asked, hands on hips. She was older than the boy by around two or three years. Her straight, dark brown hair had been cropped just below her ears and parted in the middle.

"I am your Papa!" his smile remained muted although his eyes warmed.

"Papa?" the girl replied with some disbelief.

"Yes!" had he really been away so long that she no longer recognised him? His face creased at his daughter's incredulity. He crouched down, threw the knapsack to one side and opened his arms to welcome them both. After a moment's hesitation the little girl responded running towards him and crying.

"Oh Papa!"

He held her tightly in his arms as she cried. If he had been moved by her tears he hardly showed it. She swivelled in her father's arms, still clinging tightly to his neck and called to her brother.

"Albert!" she shouted. "It is Papa, Come and greet him!"

Albert had only been a baby when Yves had left to fight and had no recollection of his father, except for some dusty old photographs that his mother showed him intermittently. The man in front of him did look somewhat like the man in the pictures but he was much thinner in the face and unshaven. His scruffy appearance and frightening stare reminded him more of the prisoners of war that the Germans marched up and down from the harbour.

"Don't be frightened!" she continued. "He will not hurt you, he is our Papa."

"The same as the one in the pictures?" Albert whispered nervously.

"Yes!" she replied, chastising him.

Albert sidled up to Yves, shuffling his feet as he approached, kicking up dust with his sandals, heavily worn down at the heel and scuffed bare along the toes. Once within arms length Yves swept him up. He then stood erect lifting them both together, one forearm taking the strain for each of them as they sat legs dangling.

"Your bag!" his daughter reminded him about his knapsack that lay in a heap on the floor.

"I will collect it later Agnes."

As he carried them both towards the house, Agnes called out to her mother.

"Mama, mama, Papa is here!"

Hearing the cries of her daughter but not quite making out what it was that she was saying, her mother rushed out from the kitchen along the short hallway and out into the bright daylight. On seeing Yves carrying the children she stopped in her tracks and put her hands to her face in disbelief.

"Yves," she muttered. "Is it really you?"

Yves leaned down so that the two children could jump off. They stepped aside as their mother and father embraced. The couple held each other tightly for what seemed like an age, Bertha sobbing openly with joy. Eventually they released each other, standing back whilst still holding hands, arms outstretched. He looked her up and down as if he was making sure that the woman standing before him was indeed his wife. She was much shorter than his six feet and was much fatter in the face with her light brown wavy hair parted off centre and held with a hairclip to stop her fringe from falling over her eyes. She wore a short sleeved, dress that had a large floral pattern in red and green printed on it. A short knitted cardigan hid her chunky arms. Her eyes were warm and inviting. Even now, in these times of austerity, she still managed to keep herself looking presentable, unlike Yves who was completely bedraggled. When he had left for war he had looked so dapper in his army uniform, grey woollen hat, double breasted greatcoat fastened to the chest revealing a starched white collared shirt and plain grey tie. A thick leather belt tight around his midriff and his black regulation boots polished to a shine.

"What are you doing here?" Bertha asked, still not quite believing her luck. "Have you escaped? You know there are Germans right here at La Chaire, they are in the house as we speak, quickly, come inside before they see you." She tugged at him, encouraging him to follow her into the house.

"How come you are here?" she frowned. He saw the doubt in her eyes.

"When the Germans took France all its armies were disbanded," he explained.

"Were you not imprisoned?"

"For a while and then we were released and sent to Paris to have our ID cards stamped so that we could come home. I returned to the island with Klebere Chapon, the hairdresser from town."

Bertha nodded as she recognised the name.

"Come let's all go inside, I bet you are starving."

As she led him inside they continued their conversation. The two children brought up the rear, Agnes skipping and Albert kicking stones.

"You have lost so much weight Yves, I hardly recognised you," she said

"What do you expect— there is a war on and food is not easy to come by, especially when you are on your own."

"So how did you eat?"

"Some locals took pity on us but there were times when we had to steal."

"Yves how could you?" she admonished him.

"When you are hungry you will do anything for a meal!" he explained.

"I know," she replied. "People are forever raiding our vegetable patch. If it wasn't for the Germans next door, I am sure we would have nothing."

"You do not fraternise with them do you?"

"God forbid no! They try and make conversation but I will have little to do with them and I have told the children to do the same."

Once they had stepped into the house they made their way into the kitchen. A warm glow came from the hearth filling the room with a cosy heat, giving the place a homely feel. Yves plonked himself down on a plain wooden chair by the kitchen table near to the kitchen range. This was his favourite spot in the house and it felt like he was putting on a pair of familiar slippers.

"The water is still on the boil," Bertha said moving towards the black stove. "I will make you a cup of tea."

"You have tea?" Yves was amazed.

"Not proper tea," Bertha smiled at Yves as she corrected herself. "It will have to be nettle tea I'm afraid, or would you prefer carrot tea?"

"As long as it is wet and warm!" he returned her smile.

"Nettle tea it is then!" she declared trying to make him feel at home.

"I notice that there is a fire in the hearth," Yves said as Bertha passed him a cup.

"Wood is at a premium but we manage to get by," she informed him. "If we want to cook anything substantial we have to walk up to the forge at the top of the hill. The blacksmith has to keep his fire going and he lets us use it on occasion."

Agnes danced around the table, Yves stroked her hair as she passed and Agnes smiled affectionately at him. Albert stayed close to his mother, never taking his eyes off his father. The spaniel continued to stiff at Yves' heels.

"Where do you get the wood from, for the fire?" Yves enquired.

"In the woods and the garden roundabout, but we have to make do with scraps because the Germans take most of it," Bertha told him.

"I noticed smoke coming from La Chaire."

"They use the trees from the garden to make their fires."

"Have they ruined much?" he asked as he took a large sip of the tea she made for him.

"A little," she said. "To be honest I have not been into the garden much since you left. I do not feel safe with all these soldiers about."

"That's understandable." Yves nodded.

"You will have to go and see for yourself but leave it until tomorrow when you are better rested and refreshed."

Yves saw the sense in his wife's advice, although the thought of the garden being decimated filled him with anxiety. Agnes came and sat on his knee which dispelled his fears for the moment. Still Albert watched him warily from a safe distance, toying with his model truck as he kept on staring.

The next day Yves was up bright and early, eager to survey the garden and to set about a plan to get the place back in order. He marched across the main terrace, in front of La Chaire, ignoring the guard on the door and stopped to survey the stumps of the palm trees that once graced the entrance. He shook his head disapprovingly then shrugged his shoulders. If this was the limit of the damage done then he could live with that.

The Wichuriana roses on the pergola had run riot over his three year absence. In places they had been cut back to allow access along the path but this had obviously been done without any care or consideration. Green suckers sprouted from their base, many of the original runners were dead or dying, their stems faded to brown and stratified, hardening their barbs to the point at which they posed a significant snagging hazard, tugging at clothing and tearing at skin without compulsion. Those stems that still grew were showing signs of budding. The clematis plants that had for so long bedecked the steep walls were in disarray. Many had died, left unwatered, hanging limply in dense clumps. Those that had managed to survive were opening up their blossoms ready for their early summer display of colour.

He paced the narrow paths and steps around the south facing garden, checking on the health of each and every plant. The evergreens were all generally in good shape, if they had not been removed for use as firewood, so they just needed cutting back and shaping. Most of the smaller shrubs, the azaleas, hydrangeas and rhododendrons, were of limited value as timber and so had escaped the axe, all of them needed severe pruning. The upper rose garden was quite unscathed although he did notice an attack of canker on some plants and serious greenfly infestation on all of the others. The miniature roses fought against these odds, throwing out green shoots and trying to bud. At the summit of the hill, near pulpit rock, some of the trees had been felled. He paused to stand in amazement at the Monterey Pine, standing tall and proud, completely unscathed.

As he descended the steps he worked through jobs that he needed to do, prioritising them in his head. The amount of work did not phase him. He had guessed that he would have a lot to do to get the garden back on its feet. As he reflected, his attention was drawn to profusion of weeds and wild flowers poking out from the flower beds. He sighed wistfully; weeding was a chore that he hated.

Following a brief stop for sustenance at the cottage, Yves set out to inspect the North facing side of the garden. As he crossed the brook he could see that the collection of rhododendrons had grown thicket like in his absence. The once coutured paths were now so heavily overgrown that they were nigh on impossible to penetrate. The dense vegetation, albeit festooned with a vivid display of colour, would need to be cut back. A noise heightened his senses. He endeavoured to locate its source. The sound was repeated and then again. It was easily recognisable, somebody was striking at timber. It had a sonority that was quite distinct. Now attuned to the sound Yves moved in its general direction.

About halfway up he came to a clearing. The signs of activity were there for all to see. The shrubbery had been cut back to the ground in a wide arc. The pale brown stems contrasted against the dark soil. Branches thick and thin had been sorted and placed in piles ready for transportation back to the house. Yves stared in horror at the carnage. The thwack of blade on wood continued unabated so Yves pressed on. He came upon a small detail of German soldiers, four in total. Their field grey jackets had been discarded and left hanging on one of the bushes nearby. It was heavy work, judging by the sweat patches underneath their armpits. Braces held up loose fitting grey trousers and all had their sleeves rolled up.

They were taking it in turns to wield the axes. Two soldiers took aim and chopped at the wood. The other two removed cut boughs and stripped them of leaves using machetes. They painstakingly cut off smaller twigs to use as kindling. Yves called out to them.

"What do you think that you are doing?"

The soldiers stopped momentarily and looked at him incredulously.

"What is your business here?" One of them asked. He leant on the shaft of his axe, glad of the breather.

"I am the gardener here!" Yves said with all the authority he could muster.

"Who has need of a gardener in times of war?" a second soldier laughed. "You would be of more use working in the fields. There won't be much of a garden left soon anyway."

The others joined in the laughter, mocking Yves' pomposity.

Yves was not deterred.

"War or no war this garden is my responsibility and now that I have returned I fully intend to keep the garden as it should be."

"The war may be over for you but for us it is not and we have our orders!" the first soldier replied.

"You can go elsewhere and forage for firewood there are plenty of other sources around and about," the anguish on Yves face was there for all of them to see.

"Why would we do that when there are plenty of trees and shrubs right on our doorstep?" The first soldier asked.

"Because all these plants are special, some are very rare." Yves explained, his hands held out, palms up displaying the passion he felt for the plants.

"That's as maybe but we have been given a task to do and we cannot shirk from our duty," The first soldier picked up his axe to continue his work. "In times of war sacrifices have to be made, I'm sure you'll be able to replace them once this godforsaken fight is over."

"That is the whole point!" Yves stepped forward to force the issue, "Many of these plants are irreplaceable."

"Then that is a shame," the first soldier seemed almost to sympathise with Yves pleas, and then he dashed them. "But we have a job to do so step aside, these axes are sharp and you might get hurt."

"Who is your commanding officer?" Yves demanded.

"You will get no joy there!" the second soldier glared at Yves over his colleague's shoulder.

"We will see about that!" Yves returned his stare.

"Go home to your wife and children before we are forced to make them fatherless!" the second soldier was unequivocal.

Frustrated and angry, Yves turned and made his way slowly back down the hill towards his house. The soldiers resumed their work, their laughter and the crack of timber ringing in Yves ears as he left.

Yves stepped disconsolately from the garden onto the road. As he did so a black Wolseley purred past him. He was so wrapped up in his own thoughts that he did not even bother to look and see who was in the car. Anger and frustration rather than curiosity occupied his mind. The car pulled up to a stop a little way up the road just before the entrance to La Chaire. The nearside rear window slipped silently into the recess of the door and a voice called out to him. Yves never flinched, he just trudged on back towards the cottage. It was only when the car horn sounded that his machinations were interrupted. He could see the German soldier at the wheel gesturing to him. The sight of the all too familiar field grey uniform with its black insignia and lapels fuelled his angst. He was about to turn away and ignore the soldier when the officer in the back of the vehicle stuck his head out of the open window and called to him once more, this time a little louder.

"You, come here!" the officer ordered. His tone was officious. Yves was intelligent enough not to ignore a German Officer so he stepped towards the vehicle. "Who are you?" the officer asked.

"My name Le Bloas," Yves replied, his natural reticence manifesting itself as arrogance.

"I have not seen you around these parts before, what is your business here?"

"I live here, in the cottage next to La Chaire," Yves explained. "I am the gardener."

"Then why have I not seen you until now?" the officer looked intently at him.

"I have just returned from France." Yves chose to meet his stare.

"And what were you doing in France?"

"Fighting!" came the terse reply.

"Explain!" the officer commanded. Yves deliberated briefly and then decided to play ball.

"I was a soldier in the French army till the Vichy government disbanded us."

"Then you are one of the lucky ones," the officer's tone softened. "For you the war is over, you have been returned to your loved ones. The rest of us are not so fortunate."

"The war is not over for me, or my family!" Yves irritation showed.

"Your liberty maybe somewhat compromised, that is true, but at least you have the comfort of being close to those whom you care for the most. You are not being shot at and your life is not at risk. Mrs Riley at Rozel Manor has spoken very favourably about this garden, she says it is quite special."

"It is!" Yves replied.

"Explain!" the officer demanded.

Yves knew that he had to reply otherwise he might end up with a beating, or worse.

"Many plants survive here when to all intents and purposes they should not."

"And why is that?" the officer was intrigued.

"Who knows?" Yves shrugged his shoulders. "Climate, soil, location?"

"I see," the officer mused. "And what value would you place on these so called rare and exotic plants?"

"They are priceless!" Yves answered enthusiastically. Only after his impulsive reply did he realise where the line of questioning was going. So he added an addendum. "But, like so many things of beauty, their true value can only be appreciated by the connoisseur. Cutting them down and burning them is like destroying a masterpiece."

"You should not be so harsh on the soldiers, they are only following orders."

"Your orders?"

"Yes."

"Then you are as foolish as they are ignorant."

"Watch your tone Mr Le Bloas," the officer bristled, "lest you earn yourself a beating."

"I cannot see that there is much in the way of damage," he observed.

"Little has been touched near the road but if you go up into where the rhododendrons are you will see the devastation there."

"I thought bushes like rhododendrons were used as firewood in their native country?"

The informed question was not lost on Yves.

"That is true, but in the mountains of Nepal they are not just hacked down indiscriminately they are trimmed and pruned so that they continue as a resource for the community."

"We could do that could we not?"

"Indeed we could, if your men were educated!" Yves risked censure by being so bold.

The officer chose to ignore his last remark and decided to take a closer look at the garden.

"Wait here till I return!" he commanded.

Yves did as he was told.

The officer stepped out of the car and it was a good hour before he returned.

"The place is a mess!" he said as he dusted off, rogue leaves and other debris from his tunic.

"What do you expect?" Yves replied. "I have been away fighting for the last three years."

"You will put the garden back in good order!" the officer instructed. "Once the place is tidied up I shall return."

The officer dismissed Yves with a sweep of his hand. The conversation over the officer was about to return to his car when the two soldiers returned, laden with the firewood Yves had seen them cutting. Yves' curse was audible. He glared at them as they approached. The officer called them over, his voice terse and unforgiving. They attempted a salute, which was difficult when their arms were otherwise occupied.

"Heinrich, where have you taken this wood from?" the officer asked.

"Up there among the trees," Heinrich replied.

"Who gave you permission to cut there?" the officer's tone was harsh.

"Nobody," the soldier replied somewhat bemused by the questioning. "We were just told to fetch firewood."

"We were just following orders." The other soldier piped in.

"And you, Helmut, do not have the wherewithal to distinguish between tree and shrub?"

"Sorry Feldkommandantur!" Heinrich snapped his heels together and bowed his head apologetically.

The Officer spoke with the cold air of authority. "Has it escaped your attention that this area is a garden not just a wild wood?" The soldiers shook their heads. "Does this land around the house not strike you as more like a garden than a coppice?" This time they just shrugged their shoulders. "It is plain for all to see that this is a garden full of cultivated plants and as a result should be afforded the respect given to any person's property. Whilst we have need to commandeer residencies it does not mean that we should treat the place with disregard."

"Firewood is not easy to come by," Heinrich was bold enough to offer his opinion.

"I appreciate that commodities are difficult to come by but do we really need to be so uncivilised and ruin what little beauty that is left?"

The difference in class between the officer and the soldiers was apparent. His aloofness had not been lost on the rank and file soldiers under his stewardship. They had earned their stripes, he had inherited his and that rubbed against the grain. He detected their reluctance to embrace him, and more often than not chose to avoid their company rather than risk the embarrassing silences that all too often ensued. Hailing from Bavaria also made him quite distinct from his compatriots, who viewed his Bavarian arrogance with contempt. Theirs was a world filled with raucous behaviour, while he appreciated the finer things in life, fine art, literature and the classics.

"With due respect Feldkommandantur!" Heinrich began but was cut short as the officer raised an open palm to stop him.

"Do you not have on ounce of initiative?" the Feldkommandantur growled. "That settled, you can carry on with your business."

The officer dismissed them.

As they neared La Chaire Albert and Agnes ran out from the cottage, pursued by their little black spaniel Pip. The dog made a bee-line for the soldiers, yapping and snapping at their heels. They could not see the dog, burdened as they were by the timber, which made them unsure of their footing. They kicked wildly in the general direction of the barks, an action that irritated Pip further, causing him to growl and snarl in between barks. A sudden yelp sent him scurrying away. The two children complained as they chased after their injured pet.

"That bloody dog!" Heinrich cursed. "I swear that one day I will put an end to its infernal racket."

Chapter 16

La Chaire 1942

Yves wasted little time in beginning repairs to the damage caused by the occupying soldiers. He set about replacing lost or injured plants using skills that had been passed down the generations. Plants that were propagated by seed had the seed taken from parent plants that had survived the onslaught. Yves also used grafting and layering techniques to produce plants of a hardier variety.

Whilst he was busy working on the rhododendron thicket Albert searched him out. So involved was Yves with his work that he did not realise that his son was standing right behind him. It was only when he stood up to stretch his stiffening back that he noticed Albert standing, silently watching him. Yves' heart missed a beat as he was startled by the boy.

"What are you doing?" Albert was genuinely interested.

"Soil layering"

"What is that?" Albert continued his enquiry.

"Covering the stem with soil and leaving it to root."

"Is that all?"

"Pretty much, except that once the stem has rooted it is separated from the parent plant."

As if to demonstrate what he had just explained, his father shovelled a pile of topsoil over a long stem which protruded out from the main plant. It struck Albert as odd, seeing the leaves at one end of the leggy stem poking out from the soil and the other end still attached to the main plant.

Albert soon lost interest and decided to go off and play. He pretended that there were German soldiers hiding in the bushes all around them. Yves was unsettled by Albert's presence but did not show it. He was a solitary man at the best of times, preferring his own company, unless it suited him otherwise. Gardening suited his persona. Long periods alone in the garden were times when he could reflect, alone with his thoughts, cogitating on this and that. The fresh air brought with it freedom of spirit even in these oppressive times when anxiety and depression preyed on idle minds.

The thought that his beloved garden might be completely decimated filled him with dread. It was not just the selfish need to preserve a way of life that was so dear to him, but the realisation that if the garden were to disappear his livelihood would be lost and those that relied on him would likely be cast out and left destitute. He could not get away from the feelings of guilt that ran through him but he had to be pragmatic about the situation. If he played the situation carefully he might just tread that fine line that many on the island had to tread in order to survive.

Albert disappeared along one of the many paths, seeking out the enemy, stalking the undergrowth for snipers. He shot a few and took a couple of near misses, the situation was dire and the odds were against him. He decided to make a dash for freedom and to raise the cavalry to push back the overwhelming odds that surrounded him. As he ran full pelt his escape was blocked by a tall, dark figure, whom he ran straight into. He looked up at the tall stranger, who was dressed in German army uniform.

"Chasing soldiers eh?" the FeldKommandantur observed with a welcoming smile.

Albert was mortified. He took a step back before his muscles turned to stone and rendered him completely immobile. He was like a rabbit caught in headlights.

"What is your name?" the officer tried to be accommodating.

Albert could not speak.

"Come on little boy, I will not bite you!" the officer said softly. "I have a young man just like you at home," he added.

"Albert," Albert mumbled looking down at the ground.

"You'll have to speak louder than that!" the FeldKommandantur instructed.

"Albert!" Albert said a little louder.

"Are you enjoying your game?" the officer endeavoured to make light conversation.

Albert nodded, still terrified at being in the presence of the officer. Even at this tender age he recognised the difference between a regular soldier and those in command.

"This garden must be full of adventure for you," he observed.

Again, Albert said nothing, he just nodded.

"We have a garden much larger than this in Bavaria," the FeldKommandantur told him. "We have many trees and shrubs there but they are not as cluttered. We also have a large lake, well stocked with fish and an ornamental pond."

Albert could not help but be impressed as his imagination was fired. He had visions of ships in battle on a vast lake.

Recognising that Albert was frightened the officer ruffled Albert's hair.

"Off you go and play Albert," he said.

Not needing a second chance Albert turned on his heels and dashed back to his father. Soon after the FeldKommandantur re- appeared, making Albert run behind his father for safety.

"Good morning Le Bloas!" the officer greeted him.

Yves returned to his work, showing his disdain for the officer. The FeldKommandantur was incensed.

"It would pay you to be civil to me!" he snapped.

There was an uncomfortable stand off as the two men considered their next course of action. As Albert hid behind his father the threat was not lost on Yves. Here, at this moment in time, all aspects that played on his emotions came together. When he looked up at the FeldKommandantur all he could see was the enemy. He had spent three years of his life fighting men like this, shooting to kill and dodging their bullets into the bargain. He had seen compatriots die all around him and he had suffered the ignominy and humiliation of the trek home, abused by the Germans at each and every opportunity. His antipathy ran deep and he was resistant to any approach from the likes of this officer. But then there was the garden. When the Nicolle family left on the boat to seek sanctuary first in England and then in Canada, they had entrusted their prize garden to him. It was a responsibility that he was committed to, as well as being a labour of love. Then there was Albert and the rest of his family. Maybe he could live without the garden but he could not see his family suffer as a result of his own obstinacy.

The officer considered demanding that Yves converse with him but, once more, he thought better of it. Yves sighed as the FeldKommandantur took a couple of steps back down the path. The footsteps stopped and the officer turned to speak.

"Tomorrow I expect a full tour of the garden!" he ordered.

Yves stopped shovelling but did not turn to acknowledge the officer.

"I shall expect you at nine o'clock prompt, outside of the main house."

Yves decided to finish for lunch and made his way back to the cottage with Albert holding his hand tightly. As they approached the cottage he was waylaid by his daughter.

"Papa," Agnes called, visibly concerned, "have you seen Pip?"

"No Agnes I haven't," her father replied, "but then again I have been up in the far reaches of the garden all morning, when did you see him last?"

"This morning when I went to the beach to fetch sea water for Mama."

"I'm sure he will turn up soon," Yves attempted to reassure them. "He's probably sniffed out a rabbit or something, he will return when he gets hungry."

"Do you think so?" Agnes whimpered as she cuddled up to her father for comfort. Yves picked her up and carried her back to the house.

The FeldKommandantur was true to his word appearing once more up the drive at around nine o'clock the next morning. The black car staggered to a halt a few yards away from where Yves sat. The officer emerged, ducking to avoid the top of the doorway, and adjusted his hat as he stood upright. He stepped over to where Yves sat whittling away at a piece of wood.

"Good morning Le Bloas!" he greeted Yves in a business like manner.

"Bonjour," Yves grunted reluctantly

"It is good to see that you are prompt!" the officer remarked.

Yves could have told him that he had been out and about since dawn but he chose to keep quiet.

"Shall we commence?" the officer asked politely.

Yves put down his whittling and dragged himself up from his sitting position and strode off in the direction of the south facing part of the garden.

"Ah a camellia!" the FeldKommandantur observed. "I have a whole avenue of them on my estate. Planted along the west wall they form a glorious spectacle in winter."

The officer took a closer look at the plant, with its waxy leaves and fading red flowers. He took out a small notepad and pencil, jotting down some information or other and looking along the path before making a small sketch. They moved slowly along the garden paths, Yves careful to answer only when spoken to and then to say only what must be said. The officer scrutinised almost each and every shrub, making notes as and when he saw fit. They had almost reached the end of the walk through the south side of the garden when they came upon a large tree. Yves stopped at the tree which was about twenty feet in height. It was full of bundles of little white flowers, shaped like tiny bells that are often seen in fairy pictures.

"These are like Lily of the Valley," he remarked, pulling a branch down so that he could smell their fragrance.

"Oxydebdrum Arboreum," Yves said casually.

"Ah!" the Officer exclaimed, "Lily of the Valley tree. These blooms are almost identical to the plant and they are so fragrant. Does it not originate from South America?" he enquired. "Argentina I think."

Yves nodded.

"I have read about this shrub," the officer enthused. "Overnight it turns from a pretty but nondescript tree with green foliage into this mass of white blooms that we see before us now. It is most striking, is it not?"

Yves felt the urge to respond but did not.

"And in autumn, when the first frost strikes, the whole tree turns flaming red," the FeldKommandantur enthused as he scribbled vigorously in his notebook.

Just before they were about to leave the south garden the officer stopped once more.

"Now that shrub over there is interesting," he declared.

Yves took a cursory glance in the direction that the officer was looking.

"Over there among the long grass and greenery," the FeldKommandantur pointed in its general direction. "The one with oval leaves set alternately up the stem."

"It has green flowers," Yves stated.

"That is odd!" the officer was enthused. "And what is it called?"

"Its common name is Back Brush," Yves told him.

"You would not notice it unless it was pointed out to you," the officer commented.

The FeldKommandantur carefully made his way through the undergrowth until he was right next to the sapling. It had a tall woody stem, standing erect with branches starting to emanate along its length. He stooped to examine it, holding one of its florets between his thumb and forefinger.

"What delicate flowers, and they are so green."

As the two men stepped back onto the road to begin viewing the north side of the garden, Agnes and Albert appeared. This time, rather than being exasperated and anxious, Agnes was quite subdued, wearing a hangdog expression as she kicked the dust in front of her. Albert copied her, although he could not resist frequent glances each and everywhere just in case there was something more exciting afoot.

"No sign of Pip then?" their father enquired as he approached them.

"No Papa," she sighed, "we have searched everywhere for him."

"Have you tried down by the beach?" he asked.

"Yes and along the harbour and up by the railway," she informed him.

"I thought I told you not to stray so far?" Yves tone changed as he looked askance at the officer.

"You should listen to your father!" the officer commented.

"Go and play nearer to the house and stay out of the way of the soldiers!" e chastised and then in a softer voice said, "I am busy right now, but perhaps later this evening we might take a stroll around the area to see if we can find him."

Reluctantly Agnes trudged back towards the house. Albert let go of his father and followed his sister.

As the two men stepped onto the zigzag path that wound its way to the top of the northslope, the officer took the opportunity to strike up a conversation.

"Those are two lovely children that you have there," he remarked.

"They are."

"What ages are they?"

"Albert is six and Agnes is eight."

"I have three children!" the statement hung in the air awaiting a response but there was none forthcoming.

Yves lack of empathy cut deep but the FeldKommandantur hid his frustration. He and Yves had a lot more in common than the gardener was aware of. He thought about telling Yves that his children were in fact safely ensconced just across the border in Austria but that his wife was incarcerated in a dark cell, in Linz, facing a charge of treason. The FeldKommandantur pulled out a tiny silver knife from inside his jacket pocket and played with it between thumb and finger. The glint of the knife caught Yves attention.

"It is my wife's," the officer revealed with some sadness before returning it to the safety of his coat pocket. He took a moment to collect his thoughts and then looked up at the mighty Magnolia tree standing opposite Yves' cottage.

"Magnolia Cambelli!" he declared, looking up at the large tree with great admiration. He took some time to walk around it before recording his thoughts in his notebook.

The note- taking unsettled Yves.

He followed the officer upwards along the winding path, with its puddlestone walls to their left. Set in the walls were alcoves and recesses, where plants that had been strategically placed, now ran wild. Yves made a mental note to tidy them up. The officer continued to write his observations as he perused the many palms, yuccas, azaleas and hydrangeas that lined this section of the garden. At the summit he stopped to look back over the south facing garden from their elevated position on the north side.

"This garden is wonderful. It reminds me so much of my childhood. I had a picture on my nursery wall that is reminiscent of La Chaire; it contained exotic vegetation, palm trees and the suchlike." There was a genuine sense of wonder in his voice. "If war could be fought with flowers these beleaguered islands could conquer a continent." The officer concluded. Yves was not at all enamoured by this last statement and it showed on his face as he strode off up the path, leaving the officer to chase after him. The rest of the climb was conducted in silence with the last plant to be noted being the Monterey pine at the summit.

"This tree would keep a house warm for a year!" The FeldKommandantur observed, trying to lighten the atmosphere. "Mind you they would have to be desperate to climb all the way up here just to get some firewood."

The tour had seemed thorough and exhaustive, leaving Yves feeling drained. He felt that the secrets of the garden at La Chaire had been laid bare. All he could do now was watch and wait.

Yves got to task on all areas of the garden. He tidied up flower beds and trimmed back bushes and shrubs. All waste wood was carefully stacked by the roadside so that people could help themselves. The walled garden behind the shed that housed the well was tilled in preparation for planting crops.

As was his routine, Yves came in from the garden just as the light was fading. He washed off the dirt from his hands in the pot sink beneath the kitchen window. He sat down at the bare wooden table with Albert and Agnes sitting in readiness either side. Bertha had prepared them a shellfish stew made from winkles, limpets, prayers and cockles. She had used nettles as a herb and the salt she had used came from evaporating the sea water that had been collected by Agnes. Potatoes, carrots and onions, grown in the vegetable patch, added much needed nutrition. Bertha ladled the stew into four bowls and then placed one bowl each in front of her hungry family. Yves broke off small chunks of bread from the loaf that sat in front of them in the centre of the table and gave a piece each to Agnes and Albert. As Bertha sat down they tucked in and the meal was eagerly consumed. Afterwards, Bertha made them all a cup of carrot tea.

Once the meal had been finished and the table had been cleared, Yves went upstairs to fetch one of his prized possessions. He returned carrying a large leather tome which he duly placed on the table with great reverence before sitting down in front of it and carefully untying the thin leather strap that kept it bound together. Agnes and Albert were fascinated by the book. They sidled up either side of their father and waited with anticipation to see what would be revealed. Albert, still being on the small side, had to stand on tiptoes and crane his neck to get a good look. Yves took pity on him and lifted him onto his lap so that he could get a grandstand view. Agnes had seen the books many times before, resting silently up on the shelf in her parent's bedroom, just tantalisingly out of reach of enquiring minds.

Slowly he raised the front cover.

Each page was separated from the next by a sheet of tissue paper. Through the translucent protective layer both Albert and Agnes could make out the outline of a flower situated in the dead centre of the page. Yves unveiled the tissue paper to reveal the drawings in all of their glorious detail. They did not have the artistic interpretation of the camellias painted by Clara Maria Pope so many years before, but what they lacked in flair they made up for in accuracy and attention to detail, yet these had been painted by a humble gardener. Each flower was delicately drawn in ink. Calligraphic lines added shadow and structure to the sketches, the attention to the finest detail was impressive. Drawings taken from individual parts of each plant were to be found around the edges of the page. Again the attention to detail in these exploded addenda was impressive. Details showing everything from petals and sepals, to anther and carpel, size, orientation and location of leaf, stem and bud. If this was not enough, Yves had richly annotated his pictures showing them to be working documents as well as a labour of love. The children were not disappointed.

"What is this book for Papa?" Albert asked.

"I use the books to keep a record of the plants I work with."

"Why?"

"Over the years I have tried and tested many ways to get plants to grow. Some of these are secret, others I give or sell to other gardeners."

"Why would you keep them secret?" Agnes enquired.

"To maintain the magic and mystery of how plants grow," Yves turned his head slightly and cast a knowing glance at Agnes.

"Do they really grow by magic?" Albert wanted to believe.

"Indeed they do that and a little know how," Yves smiled at Bertha who smiled at the loving picture of her family together around the kitchen table. "And some people will pay handsomely for me to make that magic work in their garden."

"I wish Pip would return soon!" Agnes complained.

"He will come back when he is ready," Yves said giving her a little hug to console her.

"Now then you two, let's get you ready for bed!" Bertha interrupted turning from the sink and drying her hands on her pinafore.

"Must we Mama?" Albert pleaded. "Can we not look at some more of Papa's pictures?"

"Perhaps tomorrow," Yves said as he ruffled Albert's hair. "Now do as your mother says and get ready for bed."

The next morning saw their father going about his business once more.

Ideas developing in his head overnight had provided for a restless sleep. As dawn broke he rose and partook of a simple breakfast. After a brief discourse with Bertha he threw his regulation army knapsack over his back and strode purposefully out of the house, followed by Bertha and the two children. He jumped on the old bicycle that lay propped up against the wall outside the front door. The whole family laughed as he wobbled his way along so slowly that it looked like he would collapse in a heap at any moment. Eventually he gained control and even managed to give them a wave as he cycled away.

Their father's departure coincided with the appearance of a number of soldiers from the main house. Under orders they stepped out from the entrance and assembled on the gravel area in front. Their appearance caused the family much amusement. Here were a group of men dressed only in tight black trunks and jack boots, standing in the cool air of the morning breeze, each holding a rolled up regulation towel under their right arm. On the call they stood to attention. The officer, similarly attired, barked another order and they set off at a march down the slope towards the beach. Agnes, followed by Albert, still in their nightclothes ran alongside the men, mimicking their marching style. Bertha could not help laughing although she tried to disguise her mirth.

Heinrich and Helmut brought up the rear and the expression on their faces showed that they were none too enamoured by their ridiculous appearance. The mocking gait of the children served only to heighten their irritation, so much so that they risked censure by breaking the regimental march in order to turn their heads and scowl in the direction of the children. Unperturbed, the children continued to walk alongside until Bertha's fear for their safety overtook her initial mirth. She saw the intimidation and anger in the glare given by the two soldiers.

"Agnes, Albert, come back here right now!" she shouted.

The two children ceased their mockery and ran back in the direction of their mother. She saw the two soldiers look back over their shoulders one last time and the look they gave made her wither.

"You mustn't go near the soldiers!" she scolded.

 "Yes Mama!" they replied in unison.

Bertha hurried them back to the relative safety of the house just in case.

Later that day their father returned. He hurried indoors in the hope that his furtive movements had not been seen by any keen eyed guards. He nipped into the kitchen and then made his way to the scullery via the door at the rear of the kitchen. Once there he took off his knapsack which seemed to have a life all of its own, and placed it carefully on the floor. Something inside the sack wriggled and struggled.

Bertha, who was preparing the evening meal, caught only the briefest glimpse of her husband as he dashed by. She called out to him but he ignored her. Her concerns raised, she turned from the sink and followed him into the scullery, drying her hands on her apron as she went.

Yves saw her coming and waited by the door till she entered. Once inside, he closed the scullery door. A small window in the centre of the outside wall allowed enough light into the room in order that they could both see each other. There were a few bits of bric-a-brac in the room but nothing of any significance except a large bread oven to the left of the small window. The entrance to the oven was a couple of feet above floor level and had a roughly hewn semi-circular shape.

In the silence Yves undid the ties on the knapsack and gently eased it open, out rushed a chicken in a flutter of brown feathers. It had a yellow beak and scaly legs and its comb and mantle were bright red in colour. It clucked around the room expressing its dissatisfaction at being unceremoniously cooped up in a sack for a couple of hours. The bird quickly settled down and began to forage around the floor for any titbits that it could find.

"Where did you get that from?" Bertha asked, surprised at the new addition to the family.

"Never mind where it came from, it is ours now and we must look after it!" Yves replied.

"Look after it?" Bertha queried. "Don't you want me to prepare it for tonight's meal?"

"On the contrary, we will keep it safe and well fed so that it can keep us supplied with eggs. If we take care of it, it should last us a good couple of years and then, when it is done laying we will wring its neck and eat it."

"It might be a bit stringy by then!" Bertha pointed out.

"Who cares, it will still be edible. We can use its carcass in a stew if we have to."

"Where are we going to keep it?" Bertha asked. "We can't leave it outside or it is sure to be gone as quickly as we have acquired it."

"We'll keep it in here."

"Here?"

"Yes, in the bread oven, it's not as if we are able to bake any bread," Yves explained. "I will make a gate for the door so that it won't escape."

"You are aware that we are meant to inform the authorities about what livestock we have?" Bertha asked.

"I thought that was only for stock like pigs and cattle, besides what they don't know won't harm them!" Yves grinned briefly.

Discussion over Yves and Bertha left the chicken to become more acquainted with its surroundings. They pulled the door to the scullery tight shut so that the bird could not escape. Bertha returned to her chores and Yves went outside in search of branches and twigs with which to make a gate.

To avoid suspicion Yves gathered material from high up in the garden. Once he had chosen some likely sticks, he took a ball of twine and a saw from one of the large sheds and locked himself in the scullery where he fashioned a makeshift gate for the doorway to the bread oven. He placed some straw in the oven and then, after a short chase, caught the bird and lifted it into its new home. He shut the cage door and placed a rock behind it to stop it from opening.

When the children were introduced to it they squealed with delight.

"What shall we call it?" Agnes asked.

"You think of a name," Bertha charged her with giving it a name.

"I think we will call it Chucky."

"Chucky the chicken!" Bertha smiled as she said its name out loud.

"Chucky will make a great friend for Pip when he comes home!" Agnes' words of hope were not shared by her parents, who looked at each other with pensively.

A couple of days later Yves was busy in the garden. He had removed the stems from some roses that were showing little sign of maturing. He took out a sharp knife and cut one of the stems at an angle. He placed the stem on a different plant, having previously removed a section of its bark. With great dexterity he bound the two together using some twine. Once complete he marked the grafted rose stem with its name and a date.

Yves continued to air layer a number of other plants in order to build up his stock. He was working on another plant when a loud scream made him drop what he was doing and run back towards the cottage. As he approached he saw that the door to the shed that housed the well was ajar. He feared the worst. Standing by the door was Bertha, who looked ashen and distraught. He stepped across to console her, sick with apprehension. Once by her side he saw both Agnes and Albert sitting weeping behind the door.

"What is the matter?" he asked.

"Look.!" Bertha cried. "Over there, in the reeds by the stream."

Yves took the few steps to see what was afoot. There, hidden by the reeds was Pip. The mass of black fur and the long floppy ears were quite distinct. However his body was limp and lifeless. His eyes stared into nowhere, almost popping out of their sockets. His mouth was ajar and his tongue hung loosely. By the smell that emanated from him, he had been there some time.

"Take the children inside!" Yves instructed Bertha. "I will deal with the body."

"Who could have done such a thing?" Bertha cried as she took hold of the children and led them back to the cottage.

As the family tried to come to terms with the distressing discovery, Heinrich and Helmut sat at the entrance to La Chaire cleaning their weapons. They had watched with interest as the melodrama had unfolded. Yves lifted up the dead body of the dog with some reverence. He walked past the two soldiers who spoke as he passed by.

"You have found your dog then?" Heinrich called out with a knowing smirk.

Yves ignored the taunt.

As the dog's remains slowly decayed so the garden began to flourish once more. Yves worked his magic and restored the place to something like its former glory. As the garden flourished, its power to heal also blossomed. Tortured minds, ravaged by the pressures of conflict and occupation were soothed by La Chaire's colour and fragrance.

Chapter 17

La Chaire 1944

It was early morning as the first cohort of labourers trudged past the La Chaire. Armed soldiers, some with bayonets fixed, formed a guard around them, constantly chivvying and harrying, barking out incoherent orders. Albert and Agnes ran out of the cottage to watch them pass. The men at the front seemed relatively healthy although their clothes were badly soiled and their footwear looked ready to disintegrate at any moment. Yves, emerging just behind his children, marked them as Spanish, Portuguese or French. They had a Latin defiance that flashed in their olive eyes. He met their gaze and a brief nod of the head was enough to acknowledge their plight and pledge support, for what it was worth. Each man carried either a shovel or a pick. Albert was so frightened by their menacing appearance he instinctively stepped back into the safety of his father's arms. The reaction was not lost on Yves, who put his arms on his son's shoulders to reassure him.

Bringing up the rear were the Slavs, mainly Polish and Russians, their pale skin a marked contrast to the toned features of those that went before. These Slavs, which included women and children, were terribly undernourished almost literally skin and bone. Their haunted appearance was disturbing and Yves could not help but look away. Albert on the other hand was mesmerised by what he saw and could not help but stare. One of the Slavs took a moment to look at Albert. His gaunt face and sunken eyes, so deep in their sockets it must have been like looking through a tunnel. The man hardly blinked such was the depth of his despair. His cheek bones protruded through skin that looked ready to tear at the slightest touch. His emaciated lips, barely recognisable among the cracks and sores that were gouged along their length, offered little cover across his misshapen teeth. It was as if he wore a fixed grin, unable to express what he was feeling inside. Albert felt the weight of the man's stare. It was as if he had been caught up in the look of some mythological creature. The man's expression was not one that was pleading for help or any kind of solace, he had gone beyond such hopes a long time ago. The look was cold, empty and vacant, devoid of emotion. Albert was peering into the eyes of the living dead, soulless bleak, desolate. The sight sent emotions racing through his body that he did not understand. These wretched souls had little clothing to hide their humiliation and those that had any sort of footwear only had rags wrapped around to stave off the worst of the hard stony ground they were forced to march along. What he witnessed would stay with him forever. These people did not even possess enough energy to raise a finger in protest. They were hollow shells where the echoes of their souls rattled inside a cavernous emptiness. Eventually Yves himself could no longer bear to look and turned away in disgust. Bertha stepped out from the house and on seeing the spectacle grabbed the two children and ushered them inside whilst at the same time looking askance at her husband.

"They need to know!" Yves returned her gaze without emotion. "They need to understand the horrors of war."

"They are children!" she replied as they disappeared back into the safety of the house.

As Albert settled down to play with his sister in front of the hearth he was unaware of the trauma his father was going through outside. After a brief exchange, Albert tired of his sister's company and sought new adventures. He quietly got up and sneaked out of the house.

The shuffling feet of the prisoners could be heard disappearing down the road towards the harbour, the brightly coloured flowers bobbing conceitedly on branch and stem as they passed by. As Yves set about his work for the day, it struck him that the opulence and beauty of the garden was in marked contrast to people that had just passed through it. Even the scented aromas could not smother the stench of oppression that the slave labourers were subjected to.

Between the cottage and La Chaire two large greenhouses were to be found, and beyond them was a large shed. The timbers of the shed had been heavily bleached as a result of weathering, in particular the strong sunshine that bathed the island each and every summer. The vertical slats of the shed had buckled and warped over time, leaving gaps in between, through which passers by could catch a glimpse of what was contained inside. Albert was often caught, head pressed against the wood, trying to get a better view of what was hidden inside. To him it was an Aladdin's cave of unrivalled paraphernalia, all of which fuelled a fertile imagination. The shed was made even more esoteric by the fact that he and his sister were forbidden to go anywhere near on pain of reprisals. Since his return he had felt the force of his father's displeasure, ranging from a clip around the ear to a full blooded smack across the back of the legs. To even risk such sanctions required an inquisitiveness that cut across his natural instinct for survival.

Yves caught Albert straining to look through his favourite orifice, a long vertical gap that he could almost put his small head through. Albert was concentrating so hard trying to make sense of the large machine that clattered and creaked that he did not hear his father approaching. It was not until a large hand gripped his collar and hoisted him off the ground, causing him to squeal with fear, that he knew that he had been rumbled. Albert was still wary of this man he called father.

"I thought I told you to stay away from the shed?" his father growled.

"I am sorry Papa," Albert whimpered. "I was not going to go inside, I was just looking." He added.

"Curiosity killed the cat!" His father said continuing to hold him off the ground.

"Did he?" Albert had never heard of anyone called 'Crosity'. He wondered where he, or she might live, perhaps he was from St Helier?

His father could not resist releasing the faintest of smiles at his son's response and in doing so he let Albert back down on the ground and relaxed his grip.

"Perhaps if I take you inside and show you what dangers lie within then it might satisfy your curiosity, and you will not be so inquisitive in the future!" he said gruffly.

He put a comforting hand around Albert's shoulder as he led him to the doors at the front of the shed.

Albert looked briefly at the overhanging pitch roof and then at the two doors, one of which his father unlatched and pulled open. The sound of the engine became considerably louder as they entered. There were shafts of light that cut their way through the dark, shimmering with shiny diamonds of dust that danced in the musty air around them. Once his eyes had become accustomed to the half light Albert marvelled at the machine. There it was in all its glory stretching from one end of the shed to the other, whirring, sighing, coughing and clunking with an orchestral rhythm. A small wheel turned, attached to a belt that turned another, much larger wheel. This big wheel spun with an intensity that frightened Albert. He stepped back, instinctively sidling up to his father for protection. The spinning of the wheel mesmerised him.

"That is called a fly wheel." his father told him. "It is attached to a dynamo over there. That is what makes the electricity for the cottage and the main house."

Albert did not really understand but he could see that it was dangerous.

"If you caught your hand in the wheel or the drive belt it would rip it off!" His father told him. The thought scared Albert even more and he gripped his father's leg tightly.

"Can we go now Papa, I'm scared!" Albert cried, pulling at his father's arm to try and get out of the shed.

His father tugged him, reluctantly, in the direction of some large, rectangular glass jars. They were filled with a clear liquid.

"That is acid inside of the jars," his father said. "You must not go near them."

"Why?" Albert was not sure whether he wanted to know the reason or not.

"Acid will burn through your skin, right to the bone!" his father alleged with dramatic effect.

Again Albert recoiled at the revelation. As his father led him out Albert took a last look all around the old shed. The joists were exposed, along with the trusses that held the roof in place. From these joists, there were numerous herbs and alliaceous bulbs hanging out to dry, their unctuous odours permeated the mustiness. Alongside the spindly stems, lots of large brown leaves also hung limply. Albert thought that they looked like giant hands. He could see their veins raised in profile amidst their leathery skin. His father stretched up and took a bundle.

"What are those?" Albert asked.

"Tobacco leaves," his father replied, rubbing a leaf between thumb and finger and sniffing the residue it left behind.

"Are they from the garden?" Albert guessed.

"Yes."

"Can you eat them?"

His father smiled.

"Some men do chew them but then spit them out," his father explained.

"Do they not taste very nice?"

"Not really." His father clarified.

"Can I try some?" Albert was curious.

"They are not for little boys."

"Why not?"

"People usually smoke tobacco and smoking is for adults," his father's explanation was enough.

Albert tired of the shed and its curios.

"Can I go and play?"

"Off you go," his father ushered him out of the shed. "And remember," he shouted after the boy as he skipped away towards the cottage, "You are not to go into the shed."

"Ok Papa!" Albert acknowledged without turning his head.

Albert made his way to the house to find Agnes so that he could tease her by boasting that he had been into the shed. Meanwhile his father followed at a more leisurely pace carrying some tobacco leaves. Once he had reached the cottage he sat down on the bench. Having been unable to find Agnes, Albert decided to sit down on the floor next to his father and play with some of the wooden toys that were lying about. His father pulled out his penknife and began to shred the leaves, collecting them in an old battered tin. Albert stopped what he was doing and watched his father. Eventually, he got bored and resumed playing with his wooden toys. Soon after, his father stopped shredding the tobacco leaves, placed the lid on the tin and put his knife back in his inside jacket pocket.

"I am going to Becquet's," his father shouted to his mother.

Having the tin of shredded tobacco in his hand he set off in the direction of the harbour.

"Can I come Papa?" Albert cried. His father pondered the request momentarily.

"Yes but you must do as you are told, no wandering off, the beach is a dangerous place."

Albert ran alongside his father, barely able to keep up with the pace, skipping and dancing whilst shooting at an imaginary enemy.

They crossed over the road and took the narrow track alongside the high granite walls of the barracks of Beau Couperon. The path came to an abrupt end as it met the pebbled beach. There was a two feet drop at their interface. Yves jumped down without a thought but Albert stood hesitantly at the precipice. He was uncertain, it seemed such a long way. He took a deep breath and launched himself off the edge. He felt like he was flying and smiled at the exhilaration of it all. Then he hit the ground, twisting his ankle and rolling over as he lost his footing on the uneven rocks.

"Ouch." He cried as he tried to get up, embarrassed at his tumble.

"Are you okay?" His father was concerned.

"Yes Papa!" Albert lied. His ankle throbbed but he knew that he would have to go back home if he told the truth.

As his father turned Albert followed, rubbing his aching heel and fighting back the tears. Yves stepped across the stream that had found its way from the valley to the beach, before surrendering to the waves. The fresh water and the salty sea embraced each other with the softest of kisses, making the rounded rocks even harder to master. Sitting on a stool by the whitewashed wall was Becquet, watching them as he tended to his lobster pots.

"Bonjour Joseph," Yves greeted him.

"Bonjour Yves" Becquet replied.

The two men shook hands heartily, Yves stooping as Joe remained seated.

"I see you have brought young Albert with you," Becquet observed, ruffling Albert's hair as the boy approached.

Albert liked Becquet. He was much smaller than his father but somewhat swarthier in build. His chubby fingers made light work of the wicker that he wound in and out as he repaired the pots. A rolled cigarette hung loosely from his mouth, a long line of ash tantalisingly suspended from the end. Albert could see the people that had passed the house earlier, laying a railway track along the length of the harbour.

"Will there be trains coming to Rozel?" he enquired.

"No little man," Becquet replied as he bent and twisted some stray pieces of wicker into strange shapes. "They are laying a track for a large searchlight."

"What do you have in your bucket?" Yves enquired.

Albert's attention was immediately drawn to a large wooden barrel that sat outside Becquet's front door. It was almost as tall as Albert and he had to stand on tiptoes to see over the lip and into the murky water inside. He could see lots of little bubbles rising to the surface and ripples as something down below shifted and moved.

"Don't put your hand in there or the crabs will nip your fingers!" Becquet teased.

Yves picked Albert up so that he could see into the depths of the water. The bright sun reflected on its surface and so it was hard to make anything out. Joe got up from his chair, rolled up his sleeve, dipped it in the water and fished out a large spider crab. The crab wriggled and wiggled its legs in a vain attempt to get free. Albert recoiled as Joe brought the crab closer to his face. It was Albert's turn to try and wriggle free which he did successfully, retreating to a point of safety from the advancing crab. He was not sure whether to laugh or cry. To the relief of Albert, Becquet put the creature back into the barrel,

"Here Albert, this is for you," Becquet handed him the wicker shape he had been working on.

"What is it?" Albert asked as he took the present from the old man.

"It is a figure," Becquet replied. "It can be whatever you want it to be, a monster from the deep, a soldier for you to play with, use your imagination."

"Thank you Mr Becquet!" Albert said with glee. This was why he liked Mr Becquet, he was always making things for him, whether it be whittled people from old driftwood, or vehicles to put them in. "Can I go and play in the sand Papa?" Albert asked excitedly.

"Off you go," his father said and then added, "But stay away from the barbed wire and don't go anywhere near the harbour wall, understand?"

"Yes Papa," Albert dashed to where he thought was an acceptable spot and then turned to seek his father's approval. Yves nodded his assent.

"I will take the crab off your hands if you like," Yves said to Joe as he settled down on the floor beside him.

"What do you have in exchange?" Joe bartered.

Yves shook the tin he had brought with him.

"Tobacco?"

"Lovely!" Joe smiled a semi toothless grin. "How much?"

"You can have an ounce for the crab," Yves replied.

"How about two ounces and I'll throw in a couple of scallops and a few mussels?" Joe suggested.

"It's a deal!" Yves said and proceeded to shake hands once more with Becquet.

Albert glanced up from building a sandcastle to see the two men sharing a laugh. Becquet looked across at Albert and waved. Albert returned the wave.

"It's not right us sitting here while those poor people are made to suffer," Becquet said to Yves. "There must be something that we can do to help them."

"Like what?" Yves took out some tobacco from the tin and started to roll a cigarette.

"We should have a resistance movement on the island. If we did I would join it."

Yves handed Joe the rolled cigarette and then started to make one for himself.

"And how would we resist the enemy?" he asked.

"Anyway we could!" came the reply, "destroy their railway, blow up a few buildings perhaps shoot some of them!"

"With what," Yves was dismissive of the idea "our bare hands? We don't have any weapons. When the British left they demilitarised the island, leaving us defenceless. Besides, think of the reprisals if we resorted to such tactics. Resistance does not just spring up from nowhere, it starts back in London. They identify specific targets and then send agents out to recruit people willing to fight."

"Like me!" Joe interrupted.

"The problem is, Joe," Yves carried on, "that the island is not strategic and so we don't even register on their radar. And what would the cost to the community be?" Yves poured cold water on his argument. "Civilians shot in reprisals, innocent people who did not ask to get involved punished, assuming that you have the ordnance to carry out the assault in the first place."

"We could steal the equipment we need from the Germans."

"We are duty bound by the Hague convention."

"Don't give me the Hague convention!" Joe was piqued.

"Without rules there would be anarchy and many more lives would be lost unnecessarily," Yves pointed out.

"The Nazis are also bound by your Hague Convention are they not?" Yves nodded. "Yet I don't see them observing the rules. They are mighty quick to threaten us when we don't do as we are told."

Albert had had enough of playing and made his way back to where his father and Becquet sat. He could tell by their expression that all was not well between them. Their argument was becoming a little more heated and they began to gesticulate at each other. Albert stepped up to the two men as they faced each other, both intent on making their point.

"Can we go home now Papa?" Albert asked innocently.

"When I have finished my cigarette," his father dismissed Albert's plea, choosing to hammer home his point. "Remember that the island is heavily fortified, it would take months to break down these defences, time that would be better spent moving the Germans back across Europe."

"So you are saying that we should just sit here and twiddle our thumbs!" Joe shook his head.

"If you feel that you want to make a contribution to the war effort, think of us as hostages," Yves sought a compromise.

"Eh?" Joe took a last draw on his cigarette which was, by now, a tiny stub of paper burning his fingers. He tossed the stub away.

"By sitting tight we are taking up some of their military strength," Yves pointed out.

"But we cannot be seen collaborating with the enemy!" Joe returned to his original concern.

"Who said anything about collaborating?" Yves was unperturbed by Becquet's derision. "Knowledge is power and if there is a battle taking place, it is for the hearts and minds of the people. That is why there is a difference between co-operation and collaboration."

For the first time Joe was silent.

"And you really think that what we do is enough?" Joe sought reassurance.

"It's the best that we can do under the circumstances, keeping information flowing to counter the propaganda they peddle," Yves clarified.

"And maybe peddle a little of our own!" Joe raised an eyebrow.

As the day waned into a clear dusk, red and purple layers lining the evening sky as the sun set, Yves set off back to the house and harvested some of his root vegetables. It was his routine to lay the crops out on the grass, underneath the magnolia tree, soil that the damp would dry off and in the morning it would easily be brushed away. Albert, his constant companion these days, took on the task, laying them out in regimented lines, pretending that they were soldiers on parade. Then, as he realised that some had funny shapes, starting to design figures of his own.

"Stop playing with them and put them in tidy rows a few inches apart!" his father rebuked him. Albert sulked at having been chastised.

A siren sounded, marking the end of the long shift that the prisoners had had to endure. A short while later they passed by La Chaire and the cottage. Albert ran out from the house to watch them pass.

He could not have known that all they had to sustain them the whole day had been a draught of water from a dirty bucket and the odd morsel of food tossed to them by the guards. Albert was surprised as individuals took up handfuls of grass, dandelions and celandine as they walked up the lane. Once they had all moved on, Albert noticed that the vegetables that he had so carefully laid out on the grass had all gone. He looked up the lane to see the last of the prisoners turn and give him a wan smile, in his hand he held a half eaten parsnip.

~

"Good morning Le Bloas."

Yves recognised the heavy accent but chose not to acknowledge the greeting, continuing the onerous task of plucking weeds from between the cracks in the puddlestone walls. He shook any excess soil into the flower beds and placed the bedraggled foliage into a pogo, a wicker basket, placed nearby. The basket was almost full to overflowing.

"You should use a wheelbarrow," the officer suggested. "It would hold a lot more and it would not be so back breaking as having to haul heavy loads down hill in a basket."

The FeldKommandantur understood the reasons why Le Bloas chose to be so ignorant, in truth he had a grudging respect for a man who had the courage of his own convictions and enough moral fibre to stand up for principles he believed to be right. The likes of this gardener were a far cry from the spineless informants who sold their compatriots for the price of a meal or the Nazi sympathisers who followed orders without question. How he would have loved to explain to Le Bloas his true feelings but to do so would be to invite too much risk on them both.

Yves did not take kindly to people telling him how to do his job.

"Have you ever tried manoeuvring a wheelbarrow down a flight of steps?" he replied curtly.

"You are right, of course," the officer apologised. "Who would have thought that this garden, so wonderful to promenade along is so fraught with difficulties to maintain?"

In some respects a stilted dialogue was preferable to none at all. In truth the FeldKommandantur was not that bothered as his visits to La Chaire were a short punctuation en route to Rozel Manor and the much more relaxing company of Mrs Riley, a woman of breeding and well versed in the etiquette of high society. His trips to the north coast were a refreshing change from the tedium of life in St Helier. As Le Bloas worked his magic he was beginning to see that the gardens at Rozel Manor were no match for the unique atmosphere that La Chaire offered. The place had a solitude embraced as it was within the high cliffs of the north coast. Its atmosphere was esoteric, fuelled by a heady bouquet and a richness of colour that he had never witnessed before. He envied Le Bloas' good fortune and he desired what he could not have, a garden like La Chaire.

Most gardens he had visited, including Rozel Manor, had a sense of space about them. Large lawns, sweeping vistas that carried the eye towards the horizon. This was not the case at La Chaire, such delights were revealed only when you reached the summit and looked out over the sea towards France. Paths wound around the contours of the cliff, revealing their secrets gradually as you came round the bend. This element of surprise added to the garden's charm and gave the place a sense of anticipation and adventure, especially to a keen gardener like himself. Here, in these hidden arbours, the officer felt that he could let his guard down. There were no prying eyes. Here he could do as he pleased without attracting attention and without damaging his already suspect reputation. The two men went their separate ways without adding anymore to their conversation. Yves picked up the pogos and made his way towards the steep steps, the FeldKommandantur continued with his voyage of investigation and discovery.

~

Late spring saw the garden at its most glorious. The plants had shaken off their old skins, dead leaves and rotten twigs, all to be replaced by new greenstick growth and lush foliage. April showers had watered the soil and the May sunshine had begun to bathe the place in sunlight from early morning to late in the evening. The dryness of summer was a few weeks away. Flower heads grew and were sprouting, opening up into a blaze of colour. Herbaceous borders had started to blossom, not quite ready to release all of their unctuous odours but offering a tantalising whiff of what was to come.

It wasn't often that Yves would allow himself a moment to stand back and admire the fruits of his labour. Like the artist that he was, always in pursuit of perfection and forever self critical, he would move from one job to another, leaving others to lavish praise on his efforts. Having dumped the weeds in his compost, he took a cursory glance at the South Facing garden and had a moment of satisfaction at how much he had achieved in such a short space of time.

Nature, however, does not stand still and no sooner was the garden at ease with itself that it started to change and so Yves would have to work tirelessly to keep it in check. To labour and not to rest, to fight and not to seek any reward, the garden was not just his livelihood; it was his obsession. He was as addicted as any opium taker. He was as much a part of the garden as it was a part of him, a symbiotic relationship that even came between himself and his wife at times. As he stood motionless, his argument with Becquet came flooding back.

"You are creating a garden for their leisure!" Becquet had criticised.

"I am restoring the garden, doing the job I am employed to do." Yves had replied more than a little put out at Joe's disapproval. "I am following the instructions given by the States of Jersey and by the British Government."

"Which is?"

"To carry on as normal," Yves found having to justify his actions difficult to swallow, especially since he was only one of a few on the island that had actually seen active service. He was keenly sensitive to Becquet's thinly disguised criticism. "They just use it. They do not ask my permission, I am powerless to stop them."

"But why give them the satisfaction of enjoying its splendour?" The argument was a persuasive one.

"Then how would I feed my family?"

"You could work the fields?"

"I might as well tend the garden as work the fields!" Yves pointed out. "Either way the Germans profit by my labour."

There was brief pause before Yves added.

"You still tend your pots and fish."

"That's different!" Becquet began.

"No it isn't!" Yves butted in.

There was another short silence as the two men reflected on the impossible dilemma that faced both of them.

"I'm not sure what I would do if I couldn't fish, perhaps I would be forced onto the land."

"Or take the better pay and labour alongside the prisoners of war?"

"Never!"

"Neither would I!" Yves agreed. "That would be a step too far but some people do. You see Becquet, we just have to carry on as normal."

Albert was up around the summerhouse. This time he had a wooden sword in his hands, risking the wrath of his father by taking off the heads of some of the roses and other flowers that were growing. He was careful to attack only those that looked dead or dying but ultimately there were a number of innocent victims. He tossed the dead heads into the surrounding bushes to cover his tracks. As he fought with an imaginary dragon an aeroplane could be heard approaching. He stopped to see if he could see it pass by. As he craned his neck to try and get a view of the plane he thought about changing the game to fighting Germans, and his stick would become a rifle to shoot down enemy aircraft. Then he struck on the idea that the aeroplane was in fact a dragon flying overhead so it was important that he hid from its view until it landed, and then he would creep up on it slowly before slaying it and saving the island.

The Fieseler Fi 156 came into view, much to Albert's excitement. To the German's it was affectionately known as *The Storch*. It was a small reconnaissance aircraft that was seen now and again searching the coast line. Further down the slope Albert's father gave the plane a casual glance before returning to his chores, he shook his head in disapproval at the wasted effort of such scrutiny.

Albert was taken aback as he aimed imaginary arrows at the plane and 'The Storch's two hundred and forty horse power, air cooled, V8 engine spluttered and stuttered. He had made a direct hit! The faltering noises attracted the attention of the all those in the harbour, including the PoWs who were subsequently beaten for relaxing. All were voyeurs in the unfolding drama.

From his lofty position Albert could make out the pilot, the only person in the four-seater plane. He saw the distinct, dark brown, snake like lines painted over a beige background that passed camouflage. Albert thought they looked like scales on a dragon.

Albert watched entranced and with a growing sense of horror as he could see the pilot fighting to keep the plane aloft. Down below his father had stopped working. He watched anxiously as he tried to predict its trajectory. At first he reckoned that it would clear the surrounding ilex trees and ditch in the fields on the other side, but as the engines stalled and the plane dropped from the air he realised that it was heading straight for the south side of the garden. He wanted to scream out loud, stand and wave his hands in an attempt to encourage the pilot to make one last effort but he knew such gestures were futile. Instead he just stood and watched as the inevitable occurred.

The plane hit the upper part of the garden opposite and, almost immediately, burst into flames. Yellow tongues sent out plumes of thick, black smoke. Volatile oils in the leaves and branches vaporised and, in turn, caught fire. Then came the tell tale crackle of burning timber as the conflagration took hold. Yves heart sank as Albert's heart raced. The garden had already suffered at the hands of the occupying forces, and now it was under attack again, but this time Yves could do nothing to save it.

Men appeared from all around the harbour area, rushing to the point of impact with buckets, bowls, anything they could lay their hands on that would carry water. Very quickly a line of bodies was formed from the beach, up the path and into the vegetation. The Germans sought to extinguish the flames so that they might rescue any occupants of the plane.

At first the fire was so ferocious that Yves thought it would consume the whole side of the valley. Albert watched as flames licked up the sides of the tallest trees as if tasting them before devouring them. There was indeed a fire breathing dragon struggling for survival in midst of all this mayhem, would it live? Slowly but surely the yellow spears lost their venom, dwindling until all that remained were heavy wisps of smoke and a few throbbing embers, glowing red in the breeze.

As the soldiers neared the cockpit they saw that there was nobody inside. They looked around for the pilot. Maybe he had parachuted into the sea? If so they had better launch a boat, because the waters were not much above twelve degrees centigrade at this time of year.

"Papa!" Albert tugged at his father's trouser leg.

His father turned round, his face blackened with soot from the flames and drenched with the sweat of the toil. Yves looked disapprovingly at Albert.

"Go home!" he ordered. "This is no place for a child."

"But Papa!" Albert insisted. "There is a man in the trees behind the house. Come and see."

Yves followed Albert back down the slope across the road and back up the walled garden to a spot behind the cottage. There, hanging limply from one of the tall ilex trees was the missing pilot. He was suspended by his partly open parachute, his chin resting, lifeless on his chest, his arms and legs dangling loosely.

"Is he dead?" Albert asked innocently.

"It looks like it," his father replied coldly.

"I've never seen a dead man before!" Albert said.

"Go home to your mother!" his father instructed. "You have seen enough for one day."

Chapter 18

The damage inflicted by the rogue aeroplane was not considerable. It turned out to be more of an irritation than a catastrophe. Albert was under strict instructions not to go near because it was deemed too dangerous. The wreckage was quickly removed and his father set to repairing the damage.

Yves believed that he was not just a gardener; his work was far more significant than that, it was, in essence, scientific. His research, all meticulously recorded in his books, would ultimately be the family's salvation. The knowledge that he had gained from his cross pollination studies, the exploration of ways in which a gardener might get rare and fragile species to bloom might be worth a fortune when the war was over. He was not going to let the present conflagration get in his way and if a World War was not going to deflect him then nothing would.

Addiction creeps up on a person. The obsessive loses all track of time as they pleasure themselves, neural pathways become hard wired and then they are hooked. It is often the case that the addict realizes their obsession but steps into the realm of denial. In this fantasy world they create all manner of plausible reasons for their actions.

Such was the seductive nature of La Chaire that Yves had unwittingly become immersed in. Its willowy boughs massaged his aching limbs. Its scented byres intoxicated him almost to the point of ecstasy. The texture of waxy leaves left him feeling a desire to run them through his fingers for hours on end, and even the crumbly nature of the soil had him purring as he broke it up between thumb and forefinger.

From dawn till dusk, from the moment that he awoke to the point at which weary limbs succumbed to slumber, he ate and drank La Chaire. He was enveloped in a world of his own making. As he lay next to Bertha, who was fast asleep, his mind refused to rest and let go of the day. He was already planning the next day's agenda and when that was exhausted his mind would wander into fantasy. He held aspirations to maybe, one day, actually own La Chaire.

Confirmation came through about the D-day landings and there was a tangible excitement all around the island. Locals' hopes were raised and they went about their business with renewed optimism of a quick release, the Germans on the other hand became decidedly touchy and more reticent in their dealings with the local population. Speculation grew about the imminent liberation of the islands as the allies moved slowly but surely down through Normandy. Joe, Yves and many others took every opportunity to gaze across at the French coast, from Granville to Avranches, anticipating the arrival of naval warships intent on rescuing them. Most thought that deliverance was only a matter of time. As D-day had passed them by so V.E day would also come and go with hardly even a murmur about their plight. Many still hoped that freedom would not be long in arriving and the realisation that emancipation was not impending came as a bitter pill for many Germans, as well as for the islanders.

"I think the British Government have forgotten us," Joe commented to Yves as they sat and chewed tobacco on his doorstep.

"They have not forgotten that we are here, we are on an island, an outpost twelve miles off the French coast. Stuck out here the Germans are little threat to the Allied advance so why would they waste vital manpower and resources liberating us when there are much more important battles to fight on the mainland?" Yves, ever the pragmatist, vexed Joe.

"But we are British citizens do they not want to rescue their own?"

Yves just shrugged his shoulders, spat out his exhausted ball of tobacco and looked out to sea.

Germans and locals alike were now thrown together in a siege that would be played out for almost another year. Slowly but surely supply lines from the French coast petered out to a trickle and the fight for survival took a turn for the worse. Up until now the German forces on the islands had had it all too easy.

As supplies shrunk, islanders and troops alike set about chopping down anything that could be used as fuel. From old, established trees to young saplings, nothing was spared. In built up areas where the population was at its highest, avenues once lined with elm, beech and ash were stripped bare, even the stumps and roots were unceremoniously dug out and sliced up. The timber was not just used for fire; it became the fashion, borne out of necessity, to have footwear made from timber, not unlike the clogs of old.

In the light of this stampede, the German administration decided to appoint someone to manage the situation, to prevent the fracas that developed as people fought for possession of this tree or that bush. Yves thought that the newly commissioned 'Superintendent of Forestry' would give the trees on the island a stay of execution, he surmised that the post would involve some sort of management or husbandry whereby only selected plants would be culled, perhaps older, rotten trunks or those where the need was least, he was sadly mistaken. The carnage carried on unabated, in fact the pace of tree felling increased in a systematic, German, methodical approach to the task. If the felling carried on in this way the whole island would be bereft of foliage within the year.

Albert was helping his father in the garden and he had been given the task of watering the herbaceous borders, a job where he could do little damage. For a little boy it was a heavy job; fetching and carrying a water can. Albert manoeuvred the over sized can from the well to the garden by grabbing the handle with both hands and placing his legs either side so that he waddled to and fro until he reached his destination. His father shared a rare moment of joy as he watched Albert struggling.

"I want to be a gardener when I grow up!" Albert declared as he finished off the first aliquot, the sense of achievement filling him with satisfaction.

"It is a lot of hard work." His father warned as he drew on his cigarette.

"I don't mind hard work." Albert replied trying to whistle. How he wished that he could whistle, then he would be a real man.

As they shared a father and son moment a lorry pulled up along the lane and out stepped the largest human Albert had ever seen. As any young child would do, Albert stopped watering the flowers and stood transfixed, staring at this giant. Albert barely came up to the man's knee. He had read tales of mythical creatures, dragons, goblins and suchlike but part of him doubted whether they really existed. In those same stories giants roamed the forests, pulling out trees with their bare hands and eating up children unlucky enough to cross their path. They were the stuff of nightmares.

"Tabby come here!" the sound of his father's voice broke the spell. Albert rushed to his father's side.

His father was tall but the newly appointed Superintendent for Forestry was even taller. To describe him as a giant would not have been an exaggeration. As he climbed out from the passenger's side of the mottle green truck it was as if he was emerging from a scaled down model of the vehicle. Standing erect he dwarfed both lorry and driver.

Nothing much fazed Yves but this monster of a man made him hesitate, albeit briefly, before he turned his back and returned to his work, preparing the soil for the winter frosts. In that brief exchange of glances, Yves sized the man up. Most tall men were like Yves, lean of face as well as of limb but not this German. He had a crew cut hair style, a stubbly mane that exposed and exacerbated his gargantuan features. His ears were as large as saucers and his nose thick and bulbous. His mouth seemed vast, cutting a furrow across his face like a child might sculpt from a pumpkin. It was edged by collagen filled rubber lips and as he opened it to speak, a cavernous orifice appeared that might swallow a child in one gulp. His skin was pitted with pock marks from an acne ridden adolescence. Needless to say his uniform was ill fitting, taut about his large frame, hands like plates stuck out from sleeves that ended somewhere up his forearm, exposing chunky wrists, thick with hair.

This Goliath of a man brought with him the usual arrogance of office but there was something else, something more sinister about him that unsettled Yves. It was not just his sheer size but rather an air of naive self-belief as befits a person that has been promoted beyond their competence, awash with the trappings of power. He lacked the subtlety required of a proper officer, choosing to get his point across by use of brute force and blunt obduracy. There would be no grace or favour in any of the Superintendent's interactions, he would just as likely to cut down a prized exotica as he would a line of poplars that had grown along a private road for the last hundred years. He was not a person that earned respect, rather he was someone who commanded your undivided attention as he bludgeoned his way through your personal space.

By nineteen forty one over a hundred thousand trees had been felled across the island, leaving vast tracts of once untouched, innocent woodland permanently violated. Once the giant from East Germany had completed his mission there would be little left but scrub. He had earmarked every patch of gorse, every rhododendron, each and every shrub that had been lovingly cultivated, as likely kindling in the event of a dire emergency.

The officer barked a series of orders at the driver and at the two squaddies that sat in the back of the truck. Motivated by sheer terror they leapt into action, taking axes from the back of the truck and sprinting up to the nearest ilex trees before beginning to cut away at their trunks.

Albert watched anxiously as his father stepped up to the superintendent.

"What are you doing?" he queried, trying to keep his anger at bay.

"Collecting timber!" came the blunt reply. The officer barely glanced at Yves, choosing to focus on his men to make sure they were on task. He barked another order, cutting across Yves as he did so.

As if to make a point of his superiority, the Superintendent decided to walk over to where the men were cutting down the trees. Instead of following the path, he strode straight across the garden, trampling through herbaceous borders and slashing at shrubbery that got in his way with his machete. The feeling of despair made Yves nauseous. All he could do was watch, impotently, as they began their systematic wrecking of La Chaire.

It came as some relief when they only felled a few trees in total before stopping. Once horizontal, each tree was stripped of its branches and each branch stripped of its leaves. The trunk was then cut into manageable pieces and the logs were lifted and unceremoniously thrown onto the truck. The two soldiers jumped onto the back and the driver returned to his seat in the front. The Superintendent followed soon after. As the vehicle's engine stuttered into life the officer poked his ginormous head out of the tiny window and threatened Yves.

"We'll be back for more later!" he threatened.

The driver crashed the gears and the trucked chugged off back up the road past La Chaire, straining under the added weight, plumes of black smoke billowing out from the exhaust.

Yves was at complete loss as to what he should do next. He could not just sit by and watch the whole garden be systematically stripped bare, he had to do something, anything, to try and save the place. Direct intervention was out of the question but what else was there left for him to do?

Some time later the FeldKommandantur paid the garden a visit and he immediately noticed that some of the trees had been felled. Yves was tending to a flower bed under the large wall to the west of La Chaire. The two men shared a glance before the officer stormed into the house. Yves could hear raised voices and soon after the FeldKommandantur strode out once more, his face red with anger.

Next day, Yves heard the familiar chugging of the Superintendant's lorry coming up the lane, announcing its arrival before he could even see it. He jumped up from his work, preparing to greet the officer with a glare. As they met there was a stand off between them that lasted a couple of minutes before this enormous soldier spoke in broken English.

"Don't think a letter from the FeldKommandantur will save your precious garden." He snarled.

"I don't know what you are taking about!" Yves replied with equal venom.

The two gazed long and hard at each other until eventually the superintendent turned on his heels and stomped back to the lorry, his footsteps reverberating along the ground. He ordered his men back into the wagon. As he slammed the door of the vehicle shut, Yves breathed a sigh of relief. The lorry staggered into action and sped off back, kicking up plumes of dust as it accelerated and skidded on the dusty track.

As Yves returned to his work his heart still racing and his mood darkened. He realised that this would not be the last time the garden would come under threat. It would only be a matter of time before the Germans returned to pillage what timber they could.

Both occupier and the occupied watched, with more than a passing interest, the Allied progression through Normandy. Even on a still day the sound of gunfire could be heard clearly across the Manche. All day, everyday, heavy artillery pounded out a rhythm as the British and American forces pushed back the Germans. Tongues of fire amongst plumes of smoke licked upwards towards skies darkened with dust, soot and ash. Eventually St Malo fell, buried beneath a barrage of ordnance. With its capture, the Channel Islands were effectively cut off and so began the decline into what was little more than a siege.

Soldiers and civilians were left alone to tough it out until the inevitable surrender was declared. Rationing, already a daily bind, became a lot more severe and bit everyone, irrespective of rank. Bread was limited to one pound per week and there was no poultry or pork to be had. Yves' chicken remained a closely guarded secret, ensconced in the old bread oven, away from prying eyes. He had not even told Becquet about it and the children had been sworn to silence. One day, in the not too distant future its egg laying days would be over and then they would have meat for tea, for a couple of days at least.

As the siege mentality deepened, German paranoia grew and they fortified the beaches even more, laying barb wire and concrete pillars on pristine sands, alongside land mines designed to wreak havoc to whatever inadvertently stepped on them. Low water fishing was made almost impossible and only the brave or foolhardy would risk life and limb for the sake of a few shellfish. Hungry eyes turned towards the prized Jersey cattle. Their meat was anything but prime steak but that mattered little to empty bellies. However the herds were protected and often guarded against poachers and soldiers alike. From these cows came white gold, rich in buttermilk, a pint a day allowance for all, this ration was the mainstay in fending off malnutrition and starvation.

People turned, to an almost indulgent degree, to the land for sustenance in an attempt to stave off the hardship caused by the blockade. Belts had to be tightened further but the local population just got on with it, they were already adept at improvising, necessity is the mother of invention after all. The rich Jersey soil, provided potatoes as a staple but this favourite and flavoursome of root crops was also ground to make flour that was, in turn, used for baking. Much use was made of the mortar and pestle in the kitchen.

Carrots were ground to make the basis of tea and jam. Parsnips, barley and acorns formed the main ingredient of ersatz coffee. Dried elderberries that grew wild along country lanes were a more than adequate substitute for currants in cakes and buns. That is if the tree had not already been felled for use as firewood.

If the family were lucky enough to acquire some shellfish, perhaps the odd spider crab or lobster, they would use nettles to flavour the stock. Carrageen moss, red seaweed, was an adequate substitute for soap and could be collected at low tide, if you dared.

As fuel supplies dwindled, stoves and ranges stayed cold for long periods. Nothing went to waste as people packed old oil drums with sawdust, leaving a hole at one end from which a tiny flame would flicker. It would take hours to boil a pan full of potatoes.

The only place where fires continued to roar were at the local forges. Large amounts of heat were needed to soften up steel and temper it for its various uses, whether that was horses' hooves or agricultural machinery. Those lucky enough to live near a forge were sometimes allowed to utilise the heat generated and cook their meals by the fire. It was a common sight to see cooking pots circling the flames, each competing for whatever heat came their way. Yves family were one of the lucky ones, although it was a trial to get the food to the forge and back again before it cooled down.

Albert had been sent to the forge to get the potatoes cooked for dinner. Yves placed the heavy cooking pot, filled with salty sea water and enough peeled potatoes and other root vegetables for all the family, in a small wooden wheelbarrow. The wheelbarrow had been made by Joe Becquet for Albert to use around the garden when he was helping his father. It was constructed entirely from wood and in proportion to Albert's size. It was Albert's pride and joy and he played with it every day, copying his father in around the garden, fetching and carrying.

The pot was not difficult to lift with the aid of the wheelbarrow and Albert set off up the path towards the forge with gusto, the wooden wheel of the barrow squeaking on the axle as he pushed.

"Not so fast!" his mother cautioned.

"We want something left in the pot on your return!" his father shouted with an uncharacteristic cheeriness in his voice.

"You shouldn't give such a young child such a big responsibility!" Bertha scolded as she watched Albert slow down after his first few confident steps. His initial self-assurance was replaced by insecurity as the weight and the odd centre of gravity of the barrow caused it to wobble precariously over the uneven stones.

"Give the lad a chance!" Yves dismissed her concerns as he turned his back to return to his own chores. Bertha watched Albert as he made his way up the hill, stopping every few yards to rest. She was certain that he would not make it and muttered to herself as she watched him struggle.

Albert eventually got up a head of steam, turning the corner in the road so that he was now out of her sight. He trundled along, pretending he was steering a motorbike but careful not to let his imagination run away too much in case he lost control of the wheelbarrow and spilt its contents. Losing himself in his thoughts helped to pass the time, so much so he reached the junction at the top of the hill without realising it. There was no left turn as such and so he steered right into the lane, allowing himself a lean of twenty degrees or so and a screech to mimic the make believe motorbike he was supposed to be riding. The country lane twisted and turned a little before it brought him to an old granite mill tower. He passed the local shop, which was situated in the mill, stopping briefly to peer through the window. Its shelves were virtually bare of produce and so he set off a touch disappointed. There was a bakery a little further along, to the right hand side, on the road that led to Rozel Manor. Albert was sent there to get their weekly allocation of bread. The forge was nearby, just across the road and it was here that Albert eventually arrived having not spilt a drop, a feat he was quite pleased about.

Albert liked the blacksmith. He was a friendly, jovial sort of man. He greeted Albert with a ruffle of his hair, his massive, plate like hands almost covering Albert's entire head. He placed the cooking pot carefully by the side of the forge and shovelled some coals around its base. In just a few minutes the lid of the pot was rattling as the water inside started to boil. Albert watched in awe as the blacksmith went about his work. The sound of steel on steel as hammer hit metal on the huge anvil fed Albert's imagination once more. On the way back home he would be a charioteer chasing down Gauls as he fought with the Roman legions.

Albert arrived back at the house at the same time as a cavalcade of cars drew up outside La Chaire. He stood holding the barrow, staring at the vehicles as they stopped one after another. Bertha came out to see what all the commotion was about, she noticed Albert standing staring and rushed to bring him inside. She took a firm grip of the cooking pot handle with one hand and got a good hold of Albert's right hand with the other. Unable to control the wheelbarrow properly Albert got it close enough to the cottage before he was forced to let go and let it fall.

The next morning as Albert helped his father to clear up a pile of weeds and grass into his wheelbarrow, a contingent of officers strolled out from La Chaire, to take in the morning air. Most were smokers, choosing to draw on rolled cigarettes prepared by their orderlies earlier in the day. They made their way across the path and up into the South facing area of the garden. They barely cast a glance at the gardener and his son as they passed, led by the FeldKommandantur, the only one Albert recognised.

Next came a much smaller, podgy looking officer dressed in a deep blue jacket with gold epaulettes. Gold buttons strained to keep the two sides of his jacket together, across his rotund midriff. His thick thighs were hidden beneath black breeches, tucked inside his gleaming, black jack boots. The other officers, excluding the FeldKommandantur, scurried around this diminutive man, jostling for position by his side, which was not easy along the narrow path.

"This is a well stocked garden," he observed.

"The garden was once of great botanical significance," the FeldKommandantur revealed. "There are some fragile and rare plants to be found here."

"How rare?" Huffmeier was intrigued.

"Some are so rare, they can normally only be found in this climate under glass."

"Indeed!" the admiral was impressed. "So what is the gardener's secret?"

"The location, I believe," the FeldKommandantur began to feel a little empathy developing between the two of them, a common interest in things floral.

"This is a magnificent specimen, is it not?" Huffmeier enthused as he caught sight of a camellia. In full bloom it took the breath away.

"The originator, a man named Curtis I believe, brought in plants from all over the world and through careful cultivation got them to flourish here."

Huffmeier nodded thoughtfully as he listened.

The entourage moved on winding its way further up the slope.

"Is it not a travesty that our troops must freeze whilst this place is protected by so many trees?" Captain Bohde sought to discredit the FeldKommandantur. His Bavarian snobbery filled him with anger.

"You have no eye for the finer things in life do you Bohde?" Huffmeier remarked.

"We are at war Herr Admiral!" Bohde spoke with restraint, hurt by the comment. He could see the snigger in the other officers expressions, all except the FeldKommandantur who just looked away. "We have no time for such frippery."

"You are truly without class." Huffmeier launched into a personal attack on Bohde, dismissing his point of view. "You would not know a masterpiece from a child's painting. Must everything be sacrificed? Can we not enjoy the spoils of war even a little?"

Stung by the admiral's words, Bohde fell silent, flushed with anger. He glowered at the others but left particular venom for the FeldKommandantur Jealousy and a determination to exact revenge flowed strongly in his veins. The antipathy was reciprocated by the FeldKommandantur. In his opinion there were three types of Nazi and all were dangerous in their own way. All had an unwavering conviction towards Nazi dogma. The earliest Nazi's remembered when Germany was bankrupt and saw themselves as freedom fighters, partisans fighting against an old guard for a better life. Then there was the new breed, innocents, their minds indoctrinated into the fraternity, brainwashed adolescents incapable of thinking for themselves. But the worst type of Nazi were the ones that surrounded him, tin pot leaders, petty functionaries who jumped on the bandwagon and rose to prominence, filling the vacuum left as the Nazis removed any sort of opposition via councils and other legal and political forums. Eventually, the FeldKommandantur cursed, these slugs will crawl back under the rocks they had emerged from.

Yves watched the officers disappear into the rhododendron thicket. He could still hear their voices chattering in German, interspersed by the odd guffaw.

A few days after the visit by the high ranking officers, Yves was where he always was, and liked to be, in the thick of the garden, tending to its nuances. Albert and Agnes played in front of the cottage, filling the wooden wheelbarrow with all manner of flotsam as their imaginations ran riot. Albert was keen to mimic his father and so he paid attention to any dead or dying leaves, extricating them from the rest of the plant. Their mother was in the house tending to her daily chores.

It was a winter's day but the calm, clear, bright morning was quite deceiving. The air temperature was high for the time of year giving the day an almost spring like feel. The stillness was broken by the arrival of around five trucks. They came to a halt, one after the other in front of La Chaire. From the backs of the trucks several soldiers disembarked, wielding either axes or spades. Yves stopped what he was doing and came down from the garden, to see what the furore was about. As he espied the soldiers and the tools that they carried his heart sank. When he saw Captain Bohde emerge from one of the trucks accompanied by the tall, East German, he knew the game was up.

The officer barked instructions to the giant who, in turn, growled at the soldiers, most of whom scattered to all parts of the garden. Those with axes headed towards the outer reaches where the tallest trees were to be found. They set to, hacking away at the protective ilex and other deciduous trees that had established themselves over the years. Sighing boughs could be heard screaming as they cracked and split under the hatchet. Tree trunks groaned and creaked as they were bludgeoned, blows raining in with alternate ferocity. One after another they proclaimed their own death rattle, a final fracture as their lumbering resistance finally gave and a fracture emerged that ripped open their heartwood. As they tumbled down they expelled a whoosh, a last breath before being carted away and dismembered.

All Yves could do was to watch with increasing dismay as slowly but surely the green screen that had for so many years defended the exotics from the abrasive sea started to look a lot more threadbare. Patches of open water were now clearly visible from the garden. He returned to the relative safety of the cottage and sat on the perimeter wall, desperately eyeing the holocaust that was unfolding. He searched for some kind of solace, something that would help him through his pain and torment. In desperation he found himself speculating on which of the flora might survive the rigours of life by the shore. In his mind he flicked through the catalogue of possibilities. It was an exercise that gave him some comfort amidst the mayhem. Having carried out a thumbnail analysis of likely survivors, his spirits began to lift, a little. Once these butchers and had had their fill he could set about recovering the situation. There was still some hope and he consoled himself with this thought as he rolled a cigarette.

The following day the FeldKommandantur arrived. The dismay on his face as he saw the clearing created by Bohde and his East German sidekick was evident.

"Where do you keep your pots?" the officer asked bluntly as he stepped up to Yves, who was working in the pergola.

"Pots?" Yves replied perplexed.

"Plant pots! Pots for putting plants in and large ones at that!" the FeldKommandantur demanded. "Don't try and be evasive with me!" the threat was real and Yves knew that he could not ignore it.

"They are around the side of the greenhouse," Yves felt like he had made some confession but the reason why eluded him. "Why do you want plant pots?"

"It is clear to me that the garden is finished. It is only a matter of time before it is emptied so I am going to save the most valuable ones," the officer explained. "I am taking them back to Germany with me."

Yves reeled at the revelation.

"They will never survive the journey." He pointed out, shaking his head with incredulity.

"I respect your concern but this is the only way," the FeldKommandantur was undeterred.

"If you are so insistent on taking the plants why don't you let me take some cuttings for you and prepare them properly?" Yves did not really want to help but if he could save the garden then he was willing to do this small task, however onerous, in order to preserve it

"That will take time and time is a commodity that I have little of. The war is all but lost and I need to grab what I can and escape before the Allies cut off our retreat completely!" the officer dismissed the idea outright.

Yves head sunk to his chest weighed down with the burden of defeat. All the while his mind was racing, searching for a way, any way to thwart the officer. He looked up, shaking his head in disbelief. He wanted to cry, to beg the officer not to carry out this genocide and destroy his life's work. But Yves knew that any resistance was futile, so instead, he just sat on the wall, in silence, and lit the cigarette that he had been rolling up all the while.

The FeldKommandantur took out his pocketbook and walked around the garden, with a small group of soldiers in procession behind him. He stopped consulted and pointed to one shrub or tree before instructing the soldiers to dig it up.

"Dig around the base, leave enough soil and be careful with the roots." He scolded.

The first to be removed were the camellias, the double white and all the rest. There was little appreciation of the skills required to remove a shrub from the soil and preserve its fine root hairs, it was just a series of thrusts of the shovel around the base and then brute strength as the rooted mass was levered out of the ground and then dumped into an adjacent pot. Bushes that were too big up top were unceremoniously trimmed with a machete, their branches lopped off to lie where they fell. It was a desecration. The acacias went the same way as did the tamarisk and the Sikkim Rhododendrons. The yellow orange fruit of the Myrianthus were shaken off as it provided a struggle before it was eventually uprooted, not so the two wattles that were lifted with hardly any resistance. It seemed like only the Monterey pine would survive. The officer looked long and hard at the Magnolia Cambelli in front of the cottage before cursing in frustration and moving on. It was much too big to shift. He made the same decision over the wisteria.

For over one hundred years the garden had remained virtually undisturbed, in that time it had been allowed to blossom and grow. In this very garden the future had been shaped. Samuel Curtis had pushed back the barriers of botany and laid the foundations for modern horticulture, influencing a whole empire in the pursuit of 'floriculture'. Then Princess Ka'iulani, a queen in waiting, had graced the garden with her presence and that had taken on the might of the USA and almost won. It was among these floral pathways that she conceived her attack on American hearts and minds and it was here that she heard of the annexation of her beloved homeland, Hawaii. And then there was Charles Fletcher, a man that had invested almost everything that he had in La Chaire. It had not only bankrupted him it had also exhausted him to the point of destruction. If Curtis had been its spring, and Fletcher its summer, then Yves was witnessing La Chaire's winter of discontent. Where all had sought refuge from the storm, now a storm was being unleashed on the garden itself.

She was being sacrificed on the altar of expediency to the twin gods of greed and avarice. Yves watched, shackled by his own anxieties as La Chaire was systematically raped, deflowered, literally, by rough hands, who could rightly claim that they were just following orders. She was manhandled, dragged from her pedestal and subjected to an ignominious attack. Her earthen hymen rent asunder with every thrust of the soldiers tools. Her silence in the face such a violent assault was testament to her breeding.

It had taken a century and more cultivate the gardens at La Chaire, yet these soldiers had decimated the place in little more than a day. By dusk all of the available pots had been filled. In his greed the FeldKommandantur had made a miscalculation. He had thought he would be able to load the trucks there and then but time had run out.

Yves spent a restless night, tossing and turning, thinking about how he might rescue this impossible situation. Alongside the need for preservation was his feeling of antipathy towards the officer. The desire for revenge burned deep.

~

The point of no return had arrived. Albert and Agnes lay fast asleep as their father eased out from beneath the bedclothes. He was up and dressed quickly and quietly. He felt like a criminal, skulking around secretively, going about his work trying to avoid detection. To commit murder when it is premeditated requires the cold steel of an assassin. There is no attachment to the victim, no emotion, no guilt, just a sureness of mind that a life is about to be extinguished. There are no thoughts given to consequences because the assassin is confident that they will not be detected and there is little, if any, hesitation, except perhaps to make sure that the perpetrator is not unmasked as they carry out their heinous act. Some might describe such an assailant as cold blooded, even psychotic. Whatever the description, the only truth is that they are a person that will willingly destroy the life of another for no other motive than self gain. The sanctity of life is such that in the eyes of society, the assassin is a pariah. However, in times of war, life becomes valueless when it is sacrificed for the greater good.

So where is the rationale behind the so called, 'crime of passion'? How can somebody justify the annihilation of another, especially when that soul is the one that is dearest to them? Is it blind paranoia that drives the lover to kill their beloved or is it some other base emotion like jealousy or rage that a court of law may empathise with and find the culprit not guilty. What, if any, is the difference between the assassin and the aggrieved lover? They both have the blood of another on their hands, targeting their victim with unerring certainty. Why is the assassin so reviled, yet the criminal of passion is counselled, comforted and their action condoned?

As Yves stepped out of his front door, he felt a little like both. He was about to exercise what he saw as euthanasia. Was it just plain stubbornness or something more distasteful such as spitefulness, petulance or jealousy that had forced his hand? Revenge is a dish best served cold. Whatever the reasons for his actions the ultimate end product would be a pyrrhic victory in a war that already been both won and lost.

Oil of vitriol has many strange features. In high concentrations it is called oleum and its viscous nature explains why it might be mistaken as an oil but that is where the similarity ends. Also known as sulphuric acid, its hydrophilic character is positively ravenous. When poured onto organic matter its dehydrating properties removes all hydrogen and oxygen molecules leaving behind an expanded, pumice like mass of carbon, charred remains that retain their toxic assailant ad infinitum. The reaction is significantly exothermic, issuing buckets of steam, as the acid eats away at the living matter. Alchemists of old reached for oil of vitriol in their desire to seek for that most elusive of chemicals, the philosopher's stone.

Yves knew that to pour oil of vitriol directly onto the potted plants would give the game away so he was up early to prepare a more dilute solution that would have the same effect but take its course of action more slowly and only be detected, it at all, whilst the plants were well on their way. However, even the simple act of diluting the acid was not without its hazards. To add water directly onto oil of vitriol results in a heat of reaction so great that the water boils before the acid can be diluted. To affect dilution the acid must be added to the water slowly, and with great care. Even this method is not without its dangers. As the acid hits the water, the water can again boil. To prevent this, the mixture must be stirred carefully and the mixer needs to be ever vigilant to avoid any over heating.

Yves needed to give himself plenty of time to prepare the solution and to give it a chance to cool so as to avoid drawing attention. He half filled his watering cans with water before carefully ladling out small aliquots from the large glass containers, stored near the old generator. As a cold, colourless liquid the diluted sulphuric acid appeared as water, Yves would just have to hope that nobody chose to test it by taking a drink. By the time the FeldKommandantur arrived, Yves was moving from one plant to another, watering can in hand.

A few minutes after the arrival of the officer and his entourage of trucks carrying many soldiers, Albert came running out from the cottage anxious to see what all the noise was about.

"Papa, Papa!" Albert shouted to his father as he ran towards him.

"Not now Tabby!" his father reprimanded. "Go back to the house this is no place for a little child."

"But Papa, I want to water the plants with you. You always let me water the plants!" Albert pleaded as he pulled at his father's trouser leg.

"Not today Tabby, there are too many soldiers and too many wagons. You might get hurt," his father explained, distracted.

Albert sensed his father's agitation and for a moment let go of his trousers. His father continued to water the shrubs and small trees that had been placed in individual pots, in a long line outside of the main house. German soldiers strode purposefully this way and that all about the terracing. There were a number of wagons and trucks, their engines ticking over, waiting to be filled. Officers barked orders as the soldiers went about their work, carrying paintings, rolled up carpets, chairs and other items of furniture. It seemed that just about anything that was not nailed down was being placed in the back of one vehicle or another.

Fascinated by the goings on, Albert wandered away from the safety of his father's side and into this morass of activity. He stopped to stare at a large portrait of a man he had never seen before. He thought that the man was staring at him and looked scary so he quickly moved on. He saw a large rug leaning on the back of a truck, waiting to be placed. He was attracted by its bright colours. He touched it gently with his fingers. It had a warm, soft texture that he liked so he touched it some more.

"Get out of the way!" a soldier shouted as he brushed past Albert carrying a heavy sculpture that he threw onto the back of the wagon.

Alarmed by the soldier's unfriendly outburst, Albert turned tail and ran back to his father.

"Papa, are the German's leaving?" he asked.

"Yes." his father was very careful not to spill any precious fluid as he treated each plant in turn.

"Are they taking everything with them?" Albert enquired innocently.

"Yes."

"Even the plants?"

"Yes."

"But they are your plants!" Albert observed.

"Not any more!" came the terse reply.

"Le Bloas have you finished watering the plants yet?" the German officer asked impatiently, his voice barely audible above the furore. Albert clung to his father for comfort.

"Nearly!" Albert's father snapped back.

"Then get a move on and make sure that they are fastened safely!" the officer instructed before moving into the house.

Albert's father cursed under his breath.

"Can I water some plants now?" Albert pestered once more.

"I've told you no!" his father shouted at him. "Now stay out of the way."

Albert felt like crying as he shuffled his feet in the gravel of the terrace, moving to the far end of the row of plants where his father had pointed.

He watched as his father rolled the large plant pots, without spilling a drop, to the rear of one of the lorries. He then called for help so that they could be hoisted, one at a time, onto the back. He then took it upon himself to jump up onto the lorry, place each pot carefully and fasten it to the side of the truck with rope. Albert sucked his thumb as he watched his father toil. Once all the plants had been loaded, his father jumped off the lorry and a soldier raised the tailgate and secured it. He made his way to Albert and pulled him close. Albert reciprocated. The bond between father and son was re-established.

Yves was all too aware that if any acid leaked and made contact with skin or metal its true personality would be revealed. He was not without a great sense of loss but he could not help giving a wistful smile at the thought that Becquet would no doubt approve of this heinous act of espionage.

The two of them watched as one lorry after the other manoeuvred in the tight space of the terrace before following the one in front down the drive and onto the lane. Their contents rattled and teetered in the back as the vehicles made their way over the uneven ground. Last to leave were the trucks containing the plants. Albert looked up at his father.

"Are you sad Papa?" he asked.

"A little," his father replied softly.

"Is it because they have taken your plants?"

"It is."

"Will you grow some more?"

"Maybe,"

Once the sound of the lorries had diminished Yves turned to view what was left of the garden. What hit him was a scene of utter devastation. There were great holes in the ground where shrubs had been torn out, herbaceous borders had been trampled under foot and many surrounding trees had been completely decimated. It had been an act of utter desecration. The cold, winter wind seemed to have increased in magnitude, whistling through the wreckage with a bitterness and a howl of delight that signified its breakthrough. The frosty tip of the wind sought out exposed roots and fragile leaves to attack but even the cold east wind must have been disappointed for there were few bones for it to pick at.

Yves reflected on his son's childish optimism. He wondered whether he had the willpower to start all over again. He had been the latest caretaker of the garden that was La Chaire, would he be the last?

Acknowledgments

Sarah Cursham

Lucinda Cursham

Albert Le Bloas

John Brewster

Hatton Hotels

Angie Petkovic

Societe Jersiase

Jersey Archive

Kew Archive

Kew Gardens

Winchester Reference Library

Worthing Reference Library

Ancestry.co.uk

Bibliography

Princess Ka'iulani, Hope of a Nation heart of people, Sharon Linea, Eerdmans Books, 1999

The von Aufsess occupation diary Baron Von Aufsess, Philmore, 1984

The British Channel Islands German Occupation 1940-1945 Paul Sanders, Jersey Heritage Trust.

RHS gardening month by month, Ian Spence, Dorling Kindersley, 2007

The English Garden a Social History, Charles Quest-Ritson, Viking, 2001

Victorian Voices Joan Stevens, La Societe Jersiaise, 1969

Everyday life in Regency and Victorian England Kristine Hughes, Kristine Hughes 1998

www.mnlg.com
www.poetryloverspage.com
www.janesoceania.com
www.royalty.nu
www.electricscotland.com
www.livinglifefully.com
www.pfaf.org
trulyvictoria.netfirms.com
www.rosarian.com
www.diggerhistory.info
www.kew.org
www.audubonhouse.org
www.victorianweb.org
www.archivist@apothecaries.org
www.regencyreproductions.com
www.arthurlloyd.co.uk
www.victorianlondon.org
www.georgianindex.net